BOOK OF ADDIS
Cradled Embers

A Novel

BY BROOKE C. OBIE

FOR THE PEOPLE PRESS

Cover Design: Brooke C. Obie, Stephen Wilder, Lwam Essayu, Adobe Stock Images

ISBN: 0692721061
ISBN-13: 978-0-692-72106-3

FOR BARRY & JO ANN

THANK YOU FOR BELIEVING

CONTENTS

ACKNOWLEDGMENTS

I owe a great debt to the Women of the Revolution, whose spirit, work, creativity, voice, resilience, struggle, resistance and mere existence sparked within me a revolution of my own.

To Toni Morrison and Jamaica Kincaid, for their stories on the impact of slavery and colonization on Black motherhood, without which I could not have written this book.

To Chinua Achebe who gave me my first taste of Nigeria and made me long for more. To Aimé Césaire whose work taught me to disrupt the language.

To Chimamanda Ngozi Adichie for writing in Igbo and not translating it, and for offering me kindness, hospitality and encouragement as I sought to complete this book.

To Robert Antoni, whose Writing in the Vernacular seminar reminded me of the political power, resistance and brilliance of Black Vernacular English. This would be a different, lesser book without your course. Thank you!

To Susan Cheever who shepherded me through my thesis and every step of the book-writing process; for doing everything for me that you promised to do, and then some, thank you!

To Oney Judge, the bold woman who escaped the clutches of her enslaver, George Washington, and lived to defy him long after his death. To Harriet Tubman, Angela Davis, Winnie Mandela, Assata Shakur, Fania Davis--There is no Addis or Taddy without you.

To George Jackson, whose love letters to Angela Davis made me long for love letters signed "Power to the People," and then made me decide to write one of my own.

To Nina Simone, Bayuba Cante and Fela Kuti, to the writers of Negro spirituals and singers of chain gang songs for putting Black pain into melody that heals, transcends time and became the soundtrack to this book.

To Demetria Irwin, my sister in writing and in Harlem, thank you for your friendship, support, and your encouraging notes. You didn't give up when I wanted to. Thank you! To Uzoma Onukwubiri, my Igbo sister, for not hesitating to read through this work and offer invaluable insight on Igbo language and culture.

To my sisters Jennifer Jackson and Yanit Belachew, for

reading the roughest of drafts of my writing sample for grad school and finding beauty in it. For reading late-night emails about logos and fonts and press releases. For sharing the journey with me. Thank you!

To my writing support group, April Holloway and Sylvia Wall for every bit of encouragement along the way. You're true friends. To Eddie Winstead, my brother-cousin, I speak your name. Rest in peace.

To Uzodinma Iweala for letting me take you to lunch and ask you questions about how and why you wrote the brilliant *Beasts of No Nation*. Thank you!

To Marlon James for writing *The Book of Night Women* in the vernacular. I didn't think I could write my book in both the third person and in the vernacular. Then I read your book and I decided I could. Thank you!

To Tiphanie Yanique for your early notes and your encouragement.

To Feminista Jones for your sex positive framework. Addis and Ekwueme thank you too!

To Jamilah Lemieux for commissioning my first paid writing gig at my dream publication. To Kierna Mayo for seeing my worth and hiring me for the job that paid my bills while I wrote this book at night. Thank you!

To my mom, JoAnn, for immortalizing a picture of yourself in velvet. Being entranced by your beauty and your giant Afro was the first spark of my own revolution. So apt that you started it all. I owe you everything. Thank you!

To my dad, Barry, for being the first person to read my book at every stage, for taking me seriously, and supporting me always. You're the standard. Because of you, I can't ever accept any less. Thank you!

To my grandmothers, Hattie Ward and Chestina Obie, the strongest, most loving mothers of the revolution I know, whose sayings live on in this book. To Lucy Obie, owner of land, rocker of hats, daughter of my ancestors. Thank you for surviving. There's no me without you first.

Thank You God for giving me words to speak life. You are everything. This book is an homage to You all and a gift, I hope, to my people. Ike mba!

PROLOGUE:

ANAGHI EJE AKWA ONYE KWULU UDO

NO ONE ATTENDS THE HOMEGOING OF A SUICIDE

DIDO

In the kitchen of the Great House at Wellesbury Plantation, Dido hear the *clang! clang!* of breaking china and she know it beginning. She startle, dropping her spoon in the pot she were stirring. She silent, watching it sink to the bottom of the rabbit stew. (She warn't planning to let anyone else eat that stew, not that one, but she needing something to do with her hands while she waiting, so she were stirring.)

When she hearing the commotion coming from the dining room, she knowing her di nwēnu, Ambrose Burken, done fall back in him seat, down, down to the floor. Him chair done splinter up under him portliness. Him wine glass slip from him chunky fingers and it shattering against the cold, stone floor.

Dido peek into the dining room and see teeny pieces of china bowl laying out like folks been casting lots round Ambrose feets. Remnants of that stew he most likely were enjoying...at first...splattering. Dido know it were him favorite stew. She know he were gon eat it up quick, not even letting it savor on him tongue. He greedy. He take everything when he want it. Stew be no exception.

A thousand times Dido fix him rabbit stew. Except this time, there be bitterness to it. She were watching him swish the stew round in him mouth til she caint no more bear it. Aint even pray o'er it, she were thinking when he were so bold when he ate it, cause what could Dido dare do? Now, he holding him gut with both hands, him pink face turning a funny white, begging the Debil don't take him. He don't know Dido. That aint even her real name.

Ambrose crying out soft, desperate. She grunt a little when she think, He sound like when he on top of me.

Dido walk light footed into the room, peering over the great table between them. She see him struggle on the floor, mouth foaming. She shaking, bumps rising up and down her arms. She whisper,

--You all right, Massa Ambrose?
He rolling round in agony. He say,
--Help me, Dido!
--There, there, Massa Ambrose, she say. --Close your eyes and just breathes real slow. It'll all be over, by-an-by.

2

Ambrose cough and spit up a frothy mix of stew and insides. He smear the pink mess in the floor with him face. Dido knowing him chest be on fire. That mean it were working. Dido slide into a corner to wait, her mind wandering.

She cursing her brother for being so slow in collecting the roots from The Eboro anyhow. It were just like Turk to conjure a fix to they Ambrose problem that cost them time they aint got. Now Dido racing the sun, cause fore it drop from the sky, Misuss Caroleen be back, her and the nosy lot. Then Dido be the one fixed, for sure. The nosy lot always itching to get another menor into trouble to prove they a different kind of menor than the rest. The kind the no-color folks might could trust. Dido done what she got to just to stay living ever since she been dragged to Wellesbury, but even in her quiet obedience, she aint never been one no-color folks ought to trust.

Ambrose aint know it, though, so he making her the cook to keep her nearby so he can have her when he want her. Now he rolling over onto him side, shivering. Dido lock her eyes on him. He don't speak but he begging her with no words. She see him pleading eyes and her face get hot and scrunched. She breathe heavy but she don't look away while he roll on him back, howling like a sick dog.

--Mm....Mmurderer... murder, he spit.

And Dido wonder where he get the confidence.

--You right, Massa Ambrose, she say and look dead in him face. –Let Chúkwú judge me sure enough.

Dido looking at her hands now, turning them over, marveling at what she aint know they could do. Put a woman in a tight space, she liable to do anything, Dido membering her mam back in Eboeland say.

Ambrose body chickenjerk. He breathing shallow. When he seem like he surrendering to the hell she sending him to, all a sudden, Dido aint hot no more. Her blood cold and she sweat cold and everything inside her get to tightening.

Dido been slow-cooking for two week, ever since she catch Ambrose with him hands in her daughter. But this plan with the roots, she only plot it with her brother Turk this morning. Now Dido dizzy and chest hurting. She heaving up and down heavy cause the truth done set in. He dying now and her body and her chile's body aint gon be no more safe when she through killing him. She thinking bout that and crumple backward under the

3

heaviness of it, only her corner wall keeping her from hitting the floor.

--They gon come for me. They gon kill me!

She shaking when she scream it but she don't cry. Cause Dido also knowing him have to go. And she the cook, after all. Who else gon do it? And she were Taddy's ńné, and Taddy warn't but twelve years old. Who else should? Yes, he have to go, she thinking. Aint like she were sad bout it none, but she don't get no peace from it, nuther. This aint who she were born to be. This who he make her.

--You believe what you send that preacherman to tell us, Dido asking Ambrose. --That God washing away the most vilest of sins? That the wickedest tormenters of the earth can see Heben yet, if only they repent and believe? Now be the time to find out, she say, but deep in her heart she caint believe Chúkwú gon send her and Ambrose to the same place. Aint no way, she thinking. Not after the hell she already been through these many years. Her heart slow to normal and her chest loosen when she think on that. She can breathe again. She rest her forehead in a brick crack in her corner, soul tired. He choke out,

--Dido...

--My name *Ezinne*, you poor fool, she glare at him. --Shoulda known it. Bet you woulda done different by me and mine, she say.

Her head pounding so hard now she caint hardly see. She bury it deep in her hands to make it stop. To pray.

Then she talk to Ambrose in the Eboe tongue, cause what he can do bout it? --Nwe ònwe, she say. --You know what that mean, massa? It mean be free. This world be a prison for us all.

Dido been waiting for the end but the end don't come. Ambrose still moaning and rocking in him vomit and Dido growing faint. She running over the plan again in her mind and know she done everything Turk tell her to do with the roots The Eboro give him. When Turk come by early that morning, he tell her, --I been to seek out the woman who don't age!

He were grinning when he say it, caint hardly keep a whisper.

--She gave me what gon fix everything fore I even ask her for it.

4

Turk say it to Dido just when her man Pompey gone off to work at the smithy in town.

--What fool thing you talking, Turk? What woman who don't age? Don't even say who I'm thinking you mean.

--That be just who I mean, Dido. I been out in the woods to see The Eboro, the one who hear even what Ala tell you in secret. The one the no-color man caint slave. She fix herself that way, hiding in plain sight, and don't nobody dare touch her! She gon fix Taddy too, she tell me. Nightfall come and I go to her and she see inside my head and give me what my heart tell her to. I aint say a word and still she know just what to do!

Turk showing Dido what he got in a bag in him hands.

--Roots, Dido say, eyes wideing.

--The Eboro say stir these up in a stew and he be fixt, sure enough!

Dido reaching out for the bag of roots in him hands but pull back fore she touch them.

--We gon kill him with those! She say.

--Yeah, we gon kill him! What choice we got?

But Dido turn her back on Turk and shake her head.

--No. Pompey aint gon like this none at all.

--This for *Taddy*. Not Pompey.

--Pompey say he have him a plan too. And he be my man and Taddy's pap.

--Well The Eboro aint say nothing bout Pompey. She say we *posed* to do this. She already done seen massa dead. Say he gon die on *this* day. She say *what prop him up gon bring him down*. I reckon she meaning him own lands. *These* here roots.

--Don't feel right...

--I warning you, now, Dido, Misuss be back tonight with them other house menors and you see what they let you put in a stew. See if they don't get you strung up fore you pull a root out you hankchecuff.

So it were decided.

--May we live to see ourselves tomorrow, Turk saying to her in Eboe as he were leaving. It stick in her now. Aint gon be no more tomorrows.

Dido rolling over every membering of what Turk say this morning but she not membering nothing bout how long The Eboro say it take Ambrose to die. She try membering the roots they grow in Eboeland, but she been in Virginia too long. She wondering why Ambrose still living and if he not eat enough root on account of him being so fat, or if roots plain weak in this world.

She out of time to think, cause now the heavy kitchen door slamming open and boots coming straight for the dining room. She hear they stomping, shoot up off the ground and flatten her whole self into the corner to wait for what coming.

--Dido? Dido, no! What have you done?

She hearing Pompey talking to her in Eboe and know they all in trouble. Pompey don't never risk speaking they secret tongue in plain day, specially not in front of Ambrose. Still, she breathing easy cause it only be her man and she run and throw her arms round him thick neck. He pull her close into him chest. Though she a tall woman, he taller still, and he swallow her up with big arms.

--I told you I would fix it! I told you I would find a way! Now what have you done to us all?

The soot from Pompey's clothes and hands from a day of welding iron smear on Dido's face and she breathe him in like it be the last thing she ever do. She answer in Eboe too, cause what Ambrose gon do?

--He should be dead by now. I did everything Turk said, everything The Eboro told him.

Pompey hold her away by her shoulders to look in her face when he say, --That fool brother of yours told me what he set you up to. I rode as fast as I could from the smithy. Why, Dido? Why do you listen to Turk and some juju woman and not me?

She pull away from him hands and point at a writhing Ambrose. --He came after Taddy! He wasn't ever going to stop, you know it! You thought he'd stop with me but you see he hasn't! Not even this very day!

Pompey turn him head away from her, shaming, and she sorry she tell him that part. She gentler when she say, --I stopped him now, Pompey. I did. He won't ever touch us again!

--The only thing you've done is killed us all.

Him words sink into Dido and draw tears like blood in a slow drip from her eyes. Pompey put her face in him hands and say, --No time to cry, woman. We will set it right. Go and fetch Dallas in the stables. Tell him to ride as quickly as he can to Doctor Warren. Tell him to say Ambrose is dying and to come straight away.

Pompey get to folding up Ambrose's arms to make him a easy carry. Then he say, --Clean this room and start preparing supper. Misuss and the others will be home soon. When they get here, you tell them Ambrose was eating and suddenly grabbed at his chest, saying he couldn't breathe. Then he fell out of his chair. He crawled up the stairs to his room and told you to get help. Say no more than that. He clutched his chest, not his gut. Say exactly that, lest they accuse you for sure. I will take him to his room.

--Will you...end his suffering?

Dido eyes begging but Pompey scoff. He say,

--End his suffering? You think if I could slit his throat and watch him choke slow on his own blood I would not do it? You think if you and I and Taddy could stay alive, stay together, and I could still crush his skull with my blacksmith's hammer, that I wouldn't do it and spit on him after? I would wonder if you had gone mad, but I already know what this man has done to you.

Him words cut Dido cause she know it make no sense to care what little Ambrose suffer in the end. Not after all he done. It do make her feel every kind of mad.

--Pray he dies soon, Pompey say fore he scoop up Ambrose easy, even though the man be fat all round.

Pompey carry Ambrose across oak floors, through long corridors spackled with paintings of the Burken clan, generations glaring at Pompey as he take Ambrose up three lengths of creaking stair to Ambrose chambers where Dido caint see them no more.

When Dido see to it that the stable boy Dallas riding off to Doc Warren, and long moments pass, at last she seeing Pompey come back down the stairs, empty.

--He is dead, Pompey say and Dido get a chill.

--The roots?

--Too slow. I smothered him with his own cushion until he was still and cold. He is gone.

Dido run to him weeping. --I doomed us, she say.

--No, Ezinne, no. He whisper her true name, he hug her, just as strong as always, and she knowing he still loving all of her. --You saved us.

He kiss her and leave quick and quiet out the back, lest any field menor see him there and know things aint right. She watch him bareback him horse and ride off for the smithy.

Dido pick up all the china pieces, the wine glass and the splinter-up chair. She scrub away the vomit and she sneak outside with the stew pot. She look all round to make sure no one seeing, then dump it in weeds away from the house garden. She scrub the pot like she scrub herself after the first time Ambrose come up on her, rough, with no mercy. But she swear to herself she thinking of that day for the last time. He were dead now.

Dido start again on the rabbit stew. When she made the first batch, she were singing. She warn't in no singing mood this time round.

Dido stop short when she hear a heavy fist on the front door of the Great House. She walk slow to the main hall to fetch it. Almost done, it almost done, she thinking.

--Hello, Doc Warren, she say when the heavy wooden door creak open to a thin, world-weary man in a frock coat and top hat with a black leather bag in him hand.

--Hello, Dido, he say. --Tell me, what has happened to Ambrose? Where is he?

--He right upstairs in bed, Doc Warren. This way.

Dido lead him to Ambrose bed, though Doc Warren know the way. She tell him as they walking just what Pompey tell her to say.

--Massa Ambrose clutch him chest at dinner and just keel right over saying him caint breathe. Kept grabbing at him chest, he was.

--I see, he say, but don't say nothing else til he see Ambrose bloated face. --Oh, my friend!

Doc cry out and him face collapsing in when he see Ambrose, pale and sweaty. Dido soul cry out when she see him too. *Alive? Alive!*

Doc kneel down next to the bed, digging in him bag. Dido hold to the wall to keep steady. No time to break apart cause she hearing hooves trotting up out front and she feeling her heart beating in her throat. Caroleen home now. And the nosy lot. Dido get to coughing but it feel more like choking.

When she catch her breath she say, --Scuse me, Doc Warren, the Misuss home. I bes prepare her for this ugly sight.

--Yes, of course, Dido, he say without looking away from Ambrose. --Quite right, he say.

8

Ambrose grabbing Doc Warren by the arm, trying to gather him words together but Doc Warren say,

--Shush now, Ambrose. Try to save your strength. We'll fix you up, friend. You'll see.

But Ambrose eyes got a story to tell. Dido see that and she run out the room, cursing him, praying all at once.

The footman creak the Great House door open and Caroleen walk in, looking like the coldest kind of sunshine in her yellow hoop dress trimmed in white lace. Dido run toward her, down the curving grand stair and Caroleen coil up her whole body at the sight of Dido.

--Stop, girl!

Caroleen say it, thick with the French she were born to and Dido don't dare move a foot off the stair she landing on. --The way you are flying down *my* staircase, one could almost mistake *you* for the Mistress of this house!

--Begging your pardon, Missus. I warn't meaning to run...

--Get off my stairs at once! C'*est ma* house, menor girl, you understand? Not *his.*

Dido walk down the rest of the way and back away from Caroleen. But Caroleen come closer. She breathing right in Dido face, teeth clenching.

--Yes'm, Dido start, flustering, --But...

--He may own you, but this house and the money that bought it, it is mine and never mind what he thinks of it.

Caroleen tell Dido once she don't think she hate the ones she call menors. She come from France to the colonies and in all the places she been, menors just be menors. Who were she to change it? No, she tell Dido, it aint hate at all. Her nosy lot even comfort her the first time she seen Ambrose on Dido. Caroleen cry in Big Lady's lap over it, and Big Lady rock her and make her feel like being alive again. No, Caroleen tell her. Menors aint the problem. The problem be Dido.

--Where is supper, girl? Or were you not expecting us? Caroleen walk past Dido, untying her bonnet string and letting her straw-color curls fall out of it.

--Begging your pardon, Misuss Burken, she say and curtsey quick. --But Massa Ambrose fallen ill. Massa Ambrose sitting at the table eating then fell out grabbing at him chest and say him caint

9

breathe. I help him upstairs and fetch Doc Warren and he up there with him now. He don't look too good.

Caroleen throwing her bonnet into Dido chest and get to flying up the stairs herself, like the Great House on fire. Dido grab the bonnet and press up against the staircase wall to let her pass, some of the nosy lot fly close behind, well trained. Two others go to prepare Caroleen some tea and supper in case she ask for it later. But Big Lady come stand right in front of Dido and won't let her pass up the stairs.

--So, Massa done fell out. And at the table, you say?
Big Lady aint asking no question.

--Yeah, Dido say, looking Big Lady straight in the face.

--Hm, Big Lady say. --How little ole you get Massa Ambrose up all them stairs to bed, Afrikan?

--I aint big as *you*, Dido shooting back, --but I sure aint little. She push the bonnet into Big Lady's chest and Big Lady fall back enough for Dido to get up the stairs.

When she reaching Ambrose room, she try to sneak in, quiet, and stand in the back just to hear what he gon say, see what he gon do. But he spot her and start to choking again. Him eyes popping, he pointing, she hear him say, --Dido!

Everybody hear it. He shaking him head and coughing. Caroleen say, --Get out! No one told you to come, girl. See how you upset him!

Dido turn quick and take down the stairs two-by-two. She sneak out the house without seeing any of the nosy lot, but she hear two saying, --Garden menor tell me Pompey been here in this house mid-day!

--All the way from the smithy? Now what you thinking that bout?

--Hmph! Aint no telling with them Afrikans...
Dido get flush and shaky. She slip out back and run to her hut. She gotta get to her Taddy.

Taddy were too young to do real work and too old to be under anybody's constant eye but Chúkwú alone, so when Dido get back to her hut, she happy to find Taddy safe, in a corner playing with the maize doll Pompey make her.

--Come hug your mam, babygirl, she say, and Taddy come quick and do like Dido say.

--You gotta do something for your mam now, Taddy. You gotta tell me again bout Ala, Dido say, pulling Taddy down so they can sit on the dirt floor together.

--Mam, I not forgetting Ala. I just tell you again bout her whileago...

--Do this for your mam!

Dido don't want to frighten Taddy so she calm herself.

--Tell me one more time, babygirl. I won't ask you no more afterwhile. I sweard it.

--Ala belong to Chúkwú, Taddy say, --And she watching over all the earth. When your belly fat with me inside, Ala come tell you me was coming and me was a girl and me gon do a great thing. Ala tell you she gon help me do a great thing.

--You right, babygirl. Zactly right, Dido smiling and eyes tearing. --And don't forget, back in Eboeland, your mam were the daughter of a king. Don't forget it.

Taddy look up to her mam, puzzling. --What a king be, ńné?

--A king be a great leader, baby. The ruler of the land. He wise and he keep everybody safe and happy.

--Like Massa Ambrose?

Dido feel stones in the pit of her gut weighing her down, stretching out her womb til she caint hardly breathe.

--No, baby. Not at all like Massa Ambrose.

Pompey come home from the smithy then, quiet. He come up behind them and she feel him wrap them both in him mighty hands.

--He not dead. He not dead, Dido sobbing quiet into Pompey chest. He kiss them both and release them. She watch him pull up him pant leg, untie him blacksmith hammer from him ankle and set it on they teeny round table. He snatch a branch from they woodpile and a rock and he get to sharpening til the branch be a spear. Dido rocking Taddy as she watching him, and none have any more words tween em.

Fore long they hearing Misuss scream so loud she echoing through the house and clear out to the quarters. Even Taddy know Ambrose be dead and everything done changed.

In no time, here come Butch the overseer and him five watchmen clan. They come with muskets ready. Butch kick down the door to they hut and let him watchmen descend.

11

Pompey standing firm, pushing Dido and Taddy behind him, spear in him right hand, hammer in him left. He knock one watchman in the head with him hammer and the watchman dead, easy. Butch try next and Pompey stab him through with the spear, just missing him heart. Butch cry out fore he snap off the long end of the spear while two other watchmen aim they muskets and shoot Pompey in both him legs. They drag Pompey out through the quarters while he scream through clenching teeth.

The only watchman left standing pry Taddy and Dido apart and throw Dido up over him shoulder like straw as she kick and scream, --Taddy!

Taddy reach for her pap's sharpening rock and throw it square at the watchman's back. He cry out, knees buckling a little but not so much Dido get away. He shoot Taddy a glare that make her fall back in the dirt. Dido full of fear for Taddy, so she shake her head, *no*, so Taddy don't move, don't speak as the watchman turn and carry Dido out the hut.

Torches light up the quarters and all thirty-seven enslaved rush out they huts and gather round the whipping block in the clearing to bear witness to what the watchmen gon do. Dido spot her dearest friend Nnene in the crowd and she scream out, --Nnene, take Taddy! Take care her! Promise me!

She feeling the most despair she ever feel since she first lay eyes on a no-color man and him gun so long ago in Eboeland. It were Nnene what save her on the Debil ship from Eboeland. It were only Nnene what could save her now. Nnene scream her promises. --Ezinne! I sweard it to you!

Dido breathe out all she were holding in but only til she see more watchmen coming. They got Turk.

--NO!

She yelling as Butch and the watchmen drag the three Afrikans up jagged stairs to the block, lining them up by who done the worst, Turk, Pompey, then Dido. Dido member now how she say her brother's name in front of Ambrose while she were killing him, and she shaming for being so foolish. She caint look at Turk, Pompey nuther, as the watchmen bury they musket heads deep into the necks of the rebels.

--It is only the beginning, Pompey whisper in Eboe and it all Dido need to straighten up her back and lift up her head to the gates of heaven. In death, they all three silent heirs of Eboeland this night.

Dido close her eyes to pray what the preacherman tell her be the Lord's Prayer. Her mind all a swirl and she jumbling it up with a prayer she membering from when she were a chile.

--Nna Anyi no ne elu igwe, she saying.

--Ala, earth angel of Chúkwú, watch over my Taddy. Don't let her leave this earth til she do her great thing.

Dido hear her chile screaming for her but she don't dare look.

--Nna Anyi no ne elu igwe! Dido praying.

One gunshot hack through all the darkness. Then the body thud against wood and Turk head roll into dirt, eyes wideing.

--Ala, earth angel of Chúkwú, who knows my real name!

Gun blasting and Pompey make a choke sound for him head get to rolling too.

--Jesus!

Nobody seem to hear the last boom what hit Dido square in the neck. She don't thud though. She just slump, neck break and open up to one side. The crowd were humming til then. Now, everything fall silent.

Butch use him good arm to knock what left of Dido head off her body. Watchmen come and pile up them bodies and Butch pull the rest of the splinter spear out the back of hisself with a grunt. He stake what left of Pompey with the spear, grab a torch from a watchman and light up them bodies and the night sky.

Weeks pass, but not a day go by Taddy don't see her ńné, her pap and her uncle, cause Butch done just what Caroleen tell him.

--Cut off those menors' heads! I want them on a pole, so the rest of these menors know I'm not the trifling kind!

So Butch doing it and all the slaves fearing Caroleen, even the nosy lot. Butch beating Taddy every day since her kin done the dread thing. Caroleen keep Taddy close by to watch, working her hard in the garden but making sure she never see the inside of the Great House while Caroleen living.

Through the Great House windows, Taddy hearing Caroleen screaming at Butch all the time for what he got nothing to do with. --Fool husband, Caroleen say. --Bedding them while they mock me! Butch, you teach them what it cost! And my boys, my

William and Francis, if they even go *near* a menor *putain*, you direct it to me. Not while I breathe they will touch one, not while I breathe!

Caroleen screaming it, no matter that William warn't but thirteen and Francis warn't but nine and the law say them slaves belonging to man-chiles over woman any day, specially a French one. Still, she screaming, screaming, but all this time she don't never once cry. Taddy do though. Specially after Caroleen get to ranting and Butch get to beating. Butch never touch her like Ambrose, but him licks still going to her soul.

Turnt out Dido done what she set out for, cause after that, no no-color man touch a menorwoman nor girl at Wellesbury while Caroleen living, but that too far off. Little Taddy don't know none of it, let alone to be grateful for it, cause the whippings getting worser and the work days getting longer. She just know she walk by them heads every day, shrinking and stinking in the sun, and she pray and she pray, --Ala, please bring back my ńné, my pap and Uncle Turk.

But none of them coming back so she pray different.

--Ala, please let Misuss hamercy so we can bury our dead proper.

But Caroleen never hamercy. After the three heads rotting something awful, Taddy hearing Butch come tell Caroleen, --Missus, some menors wanting to bury them heads...

--Do it and die! Caroleen say. --Let birds pick out their eyes and worms eat at their flesh!

So them vultures, worms, maggots and time taking that awful smell and most everything else, leaving only sunken skulls and hair on the pole. Then Taddy plain give up.

She say, --Ala Earth Angel lie to my ńné. I aint never have no great thing. Never have no great thing in me at all.

PART ONE:

ENYE NWATA IFE KALIRIA OJU BA ENYELIE YA NYE
ONYE.

*WHEN A CHILD RECEIVES WHAT IS BIGGER THAN
HER, SHE THINKS IT IS FOR SOMEONE ELSE.*

30 YEARS LATER

-1-
ADDIS

Addis gasp and sit up in her bunk, shook. She almost hitting her head on the ceiling of her hut, but she raise her hand to protect herself in the darkness. Addis cough and grab at her neck to make sure it still be sitting on top her body. Her breathing slow up when she realize she safe in her own top bunk. Safe as a oji slave girl get at Wellesbury Plantation, anyhow. She lay back down on her bed, her heart thump thumping like a drum of war. When she get her wits bout her, she speak.

--Nnene, I dreamed of her again, Addis whisper soft in Eboe to the graying woman resting in the underbunk. It be pitch black in they hut, but Addis know her guardian be wide awake. If she aint wake Nnene with her coughing and shaking, it were only cause Nnene already been woke, waiting for the bell that signal the day breaking, and they own backs soon to follow. Addis sleep like a lizard when she dreaming, but Nnene sleeping always like a rat.

They alone, but, just like all the Eboe-talking slaves at Wellesbury, Addis and Nnene save they secret tongue for the earliest morning or latest night. Even the cock or the fox might hear and sell them out. The overseer Haynes and him watchmen got eye and ear everywhere, and they whip show no mercy. Eboe-talking get you fifty lashes, at least. Addis get even more quiet thinking bout that. She just under a whisper when she say,

--I saw Gran Gran Dido. I saw her poison Burken's father Ambrose with roots and then I saw watchmen kill her. I felt them do it. I rose up out of my body and was floating over it all and saw you as young woman and my mam as a little girl, watching the killings.

The wood boards squeak when Nnene get to shifting in her bunk.

--Then, Ala come to me again. But this time, I could see her face. She was deep black, pure as the Potomac at midnight, with deep-set eyes and lips like silver. She was dancing in the ocean. Her dress was silk, made of every kind of blue I have ever seen and some I had never seen before. It was trimmed in white like waves, and the whole ocean turned when she danced. She was singing. The *ocean* was singing, *bïa Chineke*. They kept chanting it, *bïa Chineke*, until I got hit with a wave and started to drown. Then I awoke.

--Hmph, Nnene grunt. She turning on her side with her feets hanging off the underbunk. Years can come and go but she never get comfortable sleeping on that bunk. --What is a child who doesn't even believe in Chúkwú Christ doing dreaming bout the earth angel anyway? Dreaming of Ala telling the Lord to come, hmph! I say, what for? And I tell you what an ocean won't do, drown somebody who's not set hair nor tail near it, that's what.

--Well, I don't know why I dreamed it.

--Eh? What you don't know would make a world, child. Why could you not just have itchy eyes or bump your foot on a stone to warn you of bad things to come, like the rest of us? Always these visions and dreams. A succubus must have gotten hold of you somewhere down the line.

Addis knew she were a strange, near-woman chile, but she don't think it her own fault she always dreaming what she dreaming. And it warn't no succubus that she know of. It were the overseer Haynes what done it. When she warn't but five year old, here Haynes come, with him wild hay-color hair and blood in him eyes holding a musket by the butt. Knock her clean out with it. That were the same day he kilt her pap, the same day she stop believing Chúkwú Christ were gon save her and the same day Chúkwú Christ start sending the angel to speak dreams to her. Everything done to her were strange, she thinking, so how folks think she gon turn out?

--I sure hope Taddy knows I tried my best with you, Nnene say, flustering. --Raised you to fear and honor the Lord for your mam. Lord knows I did!

Now Addis get to scoffing and muttering.

--My mam can blame herself if she doesn't care for the way I was raised.

Nnene silent. Addis know Nnene hate it when she talk bad of her own mam. But Addis think she got every right to be angry with Taddy for leaving her alone, so both lay still, waiting for anything else to happen, the cock crowing, the clanging bell, but nothing come. Addis never been one for waiting, so she steal the quiet.

--It was a beautiful dream, anyhow. I have never seen so many colors, not even in the gardens in spring. And while I was drowning, she called out to me. She called me my true name, Adaeze. Then she called me agụ. And I answered to both.

--Strange child you are! Only you would find it beautiful to drown, Nnene whisper-scream it.. --Thought you were scared of the water anyhow, eh? And agụ? What do you even know of tigers? If you saw one you would die on the spot, I'm sure!

--It's just a lion with stripes.

--Hmph!

--And if Ala is the Lord's Earth Angel, why couldn't she dance in the ocean? And why couldn't she call me a tiger if she wanted? Wouldn't she know who I am? She knew my true name, after all.

--And oceans! Nnene start again. --What have you ever seen but the Potomac out there, but you are dreaming of oceans. Lord, help me with this child!

--But you saw an ocean, once, when they brought you to this world as a child. You told me you had seen it. Wasn't it all kinds of blues and white?

Addis feel the bed shake once as a shiver go up Nnene spine, even though it be as hot and damp as every other summer morning in the hut. Addis don't know whether Nnene membering being on that great ship from Eboeland, or if Nnene fearing cause Addis dreaming of tigers, oceans and Ala, but something sure make Nnene blood run cold. Addis don't ask and the morning bell crack the silence.

Nnene hop up quick, even in her old age, picking up the quilt she shrug off in the night. She fold the quilt and reach up over her head to tap the frame of the bunk Addis still laying in.

--Best get a move on, Nnene say. The day beginning so the Eboe got to end. --You don't want Haynes n'em to come here after you, she say fore she starting a small fire in the hearth to clear out the night.

Addis climb down the bunk ladder. Her feets hit the dirt floor and she startle when Nnene wrap up Addis with mighty arms that done cradle life and death. Addis taller than her, but next to Nnene, she feel like a teeny thing.

--You seventeen now, Addis, she say, reaching up to stroke Addis long, cherrywood face and then reach for Addis thick hair she got platted down her back. Nnene hugging Addis when she say,

18

--You growing up to be so beautiful and strong. But now you just old enough a woman for it to hurt your soul when they punish you.

Addis want to scoff again til she feel the wariness in Nnene's arms. So Addis return the embrace but not the warmth, pulling back when she start membering things she rather not.

--I warn't much a woman when Haynes come and blow a hole through my daddy gut and set him body on fire, Addis say. She caint look at Nnene when she saying this. She know it hurt Nnene to hear all the bad things. So Addis just walking to the washpan in the corner of the hut by the hearth.

--Warn't but five when Haynes ole scar-up face bust me in my head and got me dreaming funny, thinking funny, Addis saying, dipping a rag in the days-old water and scrubbing her face with it. --Warn't a woman when Taddy leave me for you to raise and go crawling to Burken house with the smell of my burnt-up pap still a-wafting in the air. Don't seem you gotta be seventeen to be hurt to your soul, Nnene.

Addis stop scrubbing herself when she feel her face stinging. She trying not to be hurt bout things long since done, but time passing never been much comfort to a slave. --Sides, she say, calm, --it be my body they after now, anyhow. Not my soul.

Nnene come up behind Addis and put her hands on Addis shoulders.

--Chile, Nnene say fore she gets real quiet. --Bes you keep your dreams tween us.

Addis nod, but get to wondering if it were more than just a dream to Nnene. She turn to Nnene and smile a little.

--Who you thinking I going to tell this to? The Menor-Missus? Addis laugh and Nnene raise her voice now.

--MotherFather God! How you disrespect your mam so! Where you even hear such a thing?

--Everyone calling her that, you know. Everyone know Massa keep her like she special. But just cause he the massa of this plantation and the massa of the whole world, don't make her no more than what she is.

--You call her *mam* in my face. And we don't say *menor*, we say *oji*. So you get that straight. And Massa Burken be the president, Nnene correcting. --He ruling *Amerika*, not the whole world, she say.

--He a great warrior, defeating a whole nation of no-color folks to

19

make other no-color folks free. Why you think he got all them cannons all up round the Great House like decoration? People knowing him the world over cause he a champion, but he don't rule it all. And what he doing to your mam aint special.

--No? Addis say. --Cause that be what she act like. With her two mulatto boys, Great House-living, all three of em, like they winning some prize. Oh they tremble sure enough if the Lord come and wipe out they good fortune with a ocean wave. Don't you worry bout me telling Taddy nothing bout my dream. Nothing at all.

Nnene reach over Addis shoulder and grab the rag out her hand and push Addis out the way. --You won't be disrespecting your mam in front of me again. Thirty years ago, I raise her just like I raising you, like my own kin. I tell you over and over, she say, wagging her finger at Addis back. --You won't be doing it again. To have both me and your mam alive to care for you? You better thank your God and shake your tail! What I'd give to know what become of my mam.

Nnene take the rag, baptize it in the water and ring it out. She using it on her own face when she say, --Sides. You know I'm meaning don't tell that boy.

--Who, Ekwueme? Addis say, coy. She don't want Nnene getting suspicious so she don't make a fuss when Nnene mention her love. Addis grab the fading blue linen shift she wearing every day since spring and step into it slow, careful not to stretch the tatters at the hem that come from getting caught in garden vines and branches.

--Unless there be another boy sides him! That boy alone be trouble. *You* and that boy? There aint a word for the hitch you bring us all, Nnene say over her shoulder. --Tell that boy the dream and the fool fool have you to thinking you and he float to Eboeland on a cat's back fore night fall.

Addis grunt a little. *Sssk!* She sure Ekwueme might say, like he do anytime folks bring up Ala or Chúkwú. *Aint menor life taught us there be no such thing as magic and spirits that save? Where were Ala when my pap were kilt? When your pap were kilt? Sssk!* She already knowing there be no reason to tell Ekwueme bout Ala. Sides, they got bigger things to think bout, she thinking. Nightfall were sure coming but they warn't planning to escape on no cat. Ekwueme got him a plan and Addis smile just thinking what he gon tell her bout it this very night.

Addis reaching for her bonnet off the rusting door hook when she feel Nnene come behind her again, wrapping her arms round tight.

--Things might get worser round here for you, she say. --Might soon come. Worser than you ever thinking it could. But you gotta know. You gotta believe me when I tell you, Chúkwú hear you. Chúkwú *know*.

Addis turn to hug her and she catch some of Nnene's tears on her own cheek. But it get to be too much for her, taking on Nnene's pain and fear and mixing it up with her own. So Addis let go of Nnene quick, grab her bonnet and head straight for the Great House garden, as silent and determined as she were when she were drowning.

ADDIS

Get through the day and the night soon come, Addis thinking as she march her way to the Great House gardens, uphill from the quarters. She always starting her work in Lower Garden, where they growing fruits and vegetables in season. When she finish, she head cross the horseshoe pathway in front of the Great House to Upper Garden where they growing flowers, plants for soaps and herbs for cooking and medicine. Upper Garden also be where they keeping the Greenhouse Burken make him slaves build a few years back, where he sperimenting with all kind of funny fruits and plants that don't grow natural in Virginia.

When Addis were little, she wondering bout the queerdoings of her di nwēnu, but she don't no more. What it matter to Addis why Burken do what he do? Warn't gon change how fufu taste.

Addis reach the opening of the brick wall what surround Lower Garden and pick up a basket. She slink her way up the first peach tree at the edge of the garden, basket under one arm. She careful not to scrape gainst the glass pieces she strung up on the branches to frighten thrashers and jays from eating all the crop. Sun aint broke yet and Addis don't need it. She been climbing these trees, not making nary a sound, since she were a termite on a toad's back. She don't have to tell her feets to balance in between the two sturdy branches they feel. They just do. When she settle, she start to picking peaches and dropping them into her basket.

With the leaves giving her shield, Addis don't drop the next peach she picking. --Thank you, peach, she say, and she bite it and let sweet juice drip down her chin. Her nose flood with warm citrus and she breathe it in so deep it sting her nostrils while she slurping quiet. Addis wipe her face on her shift and lean her body back on a branch. She hold the basket with her knees while she slow-eat the peach. The ones you aint posed to have be the sweetest, she thinking.

That were the thing bout garden-working. It warn't houseworking and it warn't fieldworking. It were some place in between. Hard work, sure enough, and Nnene and Addis working the fruit garden, the herb garden cross the way and Burken's Greenhouse from caint see to caint see, but it were still better than working out in the fields of one of Burken's 5 Farms. Not just cause they could switch to plucking the trees and get some shade when the sun forsake her children and beat them down too much, but cause most all other slaves, bout three hundred in number at Wellesbury, be spread out over the 5 Farms cross the whole plantation. Haynes and him watchmen got they hands full with all the others and leave Nnene and Addis alone most hours.

Burken the only one who come check on Nnene and Addis garden work and he only come after him mid-morning ride and again fore evening come. Now he been named the president of the country, Addis thinking he gon be too busy to watch them. But she changing her mind, quick: somebody always gon be watching them.

That were the thing bout *Addis* working the garden. Sometime it fool her into thinking she free, just a moment. She even love working the ground and climbing trees, though she try real hard to hate it. Addis thinking if she like it that make everything Burken and Haynes doing to them okay. She tell Nnene this when she were only eight and Nnene say, --Chile, aint nothing you ever could say or do to make what they doing okay.

Instead, Nnene tell Addis to think of the ground, the seeds, the crop same as them.

--The crop getting just enough water, food and light to keep em alive so Massa can strip em to death, take everything from em, then throw em away when theys done. It aint omenani...least not how we know it in Eboeland, Nnene say. --Omenani different here in Amerika.

--In Eboeland, we was all mmadu. We treat everybody like they mmadu, she tell Addis. --Mmadu were the very goodness of life. It were to be honored and protected. And theys a certain way the mmadu ought and ought not to act. Aint so in Amerika, she says.

--Be Eboe, Nnene always tell her. --Keep your mmadu, nevermind what come.

So Addis feel all right bout loving the ground and taking comfort in the smell of dirt and the moist crumble it make when she squeeze it between her fingers. She talking sweet to the crop to help them grow and thanking them for they gifts when harvest time come. But she always thinking of ole man Remus to make sure she not loving it all too much. Remus were the gardener fore Nnene got the job, the one who rat out Pompey to the nosy lot and get Pompey head blown off with Dido and Turk. Ole Missus Caroleen, fore she pass on to Hell, she putting Nnene over the garden work and bring Taddy with her.

Addis member how Nnene say Caroleen done it cause she pity Nnene on account of how every baby Nnene born aint have no breath. But everybody know Caroleen aint one for pity. She done it to keep an eye on the chile, fearing one day Taddy were going to grow blonde hair and green eyes like her husband Ambrose have fore Dido kill him off. Course Taddy never did and Remus get put out to field for nothing and he die soon after, heartbroken without him garden, fool ole thing. No matter how any of em love a garden, it warn't nobody's but Burken's.

Still, Addis were grateful to be garden working for more reasons. Cause of it, she close enough for her mam to sneak her books Caroleen's granbabies leave at the Great House, fore the babies die off, anyway. So Addis learn to read the schoolbooks, memorizing letters then words then sentences. *In Adam's fall, we sinned all. Job feels the rod and blesses God.* And then she copy it all down on paper and learn to write.

Nobody never finding out or even missing them schoolbooks nuther on account of all them granbabies getting the Fever. And they daddy, Caroleen's youngest son, Francis, he either die of it too, or the heartache, one. That leaving nothing but Massa William Henry Burken. Addis eyes always peeling for him. He warn't Haynes, but he were him own kind of evil. Haynes knowing he hurting you and he taking pleasure in it. But Burken? He caint imagine him slaves not loving they life with him. To Addis, that make him the most dangerous.

--Why do they hate us, so? Addis ask Nnene in Eboe, late one night.

--Chukwuma, Nnene say, not wanting to waste her God-given time thinking bout what make a no-color man think like he do. But Addis insist. So, Nnene say at last, and Addis never forgetting it:

--Aint no soul on a plantation that aint a slave. When the nose get hurt, the eyes weep.

Addis sit with that answer for many years, but it don't satisfy her none. What she care if they hate theyself too?

A twig breaking just now, and Addis startle and sit up on the branch, half-thinking she hear Burken coming. But no. Too early. And the feetsteps be too quiet. They belonging to someone used to sneaking.

--Best not be grubbing on no peaches up there, chile.
Addis swallow the last of her peach and suck the pit clean fore she
say,

--No'm.

--Well I sure don't hear you working.

--I working, Nnene.

--Mmhmm.

Addis slip the pit into her shift pocket and get back to
picking. Harvest time done come and peaches warn't the only thing
ready to be thanked and plucked but it were bout the only thing
Addis could do without the shine of morning. She pick all that be
ready and shimmy down the tree one-handed, the basket tucked
under her left arm. When her feets hit the ground, she set down the
basket and stretch out her arms.

Then a bright flash lighting up her world. All a sudden, her
arm aint her arm no more, but it be a buzzard wing, with gray and
dirty white feathers, stained by a bloody beak. The vision make her
stumble to the ground, but she don't dare drop the basket. When
she gain her balance, she set it down, and put both hands on her
temples and rub and rub furious. She feel the prickle of feathers
against the side of her face, but still she say outloud,

--Aint nothing there. Aint nothing there. She say it just like
Nnene teaching her years ago. She shake her head free, blink her eyes
and her arm be a girl's arm again.

Just then, the cock crow and they know morning breaking.
Right on beat, here come the sky lighting up the east with orange.
Addis look up and see the sun licking up the river miles away and
for a brief moment she happy. She thinking, maybe she be a child of
the sun like Nnene always telling her. Maybe there be a God, One
who make beautiful things like how preacherman say when he come
on Sundays.

--Go day, come day, God gon bring Sunday afterwhile,
Nnene always saying, and Addis don't mind cause Sundays be when
no-color Christ saying don't work cause it be a holy day. But no-
color Christ also saying be a good slave or get the whip, she thinking.
So she aint fond of him none at all.

--Fool chile! Nnene always say when she hearing Addis say
no-color Christ out loud. --You not knowing Chúkwú Christ been
known in Eboeland long fore the no-color man come and say so?

--Nah, I aint know.

25

--You aint know Chúkwú Christ been known to ojis long fore no-color man even know? Hmph! What you don't know! What you don't know would make a world.

Addis blink and the memory melting and the sun get to rising even more and she certain it all be a lie. Maybe massas and preacherman make up even the sun so they can have they own way, she thinking. Maybe aint nothing real. Maybe she not even really here in this garden...

--You just gon stand there dreaming dawn away while there be weeding need done?

Addis hear Nnene and come back into herself.

--Sorry, Nnene.

Addis get started on weeding round the cabbages and shut her mind down so she don't have to be thinking all the time what she thinking.

Addis looking only at her hands while she digging in dirt, careful of the cabbage heads, firm but gentle when she grab at the weeds just below ground. She tell them, --Sorry you caint stay here. I know it aint so much your fault where you growing but you choking out all what be good round here. Caint have that, you understand.

She plucking up the weeds and piling them behind her as she go through three cabbage rows. Warn't nothing weeds were doing cept destroying life on top of giving her more work to do, so she aint thanking them for they gifts, but still she pitying them as she were plucking. They aint knowing what they doing, after all. But that don't mean they get to stay.

--You almost ready, cabbage! She whispering to the crop as she work her way down the row, its boxwood edges snagging at her dress every now and again. --Look how fat and green you getting for your friend Adaeze! Knew if I tell you my true name, you open up to me too. When you all the way open, I'm gon take care of you just like I promise you. Trust in me.

She keep talking as she work, like Nnene teach her, cause she knowing it making the crop in her hands feel safe and loved by more than just sun and earth. But it also keep her mind quiet. So if her words don't last through weeding thirty rows of cabbage, spinach, collards, onions, beets, beans, carrots and peas, she usually sing. Never whistle, though. Nuther at the moon nor in the sun, Nnene always saying.

--Just see don't it bring out the snakes, Nnene saying, so Addis only humming or singing.

Sometimes she singing what she pick up from ojis she see on Sundays when church going on down at One Farm or when she out on Three Farm for a homegoing. Sometimes she making songs up when her heart be light enough. But that only come after she done seen Ekwueme, and it been at least two weeks since the last time. Sometimes she humming songs bout Eboeland she learn from Nnene when Nnene feel like shaking the dust off them, though those times coming less and less as the years go on. The crop like the Eboe songs the best, Addis learn, but today, only song stuck in Addis head be one she hating.

When she were young, chiles that aint fit for working yet used to come up to the gardens and try to steal fruits. When Nnene tell them to get on, they mock Nnene with songs they hearing from they caretakers.

Run and hide, jet black woman! / Mean woman / Lawd, she mean!

Addis chase them out, sometime with rocks, and she would cry and Nnene tell her, --Why you cry for, chile? They not even knowing what they singing. They not even knowing.

Addis feeling a lump in her throat thinking on this now and she singing to set it free.

What been done to the jet black woman? / Mean woman / Why she mean?

All her singing stir up a black butterfly with tips on its wings as blue as cornflowers. Addis stick out the palm of her hand and the butterfly land right on her and it make her to membering the last book her mam ever giving her. Had a poem in it by a fella named Joseph Warton all bout the queen of the insects, the butterfly, a child of sun and summer. Addis hold her hand steady and sing her fears to the creature.

He done put some sugar in her coffee / Mean woman / It make her mean!

But she stop dead when she hearing untender feets stomping through the garden. She look up slow and see white breeches, but she don't need to see past him cotton waistcoat to know it be him.

William Henry Burken don't walk, he clomp bout the world like a man who belong everywhere him foot step. Nnene tell her he been this way ever since he were born. After Dido kilt him pap,

Nnene say it make him feel even more like everything be owed to him. Like the whole world got to make up for him emptiness. Warn't long fore he were off fighting for the king, leading troops into battle, thinking he gon win the king's favor but he don't.

King don't even consider Burken the same kinda people since Burken be colony-born, Nnene tell her, so Burken, in a fury, plot him a revolution and make him a new country where he get to be better than a king. He get to be a god caint no one touch for all time and he move through every space in the present like he sure of it.

Burken don't stop til him thick thighs near touching Addis face. She stagger back on both hands and look up at him, sun in her eyes. He look down at her like he have no inkling how or why she down there.

--Heavens, girl, stand up, him say, and Addis rise slow.

--Yessir, she say, quiet, still looking him in him eyes. Him stern face soften a bit and he say,

--You look so much like her, he almost whispering, the right corner of him mouth turnt up. But the words pelt down on her like hail and Addis scrunch up her face and recoil. Burken harden him face again. --Come with me, he say, barely looking at her from the corners of him eyes.

He walk past her and she too fraid not to follow. But what would he dare do to her? He separate plenty families, like Yandy the cobbler who don't see him wife and kids at Four Farm til Saturdays and Sundays, same as most all the men working House Farm that got families. Not to mention her pap, who Burken kill off, and her mam who Burken steal away, breed with and use on any night he like. What would he dare do? She answer her own self: anything he want.

Addis follow Burken into the brick Greenhouse inside the garden walls. She stand in the doorway while he walk down a row of saplings and sink him hands in pots of seeds sitting on a table, ready for winter planting: coffee, oranges, limes, lemons and such.

--Do you know what this is? Burken ask Addis and she cough fore she say,

--They seeds, Massa.

--Seeds, he hmph. --Well, he who knows nothing is closer to the truth than he whose mind is filled with errors. These seeds, Addis, this Greenhouse you are standing in, these are the dreams of the future. My dreams. I create here. I build here. In this place, I know the true meaning of Christ's words in the Book of Matthew, that with God all things are possible. My world is limited by nothing; neither cold nor frost hinders my creation. I hope, some day or another, we shall become a storehouse and granary for the world.

Burken turn to Addis, smiling, but him smile fade when he see her cold face. He walk toward her and she back against the doorframe. --I see you do not understand, he say. --You have no concept of the vision you are helping to manifest. How could you? It is so far beyond you.

Addis press herself into the wood casing as Burken make him way closer still, giddy.

--But be inspired, girl. Be confident that you are a part of a great, new beginning. The work you are doing, in this garden, in this Greenhouse, *for me*, will live forever.

--Won't nobody know *I* done it, though, Addis spit then bite her lip. Her gut drop down and she forget to breathe as he look to her, hands behind him back, like the hunting dogs look at meat rations. She shiver as he stand there, just close enough to do anything he wanting.

--Our cause is noble, Addis, he breathe. --It is the cause of mankind. Do not concern yourself with honor and praise far beyond your station. If you are to survive, you had better learn that, Burken say and look her over once more fore he stomp away.

Addis let out her breath. The fear done left her and now she fill up with something altogether different. Something cold and heavy sticking to her insides and she caint swallow it away. Maybe she do got a succubus in her after all, she thinking.

-3-
TADDY

Taddy! Missus Burken yelling and it snap Taddy out the rage slow-burning in her gut when she seeing Burken through the kitchen window, out in the garden, close on her chile. She were watching him move Addis to the Greenhouse where she caint see good and she don't like it none at all. He always out there with Addis this time of day but it don't never sit well with her.

--My word, girl, where is your head today?

--Awful sorry, Missus Burken, Taddy say, pulling herself away from that window, making her eyes level with Missus Burken so she know she listening.

--Ah, *bon*? I bet a good lashing will wake you. I would hate to get that brute Haynes in here but a president's wife should never raise her hand to anyone, even one as shiftless as you.

--No'm, I woke now, sure enough. Taddy wipe her hands on her apron and draw close to Missus Burken.

--Good. Now pay attention. We can't have you nodding off when we get up to Philadelphia, now can we? Not with all the important folk Master Burken will have to tend to.

--Yessm.

--You will have to be more mindful of the time now. You will start bringing Master Burken hot tea for his chest cold at half past four, but only if there are no guests in the house to see it. If so, then coffee only, do you understand?

Taddy put on her best jumble face and say with eyes real big, --*Foourr*?

--Agh, Missus Burken throw up her hands and go to the great hall clock what used to chime but don't no more. Taddy follow swift.

--HALF! PAST! FOUR! Missus Burken yelling while she pointing at the clock hands, pounding every word slow like that what gon help Taddy understand her better.

--ONE! TWO! THREE! FOUR! AND A HALF!

Missus looking round and see her womenslaves stare at her, biting they lips to keep from laughing at how strange loud she being. She clear her throat, lift her head and quieter say,

--Understand?

--Yessm. Half. Past. Four, Taddy repeat, just as slow as Missus Burken, squeezing what lonely bit of pleasure out of it she can.

--Good. With Master Burken being the very first president of this great country, we are all going to have to start making some *adjustments*. You would do well to keep that in mind.

Taddy see Missus Burken turn a bit red at the French that still drench the new Amerikan way of talking Missus trying on.

--Yessm, Taddy say.

--Well, off, then. Put the tea on. Go on.

--Yessm.

--Come, Nora. I'll have to tell you what to pack for Philadelphia. Everything must be *just so*, from clothing down to the china we use. Quality, assuredly, but not opulence. The theme is understated grace…understand?

Taddy watch Missus Burken strut away, back so straight and head so high she thinking Missus gonna tip backward. Taddy grin to herself at this new Missus Burken. But her smile straighten out as soon as she see Burken come through the Great House front door.

--Splendid time for you to come inside, darling. I've got tea put on for you.

--Mrs. Burken, we cannot possibly have tea.

--Do not worry yourself, Mr. Burken. Your troops cannot see you from here. Taddy will bring it to your study in a short while.

Taddy watch the Missus titter as Burken kiss him wife cheek. Taddy whole body tense up at the sight of it, but she have no time to figure why that be, cause just then, her youngest boy, Billy Lee, come bounding through the back door in the kitchen. He too young to work but he nine years old and were sure old enough to keep hisself out of trouble. Still, the cream color boy yelling out --Pap! Pap! when he catch sight of Burken down the hall. Taddy run and grab her chile and put her hand over him mouth.

--Hushup, now boy! She look up and see Burken's twisted face and Missus Burken's eyes on Taddy, set to kill. Taddy move her son back toward the kitchen door and out of they eyesight. Billy Lee eyes filling up with tears but Taddy caint pay no attention to it now, not after the show he done made in front of Missus.

--Get outta here right now! Get on back to the loft and don't you dare come out lest I send for you!

31

But Billy Lee aint moving. He stand there like he troubled and Taddy feel her heart slide out of her chest. Billy Lee warn't like her other chiles. He too breakable. He strange in ways Taddy don't understand. --You wanna get beat or what now? You wanna die!

Billy Lee shake him round little head.

--Then get!

At that, Billy Lee off like lit and when Taddy caint see him no more, she cover her face with her hands til her breathing slow. Taddy know she gon get it, and soon, for what Billy Lee done in front of Missus, upsetting the barren woman so.

Poor barren Missus Burken, surrounded by death. And why Taddy should care like she aint been surrounded by death her whole life too? Like her only hope in life aint death? Why Taddy should care the French done kilt up Missus family in Paris for what role they have in funding Burken's war with some king, with only a niece, Sabine, who survive. Burken bring Sabine to Amerika and marry her off to a wealthy man up North who make sure Burken get to be president. Now he and Wellesbury and Amerika be all Missus got left. And just why Taddy should care? Whole country seem to cry over Missus Burken's trouble. Aint no need for Taddy to be one of em, she thinking.

What good a chile be in Missus Burken's hands, no how? Same hands that take a candle to Taddy and burn up her elbows til they char and crust over. It been more years than Taddy been a mam since she been beat by any cowhide whip or ebony brush what hurt worse than thorns tearing flesh up with every lash. But it aint been no time since Missus Burken burning Taddy hands, heels, fingers, toes, elbows. Burnt her arm hairs clean off soon after Basil Lee were born. Beat Taddy with the heel of her shoes after Billy Lee were born a few years later. Aint no telling what Missus Burken gon think up to pay for what Billy Lee done now, putting the Missus' shame out like that.

Warn't really Missus' shame, no how, to a thinking person, sides what she done to Taddy. Burken be the crook what steal from Taddy's womb and Missus both.

Still Taddy hot with fear thinking what Burken mighta done if one of him military friends been here to hear what come out Billy Lee mouth! Forget the tea. Just imagine! Burken sure warn't the only massa breeding with him womanslave, but don't nobody talk bout it straight out. And Burken done got everybody believing he this upright man, a servant of God. --Think of how they will write of me! Burken always telling the Missus, in good and bad times. Aint a body in Wellesbury Burken wouldn't bury alive to keep dirt off him good name.

Taddy thinking bout it all and worry for her baby boy. She caint say what be worse, what Burken woulda done or what Billy Lee gon do. He were a strange boy; eyes always wide open. Basil Lee be the oldest Burken boy, but stuff he don't know, seem Billy Lee were born knowing. It cut Billy Lee, being a bastard menor chile, in a way that make no sense to Taddy. It were like he got a taste of a life outside menor life that Taddy don't know nothing bout and it hurt him to live, knowing the good life he musta come from were just on the other side of him own hands.

That's how Taddy knowing Billy Lee know what he done just now, yelling what he yelling. It were like, to Billy Lee, if he say it loud enough, if he call him Pap in front of God, then it gon change him life. It scare Taddy.

She knowing not only her baby gon always be brokenhearted on account of this way of thinking, but he also gon be quick to the grave.

--We not teaching our chiles to fear death like them other menors, she member her man Bernard saying to her once, when her belly were fat with Addis. Taddy smile at Bernard back then when he say it, nod even. It all sounding like a nice way to think, like they might could be different, do something different, and that were gon change they life.

But the truth were, Bernard got deaded quick the moment he jump bad with Burken, and he leave her here all alone, all while he not fearing death. And Taddy got two sons to raise now. She gon teach them all she know to do: stay alive.

Taddy thinking on these things when she see Haynes plod through the Great House door just then, tall and gruff. Unshaven. Sweat sliding down him face, over the deep scar slashed just under him green eye, cross him cheek and down him thick neck.

Taddy hear Missus Burken near choke at the sight of Haynes before her. --Master Burken, a word in your cabinet, please? Missus Burken say stern.

--Of course. I will be just a moment, Haynes, Burken say fore he disappear with Missus into him cabinet. From her kitchen corner, Taddy don't hear Haynes move, but she know he hearing what Missus Burken saying if she hearing it herself.

--I don't want him in this house, Missus Burken spit between her teeth.

--I am quite aware of your feelings, Burken say quiet but firm. --But you will not dictate to me whom I can and cannot have in my own home.

--He gets out of hand. He kills our property!

--Accidents, Mrs. Burken, accidents only. And I will remind you that you have no property, though he has done plenty of damage to my property at *your* bidding and without complaint from you, I'll remind you.

Taddy jump when the teapot whistle. She take a china cup and crunch up dry mint leaves into it and pour the boiled water over top. She drop in a cube of sugar, a dollop of honey and dash of milk. Been a long time since they having sugar round them parts, what with the War just ending, so, when the other womenslaves aint looking, she drop a sugar cube in her apron pouch for later.

--The property is mine, Haynes is my overseer, and answers to me alone. Do not worry yourself about him when your place is to be silent on such matters.

--I am silent!

Missus Burken say too loud fore she get quiet. --I hold my tongue over and over. I see things I can never speak of. Things your own mother feared about...

--You will not speak of my mother...

--I ask you only this because he frightens me, she say softer. --Mon cher, I ask you only this.

Taddy put the china cup on a silver tray with a teaspoon and turn to leave the kitchen when she see Haynes standing there, arm leaning on the doorway watching her. The other womens nowhere in sight. Just him. Scraggly. Scowling. Long sleeve shirts, no matter its summer, to cover up the cuts and scars all over him arms.

This the man who blow a whole clean through her Bernard, leave her with no love, no protection. It make the hair on her neck set to run off, and every sense in her body say follow. But she tighten up her face and straighten her back so he knowing she aint afraid, that nothing he could do be worse than what he already done to her. Then she thinking different; always something worse to be done.

Haynes push him blonde tangles back from him face and him cheek gash show real good with all the summer light coming in through the kitchen windows.

--And what about you, strumpet? You aint scared of old Haynes like the Missus.

Taddy know better than to gas him with a no, so she stay quiet but look him dead in the swampy green of him eyes.

--Know how I got this scar, wench?

--Everybody know your daddy what cut you up.

He laugh low and stomp closer to Taddy, slow and she stand her ground.

--Everybody thinks they know me.

Taddy hear Burken near yelling now. -- Haynes is not only faithful and hard-working, he is the son of my father's overseer and he is what is keeping us safe. You think these menors would behave half as well without him here?

--William, listen!

Haynes moving in even closer to Taddy and point to the top of the gash whispering to her.

--No, no, no. My daddy only start this scar, way back here, you see? I finished it, though, Haynes smirking, motioning the cut of a blade with him finger. But Taddy aint scaring easy.

--Taunt me all you like, but you know you caint touch me, Massa Haynes. Everybody know it!

Burkens arguing loud still.

--Haynes has been a brother to me since childhood. You know all of this. And with Francis dead, he is the only brother I have, the only one who stood with me before the battles and the wars and the glory. What's more, you will not dictate to me who I can and cannot have in my own home.

Taddy hear Burken move toward him cabinet door fore he say --We will not speak of this again. You will learn to control your temper in my presence.

Burken's coming. He's coming, Taddy keep telling herself as Haynes inch closer.

--Careful, now, strumpet, Haynes snarling right over Taddy's face. --Even the thickest tabacky leaf can still get smoked.

--Haynes! Taddy hear Burken call for him overseer and she never been so glad to hear him voice.

35

--Haynes? Come now. I am ready for our appointment, Burken call again. Haynes squint him eyes at Taddy, swipe an apple off the table and stuff it in him pocket. Then he back away from her and turn to walk out the kitchen, straightening hisself up, walking like what he think a gentleman look like, smirk still on him lips.

When he far enough away and catch up to Burken, Taddy let out the breath she been holding deep inside and her hands start to shake. She grip the tray tighter and come out the kitchen with the tea.

--Massa Burken? Got your tea here.

--Ah. Thank you, Taddy, I will have it on my walk, he say and take the cup, leaving the tray in her hands.

--Yessir, she say and turn to leave but Burken stop her.

--Oh! Taddy, you will find a letter on my writing desk in my cabinet. My secretary has gone on ahead of me to Philadelphia, so you will see to it that my letter reaches the Post. Send it on with a footman without delay. Then go to your quarters straight away. I will have further instructions for you there once Master Haynes and I are through.

Even after two chiles and all these years, warnings of Burken's coming instructions still send a shiver up her back.

--Massa Burken, who gon fix dinner if I in my quarters, sir?

--Mrs. Burken has given instructions to Nora for dinner. You concern yourself only with me. Now move swiftly before the postman turns in.

--Yessir, she say.

As they walk out the door, Haynes say, --You sure you want that menor round your papers, Will?

Burken place him hand on Haynes shoulder.

--My dear Haynes, you place her far above her station. She is a simple girl. Your worry is for naught. Now tell me, what are the production numbers today?

When Haynes and Burken clear off and Missus be nowhere round, Taddy open the door to Burken's cabinet. She back herself inside and shut the door.

-4-
BURKEN

My Dear Richard,
    I regret to be leaving Virginia without first visiting you in Richmond as I intended. I have had the pleasure of observing your fine leadership of our Virginia troops from afar and I am quite proud of your progress with them. As I have assured you time and again, I could not have more faith in an Adjutant General for Virginia than I have in you, and it would please me greatly if only you began to believe what I say is true.

    I understand, respect and echo your hesitancy for the task. I am forever humbled to be elected to serve our country as its first President and am overcome by a consciousness of its being a trust too great for my Capacity. Indeed, though my heart is strong, there are far older and wiser teachers surely who would have made fine leaders. I feel as though Isaiah's prophecy holds true even today, "and a little child shall lead them." Nay, even now, the wolf lives with the lamb, the leopard lies down with the goat, the calf, the tiger and the yearling all together.

    I know you smile as you read these words, as you should. Because you are like a dear brother in arms to me, I am confident you will not tell my darling wife I have likened her kin to goats. After our taxing history with the French, who would believe we would fight with them as brothers, take them as wives? Indeed, a common enemy fast turns foes into lovers. The fraternité we have fostered with the French in our hour of need proved itself invaluable to our survival and renaissance as a free people, and at great expense to the French, I dare say. I pray it remains strong throughout generations.

Even the British are finding our shores a pleasant home for themselves, with hopes for a new future here. Nonsense, one would have surely scoffed in response to such a notion just a dream ago. And half a century gone without need to take up arms against rebelling menors, save for those incidents in New York a few years back, stamped out quickly and quietly enough. In our waking lives, my dear Richard, we can never measure how quickly the tide can turn.

Though we both have worked hard for this gloriously strange peace, I cannot help but believe good fortune also sleeps on our side. And where else would she lay her head than the bed God has claimed for God's magnificent own? I do believe it to be some kind of destiny that has thrown us upon this Service. I hope that our undertaking of it is designed to answer some good purpose. The eyes of History shall surely hold their gaze upon us. In secret, you and I shall ensure the other does not blink.

I do hope you will visit me in Philadelphia. I will now be residing at Morrison House for the duration of my stay in the Capitol. Robert Morrison has been most generous in volunteering the house for my services and you know how I love that house. When we settle, Mrs. Burken insists upon entertaining regularly on Thursdays and she would love for you to join us. She has been in a most dire state as of late. It seems every other month marks the anniversary of the death in the womb of one child or another. Compounded by the years, I would suppose it to be unbearable for any mother to take after while. You know her to be a wall of fortitude, a brightened spot in any dark turn, but that is simply her as a wife. Who can comfort a childless mother? Who but God?

I have always considered marriage as the most interesting event of one's life, the foundation of miserable happiness. I dare say I contribute to her pain. Though, as any wise couple, we ne'er speak on it. I am more sure than ever: to be a husband is to bear the weight of the world on one's back, pleasing God first, then Country, then wife, then self. I oft wonder who shall meet a husband's needs.

Cursed is a man with no menors in his possession. Indeed, ownership is the only true mark of a gentleman. Our wives belong to us, most assuredly, but what power they wield o'er us, as well! To be made to feel lack due to a woman's own shortcomings—perhaps it is a queer trait of the French. I darn't speak a word against my own mother, but if my father had lived, he could surely tell me if there's any merit to this pondering. Whatever the root of it, I pray you never know it.

It is so: God has not seen fit we birth a living child together. But God has been gracious in giving her a role in the birth of a nation. I pray, one day, for her sake, it shall be well and enough.

All the more reason you must come, dear Richard. Friendships with equals are scarce between men like us and I do not shame to admit I will be happy to lay down a few burdens at the doorstep of one who would understand. It would also please me that you make the acquaintance of my Secretary at War, Stanton Thompson. It is my wish that he groom you for a future secretary position. Not to mention a visit from you and your lovely Ernestine would draw a smile to Mrs. Burken's lips, at last. If anything can, it is the combined magic of the Lawrences. So you will both come, then, to our first State Dinner, Thursday, a fortnight into next month.

We earnestly await your arrival and pray your safe passage.

I am,

WHB

-5-

HAYNES

Burken and Haynes stroll through the shade of the trees of House Farm to escape the wrath of the sun, and delight a bit in the breeze coming off the Potomac. Still, Haynes get no relief from the itchiness of him cuts and scars under him long-sleeve cotton shirt. He want to pull the shirt off and jump head first into the river, but he know it would embarrass him friend to know the cutting still going on, so Haynes just slip a straw hat on him head to hide the frowning, and keep on telling Burken the afternoon count of cotton and tobacco pounds picked on each Farm.

Burken taking sips of tea, saying --Hmmm, and compare it in him head to the previous day, week and year.

--We have got to get them to produce more, Burken say. --I am baffled they don't take more pride in their work. I tried just today to get the garden girl to understand the remarkable work she is a part of, but to no avail.

--You always been too kind to see the worst in people, Will. I work with them menors day in and day out, and I aint never met a more shiftless people.

--Unfortunate, really...

--I'll increase the whippings, shorten the rations. See how they like that. They already got rough sackcloth to make clothes with, but I can always get corn sacks. They the roughest kind.

--No, no, not yet. We must inspire them. I'll talk to Pastor Moore before Sunday, see what he can do to breathe life into them.

Burken and Haynes walking over much of the House Farm grounds like they do every day, the willow grove behind the brick walls of Lower Garden and the greenhouse, the shore of the Potomac behind the Great House, the stables just off to the side, the walls of Upper Garden, and back round to the Great House gate where seven cannons from the Great War all lined up in tribute. Haynes like to see the cannons. It remind him of fighting longside Burken in the Great War. Make him to member how close they got then, on the brink of death. He like these walks too. He think they make them friends, lifetime friends, brothers, even, like Burken just say. But a bit of him know that caint never be, not really.

Even when they was just boys fighting against imaginary

First Peoples in the afternoon sun, they was different. Burken's pap, Ambrose, would call to him son for a evening of reading stories and history and poetry and propriety. Haynes pap, Butch, call to Haynes for a evening of whippings for some menor or other who done got out of line. Butch would thrust the leather and bone whip into Haynes hands and say, --Straighten him out, boy! Take your arm all the way back and bring it forward hard, like I taught you. That's it, Rutherford! Again!

Again and again and again, Haynes crack that whip on this particular menor three times him own size and see the menor refuse to cry, though him back be split open, flesh spilling out and blood and water. It making Haynes feel something he never feel, that first time. He feel sticky on the inside, like things not sitting where they posed to be. But Butch keep yelling, --Harder! Make him cry like a menor baby, Rutherford! What are you doing?

But the menor still refusing to cry, so Butch taking over, angry now cause he feel this menor showing up him boy. And the stickiness growing in Haynes. That night, he ask him pap why the menor won't cry and him pap say they just like dogs, got to train them to feel things like pain and shame. They warn't the smartest, him pap say, but afterwhile, the lesson take. Haynes say he don't want to teach no lessons, say it make him feel sticky to see all the blood and him pap say, --I'll show you what's sticky, and he take a flint blade and slice a little piece off Haynes cheek, but Haynes don't cry nuther.

--You think these falootin folks gonna hire you to do anything but overseeing? How you think you're gonna feed yourself when I aint here? You better get good at it, and fast.

It stick with Haynes, what him pap saying, but still he don't believe it. When him best friend in the world ask him what happen to him face, Haynes don't yet tell him. He just say, --Will? My pap say nobody gonna hire me to do nothing else but overseeing. That I gotta get good at it, if I to feed myself when he gone.

Burken ask again what happen to Haynes face and Haynes tell him bout the menor who won't cry and what him pap done and Haynes member the look Burken giving him like it were yesterday. It were the look of pure pity, like somebody caring for a sick dog without all him parts. It were the day Haynes knowing he and Burken caint be friends, nor brothers.

It were what made him go back to him pap's hut that night and finish off the cut in him cheek, all the way down to him neck. It didn't feel good, it hurt like the debil. But Haynes notice the stickiness on the inside go away a little. Still it scare him pap and Burken too, so he cutting him own thighs, then him stomach, then him arms where folks caint see easy. Him pap slap him silly when he see it, then beat him, but Haynes not stopping, so Butch just making the boy wear long sleeves and long pants all the time so nobody see what he doing to hisself. He and Burken playing less and less, talking less and less and Haynes getting less and less sticky.

After Burken's pap die, Butch spending all him nights in the house with Caroleen and it make Haynes to feel what he aint felt in a long while, happy. He thinking he gon finally have a mam again, he and Burken gon be real brothers, but it never happen. When he grown, Caroleen making him head overseer after him pap get drunk and drown in the Potomac. Still, it be years fore Burken and him getting close again, not til after Burken younger brother and chiles dying of the Fever and Burken got nobody else. Not til Burken and him riding out to war together, first for the king, then against him. Still, Haynes always knowing they bond were not much more than a gentleman's bond with him rabid dog. But Burken been good to Haynes, he know this. He grateful. He love Burken like a brother, all the same.

--I am sorry for Mrs. Burken, Haynes, Burken say when they reach the white porch of the Great House. --She is excitable and too often speaking out of turn.

--Sorry to scare her, Will.

--Nonsense. She is a silly woman. And you are family. You always will be.

Haynes nod and smile and know this be as good as he could hope for, the scarred-up pup of a great, powerful and loyal man. He turn to leave and Burken ask, --Won't you sit on the porch with me awhile? These old rocking chairs are still good, yet.

But Haynes get to feeling sticky again, want to scratch at him scars and don't want Burken to see. --Best be getting back to the Farms for the evening round-up, he say. But Haynes don't go to the stable to get him horse, he go back to the overseer cabin and take off him shirt, slow. He sit in him pap's old rocking chair and eat at the apple he swipe from the kitchen with one hand, run him nails over him scars with the other. He look down at hisself and see aint much more room on hisself left to cut. He thinking how he aint snatched up a menorgirl in a long time. The words of Missus Burken crawling round in him mind, --He gets out of hand. He kills...

Haynes get to thinking bout that girl Addis, what Burken always tell him he caint touch. Haynes thinking of her and scratching and feel the stickiness melt a little, and he like it. He lean back into him chair and get to rocking and scratching. He making hisself a plan.

-6-
EKWUEME

When he sure no one looking, Ekwueme wrap the warm knife he just making in a strip of cowhide and tie it to him thigh under him loose cotton pants. He been doing it for months, make a weapon and hide it, then make another to meet the quota...so long as no one eyeing him, specially not the older blacksmiths, George and Luther. They liking Ekwueme well enough and he liking them too, but they far too chummy with the watchmen for Ekwueme to trust.

He thinking these men hoping to be watchmen theyself one day, and Ekwueme aint the only one who thinking it. Kelvin, Larry, Joe, Randy, Chester and Ant, all the ojis he plotting with, telling Ekwueme long ago, --Don't say nothing you aint got to round George and Luther! So the rest of the blacksmiths keep the weapons they making, the plan to escape, and all they Eboe talking to they self.

Ekwueme spend the rest of him day at the smithy smiling while he hammering. He not thinking bout what he working on right now, what Haynes come by whileago to tell him to make, cause if he do, he know it make him stomach turn. So he think what he always thinking bout when he wanting to smile: Addis. George and Luther always teasing him when they catch him in a grin, but Ekwueme don't mind it none. George and Luther both got they own women Burken and Haynes give to them, but they never smiling like Ekwueme, so he just feeling sorry for them. Not every man get to choose him own woman and those who do don't always get a woman who choose them back. It make a world of difference, living with a woman who got a choice.

Ekwueme were lucky. He knowing when he first see Addis that he were going to love her as long as he were breathing, and maybe even after, if there were an after. Ekwueme warn't much on Chúkwú, Ala, none of the gods of him people or no-color people, nuther. Young as he be, he seen too much to believe in what he caint see. He believe in hisself though. And he believe in Addis. If he aint have plans to get far from under Burken, he'd be asking Burken to let them marry.

Addis were a sturdy woman to him, a woman with two feets

45

on the ground, even though the dreams and visions she having sometimes take her out of herself and scare them both. To Ekwueme, them dreams were the part of her that always gon float away from him, to a world he caint lead or follow to. He always fearing the day she be more dream than flesh and fly out him reach for good and it make him cling to her all the more.

She were a girl who think she difficult to love, not cause she don't deserve love; if anybody worthy of it, Ekwueme know it be her. She just don't know it herself, cause Haynes knock it out of her. But her spirit touch him fore her fingers ever did. She were the chile of warriors and she live to honor her Gran Gran Dido and her pap, even her Nnene. Above all, he know she don't want to shame her Nnene, who been everything to her. He wish she would see her mam Taddy warn't so bad. He wish she would know what her mam been up to, but he warn't gon be the one to tell her nothing bout her mam. He know she aint wanting to hear nothing bout Taddy ever and he know it be for her own safety she don't know everything he know, so he let that drop and just love her. He love her easy.

He love that she got people to fight for and she do it, and he get to be one of them people. Ekwueme have no more pap and him mam were sold away with him two brothers and a sister so long ago he not even sure the woman he dream of at night even be what him mam ever look like. He fight for them anyway, in case they watching somewhere, and he sure fighting for hisself.

To share that fight with somebody who see him like Addis see him mean everything to Ekwueme. After weeks of fighting the world in they own way, when they get together, they just get to rest awhile. They never fight each other. Not that they say ever, --Let's never fight; It don't need to be said. He know the moment he seen her she were someone he could be tired with. He always know he gon protect her against anything, but when it were just the two of them, in the shield of the willow trees of they secret spot, they both could put they fists down for a spell. He get so tired being at the ready all the time.

She warn't no total safe place for Ekwueme by no means, though; nobody who don't know they worth loving can ever be a safe place, and Ekwueme know that. But he don't blame her for it none. He love her still. It warn't even her cool breath on him, nor the lavender oil she braid her soft, krinkly hair with. It warn't the stillness of her black skin, like a moonless, endless night, or her sweet syrup eyes that show him true self when he look into them. If he could write, wouldn't be no space nor words for the folds on her full lips and the nose that line up perfect with them when she turn to the side, the true print of Afrika on her face. Still, it warn't none of that what make him love her.

It were that she let him need her to the point of death. She let him fill him own silence up with her. He know it be too much to ask of a person, too much a burden to be somebody's wholeness, and he don't mean to do it to her. He don't want to put that on her cause one day she gon buckle under the weight of him. He know it and she know it. But she forgive him for it anyhow. She never lie to him. She believe in him too. He promise her freedom and she trust him to bring it to her and that give him all the joy he could need. He living to see that promise through. And only one month more, it be done and it gon make him who he always want to be. As long as he doing right by Addis, he never shaming hisself. He being just the man he posed to be.

Ekwueme wipe sweat from him brow and fill him nose with the bitter blood smell of melting iron and burning leather. It please him, even standing over the fire pit in the heat of summer. He imagine the flames testing him to see what he can bear and he hammer harder to prove nothing can bend him. This time, when George and Luther catch him smiling, it be because he feel he winning. Still, they stop working to laugh at him again.

--This menor Eddie outchea grinning like a fool again when he don't think we watching!

--You know it aint nothing but that gal he got. I swear she done put roots on the boy or something, Lawd!

--Shoot. You know the boy aint got no chest, he grinning like that!

Ekwueme curl him lips into a smirk and say, --Tssk! See what y'all old menors know! Take a chest as big as mine to love like I love, huh! Maybe y'all menors oughta try treating your gals like I treat my Addis and see don't you grin too!

--Aw, get on, boy! Luther shooing Ekwueme and they all laughing.

Then Ekwueme look down and see he finished what Haynes tell him to make. It be a iron trap for the mouth, to shut up screams, and it get Ekwueme thinking bout things he don't want to think. He don't feel no type of way when he fashion a horseshoe or spikes, nails, not even bayonets or swords or pellets. But he know a iron trap gon choke somebody. That's just what Haynes like to do. He steal your voice along with everything else.

Haynes probably gon tie it to a woman, Ekwueme thinking. Maybe it gon fit right over a free man's mouth to make sure he caint tell nobody he aint no slave. But Burken aint never been known to snatch free mens from up North like Sheriff Turner do, the one who own the next plantation over; Burken sure caint do it now that he president of the country. Warn't gon look right. Burken taking great pride in folk thinking he fair and good and, above all, Christian.

Funny how Burken never care bout how owning some 300 peoples gon make him look. But trying to make sense of how no-color people think warn't nothing but a conjure for a headache. Still, that trap Ekwueme make with him own hands gon be round somebody mouth, and soon. If he don't know nothing else, he know that much.

Ekwueme fasten leather straps to either side of the trap and two more to snake up round the nose and over the head. It were a trap fit for a rabid dog, sure enough. He hold it up in him hands, then over him own mouth. He wonder, even if he do right by Addis, if he ever gon be all right hisself.

-7-
ADDIS

Supper bell ring in the distance and Addis know the day be done. She look up and grin too wide when she hear the hooves of a pack of horses coming close.

--Whatchu grinning so for? Still got work to do, you know.

Addis look up to see Nnene catching her from clear across the garden. Nnene old but her eyes be like a hawk and Addis never could get away with nothing.

--Caint a chile be happy to hear the supper bell? She ask, still smiling.

--Hmph, Nnene say and she keep hoeing, knowing all the while Addis smiling cause them pack of horses carrying blacksmith boys back from Burken's smithy in town, and Ekwueme be one of them.

Addis hear the hooves getting closer and closer and know Ekwueme soon be back on the plantation. Not even Nnene's bird eyes could see what Addis and Ekwueme gon be up to this night.

When the sun start setting, Addis follow Nnene back to they quarters for supper. Fore they step all the way inside, they both removing they shoes and hanging up they bonnets. Then they wash they hands in the washpan. Nnene strike flint against the firesteel then light up the wood soaked in olive oil in the hearth. Addis dip a candlewick in the fire then set it in the lamp on the table. Nnene sit to the table and get to hemming up one of Missus dresses while Addis grab a water pitcher and pour it in a pot. Addis take four yams out the corner by the hearth, set them in the pot and place the pot over the fire.

She hear a knock at the door and know it be the ration lady come to give them they meat share. Nnene always refusing the meat ever since Addis can member. They never ate none. --Poison the mind, Nnene always say. --You never knowing what spirit getting mixed up inside you when you eating meat, she tell the ration lady, but it don't keep the lady from coming by anyhow.

Addis open the door and see a face she aint never seen. She stand firm in the doorway and ask the tall, copper-color lady who come by, smelling like sunflower oil,

--Who you be?

49

--Pardon. I just come by with meat rations for y'all, the woman say and sit her heavy basket of rations down on the ground.

--Don't sound like Betty. Who that there? Nnene asking from her table, back turned to the door.

--My name Chinü, she say. --Betty not feeling well today. Thinking she might have the baby fore long. So I doing the meat rations for awhile.

--We don't take meat rations here, Addis say. --Betty shoulda told you that.

Chinü shrug and smile. --Well, she aint. I hear bout menors like you though, what don't eat meat and all. I just caint imagine it any. Me and my daughter, Chima, we barely fill up off what they give us.

--Chile, move up out the way and let the sister in, Nnene say.

Aint no kin to me, Addis thinking, but she never say. She back up and Chinü nod to her, pick up the basket of rations and walk inside to sit at the table with Nnene. She sit the basket down in the dirt and let out a deep sigh at the rest she find in Addis chair. Addis close the door slow behind her, wondering how long this lady gon stay.

--Everything got a spirit to it, is all, Nnene saying to Chinü. --And we aint eating no spirit what been scared or tortured. We grow our own food out back in our own garden, we love it while it living and we love it in dying and they know it. We eat good, clean spirits. Nothing else.

--Now that you saying it, I member my own mam say something like that long ago. Still, me and my baby eating meat just the same.

Nnene lean across the table and look Chinü in the eye. --I know you, and your mam. You Lydia's chile. Grown chile, I reckon. Your mam say she name you God Hears cause you be a answer to her prayer.

--Yessm, that's what I been told.

--It aint just bout the spirits, Addis say, leaning up against the door, tired of hearing bout mams and chiles. --Sometime you just gotta have your own.

Chinü nod at Addis like if ever there was a feeling worth starving over it were to have your own something. Addis look over

50

and see Nnene beaming at the table just a little fore she say,
  --Chinü, you keep our rations for you and your babygirl.
Any leftover, leave some with Cleveland and Jobell round the way.
They got little ones need feeding.
  Chinu smile as wide as a chile what never been slaved. --I
thank you, kindly! Me and my babygirl do.
  --Aint nothing, Chinü. We all nubs on the same hand,
Nnene say and she look to Addis to make sure she hear it.
  Addis pull up a smile and nod to Chinü, but she wanting
nothing more than for the nub to get on with her business so Addis
could do the same.
  --Bes be leaving, now, Chinü say and take up her basket.
--Nice seeing y'all, she say as she go bout her way.
  --Night, chile. Be safe out there, Nnene call after her as the
door closing behind Chinü.
  Addis hear the sizzle of boiling water spilling up over the
pot in the fire. She clean forget her yams boiling. She take the pot
off the fire and set it in the dirt. When the yams cool a bit, she peel
them at the table with a blunt knife, chop them in chunks and pound
them in a bowl.
  --Don't mash all the juice out now...good. Like that, Nnene
tell her. --Now mix the plantains in...uh huh...and put more water
in there. Make it sticky now. Ball it up.
  Addis been making fufu all her life it seem like, but she
never mind it when Nnene tell her how anyway. It make Addis feel
something warm, like all the while she cooking, her spirit walking
home. Nnene start to singing in Eboe and Addis join in.
  Children of the Sun, wake! She is calling
  Got to get up and be gone, hey! Night is falling.
  And she burning and she burning say! By the morning
  When we rise with her again all the rest will pass away.
  The Sun! The Sun! Yes, she know her children
  The Sun! The Sun! Yes, she know her children
  And she burning and she burning say! By the morning
  When we rise with her again, all the rest will pass away.
  Soon, they eating. Addis swallowing her hot food too quick
and it burning up her throat. It making her choke, too, but she keep
going so she can meet Ekwueme when she promise.
  --Whatchu rush for, chile? Caint even swallow proper,
Nnene say.

--Gotta check my lines. You know I can only see em straight in the dark.

--Well dark aint going nowhere no time soon and neither is that garden, you know.

--Sooner I gets done, sooner I gets back and can start on that sewing Missus wanting.

--Hmph, be all Nnene say and Addis know Nnene be wise to exactly why she leaving the hut, or at least knowing it got something to do with Ekwueme, but Addis glad Nnene just let it be. She finish off her food, wash her and Nnene dishes and rush off to the garden.

But she don't stop to check her lines. She run straight through and keep going past trees and brush. When she were little, Addis used to run through here so quick for fear of the stories Nnene tell her as a chile, what Nnene learn from her mam in Eboeland bout the Baobab trees and how they come to life at night and carry off bad chiles in they roots. Now Addis knowing it aint the trees she got to fear. Trees be hiding places. To a oji, trees be life itself. The watchmen be what come to haunt the night. Burken be what carry off any chiles he like, good or bad. Haynes be the one to fear.

So Addis don't look to the left nor the right, but just keep running fast and strong and quiet. If anybody were gon catch her, she thinking, least they gon have to run they legs off.

Addis run clean to the clearing a half-mile from the gardens, guarded by willows. That's they spot. Always have been. And there he be, waiting for her, shining in the night like the son of the sun. Addis and Ekwueme lose all reason at the sight of each other and they run into each other's arms, awash with glee.

She snuggle into him chest and breathe him in deep. He smell to her like he always smell, like a hard-working man, a gentle man, strong as iron, and nector-sweet to her nostrils. She place her fingertips beneath him thin shirt, tracing the healed welts that cover him back like a spider web. She know the genesis of each one and each time she trace them she membering.

She run her fingers over the thick ones that cross him from shoulder to shoulder. *These are from when he laid on top of his dying father to protect him from Haynes' whip.* She move her hands down to the short fat ones on his left side. *These are from the first time he tried to run away as a boy.* She move up to the right. *These are from the second time.* She move to the cluster round the base of him back. *These are from when I knocked over an entire barrel of cotton and he told a watchman he'd done it.* She making her fingers do a healing dance cross him back, calling on they ancestors with every stroke.

Ekwueme place him rough hands on each side of her face and she lean into him hands like cushions. In between him two hands she feel more safe, more loved than she ever feeling and the weight of it crack her chest open. It were a living pain that she don't mind much cause it remind her that living aint got to be all bad.

She open her eyes and see Ekwueme staring back at her. She reach up to him mouth and kiss him full, not fevered but slow, like warn't nothing past nor future coming nor gone.

Ekwueme pull him lips from hers long enough to tell her in hushed Eboe,

--We are leaving this place.

--When? How? Tell me everything, she say, and lock her fingers with him own, around her face.

--One month from now! This Afrikan Kreyól free man by the name of Sayzare is coming back through here with a caravan. He is taking 12 people all the way to the place of the Yakama people, far west of here. The Yakama live in peace with ojis and protect any who respect the land and the people. We are one of the 12, Addis. In one month, we will be free!

Addis barely contain the squeal in her throat. She kiss him to keep from screaming.

--We will get married...We will have children...We will be together...

He kiss her between each thought and she close her eyes and smile.

--We will do everything...We will do nothing...

Tears try crawling out Addis eyes, slow, paying no never mind that she don't cry no more.

--One month from now, Addy. One month.

They laugh and hug again. He pick her up and spin her round til they fall to the ground, still laughing, soft. He roll over and lay on him stomach and she collapse on him war-torn back, looking up at the stars. She hear the Potomac running just round the bend and it calm her. To Addis, the warm air smell newer than it did this morning, wafting up to them from the gardens, and she take in as much as she can of its clean sweetness. The moon peek through the willows to let them know she listening, and it make Addis member to whisper.

--We will not do *nothing*, Addis coo to him in her most tender Eboe. --We will do what we want.

--What do we want? He ask her.

--Everything, she answer.

They laughing. He flip hisself over on him back and let her fall gentle on him chest. He brush her hair with the palm of him hand and she settle into him.

--Look, Addis, he say pointing to a brightness up over the trees. She turn her head to see what he see. --The North Star. It will take us just where we need to go.

--You belong out on the sea, Ekwueme. The way you read the stars. You can take us anywhere. All the way back to Eboeland.

--If that's where you want to go, I will take you there.

--That's where I want to go. And while you sail, I will write of our travels like Joseph Warton, she say.

--Joseph Warton?

--A poet. He wrote about the majesty of butterflies. He calls them children of the sun and summer. Like us.

Ekwueme laugh. --When you write of the majesty of butterflies, then I will know we are truly free and happy!

He lace him fingers together behind him head and Addis settle back into him again and smile a little herself. He say,

--Sayzare says out West, they have a oji paper and all kinds of free ojis write for it. Afrikans from all over, not just Eboes. Even some who used to be slaves. They tell other slaves how they can get free too. That is what I want to do when we are free. We both can.

--Most slaves cannot read what we write. Sounds like a good way to get ourselves caught and hauled back down here, and for nothing.

--Well, I don't know exactly how it works, I just know it works. But we cannot get free and leave everyone here to die, can we?

Addis feel Ekuweme eyes on her, she know he hoping she agree with him, but Addis turn away from him and talk other things.

--You think they write in English or Eboe for that paper?

--English, I would reckon.

--Bah. I want to write in Eboe.

--That is because you can already write in English.

--I will teach you. Then you can know too.

--Is there such a thing as Eboe writing?

--Of course there is!

--I have never seen it.

--Would you know if you had?

Addis bite her tongue as soon as she say it. She know Ekwueme want nothing more than to read and write like she do. She were always saying things too harsh. She try to soften herself this time.

--I have never seen a caravan but I know it exists because you tell me so, Ekwueme.

--Whatever you tell me, Addis, I believe it.

He unlace him hands from behind him neck and wrap them round her. Right then, all she want be to tell him bout her dream of Ala, the tiger in the water, but she order her mouth to shut. Her dreams scare him and she plain tired of being what people fear. Instead, she say,

--The Burkens, Haynes, the watchmen...they know nothing of mmadu. We are not people here, Ekwueme. We are not anything that matters. They cannot even call me my right name, so they make up Addis.

--I thought you liked Addis?

--Whose world would turn if I didn't? What do they care how they call their pigs and chickens?

--You want to call me Eddie like everyone else?

--No, I don't. Ekwueme is who I love.

--Sssk! I am as much Eddie as I am Ekwueme. Just like you are still Adaeze, even if no one calls you that. As for me, I love Addis and Adaeze. Whatever you call yourself today, I love and will love. It is your soul I love, not just your name.

Addis feel her nerves tingling and shift her body away from him a little, but she also smile a little cause she knowing he meaning all he say.

--Don't hide from me because I say I love you. I love everything about you, Adaeze Addis. Your worst faults are a credit to you and I love them madly. I would shout it if I could.

She laugh a little but she too nervous to look in him eyes. She know he already done swum down in the pit of her timeless sadness over and over and return to the surface and say, --It aint so bad down there with you. Still, she fearing every time he gon figure out he aint been nowhere near the bottom of her, cause there be no bottom to her. Every sweetness he pour into her just eek right out of her, though over the years it been leaving slower and slower. Ekwueme making her to feel like something sweet might get to stick to her, maybe even soon.

--We are our names, Ekwueme. I am not called the daughter of a king because my father and my name did not sit well on Burken's tongue. I am a made up name that means nothing and is from nowhere, like me.

Ekwueme sit up at this and take her with him. She feel him try to look her in her eyes but she caint.

--It is not so, he say to her back. --Look at me. It is not so. You are the daughter of Bernard and Taddy of Wellesbury, Virginia, granddaughter of the great Dido and Pompey. You are descendants of *Eboes*, a blessed and mighty people on this earth. Everybody's name has been made up by someone, somewhere, sometime. And even a made up name cannot mean nothing if it is yours.

She turn to him a little, her smile returning, but head still bowed. She know then what she always knowing: she never not gon need Ekwueme like she need legs to stand. This radical lover who call her worst faults a credit.

--Tell me now. Who do you want to be?

Addis look him square when she telling him, --I want to be a tiger.

Ekwueme laughing.

--Sssk! Now who is talking about things they would not know if they saw!

But her face showing she set on this thing and Ekwueme fold, easy.

--Then you are agụ, he smile and kiss her cheek.

--And when we leave here, Addis Agụ, when we are free, they will have to make up who they think we are without us.

They laughing again.

Face to face, Addis pull Ekwueme closer to her and bury her lips in the fullness of him own. She lift her shift with one hand and loose him pants with the other. Side to side, eye to eye, they rise and fall into each other and find, for a time, freedom.

-8-
ADDIS

After while, Addis and Ekwueme rest in the wholeness of what they done made together: a love that flies. They breathe like one person coming back down to earth, tired, but full and satisfied. Joyful, even. Addis search for the word she feeling and land upon bliss. Then, she membering the earth aint standing still while they loving each other. A certain part of the night be too treacherous and full of risk to they lives, so they kiss enough to last and go on to they separate sides of House Farm, Slave Row.

Ekwueme got to go up round the Great House and behind the stables, careful all the while not to rouse the horses from they sleep and cause a fuss. But Addis got to go downhill, past the gardens and past what way worser than horses waking.

Haynes living just above her part of Slave Row, off the side of Upper Garden where the greenhouse and the herbs, soap plants and spices be. Warn't never no telling when he be up, so Addis sneaking through the garden and it be faithful enough not to tell on her. But just fore she reaching the greenhouse, she seeing someone fall out its door into the dirt, sobbing soft.

Addis look round but don't see no signs of Haynes nowhere round.

--Hey, who that be? Addis say quiet. She come a little closer and see it be a woman on the ground, look bout her mam's age.

The moonlight catch on the woman's face and Addis jump back and stifle a gasp with her hand. She membering this face belong to the meat ration lady taking up for Betty while she sick. This lady tore up something awful. Face all gashed and bleeding. But Addis caint see it all and the woman caint speak cause the woman got a muzzle round her mouth and blood running from where the straps digging in the flesh to her ears and up round the sides of her nose to behind her head. Addis run to help the woman. She untie the knots of the leather straps from round the woman's head and free her from the iron trap. Addis lift the woman up and feel she wet all over, sweat and blood in a tangle, soaking up her shift.

--Hold on to me, now. My hut not far. We fix you up. The woman whimper as Addis put the woman's arm over her shoulder and drag her away slow and quiet.

--You be all right now, Addis say. The woman breathe heavy and speak slow, voice scratching.

--Haynes! I aint see him. It were too late, she gasp between words. Addis looking round in near total dark, outside what the moonlight trapping.

--Don't you worry. You gon be all right. You the lady helping out Betty with the meat rations. What your name be again? Addis struggling carrying the woman but don't dare drop her.

--My name...Chinü, the woman say between moans and breaths and Addis scoff at it.

--That's right, Chinü. The gift to her mam. The one who mean God Hears.

Chinü moan a little louder.

--Shhhh, now! It's true. God hear you, and gon save you, you'll see. And my Nnene gon help, don't you worry now.

Addis aint believing that one bit. She surprise to see Chinü living this long, the way she look. Another joke from Chúkwú. Addis drag Chinü to the hut and her foot push the door open.

--Nnene! You wake? We need help! Nnene scramble out her bunk and light the hearth so she can see.

--Lord, Addis! Nnene eyes widing all the time she looking at the woman drenching in red. --What the debil happen to this woman?

Nnene fetch the pallets they using in the winter, set them down on the floor near the fire and grab for rags.

--Haynes happen, Addis say.

--Just set her down right here. Lord, not Lydia's baby! Nnene dipping the cloths in water and dabbing at the blood from the gashes in Chinü face. --Get that shift off her, Addis. It's all right, now, Chinü, we gon take care of you.

Addis tear the shift off Chinü and see how Haynes cut up her whole body, knifing round her breasts and belly and between her legs. Warn't no stopping the bleeding.

--She were probably just finishing up with the rations, on her way home when he get her, Addis say.

--Lord, girl, what were Haynes trying to do to you? Addis, fetch her some bark to bite on then tear up some cloths and soak up as much of this blood as you can.

Addis start to move Chinü head off her lap but Chinü grab both Addis hands and make her sit still.

--I see it in your eyes. Haynes gone too far this time.

Nnene start ripping cloths and holding them fast above Chinü breasts then wiping the blood that running into Chinü eyes from her head but Chinü don't seem to notice nothing. Her eyes getting dimmer and her breathing slow.

--I got a girl bout your age, Chinü say, looking right in Addis eyes, still holding to her hands but weak. --Her name Chima. We live at Three Farm. Promise you take care her.

--Chinü...what I can do for her all the way down in Three Farm?

--I know you. What your kin done to protect you. Nobody die protecting me never. Nobody look after my Chima. Promise me you gon do it!

Addis never been so fraid. Chinü eyes looking all the way through her. Seeing she aint long for this world, Addis say,

--I promise, Chinü. I look after Chima. I promise it!

Addis not knowing if Chinü hear it though, cause Chinü eyes wide and dead. Her hands limp in Addis hands and Addis wanting to scream, wanting to cry, but everything swallow up in her throat and she don't say nothing. Don't feel nothing.

--Nna Anyi no ne elu igwe.

Addis hear Nnene start praying low and weeping, still dabbing at Chinü wounds, but Addis just get up and let Chinü head drop down. Addis grab a clean cloth and walk to the washbasin. She silent as she scrub Chinü blood off her hands.

-9-
ADDIS

That promised land where all be peace, Oh deep river...
Addis hearing Nnene sing low between sobs but Addis just sitting, leaning against the door. She don't block it nor guard it. She just leaning. For the first time in a long time, her mind blank and quiet.

Lord, I want to cross over...
Addis watching Nnene stop the bleeding with needle and thread, wash the wounds and wrap Chinü clean, naked body tight in a sheet from they winter pallet. When Nnene finish, she say,

--Get down to Three Farm and tell em what's what. Her mam name Lydia. Find Chima. Find her man if she had un or her brother, one, so they can fetch this body fore it start to smelling. Then go wake Yandy and see caint he make a coffin fore tomorrow night. I reckon he gon need to start early to get it done fore nightfall. Then you stop and see your mam. Tell her what done happen so Massa let us bury her proper. Addis, you hearing me?

Addis still leaning and staring at nothing.

--Addis!

--She aint got no man, be all Addis can think to say.

--What you say, chile?

--I say she aint got no man. You say find her man but she caint have no man if Haynes done this to her.

--Oh you fool fool if I ever knowed one. Aint you hear her? Your life aint everybody life. Now get.

Addis push herself up off the floor.

--What if the watchmen catches me? What if Haynes?

--Best not.

Addis know Nnene done say all she gone say on the matter, so she leave.

She steer clear of the gravel way what run in a horseshoe in front of the Great House. She stick to the cover of the great oak trees what line the pathway til she must skip cross the road leading out of Wellesbury, to the right and down a great hill to the other 5 Farms to the west. She steer downhill and don't bother looking round her as she run light-footed through an open field. With nothing to hide behind and the moon looking out for her own, Addis know if any watchmen gon catch her, now be the time. She hold her breath and fly like never before til she hit One Farm.

Sunday Church happen at One, on the wood benches near the backy fields or sometimes in the storehouse, when it be too hot or too cold outside. Two Farm where they growing maize, Three Farm for feeding the whole plantation and burying em too, a ditch for slave graves...food for food...a world's whole life in one farm. Four where the wheat and cotton growing and Five where the wharf be. They growing cabbages and legumes out there too but mostly got packhouses for readying crops and fish to ship off from the wharf. Addis aint never been out that far and don't see no chance she ever will, what with all the watchmen down there just waiting for runaways to try. Don't nobody land a foot they wanting to keep on the wharf nor board boat nor ship out there but watchmen.

After miles, Addis skirt the edges of the maize field and land soft in Three Farm. She caint member the last time she been to Three, but when she hit it, she find it look like all the others, only bigger, more huts, taller crops. She wake a few ojis fore she find the hut folks say belong to Chinü. She sit outside a short moment to teach her chest to breathe normal again. She wipe sweat from her forehead with the back of her hand and rub it in her shift. Then, she knock. A small-faced girl with button eyes open the door.

--I looking for Chima. That you?

--Who you be?

--I be Addis. I working House Farm.

--Yeah? I knowing you. We all knowing you down here.

--Oh?

--Who don't know the ones what come from Dido? We knowing Menor Missus too.

--Don't call her that, Addis bite, then she membering why she come and her face grow somber and Chima catch it.

--Why you here, Addis?

--Your mam name Chinü?

--Where my mam at?

--Awful sorry to tell it to you, Chima. Your mam dead.

Chima scoff. --I just seen my mam while ago, so you wrong.

--Woman name Chinü just die in my hut. Fore she go she saying she got a chile at Three Farm name Chima and I gotta find her and look after her. Now if that aint you I awful sorry.

--Nah my mam be Chinü and I be Chima but she aint dead.

You got it wrong. Ala come tell her just two days past she gon be free. We both gon be free, so,

  --Chima...your mam free now.

Addis catch Chima eyes with that and Addis don't see a girl her age no more. She seeing herself at 5 years old laying top her pap's chest, looking in him dead eyes, knowing life warn't much of nothing fore he been shot up, but now, but now...

  --No...

Addis run to Chima as Chima fall down. Addis cradle Chima and rock her slow on the floor as Chima cry out,

  --She warn't posed to leave me! She say we go together. She warn't posed to go. My mam!

  --Shhh, now Chima. It warn't her fault. She aint want to go without you, I sweard it. It were Haynes. It were Haynes.

  --Why he do this to my mam?

  --Reckon he aint think he were killing her. They think oji womens posed to be strong enough to take anything.

  --Why he get to walk this earth? Why?

  --Don't know, Chima. He kill my pap, too, and I long for the day he get what coming. It aint no comfort, I know it aint, but my Nnene say it take all kinds to make a world.

Addis feel Chima go limp in her arms, just wailing and wetting up her shift and Addis do what she aint done since she were a chile. She cry too. She holding Chima like a doll and she cry for Chinü, for Chima, for her own pap and her mam. They warn't posed to leave nuther but everybody go and Nnene be next, she know it and she cry for it. She cry for all Nnene done seen and heard. And Ekwueme. How Addis caint go nowhere near him when him pap were kilt and he needing her, he shaking and crying out, but she run from him. She cry cause he forgive her for it so easy.

We all been broke up, shook up and turnt round inside, she member Ekwueme say after, like it solve all. *That be just what this place do to us and we do all we know to bout it.*

It aint make sense when he say it to her and it still make none when she think on it now, holding Chima.

Chinü warn't the first dead body Addis seen nor touch. Warn't even the first Addis watch die. Chima warn't the first to lose a mam and break down with heartache nuther but something bout Chima's eyes stir something up in Addis. She feel those eyes in her belly and it aching. Chima cry out to Addis from a soul-place and

Addis have to answer.

Addis wake to the morning bell and find it warn't one of her dreams. Her shift still wet with tears and Chima still nestle in her shoulder, but she quiet now, worn out to sleep.

--Chima, she say quiet. --Wake up now, Chima. That be the morning bell.

--No...no...

--Come on, now, Chima. Imma tell your watchmen what happen first so you aint gotta work today. Then I go tell Yandy so he make a coffin by night and my mam gotta tell Burken, *Massa Burken*, so they lets us have the homegoing. Lemme take you to your Gran Lydia or your pap or somebody. Where your pap be?

Chima sit up and wipe her face with her hands.

--My pap gone.

Addis breathe out soft, full with relief. She know it all along. Warn't no man for Chinü. Caint be.

--He leave with the ship fore nightfall, Chima say. --He a watchman.

-10-
ADDIS

Cloaked by dark trees, Addis run with all her strength back up
through the Farms to the carpenter Yandy, what living near
the stables, near Ekwueme. When she finish telling Yandy
what been done to Chinü and he get moving on a box to lay Chinü
up in, Addis want to run straight to Ekwueme and tell him all, but
she don't. She creep up to the kitchen on the side of the Great House
and head for the loft above it, where her mam and brothers sleeping.
But someone grab her arm.

She look down and see her brother Basil Lee, the oldest of
the two, out from behind barrels of cornmeal in the corner. He
shaking him head with a finger to him lips and him other hand over
the mouth of the littlest one Billy Lee. Billy Lee bite Basil hand and
Basil open up him mouth to holler but don't make a sound. Billy
Lee, with him mouth free of him brother's hand, say in a loud
whisper —Pap up there! while he pointing up to the loft.

--Hush! Basil Lee tell him brother fore putting him hand
back over the rascal's mouth. Though Addis can only see shadows
from lamplight up there, she hear the soft snoring of a man she know
be Burken. Basil Lee pull her down to the stone floor and the three
of them hide quiet behind the barrels. --He gon be gone, soon, Basil
Lee whisper, and Addis mouth fill with bile and disgust for her mam
and pity for her brothers. How many times they been woke in the
middle of the night and made to wait behind cornmeal?

Addis doze off a little while they waiting, but it warn't no
time at all for Burken come clomping down the stairs in him heavy
boots and sleeping trousers. He walking drowsy through the kitchen
and into the Great House, and he close the door behind him. Her
brothers stay dozing in the corner, so she leave them and creep up
the loft ladder. She see her mam in a cotton and lace sleeping gown
with her back to Addis, hunching over something near the lamplight.
Addis peer over her mam's shoulder and see a newspaper, a name
cross the top she aint never seen before, *Eziokwu*.

When she sound it out in her head, she know it be a Eboe
word. It fill her with hope. For a moment she forgetting why she
there cause she knowing now for sure there be written Eboe in a
newspaper. She try to get closer to read the rest but she creak a

floorboard and her mam jump up with the paper behind her back.
 --Oh, Addis! Lord, chile!
Taddy catching her breath, turning back round and stuffing the newspaper under her bed.
 --What is this, Eziokwu?
Addis asking and her mam get flustered.
 --Never you mind that. What you doing here, Addis? Always glad to see you, of course, but you never dropping by, and never this early. What done happen?
 --Chinü dead. Lydia's daughter over at Three Farm. She were cut up something awful. Haynes done it. Nnene saying to ask you to ask Massa Burken for a homegoing tonight.
 --Of course. I'll tell him first thing. But, Addis?
 Her mam walking to her, reaching for her, but Addis wrench away, not wanting them hands on her. She turn and make her way down the ladder, with her mam peering down at her. Addis look to her sleeping brothers in the corner on the way out, then back up at her mam, who don't show no signs of shaming. Addis turn and leave fore sun rising.

Dawn burn into noon and melt into evening fore Addis even know where the day gone. She been uncomfortable, dreamlike since she leave Chima. Addis fearing Chinü and Chima crack something in her chest what been shut up all her life and now her bones crushing in on her and she caint breathe. What is it? What is it? She wonder as she were weeding. She blink and more time pass. Now they all gathering at Three Farm under torchlight.
 Near three hundred slaves come out to bury Chinü whether they knowing her or not, and most likely not. It just what they do, the ones who aint watchmen, the ones who want to belong somewhere else than Wellesbury and member another world that aint here. They all standing on three sides of the field Burken let them use to bury they dead. They facing Chinü, laid up on top her coffin in a white shift, all clean, hands folded at the gut like she sleeping. As the eldest daughter, Chima lead the procession round her mam, covering Chinü body with palm leaves and cowrie shells, all she gon need for the rebirth.
 Just a lil while longer
 Soon it all be over
 Lord I caint wait for that glory day!

The near three hundred singing, marching, dancing round Chinü. Folks beating drums with they hands, slow and steady like blood do on its last go-round through the body. The drummers knowing it might could be they last chance, what with watchmen starting to complain to Haynes bout funeral goings-on, so the drummers striking deliberate, with a message. They drumming faster and faster and dancing harder and harder, round in a circle, all the three hundred joining, and Addis swear she hearing the ocean.

Addis feel faint and look all round for Ekwueme. She feel a fever when she see him over the crowd, bending him ear to her mam. Taddy let her fingers curl round Ekwueme arm as she whispering to him and Addis near choke on spit. She start for them but Nnene grab Addis arm and hold her still with one hand. So Addis look down at her feets til the fever break.

--What is it, chile? You wandering lost all the day.

--They names, Nnene. They names. Chinü, Chima. It be just like you tell me when I dream bout Gran and Ala. *God hear. God know.*

-11-
TADDY

Taddy wait some time for folk to clear out the homegoing and turn in for the night fore she go knocking on Addis and Nnene door. She try to knock gentle, so not to frighten them. Knocks at this hour don't never mean nothing good and Taddy aint got no good news to share.

--Whosit there? She hear Nnene say. Taddy's soft voice creep through the doorcracks,

--Taddy. Open up, Nnene.

Nnene say firm, --Addis, you open that door for your mam, hear?

Taddy member that tone. She know Nnene aint asking no question. It aint no time fore the door creak wide open. She smile seeing Addis again.

--Hello, she say, searching Addis face, hoping for warmth in it. She find none. Addis just nod to her ńné, walk away and sit down at the little table Bernard building, long ago. Taddy walk inside and close the door.

--I brought y'all some bread leftover from the house. Cinnamon raisin, Taddy say, lifting up the basket she brought with her. Nnene get up to greet Taddy.

--How you treat us! Nnene say, embracing Taddy and placing the basket on the floor near the stove.

--Take my seat, honey, Nnene say, pointing to it.

--Mighty kind, Nnene.

Taddy trace the top of the old, everstrong table with her hand. For just a moment, she get lost in the membering of her man Bernard who built her this table. She member loving and being loved. Then she come back to herself.

--I best not stay too long, though, fore they come after me. I just came with some good news for Addis.

She see Addis ears prick up, but Addis keep her head down.

--I were gonna tell you this morning when you come by bout Chinü but it didn't seem like the time. But I gotta tell you now so you know. In two weeks, you coming with me to stay with Missus as a lady's maid. We going up North to Filadelfia, to the nation's capitol! Aint that something?

Addis don't say nothing.

--You hear me, Addis? You gonna come North with your mam. With Massa being the president of the whole country now, he going to live there for a time, and you know they caint do nothing without us there!

She laugh a little, but nobody join her. She see Addis swallow hard.

--No, Addis say real quiet. She lift her eyes to meet her ńné.

--No, I aint going nowhere with you.

Addis steady when she say it and it sting Taddy. Nnene face get flush and she scold Addis.

-- You hush up, now, Addis! You going with your mam and that be the end of it. Don't act like I never teached you the order of things.

Addis stand up from the table and raise her voice.

--I say I aint going!

Taddy swallow all her secrets and say the only other truth that come to mind.

--Massa *want* you, Addis. Taddy choke back the bile that come up with them words and smile instead. --There aint no getting round it. I try reasoning with him, I did. Told him you don't know nothing bout Great House living. That you won't be no help at all to the Missus, but he won't hear none of it, Addis. He like a dog named ball. He want it all.

Taddy knowing it aint right for a mam to be made to say that to her chile. It cut her deep to say it like it be a normal thing, like a right thing every mam got to teach her girl chile, like what happens when the girl old enough for the blood to come. Just another season of life. But Taddy got to let them thoughts slip away so littler stuff can have room. She saying,

--I'm gon come by next week with some nice clothes fit to travel in. Missus like us always to look nice, since everybody want to stop Massa on the road and shake him hand once they find out who riding in that white carriage with the two white horses hitched up to it.

Addis swelling up but Taddy pay no notice.

--Don't reckon you have much you want to bring with you, so there aint no sense in telling you to pack light, but I tell you anyhow. I tell you more next week when I bring the clothes. Then we off to Filadelfia the week after. We gon get to spend some real time together!

Taddy smiling, but Addis be silent, looking like her heart done lodged like a dull bullet in the base of her stomach, so Nnene speak for her.

--Mighty kind of you to come by and warn our Addis, Taddy. Sure good on you to come by. We's thankful for it and we's thankful for the treat you left us here.

Nnene go to hug Taddy one last time and Taddy get lost in the warmth. She membering how Nnene truly love her.

Taddy sighing. When she break the embrace, she turn to leave. --I'll come again next week.

--We'll be looking for you, Nnene say. Taddy see Addis slump back down in her seat like her chest on fire. Taddy close the door behind herself and know it aint a door but a ocean what separate her from her chile, and she leave Addis to drown in it.

-12-
EKWUEME

Ekwueme run round the stables light and smiling up at the night sky. It been two weeks since he last seen Addis, two weeks since the homegoing and only two weeks more til he get her free out West. He seem to float to they spot, deep behind the gardens, in the grove.

Him heart jump when he see just her back and the way her hair fall on it. He think of scooping her up while her back turned to him but he think again. He already got him one scar from sneaking up on Addis and he warn't in no hurry to get another.

--You here, he say grinning.

She turn to him and answer in Eboe.

--Yes, I am here.

Now with no chance to startle her, he run straight for her and pick her up. He bury him nose in her neck and breathe the lavender out her skin. She rest her cheek on him and he feel more love than he ever feeling. *This is my love. This is my love*, he thinking, and he never want to end it.

--Ekwu, I must tell you something bad, Addis say at last.

--Not yet, Addy. Not yet.

--Ekwu, I must!

Addis insist on it, so he put her down and feel joy leaving him body when he do. She too far away and he caint smell her lavender no more. When he think on it now, he caint smell nothing sweet; no flowers, no fruit from the gardens like normal. The air done prune up.

--I am not going with you, Ekwu, Addis say firm, and he feel the ice cold of winter coming on the back of him neck.

He hear the Potomac get violent nearby, crashing into the river bank. A boat must be nearby, he thinking. Something coming to make the current change so.

--Of course you are going. Don't worry, Addis. Sayzare's got free papers with your new name on them. Guess what I told him to name you? Agụ! You will be a tiger, just like I promised you. You know I keep my promises!

He laughing and he going in to kiss her but she pulling back, stopping him with both her open palms in him chest.

--No, Ekwueme, listen to me. I am not going with you.

--What foolish thing are you saying? This is your chance, this is your *one* chance.

--And you must take it, Ekwueme. You must.

He backing away from her, blood draining from him face.

--Master has…

--*Master?*

He wince first, then fire start to grow in him belly. He clench him teeth, him fists in the dark. They never call Burken that. Not never when they alone.

--Master has chosen me to go to Filadelfia as a lady's maid. We leave in the morning.

Each word paining Ekwueme and get him heart to pounding.

--I am going to have a new life, Ekwueme. I am going to wear fine clothes. I am going to live inside the Great House …

--You will be *his*, he spit out.

--I am already his, she snap back. --And so are you. But after while, we are both going to be different. It is going to be better for both of us, you will see.

--You are talking foolishly, Addis.

He turn him back on her, hands to him temple.

--I am saying goodbye to you, Ekwueme.

--You think if you are going North, I am not also going North? You think I would let him take you? Yes! I will meet you in Filadelfia. We will go West together. Nothing has to change.

--Ekwueme, *everything* has changed! I have a chance now at a better life without running.

--We would be together!

--On the run from the most powerful man in the country? He would come for us.

--Let him come!

--You saw what Burken did to old Farmer. Chased him down 10 counties over just because he could do it. But you're younger and stronger than Farmer. On your own, you could get away like Linus did last year and he would never find you either, try as he might.

--And you? More cat than woman! He would find me long before he could ever sniff you out!

Ekwueme pacing side to side, feeling him blood thicken and

slow in him veins. He knowing he getting too loud but he don't care. Then he start to member the part of the plan that matter most.

--You do not understand, Addis. You *must* be on that caravan. If you want to be free of me, I swear I will stay behind. But you *must* go West. You don't know what is coming.

--I know just what is coming, Ekwueme. That is just it. I am trying to help you.

--Help me?

He still pacing, digging him fists into him thighs as he walk.

--I know you are scared, Addis, but I am scared too. We are scared together. We will protect each other, like we always do! If we get caught, we will die together rather than return here. I will never let harm come to you. I will dedicate my life to the destruction of your enemies. *My* enemies. You know what I speak is true.

He grab her hand and place it on the welts on him back that mark the membering. --So what is it that you really fear?

--This is what I *want*.

--You lying!

He break with Eboe now. Eboe be for truth telling.

--You want free most of all us here! You die for free if it came to it and leave me here alone to get it. You think I not knowing it all along?

Addis look like he knock the wind out her chest and he regret he say it right away.

--You right, she say anyway. --You zactly right. This me. Your Addis. Addis what caint love nobody but Addis. You see now? I helping you here. I saving *you* this time.

--You think cause I know Addis I caint love Addis? I pay *skin* off my back for Addis cause you mine.

He grab at him chest. --You fool fool if you thinking I let Burken touch what mine.

He run to her but she back away.

--I aint yours. I aint nobodys. You lose skin for me, sure enough, but you aint bought me with it and I aint going from Burken's slave to yours and calling that freedom.

--I aint mean that. You know I aint mean that...

--But you did. I love you, I do, but I don't belong to you and you got to let me go if I say so.

--Don't send me away from you...

--Listen to me, now, Ekwu. There is a girl named Chima at

Three Farm. We buried her mam two weeks past. Find her and take her with you instead of me. Give her my papers.

Ekwueme don't listen.

--You hating your ńné and what she got to do with Burken. You hating Burken more than the Debil hisself. I know you!

--Yes, Ekwueme, you know me! I love you all I can. I swear I do. If I could be Nnene and live my life for other folk, I be her instead, but she aint my mam. Taddy be my mam! She do what she must to survive and that be all I know. Aint no getting round it. She my bone and I her gut and that be the end of it.

--You lying! Ekwueme don't want to hear no more but Addis won't stop.

--Cause I loving you all I can, I do you one thing different. I stop you from dying for me a fool, like my pap. Like my gran pap fore him. I not doing that to you, Ekwueme.

Him head start to pounding. He just knowing Addis don't mean it. She caint mean it.

--Aint that why you chose me? Cause I die for you if it came to it, like your pap? I know you!

Addis turn from him but it's her time to listen.

--All us got one thing what keep us living. Mams got they chiles. Some got Ala, Chúkwú, and they hope in that. Ekwueme got Addis. That be all I got. I live with you or die with you. That be all I got.

Addis wipe her tears in her shift sleeve and look him eye to eye when she say,

--Well then you aint got nothing.

Him eyes grow wide cause he knowing she mean what she say.

--Sorry, Ekwueme. I tell you true. I going.

Hate boiling over in him ears making Addis words ring empty, echo empty.

--I will kill him if he touches you!

He yell too loud, Eboe rippling in darkness. But if anything come for them just then, he know he gon kill it or die trying to. He raise him hands up, ready.

--Why? Addis whispering. --You gon rob my brothers of they father, a wife of her husband, and me of a better life, a safer, long life? I aint got no choices in this world. But this one thing I choosing, that you live apart from me where you be safe and I be free of guilt. I don't want to die and I don't want you dead cause of me. Let me have this one choice.

He feel frozen. It hurt to think, so he don't. He feel her reach up and grab him outstretched hands and bring them down to him waist, and hold them tight. But he caint look at her. She whisper, --Be free! Free of everything that has a hold on you. Even me. Get on that caravan. Go West. But please, take Chima. She must leave this place. Take care of her please. She aint got nothing nuther.

She squeeze him hands, look on him a last time. --Ka omesia, she say and leave him standing still, never looking back. This caint be the last time he see her, he thinking, and it make him body come alive again. He yell after her, --No ka omesia between us!

She start to run, and Ekwueme sure he done scream loud enough to wake what dead.

--He won't touch you! He won't touch you!

He yelling, but Addis a withered bloom scattered in the wind. Too many pieces going too many different ways and he don't know which part to chase. He grab at him head with both him hands at first and buckle over, down to him boots, at the loss he feeling. He knew it were coming, this day when she would leave and take clean air with her. It were only a matter of time, he always known it. But loving her were like working hard over fire; when he see what it create, he know for sure it be worth the times when it burnt up him arms.

Ekwueme take him a moment to feel it all. He lean under a willow and hold him head in him hands and let the fire in him gut spread all through him. Then he ready to think that this loss warn't no different from the loss of him pap or him mam or him brothers and sister. What else a menor life be but loss. He get him breathing under control first, then he learn to stand again. Menor life be loss, but he warn't gon be no menor much longer. He forgetting him pain and member something bigger happening than Addis not loving him. Addis were posed to be on that caravan in two weeks, far from Burken and Wellesbury, both, and now he done all but deliver her up to the lion's mouth.

--I fix it, he promise hisself. --Gotta set it right, he say and he march toward the stable ground, fists at the ready.

-13-
NNENE

The fool done run off, Nnene thinking, fearing, really, when she wake up and see Addis not in her bunk. She done run off with that boy and that be all for em both, Nnene caint stop thinking it, her gut all knotted up.

What if they make it? She letting herself hope for just a moment. What if they free from here for good and don't never look back? What if...

Nnene hear the latch on the door turn and Addis open it slow, specting she gon be sleep.

--Where you been at, chile!

Nnene jump up yelling fore Addis can even get through the door. Addis jump too at Nnene's bark, though if Addis were thinking right, she'd a known Nnene were up waiting for her on they last night together.

--I was...

--Don't even get to lying. I know you was with that boy. I sure hope you not stirring up any trouble. You leaving with your mam tomorrow and that be all there is to it!

--I know, Nnene! I was just saying goodbye to Ekwueme.

Nnene heart calm and she sit back down on her bunk.

--Well no sense in that. You be back after while. Up'n Filadelfia, the ojis be free. Caint stay there more'n half the year without being free directly. He gon send you back for at least a week or two to get round it. He just done it a few months back. You gon see Ekwueme soon enough...if that be what you want.

--I don't ever wanna see him. Not after Burken take me... I aint never gon be my mam, not if I gotta say!

Nnene cut Addis a look then turn away, shaking her head.

--You ought be shamed but you won't. Hear you talk against your own mam so. Lord knows I never teached it to you.

--She the one...

--You don't know nothing bout your mam! I raise that chile, just like I raise you and I tell you she done the best she knowed to do! You sat down and listen!

Nnene stare Addis down til she sit and look away. Nnene swallow fore she confess all.

--Every baby I ever borned had no breath.

--I know, Nnene...

--Listen! Four babies come from me, filled with blood and nothing else. And do you know why? Massa Ambrose try to breed me with many men and four times I chew the bitter root to send them babies back to Heben so they aint got to know this cursed life. Burken hear what him pap tried didn't work on me so Burken never try to breed me hisself, so that one part of my hell were over. Maybe it were right and maybe it warn't but it done now. That were the best I could do for my babies.

Nnene try to search Addis for something, any kind of feeling, but Addis silent and still. Nnene ask her,

--You think I done right? You think I shoulda kill myself instead of the chiles? Or maybe kill the ones what try to mate me? Warn't they fault nuther. They a slave like all us is. Maybe shoulda kill Massa Ambrose, then? Beat your Gran Gran Dido to it? End up like her with my head on a pole? That's what you thinking, right?

Nnene rise up again, walk to the table to Addis who won't look her in the eye.

--You think you better than me? Nnene hit the table and say, --Look me in my face! You better than your mam? You think you want free more than us do? You the first Ala ever visit in a dream and say you's a tiger so keep fighting! You's special! Oh yes, *Addis Agu*! You be the first!

Nnene see Addis clench her fist and grit her teeth but Nnene far from done.

--This life you got, this the best your mam could do and you know it. You dream things bout Dido dying I aint never tell you. You see what your mam seen as a chile and still you treat her so?

--What I seen is her let my pap die and save herself, Addis stand and say. --I seen you say God hear, God know, like it matter any. I seen God send Chinü and Chima right after you say it so we know that if it be true, if God do hear and know, God laughing too. Only fool fool think it otherwise.

--From a fool fool mouth!

Nnene say, but now she understanding. --You right bout one thing, you *see*. You see what happen to other folk and yes it hurt you to see it, but it aint happening to *you*. You see your mam drag away and you see your pap run through, you see Chinü die and you think it be a message for *you*. Simple chile. Ought to be falling out with praise for what Chúkwú done spare you from. But you gon see *true*, one day.

Addis shrink to the floor but Nnene caint stop.

--You fear you just like your mam, because you is! You seeing horrors no chile ever should, and so did she. You hope that loving somebody might make living worthwhile, and so did *she*. You deal with this life the best way you know and that's just what all us do. She gave you to me to protect you. To love you and raise you like the babies I never born alive, and hadn't I done just that? Hadn't I?

Nnene leaning over the chair at the table, near collapsing from the guilt that sit in her chest and won't leave her.

--Hadn't I? She crying. Addis run to her, wrapping her arms round Nnene, holding her up.

--Yes, Nnene! No one be as good as you. You done more'n right by me. I'll be kind to my mam, I promise you that. I treat her just like she was you, I promise you!

Addis kiss her cheek and they spend they last night crying over what is and what never gon be.

-14-
TADDY

The sound of rustled horses snatch Taddy from a light sleep. Her eyes open up to darkness and she knowing it be nowhere near time for them to leave for Filadelfia and sure enough no time for horses to be woke. Somebody messing with them. Somebody bout to mess up everything, she thinking.

Taddy want to sit up in her bed but she feel her boys nestling close to her on each side. Years of lying under Burken while he snore away make her slick as a water snake, and she slip right from under her boys, their heads dropping softly on the down pillows Burken leave there for hisself, when he come. Her feets hit the floor soft and she kneel down and dig up her pistol from a loose floorboard, then she down the ladder in no time, the ladder knowing better than to make a squeak. She wrap a cloak round her dressing gown, hide her pistol in a pocket and fly to the stables, looking round in the dark to see if anybody else been woke by whoever were wrestling with the horses.

The closer she get, the louder the horses whinny in distress. Taddy hear a hammer slamming against iron. She see a trail of light spilling out the stable and grip her pistol in her pocket. Peeping round the stable door, she see Ekwueme hunched down with a lantern hammering off horseshoes, broken wagon wheels strewn all bout the grounds.

--Onye nzuzu! Stop this now, fool!
Taddy say full force in Eboe and Ekwueme fall backward at the sound and drop him hammer from the shock.

--Chineke meh! Just what do you think you are doing, eh? Ekwueme scoot away from the horse he were working on and hold him head in him hands.

--Addis, he say. --She leaving. I caint let her leave.
Taddy grab the head of a horse close to her and speak soft to it and it quiet down. She go on to the next and do the same. She just at a whisper when she say.

--Fool fool if I ever seen one. We got work to do and you know it.

--But Addis!

--Quiet now! You fitting to ruin everything with your

78

foolishness. Think, Ekwueme!

He still sitting on the ground, a mess of horseshoes round him. --Addis were posed to go West. She warn't posed to be nowhere near that man, now she say she going!

--And what of it, Ekwueme? You think cause a no-color man say he own her that she up to be owned? You think she gon pass from being Burken's to being your'n?

--No! No. I love her.

--Your love aint no excuse, Taddy say and move on to another horse. Ekwueme start to sob.

--You even stop to think how many stableboys you gonna get whupped to death for what you doing in here tonight? You think bout how we *need* Burken outta here tomorrow? You got work you posed to be doing and here you come causing problems we don't need and aint gon do no good, no how.

--He gon take her. You know he gon take her.

--You leave my chile to me. Addis gon be free, never you mind that.

--Aint never gon see her again.

Taddy finish with the horses and sit herself next to Ekwueme. --That aint no new news, chile. And now aint the time to get off the path.

She place her arms round him and he collapse on her, tears falling heavy.

Him cries seem to lull the horses on to sleep and fill the whole stable up with the peace of release.

After some time, he quiet himself and sit up again, face dry.

--I promise I take care of Addis, Taddy say. --You member what you promise me?

--I member it all, he say. --Aint gon mess it up.

--I know you won't, she say and lift herself up. --Now, I got one more thing to ask you.

--Anything, he say.

She reach her arms out to help him up. Ekwueme gentle when he place him hands in hers, and she stay steady as she bear him weight in her own hands.

--That woman aint gon let me bring my baby with us. My Billy Lee gon be here all alone. I caint let that happen.

--He gon go with Sayzare out West, then.

--When it all be over, I'mma come get him. Tell him so,

79

Ekwueme. Tell him not to worry. Keep him safe til I come.

--I promise you I'm gon do all what I say, Ekwueme tell her. --And when I be done with it, I'm coming for Burken. And he gon curse the day him ancestors set foot in Eboeland.

Taddy eyes light up at that and her smile for Ekwueme be as wide as her plotting.

END OF PART ONE

PART TWO:

NWA NNE DI NA MBA

EVEN IN A STRANGE LAND, A FRIEND CAN BE FOUND

-15-
ADDIS

Awoman dances in the middle of the ocean and doesn't drown. She is a glorious tree-sap black and her skin shines like a new morning. She wears the waves around her waist, a skirt of the deepest blues with purple tinges and white froth fringes and she dances. She is calm and happy and I watch her as my feet burn in the sand but I don't dare move.

She is singing low; she is chanting steady.

Bïa Chineke
Bïa Chineke
I mara mmá
Ibuchúkwú
Idi ebube
Bïa Chineke!

Over and over she chants until the ocean joins in

Bïa Chineke
Bïa Chineke

Harmony. Colors. Clouds plot then move in, creating a burst of sunlight on me. She spots me.

I try to hide but I cannot move. My feet are frozen in fire. I feel her eye on me. The purple waves split open and spill blood. I smell death. She is getting angry. She is chanting faster, dancing harder, singing louder,

--Come, Lord!

She reaches out her hands, commanding the clouds and they turn black as she.

--Come, Lord!

She spins in the ocean and it obeys her, a whirlwind crashing in upon itself. Her eye is still on me and I'm no longer on the sand. I'm floating in the warm womb of dark ocean and its waves whip my lashes and its salt burns my eyes, but I won't close them.

I'm far from shore and farther still from her, but she won't take her eye off of me. The ocean is vibrating, chanting as she calls to me. She calls my true name and I am afraid.

--Adaeze!

She calls me tiger.

Adaeze Agu!

A wave comes from behind me and overtakes me and I can't breathe.
I spit and choke and struggle and I start to drown. My head is below water, but
I can still see her eye, still hear the ocean chanting, still hear her calling me,
        --Agu!
My chest burns and my arms are tired. My eyes droop and then close and I am
falling into a white nothing.
        --Agu!

-16-
ADDIS

You look like you aint got no sleep at all, Taddy say to Addis as they loading Missus bags into a wagon toward the end of the caravan.

--Cause I aint, Addis say and keep loading. Five coaches they taking to Filadelfia, two of em just fill with trunks and trunks of Burken and Missus stuff. The first one in the caravan were the big white coach with the gold-color spokes and two white horses for Burken. The other buggies only have one horse each and take twice as long to catch up with Burken and Missus, but it were more for show than speed anyhow.

Burken warn't taking but seven ojis with him and two oji watchmen: The other cook, Nora, George and Luther for blacksmithing, and the footman Seth, driving Burken's coach. Addis riding with Taddy and her half-brother, Basil Lee. He warn't but twelve but Burken thinking it be high time Basil Lee make hisself useful. Missus make Billy Lee stay behind. He warn't but nine but what Missus care when her heart caint take seeing Burken in both Taddy's boys at once.

--You still having them dreams?
Taddy asking just above a whisper when she and Addis and Basil Lee settle into a coach near the rear, toward the one what carrying Haynes and two of him no-color watchmen, Phil and Cal. The two menor watchmen don't get no rest though. They gotta drive the last two coaches.

--How you knowing bout my dreams?
Addis say too sharp, then put her head down, membering what she promise Nnene.

--I knowing all manner of stuff maybe I shouldn't. That don't stop it from being so. Tell your mam, how your head be?

--My head be just fine, Addis say and turn to look out the window of the coach. She feel Basil Lee eyes burning into her and she give him a icy look over her shoulder. Basil Lee turning away from Addis and say,

--Mam, why we gotta ride all the way back here? Aint

pap…

--Hushup, Basil Lee! Twelve is well and old enough to know the way the world work.

--Why we leaving Billy Lee behind? It aint right.

--I say hush-up now, Basil!

Addis peer at her mam for the way she talking to the boy. Reason after reasin Addis aint gotta keep her promise to Nnene, she thinking.

--But he aint gon make it without us! You know he aint all right in the head!

Out the corner of her eye, she watching Taddy mood turn sorry and Addis wonder what all be wrong with Billy and what gon happen to him now that he all alone at Wellesbury. She hope even more that Ekwueme take Billy with him somehow.

Taddy grab Basil Lee by the shoulders and draw him to her. She kiss him forehead.

--If I could keep us all together, me and you and Billy Lee, *and Addis*, I would. You gotta know that. Aint none of this my doing it.

Addis feel her mam saying it as much to her as to her brother and she grunt soft.

--Where he gon stay while you gone? Addis ask through squinting eyes.

--Blacksmiths gon look after him. He gon meet up with your friend, Sayzare.

Addis eyes flash at the name. If Billy Lee going with Sayzare out West, that mean Ekwueme gon take care of him, for sure. It make her feel some kinda relief, though she don't much no why. Aint like she gon see either of em again.

Maybe that thought were just it. Aint no way Ekwueme could die in her place if he a whole world away. Aint no way she could hurt him ever again.

--We'll see Billy Lee again, soon, Taddy say, --but now you get to enjoy your sister Addis for once.

Addis look at her milk-color brother. Mama's baby, daddy's maybe, she thinking, with him wide-set eyes the color of daisies or some such color aint natural. He thinking the same of

Addis cause he turn to they mam, who deep brown as umber herself, and he say, --She don't look like us.

The coach get to moving just then, and Addis seeing Wellesbury in a slow whirl as she pass it, the red brick walls of the garden, the white of the Great House and the gravel road, the menacing row of cannons guarding the front gate, the green grass waving goodbye, all swirling together in front of her to make a fast-fading picture of the only place she ever knowing, and then, no picture at all. *I aint never gon see this place again*, she decide, and Nnene or no Nnene, Ekwueme or no Ekwueme, she don't feel nothing but good bout it.

--You looking for that boy? Her mam ask.

--Ekwueme aint no boy, she snap.

--You all children to me, Taddy say. --Member that poem I used to read you, bout the children of the sun and summer?

But only thing Addis want to be membering be the night of the homegoing when Taddy had her hands wrapped round Ekwueme, whispering in him ear. Addis nose get hot when she think on it and she turn to glare at her mam.

--How you know Ekwueme anyhow? What he got to do with you?

--You and Nnene keep to yourselfs, and you got a right to it, but everybody aint you. And if you was looking for Ekwueme just now, I found him last night. He were in a awful state. Fixing to tear up every carriage Massa Burken own to keep you from going. I stop him though. I tell him to be the one man in your life who don't try and control you. I promise him I take care of you, tell him I got me a plan just for that and not to worry. So he choose right. He let you go.

--Fool fool to trust you, Addis say, heart full of joy as much as it aching. Ekwueme were not gon save her. Ekwueme were gon survive.

--Now aint the time. Settle in. We got us a long trip. Addis lean into the corner of the coach and watch the world's colors melt outside her window. She doze off and dream of nothing.

Addis wake when the coach jolt to a halt. --Housemaids!

Footman Seth yelling.

--They calling us, Taddy say and she scoot Basil Lee's head off her lap and onto the seat. Addis reach for the door handle but Taddy grab her hand. --This aint the time to do nothing foolish. Watchmen...*Haynes* be everywhere. When your mam tell you she got a plan, she got a plan.

Addis wrench her hand away. --I aint going nowhere, she say. But when Addis step outside that coach and onto the gravel road, seeing nothing round them but trees and woods for miles, she thinking, *Let the night come! I'mma climb a tree and jump through branches and no one ever find me.*

But it aint night. The sun be wide awake and telling all, so she follow her mam to the carriage Missus Burken in. Nora meet them there and Hal open the door and help Missus Burken out her coach.

--Fetch my pot, Missus Burken say to Taddy and Taddy obey. They all follow Missus Burken through the woods, away from the peering eyes of the watchmen. --Right here, Missus Burken tell Taddy and she set the pot down. --*Hold it,* Missus Burken say and Taddy stoop down and hold the pot in place while Addis lift up the tail of Missus Burken's ivory dress and the hoop slip underneath. Nora hold Missus Burken's hands for balance as she squat down.

Missus Burken seem to Addis a never ending drain and Addis wonder how long she been saving up for this moment. Addis stomach get tight seeing her mam so low. Her life caint be so much after all, Addis thinking. A piss-covered life.

When Missus Burken done, Taddy dump the full pot far from them all and wipe one hand on the back of her shift, holding the stained pot in the other. Addis look at her mam as if to say, *don't it make you wanna die?* And Taddy look back like it aint the worst thing she ever done. Missus Burken walk herself back up to the road and Nora, Taddy and Addis take their turn squatting behind trees, then walk back to the road in silence. Long gone be the smell of Virginia pine and the stinging sweetness of the gardens, but Addis knowing just then that Wellesbury still be any place a Burken be.

The journey were long and rough, the kind of unpleasantness that make the Burkens think they know what it feel like to be treated bad. It get worse once the gravel road stop and the dirt one begin. The horses' feets catch more rocks and bumps than ever before. Half a day into the trip, they gotta stop for George and Luther to fix the horseshoes.

While Addis relieving herself by a tree, she watching Burken scold George and Luther for shoddy horeshoeing in the first place and Nora fanning Missus Burken who, for the life of her, just caint get comfortable in this heat.

Night falling and even a president aint safe on him own roads, with ransackers and such always on the loose, so, since they far off schedule and caint stop where they plan, they finding a house off the road to ask for a little hospitality.

Course the good Maryland folk caint believe they eyes when the famous William Burken come strutting up to they door. These folks aint the fanciest, so they got but one worn-out stable for all of Burken's horses and one guest room for Burken and him wife. Haynes, Phil and Cal get pallets on the den floor and all the ojis got to stay outside.

George, Luther, Seth and the two menor watchmen, Nora, Taddy, Addis and Basil Lee cram into the stable. The watchmen sleep by the door, as if they on duty, not sleeping in a stable like a common menor.

They off at first light, but not fore they all getting a portion of grits, hoecakes and sausage. Addis giving Basil Lee her sausage and save her hoecakes for the trip that only get longer. Heaven open up and even Burken's curses warn't gon close it, so they stopping again. Not on account of the slave coaches leaking water, but cause Burken been stuck in mud all the way up to him coach wheels once. He warn't in no hurry to do it again. They find shelter with a Delaware family then a Pennsylvania one a day later, and another the next, quarters getting no better for the ojis. Then Taddy look out the window and say, --We here.

Addis look out too and caint believe what she seeing. Rows of tall brick houses, smashing together along stonecut roads, ladies out walking under parasols and fine dresses of all colors with lace trim, *ojis and no-colors, both!* each going they own way with nary a thought to the other, to Addis eye. Addis see oji men and no-color men laying brick for a new building cross the way and a line of wood stands with vendors selling fruits and vegetables and cloth. Addis feel like jumping. Something new happening to her and all round her. At last.

-17-
ADDIS

A few miles off from the city, the caravan head through an open pair of tall iron gates with sharp edges at the top. They travel down a gravel path of bending oak trees with fading leaves, telling all that winter is sure enough coming. With Basil Lee fast asleep on her lap, Taddy whisper to Addis. --Listen quick, now. We at the home of Missus Burken's niece, Sabine. She kind to menors, don't own none, though her husband richer than the Debil hisself. Get her to take a liking to you. If she ask for you, Burken gon give you up, cause he never refuse him favorite niece.

--*This* your plan?

--Miss Sabi not like the others. She help you, I swear it. Get her to ask you to stay. Trust in me, she say and Addis scoff and burdened with doom all over again.

The coach bounce to a halt and it wake up Basil Lee. --We here, mam?

Taddy pat him head. --Yes, baby, we here. You be on your best behavior for your mam. Not another word out of you bout your pap. You hear?

--Yessm.

Addis lead the way, stepping out of the carriage and seeing the grandest house she ever seen. A house in three parts, it look like. A big white stone square with two-story columns all round it in a half-moon shape and a balcony on top and two chimneys on the roof on top of that. The square got two big rectangles pushing out of it and all them got three floors of windows and a chimney on each side. It put the Great House to shame.

--Where are we? Addis ask her mam.

--This the house of Scott Hamilton and Miss Sabi, I tell you already.

The double doors of Hamilton House swing open and footmen and housemaids line up down the stairs to receive Burken and him clan. --Uncle William!

Addis hear a girl say it and she look up to see a young, pale thing in a blue dress with white lace trim, long strawset curls down her back, waving her arm wildly.

--Who that be?

Addis ask her mam in a whisper.

--That be the one. Sabine Duvernay.

--*Her?*

A well-groomed gentleman with oil-slick hair and a fine waistcoat and jacket come out the doors just then to greet Burken.

--Master President!

Scott Hamilton say and shake Burken's hand, looking the man square in the eye.

--*Uncle William*, please, Scott, Burken answer and grasp the young man's hand.

--Uncle William. You will have to keep reminding me until it sticks! I cannot imagine where my wife ran off to. We've been waiting for you.

--I heard her calling her uncle from the sky, Missus Burken say to Scott as he kiss her hand. --If the poor girl has not passed on to Heaven, I would say she's up on your balcony.

--My apologies for her display, Scott say.

--Do not worry, my boy. French women in general are a load to bear, not just Sabi. And I've known my share.

--Indeed, Missus Burken huff and Burken reach for her hand.

--But, as I assured you on your wedding day, they are well worth the effort.

The men laugh, nervous, til Sabine come running down to meet them.

--Ma tante! Sabine say and wrap her arms round Missus Burken. --We were expecting you days ago. Never mind. You are here now.

--Bonjour, ma petite. My only child.

Missus Burken hug Sabine back then reach for Sabine's hair.

--Where are your pins for this hair?

--Ack, Sabine say and brush her aunt's hands away.

--Please, come in, say Scott. --Henry, Scott say to a footman, --Bring Uncle William's things up to their room and bring his workers inside to their quarters.

--What's this, Scott? Missus Burken spit. --Your slaves sleep in your home?

--It's quite big enough, I assure you, Aunt, Scott say.

--And we do not own any slaves, Sabine say. --The state forbids it, as do I. We pay our workers quite handsomely, Aunt.

Taddy pinch her daughter and Addis scrunch her face up at this woman she coulda swore was but a girl up there on the balcony, with her hair all a loose.

--Good heavens! Sanctimony is ecstasy, indeed, Missus Burken say and peer down on her niece.

--You speak out of turn, Sabi, Burken say. --You will have to tame her tongue, young Master Hamilton.

Scott sigh and shake him head at him wife. --Yes...he start but never finish. --Tea, shall we?

--Excellent idea, Burken say. --But no need for your footmen. We will stay but a short while then head on to Morrison House.

--I am sure the workers are tired from the long journey, no? Sabine say, --I will let them rest in the East Wing while they await you. Go on, she shoo her aunt away.

--I'm afraid the fear of the peasants' revolt back home may be getting to her head, Missus Burken say. --Didn't we get her out France long before she was in any danger? She was living far from the others...

Missus Burken say as she and Burken and Scott disappear to the parlor with the housemaids close behind to bring round the tea.

--Henry, please show the men where they can rest. I'll take the women and this little lad, Sabine say, winking at Basil Lee. All a sudden, a gruff voice yell out from back at the coaches.

--Me and my worker men aint sleeping nowhere a menor sleep, Haynes say and gesture to Phil and Cal. Sabine look them over then say, --Well. It is good you are in the shade, then, no?

Haynes spit on the ground and she turn and lead the women and the boy to the East Wing. Addis fearing what hell Haynes gon bring to them on account of what Sabine figure be kindness.

On the way, Sabine ask them each they names and call herself *Duvernay*, not Hamilton. Taddy pinch her daughter again and Addis just shake her head, puzzling. When Nora shut off in the first free room, Sabi take Addis, Taddy and Basil Lee into the next and close the door. Then she turn and hug Taddy so.

--I was hoping he would bring you! She say just above a whisper.

--Good to see you, again, Miss Sabi.

--Bah, with Miss Sabi, I have told you. This is your daughter? Your Addis?

--Yes this her. The one I tell you bout last spring.

--She is beautiful. She looks so much like you.

Addis scrunch her face up again. She notice Sabine got violet eyes and recoil. A succubus, she certain of it. Nnene tell her all bout what evil the succubus do.

--Thinking bout last spring got me to membering what we talked bout. You still think you could take on another housemaid here? My Addis a natural cooker and cleaner. She sew a fine dress, too. And she been gardenworking all her life.

--Say no more, Taddy. I will talk to my uncle straight away.

--Oh, it'll be a hard sell, Miss Sabi. Your uncle taking a strong liking to my Addis.

--You leave it to me, Taddy. Leave it all to Sabine, she say and cup her hand on Addis cheek. Addis frown at the touch so Sabine drop her hands and smile and leave.

Some time later, Sabine return and rouse them from they sleep.

--It's all arranged! Addis will stay, at least until the State Dinner we are hosting next week for Uncle William and his associates. After that, well, we'll have to see after that.

--Thank you, Miss Sabi. I caint tell you what it means, Taddy say, clasping her hands together.

--I tried for the boy, too, Taddy, but Uncle William would not hear of it.

--Oh, Basil be just fine with me, Miss Sabi. Massa Burken wouldn't never hurt Basil, Taddy pat him head and say, --He the safest of all us.

--My uncle will not hurt Addis, either, I promise you. Any of you. I will do what I can.

--You done just enough with my Addis. I caint thank you enough.

--It is a small thing, Taddy. A very small thing.

Taddy kiss Addis forehead and hug her but Addis don't quite hug back. Basil Lee just stare at Addis and tuck hisself under him mam's armpit fore the two disappear out the doorway. Sabine close the door behind them and get back to Addis.

--You won't have any tasks to do, she say, --except perhaps for show at the State Dinner. Until then, we can just get to know each other. Be friends, she smile at Addis. Addis raise an eyebrow but stay silent.

--Well, I'll let you settle in for now. We all take supper at 5. The servants will feed you in the kitchen. Just take the stairs to the left straight down.

--If it be all the same, I'm awful tired. I'd rather sleep than eat a thing.

--Of course. I'll have Mary leave something out for you in the kitchen, in case you change your mind. Good night, she say and leave Addis to herself.

Addis walk a few paces to the end of the room and look out the window and see gardens. She almost can smell it from her high up room. In this bit of a cell, Addis have more space to herself than she ever have. She go and sit down on her bed, then lay back on it. Not a cot nor pallet of blankets nor a rickety bunk she having to share. Addis got a long wooden bed with a straw mattress and blankets to boot. Blankets on top of blankets. She wrap herself up tight in them and let herself smile a little.

-18-
ADDIS

Night soon come and fore she settle in, Addis hear a light knock on her door. She don't know nobody here and nobody knowing her. None but...

--Addis, please open the door, she hear Sabine whisper through the cracks. Addis get up and creak the door open slow.

--Yes, Miss Sabine? You needing something?

Sabine take her candle and put it in a glass cage fastened to the wall fore she come in, check behind her and close the door.

--How would you like to be free? Sabine grin and look to Addis like it be the best idea Sabine ever have. Addis let out a sigh and say,

--Miss Sabine, I were just bout to turn in for the evening.

--Nonsense, it's only eight o'clock. And please, do not call me Miss...

--There something I can do for you fore I head back on to rest?

Sabine look sunken in. --Please sit, Addis, Sabine say and sit on the foot of Addis bed. --I want us to know each other.

--All right. What you want with me? Why you helping my mam?

--I like your mam and I like you. And I want you to like me too.

--Why?

--Of course, you don't have to. But it would be nice...

--Who are you?

--I have told you. I am Sabine Duvernay...

--Where you from?

--I am from Paris, France, it is a world away...

--They got ojis in France too?

--Of course. I have never been to a place where there are not any coloreds.

--And ojis get treated real nice where you been?

--I have never been to a place where coloreds get treated

95

real nice, no.

 --And me nuther.

 --I want to change that, though. *Help* to change it, I am meaning to say.

 --And how you posed to do that?

 --Not alone, of course, no. There are many who help slaves get to freedom, all over Philadelphia and the North, all the way down to the South, really. I have money. I pay for doctored free papers and supplies and clothes and food and shelters. You ever know of my Uncle William's slave, Linus?

 --Yeah, a cook. Got away last year.

 --I fixed his papers. He was the first one I ever did help when I came to this country. That is what I do. That is who I am.

 --I seen you with them. Burken. Your aunt. Seem like you love them.

 --I do. They saved me from the war at home. My father was titled but penniless when he was killed and Uncle William made a fine match for me with Scott Hamilton. And Scott is good to me. Everyone tells me so. And he has more money than any king from Hamilton cotton fields in the Carolinas. But sullied money is still for spending.

 --So you stealing from them. Your family you love. Stealing people who your family say they got a right to.

 --Saying you got a right to people and having a right to people, these are not the same. I love my family. It does not mean I must live as they do. I love my soul too. More, even.

 --So I'm posed to trust you when your own family caint? Your husband know what you do?

 --My husband is of no consequence and neither is your trust. I need only your silence. Taddy assured me...

 --Taddy don't speak for me.

 --This is more than you.

 --Indeed, it be life and death. You risking all our lives just telling me what you already done. Why? Don't make a lick of sense, what you saying.

 --My Uncle adores me, this I know. He saved my life, he made a fine match for me, but he sold me, too. He sold me to Scott

Hamilton and gained an unspeakable amount of money and new political allies all over the North for his trouble. I did not even know he had the right. His arms reach across oceans...If he can sell you and he can sell me, then he can sell anybody. Even my daughters, if I ever am so cursed to bear them. I cannot live in that world. I cannot live in that world.

--Your chains aint mine.

--No! I am not meaning to say they are the same. My English, you know, is not always so good. I am meaning to say something else. That chains of gold or silver instead of iron just mean you have more room to help. We all must help. We must all get free.

--So you gon save us all?

--Not hardly so! I just happen to have much money and I can spend it how I please.

--And you please to spend it freeing ojis.

--I do.

--On account of your soul.

--I do.

Addis sigh heavy and shake her head.

--It just don't sit right.

--But, why?

--Never met a no-color woman with a soul, is all.

Sabine gasp then cough then blush and there be silence. She choke back a chuckle, but then just let it go. When she start to laugh, she caint stop. She fall back on the bed and hold her gut while her chest heave up and down. Addis look up at Sabine laughing and caint know what be so terrible funny.

Sabine sit up when she finish and breathe out like she aint done in years. She right herself, straighten out her dress and reach her hand out for Addis. Addis lift her on her feets.

--Come with me. I have something to show you, Sabine say.

Sabine grab a candle off the wall and put her fingers to her lips when Addis creak a floor board. They tiptoe in silence through the long corridor, down the servants' stairway into the kitchen. Sabine look round fore she push on a corner wall and it open like a door to a wooden stair.

--Careful, she say quiet, pointing down. She hike her dress in one hand and balance the candle on the other. A cold sweat drip down Addis spine but she follow anyway.

The light from Sabine's candle trace bags of corn meal and sacks of taters and wood barrels lined up against the wall.

--Hold this, Sabine say and hand the candle to Addis as she slide two barrels away from the wall. Sabine knock soft three times then push in on the bricks and the wall under the stair open slow. She motion to Addis to follow. Addis step inside as Sabine use her candle to light three more and Addis see a whole big space underneath them stairs. And people. She see womens and chiles, huddled deep in a corner behind three men.

--It's all right, Sabine say. --It's only me and our new friend Addis. The men step aside and a woman who look bout Addis mam's age stand up.

--Addis, this is Rit Greene, the leader of this operation.

--Operation?

Addis caint make heads nor tails of what Sabine saying.

--State your business down here, a gruff man in loose cotton say to Addis when he step in front of Rit.

--She's a friend, Lew, Sabine smile at the man. --She is in need of help like you. We can trust her, isn't that right, Addis.

--I aint got no business down here, Addis say. --I were brought down here. I don't know none of you. I don't know nothing bout none of this.

Sabine sigh. --That is just why I brought you here, Addis. So you can know.

--It's all right, Lew. She's just a girl, Rit say and step forward to talk to Addis. Lew and the others settle back into talking among theyselves or sleeping, back to what they was doing fore Sabine come knocking.

--Bịa ebe a, Rit say and sit down at a table in the middle of the room. Addis move quick to join her, Sabine following behind.

--It's a thing called The Tunnel, Rit say, with a voice smooth as cream, like a daughter of Ala, Addis thinking.

--What that be?

--The Tunnel lead from Florida straight on up to Canada.

Stations, stops, safe houses slaves can go to on the journey to free.
--Rit is on her 14th trip! Sabine say, --She's led nearly 300 so far, herself!

--Never lost one, Rit say.

--How you do that?

--Cause everybody do they part and I make sure none turn back, Rit say and open up the pack slung on her shoulder for Addis to see the pistol inside it. Addis try to hide her shock.

--What you need Lew for if you got that? Addis asking.

--Saves bullets.

Addis smirking and loving Rit right away. She want to know everything bout this woman.

--Aint you fraid?

--More fraid for those I leave behind. I pick up people plantation to plantation, state to state, wind up with bout twinny, twinny-five or so, therebout, but some plantation got twinny-five people to a acre. Three hunned people a lot of people. And three hunned people aint nothing at all.

--You do what you can, Rit. You most of all, Sabine saying.

--And now, you got one more with Addis.

Rit look Addis deep in her eyes and when she seem satisfied, Rit smile and ask Addis,

--I dị njikere ịla ụlọ?

--When do we leave? Addis answer, all a sudden light and full and hoping.

-19-
ADDIS

Addis spend her days at Hamilton House following behind the housemaids, mostly for Scott Hamilton's sake. Sabine make such a fuss bout keeping Addis round to ready the house for the first State Dinner, so Addis put on the show. But at night, Addis tiptoeing down the hall, creep down the stairs to the kitchen and creak open the secret wall to the cellar. She knocking three times fore she opening the door to the hideout, then she sit at Rit's feets and hear all her stories.

--I marry a free man in Maryland, thinking he gon buy me free, too, Rit tell her. --Then when he don't, I thinking at least he make me free by proxy. But don't none of those things come to be. My husband telling me to forget bout freedom, but I never forgetting it.

--When a man in town tell me where I can run to, I listen. The man send a message off in Eboe to a hideout some miles away to tell em that Rit Greene coming. When I get there, a ole free couple hide me and give me food and clean clothes and tell me a new place I can hide in a few days. They send off another note in Eboe to the next spot and when a few nights come, I run all night, making no stops, hiding in the shadow of the trees til I reach the shed the couple tell me bout. Two free mens owning the shed and they do the same as the couple: clothe me, feed me, clean me up and send a note in Eboe to the next peoples.

Addis stare at Rit, eyes wideing with every detail of this wonder woman's life.

--Everybody knowing Eboe, Rit? Addis asking.

--Phrases, at least, Rit say. --Everybody helping on The Tunnel at least knowing how to warn of danger or say who coming and when. Since they be so many Eboes down them parts, Virginy, Maryland, Carolinas and such, that just be the language folk decide on, I reckon, in case of trouble. Even a learned no-color man caint make heads nor tails of the Eboe script, lest somebody teached it to him.

So Rit telling Addis how she, a Guinea, along with the Angolans, the Yoruba, the First Peoples whose nation were stolen from them and even the no-color Quakers learning bits of Eboe to stay safe. She telling Addis how in Afrika, they all they own people, with they own land and they own tongue and they own wants. But here, in Amerika, they all got to be one fist.

--It aint the way it posed to be. All Afrikans ought to have they own place in the world. But this world mush us all up together.

Rit tell Addis bout how long and cold it were, them nights she spend running alone, nothing but the North Star to guide her. How even when she make it to the next safe house, she wake-up in sweats, the sound of dogs nipping at her heels in her head.

--What be the worst part when you out there? Addis asking.

--The loneliness, Rit say, no question, and Addis nodding.

--I don't know what be worse: living alone or dying alone.

Rit tell her how she think of her husband in the night when she surrounded by slave catchers. How she long for him to show up for her, stand up for her, fight them off and win, like he promise her he would. She confess he never really promise her that. Never did nothing, never said nothing to make her think he would be for her what she dream he would be.

She confess she make it all up in her head that the paper she sign with a X on her wedding day meant something like safe, like warm and free. She never knowing much bout what love be, but she always imagine that be how it ought to be like. But it never were for her. And all them times she were surrounded, nearly caught, nearly kilt on the way, her husband never come for her. He never heal her heart nor bind up her wounds. He leave her to fend for herself, and you know what?

She tell Addis, --*I did it.* I did.

Rit surviving by the grace of God and that be all, she tell Addis. For all the help she get from strangers, too many times with dogs on her trail, yet she escape, she believe with no doubt, God hear. God know. Chúkwú were the only one with her through all things. Chúkwú give her the North Star to follow, to wish on, to hope for.

And that star leading her all the way to New York. There, The Tunnel folk help her get a flat and a job as a seamstress and she work and live and breathe free for six months. Then she wake up one night all a sudden with a heaviness in her chest that won't let her rest and she just know, she caint stay there no more. She just caint stay there. She got to go back and get more folk. Her brothers and they wives, her babygirl, even her man. She caint be the only one what get free.

--So, I go back, Rit saying. --I go straight home, same way I come. But this time, I find in my home a woman my husband done laid up with. He saying he move on, he don't want to move up North so I can stay free, that I done abandon him so he got him a new woman. All the nights I long for that sorry sucker, waiting for him, praying for him come welling up in my soul and I like to break him in two. I knock over the whole kitchen table and the few chairs tween us. Then, I pull out my pistol to whip him or kill him, one.

Rit set her pistol on the table tween her and Addis and Addis eyes near out her head waiting to hear what come of that fool fool man.

--I never gon know which I were gon do to him, Rit say, --Cause just then my babygirl wake up from sleeping and come to me. She crying, out, *Mam*! So happy to see me again. So, I put my pistol away quick to have both hands free to wrap round my chile. Sara Elizabeth her name. I pick up Sara Elizabeth and kiss her and walk right out that house with nary a look back, and haven't since.

Addis lean back on her hands, taking in all the magic she sure live inside Rit Greene. She long for but a drop of it.

Rit say she take her brothers, they wives, her mam, her babygirl and ten others with her that trip. She stay in New York a few more months and just keep going back and back.

--But why weren't it enough?
Addis asking.
--Whatchu mean?
--*Freedom*. Once you get your family free and you starting over, why weren't it enough? Why you keep coming back?
--For my babygirl. She caint live free in no world that aint free. You think it gon last? A few hundred get free, few thousand

even, but the whole world aint free? It be a lie and the Debil tole it.

Addis see Rit mean it but Addis don't agree. She thinking she sleep just fine when she get herself free. If she get Nnene and Ekwueme free, she thinking, it gon be plenty enough for her. But she like Rit too much to show all herself, so she just say,

--Lew your man now, huh?

Addis smirk, bold. Rit cut her eyes at Addis at first then she laugh deep from her belly.

--Chile, go on, she say and Addis laugh too.

--That be real nice, Addis say, glad. Rit look off to Lew and her face turn serious.

--Lew'll die for me, you know. He prove it more times than I got fingers to count. He see me. He know I worth something and he treat me like he know it. I been in danger since the day I were born, near seen the face of God when I brought my babygirl into this world. I been pushed down, beaten, walked over and forgotten. Clean erased. But I'm here. I been through the worst of it with nobody but God and I knowing now aint nothing I caint survive. But Lew? In this world, I tell you. Lord knows in this world you just need a little something every now and then. Just something so you know God hear you when you say you tired. You just dog tired. You right, chile. That be real nice.

Addis seeing then what everybody tell her. That she always been protected. She always got someone to fight for her and she shaming for not ever seeing it. She look back to Rit and see lostness in Rit eyes.

--Still aint enough, huh?

Addis ask and Rit shrug and the corners of her mouth turn down.

--Still the loneliness. It don't go away all the time. When you been through something caint nobody touch, even if they love you, even if they want to, they's always gon be the loneliness.

And Addis know. For all Ekwueme do to show he love her, that he don't hold nothing against her, she knowing he don't understand her. And Nnene fight tooth and nail for her, but they nothing alike outside the loneliness. That be the one table Rit and Addis and Nnene and even her mam can sit at together in silence. It pierce the space between them and knit them closer than blood ever could.

--Can you ever fix it?

Addis begging and Rit sigh.

--You wanna fix it, you wanna be fixt and you wanna crack it open and spread it round, share it so it won't be so heavy sitting in you. But it just be yours and you just got to sit with it always.

Addis sigh too now.

--Unless you run, Addis say.

--Unless you run, Rit answer. --Stay moving, stay fighting and the loneliness caint catch you. You got to outrun it.

Addis breathe deep and smile. She ready to run.

In the early morning hours, just fore the sun come up, Addis close the wall back up and sneak up the cellar stairs. She try to slip up to her room through the kitchen, but fore she make it to the stairs, she hearing loud whispers from down the hall. She tiptoe through darkness and get closer to it.

--I don't know what else I can do for you. How can I prove to you that I love you?

--You do not have to love me, Scott. I know what our marriage is for. What it's done for you. For my uncle. For me. I am grateful to you.

--Well show it!

He yell then get soft. --I am patient with you. I give you everything.

--Scott...

--I give you *everything*. I am good to you. Am I not good to you?

--What else can I say to you I have not already said? Yes! You are good to me. Too good, perhaps. What can I do about it?

--You can love me.

--Scott, please...

--No, you run amok all over town, you go off God knows where. You embarrass me in front of your uncle and I allow it! You have secrets from me, I know you have secrets from me and I just want to know them. I want you to know me. I know it will take time. But I had hoped by now...

--Please just give me more time.

Addis hear footsteps in the study then Scott say, --I will give you more time. For us. After this State Dinner, after your uncle gets settled in and I have assured his allies are in place, I am going to take you away from here.

--Away?

--Yes, Sabi. Look. This map holds the key to our happiness. It leads to an island I purchased for you. For us.

--Scott, I cannot...

--It is in the Caribbean. We will spend the winter there. Maybe come back with a baby to make us a real family.

--Scott, please...

--Gentlemen say their women go mad from the heat down there, but you will not, I am sure of it. You will like it there, with sun on your face. You are too pale and excitable. The beach will calm you. We will be happy there.

--Scott, I do not want to go anywhere. I like it here. My family is here...

--I am your husband, Sabine! I am your family now.

--Let us get some sleep, all right? It is nearly morning. It will all be better in the morning, you will see, my darling.

--We will discuss it again after the party.

--Yes, Scott, as you like. After the party.

The cabinet door slide open then close behind Scott and Sabine as they head to they chambers. Addis hide in her corner while Scott lead the way with a candle in one hand and Sabine's hand in the other. When Addis don't hear them no more, she head straight for that cabinet.

The moon shining through the windows give her just enough light to see it on him desk. The map, Sabine's island X'd and circled. Addis never felt a stronger urge to move in all her life. She near possessed when she grab the weights off the map and roll it up tight in her hands. She slip back out that room, too fraid to check and see if anybody see her, if anybody hear. She run and run til she get to her room, shut the door and turn the lock on it. She fold the map up small as she can, near tearing it, she work so fast. She shove the map in her sack then throw it under her bed and sit on the floor, staring at the door, waiting for her breath to come back.

-20-
BILLY LEE

Night fall on Wellesbury Plantation and Billy Lee sneak away from the blacksmith quarters, up round to the loft above the Great House kitchen where he used to live with him mam and him brother. He climb up the ladder and feel through the darkness for the bed he used to sleep in, whenever him pap didn't come claim it for hisself.

Billy Lee crawl over the bed and find the oil lamp and strike the flint against it to make the room a little less cold, little less lonely. He stare deep into the flame and find him own eyes staring back in the glass. He see hisself and never feel more alone.

--Everybody leave you, Billy Lee say to hisself.

--They think you out your mind so they leave you here. Nobody want you. Nobody love you, he say, him voice rising and rising. Staring at the fire start to hurt him eyes but he don't stop cause it take him mind off the hurt in him chest.

--You aint out your mind, tho, Billy Lee. You aint nothing, he say. --Nothing but alone.

-21-
ADDIS

When morning flood the room, Addis wake up on the floor, still leaning against her bedframe. Fore she do anything else, she check under the bed for her sack and pull out the map. She unfold it, unroll it and put it up above her head and read it. Philadelphia. Florida. Atlantic Ocean. Caribbean. Sabine's Island. She roll it back up, fold it as small as she can, drop it in the sack and stuff it back under her bed.

Addis hearing all manner of commotion in the house and get up to look out her window. She see countless carriages and servants carrying in all kind of sacks of meats and vegetables to be cooking. Other servants carrying buckets of white flowers. And still others out working the yard, trimming the bushes and pruning the last flowers before fall come. The week be over and the night of the State Dinner come. Addis been so in tune to Rit and her world, she plain forget bout her own. This week were all Sabi promise her, all she say she can do for Addis. Now Addis knowing tonight she gon have to go home with Burken and she loathing the light of this day.

She grip the windowsill and feel her body start to burn up. She get dizzy and hold fast to the sill so not to fall. She try to right herself but she fall to her knees when her head get to pounding sharp, then the bright flash come. She closing her eyes and holding on but when she open them, she see her brother Basil Lee laying on the ground outside her window in the night with him face twisted up with the look of knowing on it, him very last look fore him very last breath.

Then, she see the youngest, Billy Lee, in the pit of Hell, fire round him on every side, and he just sitting there, still and smiling. She watching her mam standing over them weeping and Addis hear herself weeping too. She see her mam turn and face the barrel of a gun then Addis hear it boom. Addis scream and scream til she hear knocking at her door and someone yelling her name.

Addis shake her head and the world come back. Out the

window she see it be daylight again, servants rushing round the yard, same as before. She look down at her hands and see them bloody and scratched, the work of her own nails. Addis drop to the floor with her head in her hands and rock and cry. She aint never seen what yet to come, only omens or memberings of what been come. Could it be, her mam dead and brothers too? It fill her chest with rocks and she weighted to the ground. Then she finally membering someone be knocking.

Addis get up quick and straighten her shift out and look round to make sure the map aint poking out nowhere fore she unlock the door and Sabine come barging in and close it behind her.

--What in God's name? Are you all right Addis? Why were you screaming?

Sabine grab Addis bleeding hands in her own. --What happened here?

--Nothing, Addis say quick. --Just a spider is all. I were trying to kill a spider.

Sabine squeeze Addis hands in her hands and laugh.

--Is that all? It is good the house is already awake or you surely would have done the job.

She walk to the bed and pull Addis down with her. --Sit. I have the most wonderful news.

But Addis caint concentrate on what Sabine saying. Her neck still hot from the vision, her head still dizzy. She shake her head and her sight and mind get a little clearer.

--Are you sure you are all right? Sabine asking.

--I'm fine. You say you got news? Is it bout my mam and brother?

Sabine grin so wide Addis think her mouth gon leap off her face.

--It is happening tonight.

--The dinner? Yes, I see...

--No, Addis. The escape!

Addis eyes get wide and Sabine continue.

--The trunks of new clothes I ordered came just this morning as the flowers and bakers arrived. The paperman came soon after with news for me that he has got all the documents in order. He is going to come by tonight with a wagon with room for all of you. You will dress in the fine clothes and ride in the wagon with your free papers all the way to New York City.

--But the dinner? How we gon...

--It is perfect, don't you see? You will all sneak out while the guests drink the night away. You will slip out into the night and go as far North as you can safely go. You will rest in a safe house when you can go no farther and you could be free by morning!

Addis let them words wash over her. Free by morning. Free by morning. Free by morning. She thinking when she get free how her headaches gon be gone. She close her eyes and smile. She open them when Sabi hug her and for once, she hug Sabi back. Sabi hold Addis at arms' length and Addis get a look at the strange woman with the violet eyes.

She look at Sabi and hear Nnene whisper in her ear, *It take all kinds to make a world.*

After while, Addis head down to the kitchen and join the many housemaids who must been called specially for this dinner tonight, cause Addis never seeing none of these women the whole week she been at Hamilton House. One housemaid look to be in charge cause she barking orders at everybody, including Addis, telling at least ten where to fetch they own bucket of water and rags so each can start mopping a spot on the grand ballroom floor til it shine.

Next, she wiping down walls in the dining room and dusting off windowsills, until she hear Sabi say,

--There you are, Addis.

Sabine take hold of Addis elbow and whisper to her.

--These workers are well-paid, Addis. You need not be here.

--Wouldn't mind being well-paid for my labor, for once, Addis say.

--I promise you will leave here with a month's pay, as well as rations. Plenty to start your new life! Try to rest now. The dress you will wear out of here tonight is in the closet. Your uniform for tonight is on your bed and underneath the bed is a sack with more things for tonight. Don't forget it.

Addis near choke when Sabine say she been under the bed. Sabine find the map, Addis sure of it. What she gon think? What she gon do, Addis wonder. Will Sabi call the whole thing off? Addis aint even got not use for a Caribbean island, she thinking. What she steal it for anyhow?

--I'll see you tonight, Sabi smile then disappear into the kitchen and Addis walk up to her room with her gut all knotted up.

In the afternoon, Addis peak outside her window and see the service carriages clear out to make room for Burken and him guests. Addis change quick into the black cotton dress the housemaids wearing. She pull on her booties and a bonnet then she get to the closet to see what Sabine bring her to change into.

She open it and see a satin dress, a queen-color blue one, and she gasp when she touch it. Addis seen Missus Burken having dresses like this but never touch any for herself. It make her feel warm. Like somebody seeing her like she wish she could be. Addis run her fingers along the fur-lined black cape what go with it. She close her eyes and swear she smelling salt and hearing ocean waves. It scare her eyes open.

She close the door and sit down on the bed then she membering the map. When she get the gumption, she lift up the covers and see the sack Sabine stuff under the bed. A white cotton nightgown with heavy silver buttons, a white bonnet, a petticoat. An apple. Nuts. Some bread, cheese. Addis wrap everything back up into the sack fore she reach further under the bed to see her own sack. She open it slow and breathe out when she see the map still there. What in the world she can do with a map, she thinking, cursing her own self for what she might bring on herself for stealing it.

Then she knowing she never had no use for it cept to keep Sabine from leaving. She shake her head at her own self. Like that be the only map Scott Hamilton having. Like one map gon stop him from taking Sabine away from her work on The Tunnel, if he want to. Maybe the island be what gon save her life, Addis thinking. Aint no telling what gon happen to Sabine if she get caught. Maybe they aint stringing up the president's niece, but maybe they sending her back home to her own war in Paris, where she caint do no more harm.

Addis hear horses outside the window and know folks beginning to arrive. She look out and see so many carriages and coaches crowding in. Then she see coming down the gravel drive that white carriage, the two white horses with footman Seth at the whip. Maybe her mam and brother be close behind. She have to know, so Addis running down the stairs to the kitchen, but run straight into the head housemaid.

--There you are, girl. Take this into the parlor.

Addis take the tray of tea and biscuits and try to member where the parlor be or which one of the many rooms she meant to find. She wander round the halls seeing room after room painted in glory, each a different color, dripping with chandeliers, trimmed in gold, but she aint knowing if any or all be the parlor. She lose track of the minutes she spend wandering, tea getting cold and useless. She stay in the shadows of all the fine people gathered in the great hall, some by her own doing, but most cause no-color folk been trained to unsee her if she aint of no use at the moment.

She strain her neck looking for her mam and brother on the skirts of the party, but through the crowd she only seeing Burken. He in him finest wear, him dark blue military jacket and shining gold buttons, gold tassels hanging from him shoulders. Addis crouch behind the tea pot and watch him smiling and shaking hands with all sort of folk, women in chiffon gowns and men in long jackets with feets to them. She watch Burken grab the arm of a tall, sturdy man in military dress, him coffee color hair slick back and tied. Burken walk arm and arm with this man away from the crowd, farther down the grand hall til they disappear into a room. Addis look all round her and see nobody watching her, so she follow them, thinking maybe she gon find out something bout where her mam be. She follow the sound of they whispers bouncing off the walls.

--Mr. President, I am gravely concerned.

--My dear Richard. Is the party so much of a failure?

--Sir, I have heard troubling whispers of revolt. A slave uprising coming soon.

--That is troubling. Where have you heard such whispers?

--My networks tell me menors are organizing as far south as Florida and as far north as New York.

--Menors organizing in every state? Preposterous. Where are they getting their numbers? Are they armed? This kind of revolt,

111

should it exist, surely has been organized by learned men. Surely no menor or group of menors could be behind this. Any word on where they would get such vast funding?

--Quakers, I would imagine, Mr. President. Abolitionists are growing in numbers in every state. And what's more, you know we lost upwards of 30,000 slaves who escaped North during the War, not to mention the menors who were already free.

--Indeed.

--I have the state militia on alert, in case of attacks in Virginia, but other states need to be on guard. I fear there is great wealth behind this treacherousness. Those who are against you are loudly so and call *themselves* patriots. An article was published in the *Massachusetts Gazette* just prior to my departure for Philadelphia. It's written by a Virginia lawyer, Jamison Harriet.

--Yes, I know his family. Good man.

--Allow me to read it to you?

--Of course, of course.

--It reads, *President Burken wielded the sword in defense of Amerikan liberty, yet at the same time was, and is to this day, living upon the labours of several hundreds of miserable Africans. Ages to come will read with Astonishment that the man who was foremost to wrench the rights of Amerika from the tyrannical grasp of Britain was among the last to relinquish his own oppressive hold of poor unoffending coloreds. In the name of justice what can induce you thus to tarnish your own well earned celebrity and to impair the fair features of Amerikan liberty with so foul and indelible a blot?*

--Well! A spirited opinion, to be sure.

--Mr. President, he is not alone. Several articles like this have been published in newspapers up and down the coast. I do not share this with you lightly or to upset you. I wish only for you to know your enemies and, greater than this, that there are hundreds of thousands of men who would sooner lay down their lives than to see your life or your vision for this country sacrificed to rebels. I have called my troops to me from Virginia and they should be arriving to help me protect you any day now. Rest assured, Mr. President, your allies outweigh your foes. The steadfastness of your character is unquestionable. Your legacy as the father of this nation is unshakeable.

--You are a true friend, my dear Richard. A true friend. I do not believe it necessary to bring the Virginia army here over a few whispers.

--Mr. President, I urge you, until such time as my troops arrive: secure yourself and your family with guards.

--Richard...

--Mr. President, I insist. We must control these rebels before we get too comfortable.

--Richard, I thank you for your loyalty and your concern, but your whispers and an article in the *Gazette*...

--Several articles, sir.

--...are not enough proof of a credible threat. Troubling, it is, most assuredly, but if the freedom of speech is taken away, then dumb and silent we may be led, like sheep to the slaughter. Bring these concerns before my cabinet tomorrow morning and we will see how we can stomp out any rebel rumblings before they manifest. We will guard against the impostures of pretended patriotism.

--I serve at your pleasure, Mr. President.

Addis hear them shifting inside the room and she turn quick to leave. She do her best not to sprint, to keep the tray balanced, to breathe normal, but she fail.

--Addis.

Burken voice stern when he call to her and she stop dead. She turn round slow, tray in hand.

--Evening, Massa Burken, she manage but don't move. Burken and the Adjutant General catch up to her.

--I'll leave you, Mr. President, Richard say, and Addis watch him walk on by, reentering the crowd in the grand hall down the way, never looking back.

Burken nod at Richard then circle Addis. --Hamilton House suits you, he say. --You look almost like a lady.

She nod but her voice stuck. He stop in front of her and lift her chin with him hand.

--Are you happy here with my niece?

He ask and she find her voice right away. --Yes, so happy. Misuss Sabine a wonderful misuss, she say and Burken nod.

--Sabine is the light of him life. The only daughter I will ever

113

know. What could I refuse Sabine? Nothing. Nothing.

--Even so, he say, --Sabine is too young to understand the ways of the world. A man's world. I rather hoped Hamilton would teach her, but to no avail. She is far too spirited, he say. --The war in her homeland has her all riled up.

Addis holding her breath, just waiting for him to find a new plaything.

--You understand, though, don't you, Addis? The way of the world. The God-given order.

Burken breathe hot on her face and she get cold all a sudden. She crane her neck to look him in the eye, what Nnene tell her never, never to do.

She bite her teeth together and lower her head slow, to keep from screaming. She firm when she shake her head no.

Burken straighten up him back at the sight of it. He clench him fists at him sides and Addis bite the inside of her lips to punish her own self. She don't dare ask herself why it aint enough for Burken to own her but he got to taunt her with it too. Nobody ever think to ask that question. So she chewing a hole in her lip and hating how she caint just be right but that folks got to hear her be right. She got to be loud and right. Strong and right til everybody agree. Nnene, Ekwueme, her mam, she thinking, like they fights be anywhere near what she facing with Burken. But these be equal things in a chile's mind so she sink her teeth through her lip for never think through the consequences fore she say or do anything. She dig her nails into her palms. Got to be right, she thinking. Dead and right, just like her pap.

--You have lived an unbothered life in the garden, Burken finally say. --Your eyes have not seen enough of the whippings that take place in the fields. Daily, they happen, Addis, I assure you. Your ears have not heard enough of the cracking whip on a fleshy back.

Burken take two fingers and stick them up her nose to lift her head up to meet him in the eyes. --Those wide nostrils you possess have not smelt enough blood as it streams down, like copper and dirt wafting in the air, like money poorly spent. Choices poorly rendered. You have not yet been filled with regret, Addis, but tonight, tonight you will know regret. And shame. And finally, your place.

Burken snatch him fingers from her nose and wipe them on her dress. He brush past her and Addis let her whole body shake. The teapot get to chattering on her tray and she disappear into the closest room and leave the whole tray on the floor. She lean against the wall to catch her breath. She got to get back to the cellar, got to leave with Rit or it be all for her, sure enough.

When she no longer see even a shadow of Burken down the hall, she walk brisk toward the kitchen. As she pass the great hall, she see her brother Basil Lee playing the fiddle while folks dance and clap. She see her mam cross the way, against the wall, looking on, full of love at her son as he play. Both alive and smiling. It were just a waking dream, then, she thinking and sighing. She want to run to her mam, but then she membering Rit and the others. What if they go without her? What if she left here with Burken? So Addis don't wait, don't stop. She head straight back to the kitchen. Housemaids and butlers bustle round her and nobody notice her but one footman. Tall and brawny with wrinkled brows. She watch him eye her as she slip up the stairway to her room. Addis run through her bedroom door and lock it behind her, case that footman come after her.

A few minutes pass and she hearing nothing in the hall so she go to the closet and pull out the dress and cape and ball them up in a fury. She reach under the bed and grab Sabine's getaway sack and stuff the dress in it. Then she reach for her own sack with the map in it and stuff Sabine's sack in her own. It look bulky. Too heavy to run with if they need to run. She decide, if she must, she gon leave it behind.

But not yet. She sit on the bed and wait and wait what seem like an hour. She come to and the room be pitch black. The sun done set. She thinking the dinner must be starting by now. Housemaids and footmen must be lined up round the table in the dining room. She have the kitchen to herself now, for sure. She get the courage to throw the sack on her shoulder and peek outside.

Darkness all down the hall and that be just how Addis like it. She creep, mindful not to creak a board in the floor as she go down, down the stairs, into the kitchen. She got one shot for the cellar door and she take it, stopping for nothing, not even to look behind her. She close the cellar door and fly down the stairs, sack bouncing against her side as she go. She set the sack down and move the barrels in front of the secret door. She knock three times and enter, dragging the sack behind her.

--Addis!

Sabine say it then lower herself to a hush.

--I have been looking all around for you. Get changed, hurry. I've had the kitchen cleared out, but we don't have much time. The coach is waiting.

Addis rush to put on the petticoat and the dress and the cape in a corner, careful not to tear the tender buttons. One of Rit's girls help her fasten it up and put on her bonnet as folks start to gather they packs and hats and cloaks. Sabine give them all they free passes with they names on it. And then, the twenty of them, they ready as they ever gon be.

Sabine run to Rit and throw her arms round Rit's neck.

--One of these days, Rit Greene! One of these days you will take me with you. When I have done all I can and have no more to give, you will take me with you. Please. Promise me.

--I promise you, Sabi. When you done all you can, when you got no more left to give, I take you with me. Rit Greene aint got nothing but her word and you know it be good as gold.

Sabine laugh and say, --Don't I know it.

She kiss Rit's cheek and back away from her, wiping her eyes. It get everything to stirring inside of Addis. Addis thinking bout her mam. Hadn't Taddy suffer all she can? And Basil Lee. Addis don't know her brother much at all, but the way he growing, learning what separate him skin from hers, learning to be content separate from her, she won't never know him. Him soul won't never be safe. The stirring turn to welling in her and she full up til she caint stand still no longer.

--Wait! Addis say, --I caint leave here without my mam.

--We do not have papers for your mam, Addis, Sabine say.

--She right upstairs, my brother too, and they gon die if I leave them here. I caint leave without them. I caint!

--Think, Addis! Look how you are dressed. You cannot go

back up there unless you are getting on that coach!

But Addis grabbing all her stuff and heading for the cave door.

--Addis, wait, Sabine say, but she too late. Addis mind made up and she open that door to fetch Taddy and Basil Lee. But something stop her cold. Addis hear Sabine come up behind her but Addis aint step but a foot outside the cave beneath them stairs. She see him standing right there in her face.

-22-
ADDIS

There in the cellar, Scott Hamilton standing, eyes darting from Addis to him wife and back to Addis. The burly brown footman there too, the one who seen Addis run to the kitchen while ago, and Addis knowing he the one caught them. Scott Hamilton peer past both women and see inside the cave.

--What are you doing? Scott say slow and stunned. --Just what do you think you are doing?

Sabine step in front of Addis and the cave and go to Scott. She lay her hands flat on both him shoulders. She try to reason with him but he don't hear her. He don't see her. He looking past her into the cave. He digging in him pocket before he wrench hisself away from Sabine and pull out gold coins and give them to the footman.

--Reuel, take this girl to the president's abode at Morrison House, without delay. Wait there and see that she is in their custody before you return. Say nothing to anyone but that we are through with her, do you understand?

Reuel nod and Addis don't try to fight this heft of a man who grab her by the arm that be holding her sack. All her fight be in her lip. It always were and she cursing it this very moment.

Sabine try again to grab at Scott, to reason with him but he throw her hands off him.

--You do not speak! You do not move!
Scott wave him finger at Sabine, gritting him teeth so hard him cheeks red. Him finger become a fist and he slam it down on him own thigh. Sabine scream and jump a little.

--You vile woman. You treasonous, vile woman! After all I have done for you. After *everything* I have done for you!

--I am sorry, Scott, please!

--Get out of the way, he say fore he push her aside and she fall to the ground. Addis look down at her with fear but caint help her cause Reuel got her good by the arms and he dragging her up the stairs. She too breathless for even her lip to be of use and she make not a fuss at all.

Reuel drag Addis out through the kitchen door and over to the stables. She see a caravan and coachmen sitting atop they horses looking at her, nervous, and it sting all over her body. She only steps away from freedom. Warn't nobody getting away this night. She fearing for Rit, for Sabine. All those chiles. All the men and women of the Tunnel.

Reuel press her up against a stable door with one arm and grab a rope with him other. He lift her sack back up on her shoulder then tie her hands tight together. So tight she caint near feel them. She whimper a little and it be the only sound she got the strength to make all night. Reuel don't say nothing, he just leave her to grab a saddle and when he turn him back, she take off running.

She think to try the caravan but change her mind quick and head off the other way. She try not to look back, not to make a sound, but her sack falling off her shoulder, scraping the grass, though it caint go nowhere with her hands tied up. She just keep running straight.

Addis look down and her feets aint on the ground no more. Reuel dead silent when he lift her up and throw her over him shoulder and head back to the stable. She look all round, but don't nobody pay them no mind. She see the coachmen for the caravan get down from they horses and stand in a circle, talking amongst themselves, looking ready to break out, empty handed. She want to beg them to wait, to help her, to take her with them, but she caint let another life be on her head. So she stay silent as Reuel tie her to hisself, put a satin blue saddle with gold tassles on him horse, and ride on through the night to Morrison House.

Warn't but a few miles til they on the other side of town, where street lamps lit all over, the gravel give way to cobblestone and the houses smush into each other in rows. They keep riding til they get to a wooded gravel way that lead up to a gate.

Reuel rear him horse back and it kick the gate open and they keep riding down the drive. A half-mile or so down, they come upon Morrison House. Reuel ride round back and Addis eyes wideing when she see the no-color watchmen, Phil and Cal, coming towards them, still in Filadelfia, all this time later. Addis get to fearing Haynes still round there too. She looking round as much as she can, tied up to Reuel, but don't spot hair nor tail of Haynes, but that don't mean nothing at all and she know it.

--State your business, menor, Phil say, pointing him rifle at Reuel so he stop him horse.

--I am from the house of Master Scott Hamilton and Mistress Sabine. My horse bears the blue and gold Hamilton family crest to assure you of these truths. I am returning Master President's property to him, as his niece is through with her.

--Whoo! Fancy-talking menor, we got here, Cal!

--I see him, Cal say and spit.

Reuel untie hisself from Addis and jump down off him horse. He lift her down slow off the blue satin saddle with the gold lettering and tassles hanging down, and she wonder if that be all Hamilton giving him, a satin saddle, to turn in Rit and all them with her. If he think this saddle were gon keep him colored self safe in a no-color world, shame on him, she thinking.

Reuel bend down to her ear as he untie her and say real quiet, --I thought you were stealing. Scott Hamilton is a good man and I saw you sneaking about and I am sorry for the trouble I have caused you. I could see no way around it.

Addis look him stern in him face and say nothing but Reuel just shaking him head. He untie her wrists and Addis still aint got feeling in them. He lift her sack back up on her shoulder.

--What you got her all tied up for, anyhow, fancy menor?

--It was a long ride, sirs, and I did not want to be responsible for losing the property of Master President. I was instructed to ensure she was in the custody of Master Burken before I left and I have done so with you gentleman.

Phil and Cal nudge each other and scoff and spit. Reuel bid them good night and take one last short look at Addis before he ride off and leave her to them.

--Well, now. We got ourselves a fancy menorwench, to boot!

Phil push her cape off one shoulder and grab at her satin glory until her shoulder peek through the seams. Cal circle round

120

her, smelling her, and she just whimper and shake her head, shake all over and say, --Please!

Phil grab again at her dress and her shoulder come all the way through where he rip off the fabric and Phil and Cal laugh and laugh. They stopping when they hear hooves on the gravel. Burken coming home.

--Get in the kitchen, Cal say and spit promises that they be back for her later.

Addis watch them walk toward the carriages, fore she go round the back to a door. She walk inside and see a candle on a table and a hearth not far off. She reckon this be the kitchen, so she hang up her sack and cape on hooks by the door. She still shaking when she take the candle off the table and light up the hearth with it and stare into the fire. She lose herself staring into it. She bite her teeth together to stop from crying cause she known it all along anyhow. Aint no sense in crying. Ala always come to tell her in her dreams that Addis gon drown. The visions tell her she aint never gon fly. Fool fool to hope it. How dare she hope it?

She push all thoughts of Rit far from her. What gon happen to Sabine on account of her? Addis don't want to think bout it. Death a hungry dog what follow behind her and him jaws snatch up anybody she lead him to. Cept Ekwueme, of course. Ekwueme the only one she ever get to save when she push him away from her. But he warn't gon save her back, not this time.

The door creak open and her mam walk in slow and close it behind herself. Addis try to speak, try to cry but nothing come out so she just run to her mam. She wrap her arms round her mam and lay her head on her mam shoulder. She confess everything, how Sabi play a part in the Tunnel, how Rit hiding more than a dozen folks with her, how Scott Hamilton find out because Addis let Reuel spy her acting strange and how aint no telling what become of them all, now that Scott Hamilton know.

--Shhh, baby, Taddy say and unfasten the trail of buttons down Addis back. She slip Addis out the gown and ask if she got a dressing gown for bed. Addis go to the sack she hang on the wall and pull out the high-collar white cotton shift with the silver buttons at the neck Sabine giving her. Taddy help her slip it on then Taddy go sit in a chair by the hearth.

Addis follow and sit down on the floor in front of her mam. She cry and cry in her mam's lap thinking she done it now, and warn't gon be no time til Hamilton come marching up the walk accusing her of conspiring with runaways. She gon swing for sure, she thinking. Won't be no reprieve for Addis, not after this. And all a sudden, she want nothing more than to live.

-23-

ADDIS

In the drafty, stone kitchen of Morrison House, Addis sit at Taddy's feets, and lean deep into the corner Taddy's knees making. She rest her cheek on Taddy's thigh. Addis stare into the hearth, empty, and watch what's left of the fire lick the wood, fighting its way back to life, as Taddy start braiding Addis' thick curls. Addis nose fill with the sweet liquid Taddy perfuming her hair with. Rose oil. And Addis find comfort in it. She feel her mam tugging gentle at her hair and then parting it in a sort of zigzag down to the base of Addis head. Taddy start to braid tight one half of Addis hair, forehead to nape.

Addis get lost in the old familiar feel of Taddy's fingers massaging her scalp. It been so long since Taddy been any sort of mam to her. She warn't but five years old the last time her mam braided her hair or spoke comfort to her. Not even as her pap lay cold with a smoking hole from Haynes' gun through him belly did Addis member Taddy holding her this close. Instead, Taddy call Nnene to the hut while Addis just sit in the corner shaking, not speaking.

When Nnene try to wash out the bloodstain in the floor, Addis start screaming. --Make her stop, Nnene! Make her stop! Taddy say, and Nnene come sit in the corner with her and draw Addis into her lap, holding a bloody hand over Addis mouth and saying it gon be all right. Taddy move her things into the loft above the Great House kitchen that day, Nnene move her things to the hut with Addis, and Nnene the only mam she ever know since.

Addis trying not to member this, fighting against the dull aching she feel for the chile in her, left with no pap and no mam. She don't want to think on it now cause now her mam here and protecting her, speaking comfort to her and braiding her hair. This mam try to save her. It warn't her mam fault it didn't work, it were her own. Taddy love her, she sure of it. She rest her head in her mam's lap again as Taddy braid. She don't even try to stop the tears now. Taddy keep braiding, just tight enough for it to last awhile, but not so tight it hurt.

After while Taddy say in Eboe,

--You know, I was still a child when my first di nwēnu had me? This was the first Burken, Ambrose, of course. Though what the first one didn't take from me, the second surely has finished off, now. I couldn't have been more than twelve, though it is sure hard to say. The years just sort of melted together after that, just a long stream and nobody can find where it starts or ends.

Addis get a little peace hearing her mam speaking Eboe. She aint hearing it from Taddy in so long. Not like this. Not since Taddy used to teach her and her pap small words at the same time. She like hearing it. It mean to Addis that her mam don't really want this life. Her mam member they true home, though neither aint never been.

Taddy finish one braid and twist together the end of it with her finger. It curl up at her touch and Addis watch it fall below her chest. She feel Taddy cup Addis chin and forehead gentlelike in her hands and guide them over to rest on Taddy's other thigh. Taddy hum a melody and Addis know it right off; It be her pap's song. He sang it when it were time for bed. Taddy humming and dipping her fingers in the rose oil again and tightly braiding the other great bunch of Addis' cotton curls.

Addis thinking of her pap strong now and it making Addis to membering the blast that come from the barrel of Haynes' gun. She membering that hiss sound her pap make as the air leaving him body, the last sound he ever make. Addis membering and she try stuffing down the angry again. She spitting out the venom creeping in, uninvited. She think on other things, and ask her mam where her brother gone to. --Off to sleep in the quarters out back, Taddy answer and keep humming. Then, Taddy say,

--We are the president's slaves, and there's some to-do in that. We get nicer things, folks say. What Haynes did to Chinü, that will never happen again. Burken has promised it, and he has too much to lose now, if word got out that is how he treats slaves.

Addis shift in her seat a little at the words, *how he treat slaves*. Like there be a good way! She thinking. And what she care bout what

Burken got to lose? And aint no man losing nothing much but gold over the killing of a oji woman. She start to feeling uneasy again bout her mam.

--Did you know I got to go all the way to Paris, where Miss Sabi is from? That is a whole other world I got to see with Burken when I was your age. It was beautiful. Ojis were free over there. Probably the closest I will ever get to Eboeland.

Taddy dipping her hand back into the oil, sprinkling the hair again as she braiding. Addis feel a rising in her throat. She ask,

--Ńné, why are you telling me this?

But Taddy keep talking.

--It isn't freedom, to be sure, but sometimes you even get rose oil gifts and fine shoes the Missus is through with, like this gown you got here from Miss Sabine. But still, a slave is a slave, Addis. You must know that. You must learn that.

Addis weeping now as Taddy weaving the last strands of hair into the braid, twisting the end to match the curl of the other.

--Ńné, what do you prepare me for? A homegoing?

Addis bear her nails down into the palms of her balled-up fists. She feel Taddy's arm round her neck, slow and loving, pulling Addis back to the comfort of her lap. Addis don't resist. She let her mam stoke her hair and she sit there, suspended, as her mam talk to her.

--With your pap, though, there were whole moments when I didn't feel any burden at all. I never felt more precious than when he looked at me. That boy back at Wellesbury. That Ekwueme. He looks at you like that. I watch you sometimes, and I see him with you. Bernard comes flooding back to me.

Addis feel Taddy's bony fingers dabbing rose oil on her neck and shoulders. But the thought of Ekwueme seeing Burken lying on top of her make Addis lurch up on her knees, away from her mam's touch, spirit and throat on fire. Fool fool to trust her mam, she knew it all along.

--Does it please you? To perfume the dead body of your daughter? That is what you are doing! You brought death upon my father, and now me!

Addis turn to accuse her mam but Taddy look away into the

fire and any love Addis have left for her go into the fire too. This woman in front of Addis be a soulless pot, she thinking. Taddy finally speak but don't move her eyes from that hearth.

--You know, I blamed my own ńné, too, for the longest time for what she did. Your Gran Gran Dido. She was foolish. Killing a no-color man. Taking everybody with her. Leaving me here. My father, too, left me here. Your father, too, left me here. *My* pain, *my* burden was too much for him to witness. He could not love me enough to stay.

Addis seething at this. That this woman think her pap ought to wait round to see Burken take Taddy from him. And now Burken coming for Addis and this woman dare accuse her pap for not living long enough to see?

--Love, Addis. Love will stay. It survives with you and lets you have your burdens. Love doesn't leave because your pain is too heavy.

--Enough!

--Don't think me wrong, Addis. Your father stayed alive for me and you as long as he could bear. You are too much like him, and I fear for you...and I am proud of you, all at once.

Addis get a chill hearing this and start fearing this aint the last time Addis gon have this talk. Addis might could do this dance with her own daughter one day...maybe even a daughter of Burken's. The man sure aint got no kinda shame, she thinking. Addis stay still and quiet, perched up like a cat. She turn away from her mam again til she figure what to feel.

--Why did you come back from Paris, if all the ojis were free? Why not stay there and save us all this misery?

--I have never met ojis like the ones they got over there. Free. Educated. That is where I learned to read and write. But I came back because of something my ńné told me when I was young, before she died. It stuck with me always. She said I had to do something great. That the earth angel Ala would help me. So I came back with Burken to do it.

Addis see this moment in her head, time and again, her Gran Gran Dido, young and beautiful and alive, holding chile Taddy, telling Taddy bout Ala and the great thing Taddy gon do.

--Did you do it, Addis ask, --what Ala said?

Taddy smile wide and answer quick.

--Yes. I know now. The only great thing I have ever done, the only great thing I will ever do...is you, Addis.

Addis turn away from her mam. Before she can respond, Haynes breaking in through the kitchen back door. Even from across the room, they smelling the stink of moonshine oozing from him scarred up skin, him gristled blonde beard still wet from careless guzzling. Addis see a tiny no-color servant, not too much older than her, peering out from behind Haynes, eyes wide and fearing.

--Do I hear you talking menor gibberish in here!

He slurring, pointing an angry finger at Taddy.

She answer quick, skillful,

--Nawsir, Massa Haynes! She say. We warn't talking no menor gibbritch here, nawsir! We talking just like reglar menors sir. I's just braidin lil Addis hair like Massa wanted, then I sending her right up to him! He ask me for her, special, at dinner tonight.

Haynes don't move no closer to Addis but him glassy eyes do, piercing right through her gown. Addis lowering her eyes so not to meet him thirsting gaze. All Addis fears come to light at the sight of him still here in this place. He should have returned to Wellesbury by now, she thinking, but still he linger.

She membering the icy feel of him eyes on her, and that even the muscles pulsing in him neck seeming to hate her and desire her all at once. At least if he here, he aint nowhere near Ekwueme and he can escape, she thinking, then she choke on the thought of Ekwueme. She decide this be the very last time she thinking of him.

--You best hurry up and get that gal up to him, Haynes say.

--Don't make me come back for her.

--Yessir, she be up directly!

Haynes look to be satisfied, so he dragging the quiet girl by the arm cross the kitchen and up the stairs to him bedroom Burken giving him, far down the hall from Missus Burken, but an in-house room, for once, all the same.

When Haynes were done stomping him boots up the stairs and down the hall, Taddy get up from her chair, and kneel down in front of Addis. She grabbing her daughter's hands in her own and trying to look her in the eye, but Addis too buried in her own shame and doom. Taddy holding her daughter's face, raising Addis chin.

--I held him off as long as I could. Years I have held him off, tried to keep you away. I failed, but I am not leaving you. I choose to stay with you and you can choose too. This is your lot to carry, and you just pray Chúkwú help you bear it.

Addis go numb as Taddy rise up off of the floor and pull Addis up with her and guide Addis onto the chair. Taddy stand behind the chair now and tuck the ends of each braid up into itself. She dab her daughter's neck with rose oil once more.

Addis say, --I could leave here, you know. I could go find the safe house Rit was heading to. Be free.

But Taddy keep talking like Addis never say a word.

--Lock up your mind, in a place where he cannot get to you. Do not think of Ekwueme. Do not think of yourself. Think nothing. Feel nothing. Be nothing. Just for a while. It will not last too long, if you don't count the seconds.

Taddy reach for a bonnet lying on the table next to the hearth and fasten it neatly over Addis' braids, ruffled up just like the collar of her gown.

--There, Taddy say. --Choose life, my omaricha. My precious girl.

Taddy kiss the bonnet and Addis turn to stone. She think to tell Taddy she warn't gon stay after all, that Taddy were gon die just like Addis seen in her vision this morning. But something inside her know it be too cruel and probably not even true. Instead, she crane her neck up to her mam but look through her. --I choose a better life than this.

Taddy look to be helpless but like there aint no more fight in her today, so she break the Eboe.

--That life aint mine to give you. Now get on up to Burken fore he send Haynes down here to fetch you. Make a right off the stairs, first room on the left. Careful you don't go too far. Missus Burken laid up one of them places.

Addis rise from the chair without another word. Taddy call out to her, --I am staying, Addis. I will be right here when you get back, she say, and Addis don't feel no way bout it at all.

When Addis reach the top of the staircase, she grab a candle from the hall dresser to light her way. She quiet her footsteps and refuse to breathe when she reaching Haynes door, as to not alert him to her presence. Through the door, she hear him grunting and the tiny girl whimpering. She drown this out with the sound of her heartbeat thumping. Think nothing, she tell herself as she get to the door she know Burken lurking behind.

She look down the hall and see the other room her mam say Misuss Burken sleeping in and Addis get to thinking. Does she lay awake waiting to hear? Does she lay there and listen? Will Burken return to Missus when he is through? Addis wonder, as if any of it matter. The collar of her nightgown start to choke her. Shut down your mind, shut down your mind, shut down your mind, she say to herself. A homegoing song from Wellesbury get to playing in her head:

> *Going back to Eboeland,*
> *Gotta get back to me Eboeland*
> *Jesus be a-waiting for me*
> *Keep your head up to the sky now chile,*
> *Don't miss Em when They passing by*
> *To take us back to Eboeland with Them!*

Addis swallow empty and she open the door without knocking.

-24-
TADDY

B ack in the kitchen, Taddy wrestling with her hands inside her apron, unable to think of anything other than Burken's hands on her baby. Taddy slink into the chair, too tired to feel anymore, and she listen to the heavy, booted footsteps of her daughter climbing the stairs.

How could I do it? How could I do it? She thinking.

Hadn't she done her duty with Burken? Hadn't she borne him two boys? Hadn't she laid down more than a dozen years for him without a fuss and he couldn't even spare her baby? It was too much.

--I done everything to keep him off her. Kept her far from me so long she grow to hate me for it! And for what? He still takes her from me.

This warn't the plan. Taddy feel the fool for thinking there were anything decent in this man who kiss her hair when he lay on top of her and coo at her when she weeping quiet. No, not this man. This the same man who take up with her after him own pap did. The same man who put a hole through her Bernard and through her whole family.

--Father my chiles then try to father more chiles with my chile, this SAME MAN!

Her blood racing through her til she caint stay seated no more. She pacing round the room so quiet, but her blood burning up everything on the inside. She deciding.

--Addis. She my great thing I done. She what my ńné told me I gon do. I was her great thing she done and she warn't afraid to die for me! She warn't afraid! I done staying. I don't choose this life! Took my Bernard. Took my Addis. I aint afraid!

She digging in the cupboard quiet as can be, but her insides be screaming.

-25-

ADDIS

William Henry Burken smiling like a spoilt child when he see Addis walk in. She look to him and see a emptiness behind him eyes. Addis wonder how long that emptiness been there. Since her Gran Gran Dido kill him pap? Since him mam forbid the taste of oji women from him tongue? She been trained to see him pain. He been trained to be blind to hers. Caint you see me? She want to ask him but for once, her words stuck deep down, so she decide her whole self might as well follow.

He unbuttoning him own nightshirt and looking to Addis, but Addis aint there no more. Though she placing the candle in a holder on the dresser and walking toward the bed when he motion for her, she be far away in another time. He bring her down on the bed, gentlelike. She don't even bother to remove her shoes. He lay her there and kiss her neck, clawing at the high collar of her night gown.

But she back at Wellesbury on Three Farm, preparing Chima for her mam's homegoing, painting uli on Chima's arms and hands and face to give her beauty and strength. She painting circles collapsing in on theyself to show that the spirit live on and never end. She painting the shining moon cause Chima yet got life in her body. She painting the sun cause the sun know her children and she gon protect her kind. Addis thinking how her and the other women painting up Chima and singing, jumbling up the homeland with Heaven.

> There be peace chile in Eboeland,
> Gotta get back to me Eboeland
> Jesus there be waiting for me.
> You aint ne're felt the peace They bring,
> Don't miss Em chile the King of Kings
> They take us back to Eboeland with Em!

Burken ripping at her collar too fast and the beautiful

buttons tearing from the cloth. The silver buttons dropping heavy on the floor, jumping and rolling. *Clang! Clang!* It snap Addis back from Wellesbury to the room where the pap of her brothers laying on top of her, groping her, still grabbing at her neck. She caint breathe.

She saying, --No, but he don't hear her. Louder, she saying, --No! And again, --No! and she pushing her balled fists into him chest, finding her strength and her voice again.

He growling at her, him hands clasping her wrists down to the bed.

--Now, girl, this here is the one time you don't have to do anything at all but just stay quiet. You be sweet to your Master and I'll be sweet to you. Didn't your mam tell you? Just stay quiet.

She turn her head to avoid the spittle, the stink of Burken's breath hot on her face. He calmer now, nestling him bristled face on her cheek, getting him lips right close to her ear.

She wrench her head as far away as she can, still pinned to the bed by his knees and his fists round her wrists. --NO! She scream and her knees shoot up into him chest, and he grunt, winded. He release one of her wrists and swat her face like he would a bothersome fly interrupting a meal. He pin her down again.

He release one hand to grab at the hem of her gown, lifting it up. Her freed hand claw him face and he howl in surprise. With the full force of him hand, he slam into her face again. She feel her cheek welting but don't have time to cry cause now he wrapping him hands round her neck and pushing her legs apart with him knees. With her hands and feets free, she groping the bed for any kind of help.

She losing consciousness and hope til she feel her right foot knocking up against something hard and hot and she know she touching the bedwarmer. She twisting with all her might to get to it, grabbing desperate for the handle. He oblige her by taking him hands from her neck, grabbing her shoulders and throwing her in the direction she squirming in.

--You just be still now, like I told you, he say, scratching him whiskers against her lips. --You be very still now. Be good to your Master, he say.

He grab at her neck again with one hand and free hisself from him trousers with the other, lifting hisself off her just long enough for Addis to grip her hand firm on the bedwarmer handle.

She taking the last of her strength and she swinging the bedwarmer out from under the cover, over and up at him face. She missing him the first time. She hitting him when she swing back again. Back and forth she swinging and she not even feeling the embers that falling loose on her from the pan, burning into her own chest. She swinging until she hearing the loudest crack she ever hearing. And then a stunted groan.

Like a egg she drop when she were careless with the chickens, Burken's skull caving in with a slow ooze at the forehead. He slumping over on him side, him legs still entangled with hers. A slow breath slip out of him mouth. Him eyes wide with surprise and still fixing on her, but they dead man's eyes.

That horrible face, that crater in him head. She don't want to be seeing it but her eyes fill up with it. She wanting to move but she caint. Him eyes stairing deep into her and burn theyself in her memberings. She caint get up, caint scream, caint even look away til the bedwarmer slip from her hand and clamor to the floor. She gasp, then know she got to move. She kick him legs off her and back out of the bed, to the floor on her hands, away from him crumple up body. Addis knowing now she as good as dead and aint nothing left to do but run.

She springing out of the room and down the hall in darkness, trying to stay quiet. She seeing the shadows of the candles at the end of the hall on the dresser. They signaling to her that the staircase be near, and then the kitchen, and then the door. She fearing all the time, but the candles mean it be almost over. That give wings to her still-booted feets. She nearly to the staircase when Haynes come bounding out him room, half-dressed, messy and stinking. He scoop her up like she nothing, her feets still kicking like they never left the floor. He round the corner with her wriggling to get free.

--You think you can get away with me in the house? Ignorant menorwench!

He snarling at her. He taunting at her.

He slamming her body against the hall dresser by her shoulders, and the jolt snuff out the candles. He tightening him grip and there is total darkness now.

--Don't you know I'm always watching? He grabbing her by the neck with one hand and reach down in him boot with the other and fetch him hunting knife from its sheath. With him hand so tight wound round her throat, she caint even let out a sob, so she waiting out death in near silence.

--You think you something special with that pretty face. You think your own master caint have his way with you when he want to. Saying no to him. I heard you! What if I cut out those eyes? Always tryna work your menor wenchcraft on me with them.

Addis trying to squirm but he on her so firm it aint no use.

--Too long Will tell me I caint touch you. Not anymore! I got to teach you. I am the overseer, aint I? You aint nothing special round here.

She caint see him, but she feel the spray of spit land just below her left eye and she cry out in disgust. But he gripping her neck so tight she caint struggle when she feel the cold blade of him knife slow slash her. He cutting deep in her face from the right side of her forehead, over her eyebrow and clean down to her left jawbone. She gargling out in agony, gasping for air and clawing at the hand round her neck.

Blood spilling out hot from the gash in her face, into her eyes and mouth. She near choking on it. She sputtering to breathe and kick but she caint get no air.

--You're gonna spend the rest of your life a ugly dog nobody wants, he whisper close to her ear. --How's that feel? He laughing.

Her feets rest on nothing but the dresser behind her. She seeing a light surrounding Haynes, an unholy halo, but she refusing to accept this end. She find one more strength in her, kick out her foot and land it square on him privates. He let out a grumble and him knees buckle. Then Addis hearing a loud clang and a groan as Haynes dropping both the knife and him hold on her neck. He slumping over on the floor, moaning, and Addis fall with him, coughing and gasping, finally breathing deep.

She look up to see Taddy with a great skillet pan in one hand

and a candle in the other, standing over Haynes. When Haynes groan, Taddy blow out the candle, drop it, grab Addis arm with her free hand and drag her up to her feets then down the stairs to the kitchen.

Taddy yelling out in Eboe now, cause she know they both done for anyhow. --Fool of a girl! You've brought death on us all!

When Taddy reach the kitchen, she grabbing bits of bread, meat, and cheese and throwing them into Addis sack on the wall. But Addis caint move and she still standing on the stair. She stop breathing when she hear the sound come from Missus Burken own mouth. It be the sound of total loss, a despair only the deepest part of the soul can know. Addis recognize it cause she cry out just like it when her pap were run through. Now she know Burken really be dead and she aint dream none of it. She know Missus Burken just found him oozing head and beady eyes.

All of Morrison House seem to be waking up now. Boots coming from all directions. But Addis stopped on the stairs and aint moving. Taddy slapping Addis bloodied face and pulling Addis by the arm the rest of the way down the stairs. Taddy shoving the sack into Addis hands and dragging her to the door.

--Go from here! Find the safe house, like you said!

Taddy opening the door wide and she hearing boots descending the stairs behind her. Taddy grabbing Addis fur cape off the door hook and looking out both ways fore she tossing Addis and the cape out onto cold ground. She yelling,

--Go as North as you can and never come back! The day you stop running will be the day you die!

Taddy slam the door shut, and Addis knowing she warn't never gon see her mam again.

A single blast from the barrel of a gun and a gurgling shriek finally snap Addis to her feets. She grabbing her sack and cape and she making for the woods with no thought of even breathing. She only yards away, but she don't even hear the dogs set loose behind her. The onliest sounds still ringing in her ears be the blast, that shriek. She know Taddy be dead, Ekwueme be so far away, and she all alone in this world.

END OF PART TWO

PART THREE

E TIE DIKE N'ALA, A NU UZU

KNOCK A VALIANT MAN TO THE GROUND AND

THE OUTCRY WILL BE TREMENDOUS

-26-
ADDIS

Addis running blind in the dark woods out back of Morrison House. She scrape against a thick sharp branch and she gag on a cry when her leg wet up with blood and stick to her dress. Then she hear them. The dogs barking mad and Haynes growling, --This way!

She looking back and seeing lanterns not too far behind. She looking forward and seeing nothing but dark, she looking up and see salvation in the thick rooted trees all round her. She tear off her cape as she running, rubbing her bleeding leg with it quick and throwing it to the side of her, hoping she trick the beasts. Then she run out every breath and hope she got in her fore she scamper up a tree just as the dogs descending on the cape. They barking and biting at it like mad, sniffing and scratching up the tree the cape laying in front of, not so far away from the one Addis peering down at them from. She cloaked only in darkness and what leaves the season leaving behind.

--Over here! Boy, get here with that lamp!

Addis see her brother running fast to get to Haynes. He don't see the stump right in front of him and him foot catch it and he cry out as he falling and the lamp come crashing down, snuffing out what little light he have.

Haynes out of him skin. He grab him musket and point it at Basil Lee chest. --Stupid menor dog! What you go and do that for? You in on this too? Huh?

--Nawsir! Basil Lee screeching, backing away on him hands. Addis caint see much of Basil face from her tree but she hearing and fearing too, for herself and her brother. She see the no-color watchmen, Phil and Cal catch up, then the blacksmiths George and Luther and the two menor watchmen follow. Haynes cocked and ready.

Phil say, --Haynes, what you doing now? The boy aint mean no harm dropping that lamp. He just a boy, now, Haynes, come on.

--You stay out of this, Phil, Haynes say. --For all we know, all the menors in on it.

Haynes point him gun at George and Luther then back at Basil Lee. Then Haynes slam the gun butt into the ground and cry out like a slaughtered hog. --They killed him! They killed him!

Basil Lee get to whimpering now but it just make Haynes fix him gun back on the boy, coming ever closer to him. --Greatest man ever lived! Felled by a menorwhore. Greatest man ever lived...

Haynes wipe him brow on him shoulder but don't take eye nor gun off Basil Lee.

--The girl what killed him, Massa Haynes, George say. --And she getting away.

--She aint going nowhere, Haynes spit. He take one finger and point upward. --She's up there in them trees. Aint that right, wench!

He scream and the dogs stop they barking. Him voice echo up to her and she never been more quiet in her life. --We'll get her, he say. --Though it'll be mighty hard now that the boy here done snuffed out the light, he say, shoving him gun barrel into Basil Lee chest.

--Massa Haynes, we just use this light me and George got here, Luther say, holding up him own lantern. --Plenty sticks out here, we just make us a torch with the oil that spilt out the lamp is all.

Luther get to picking up sticks and Haynes put him gun down at him side. --Suppose you're right, then, Luther. Best we stop wasting time, say, Cal?

--Right, boss, Cal manage.

--He was my best friend, is all.

--We'll get her, Massa Haynes, George say. --We'll get her.

Haynes nod and pick him gun back up, cock it and blow what left of the lantern away.

Basil Lee scream out when fire erupt round him where the oil spilt. He try to jump up but Haynes take him gun butt and crack Basil Lee skull with it and kick the screaming boy into the fire.

Addis dig her nails into the bark of the tree and press her bleeding face against its branches but she don't look away from her brother, though she caint scream like her heart want.

The dogs barking again and run away from the fire and the two menor watchmen run right after the dogs, fearing for they lives. Luther and George scrambling to get to Basil Lee out the fire and roll him round on the ground to put the fire out, but the boy be limp.

Haynes grab a thick branch and stick it in the fire til the end of it light up strong. He wave it in the air and look up, shouting,

--You see what you make me do? Haynes moving slow through the trees with him torch waving in one hand, gun in the other. If only it was spring, Addis thinking. The leaves in all they fullness would sure bend they ear to her and give her shelter in darkness. But it aint spring and it warn't gon be long now fore he spot her. Fore he finish up what he done to her face, and her mam and her brother.

--I'm gonna take everything from you! I swear on your life, I will stay alive until I see your body cut up and burnt! Do you hear me? Do you hear me!

Addis look once more at Basil Lee lying so still in George's arms now, Luther bending over them. Her brothers was posed to be the safest ones. Addis ask her mam to die for her and her mam done it cause she know at least her boys be safe. Burken blood were a guarantee, if childhood warn't. But who gon honor it in Billy Lee now? Missus Burken? Addis knowing her littlest brother gon be dead on sight back at Wellesbury. Just like she dream it. Swallowed up in the middle of Hell.

She think of her own pap too, all of them blown away by the barrel of Haynes' gun. What she got left he can take? What she got left? She look down at her hands and though she caint see them, she feel them pulsing and bleeding. Then her nose fill with the smell of burning flesh and wood and smoke. She look down to earth and see fire at the base of her tree.

--I'm gonna smoke you out, dog!

Addis look round and every tree round her on fire and it rising fast, like there aint been rain round them woods in weeks. She start to feel heat on her feets and tears gather at the corners of her eyes. She think of her mam, her pap, her brother. Who else gon die for her? She nestle into her tree branch, hold it tighter and decide to end it herself.

When death come on, the world get awful still. Things still don't make no kind of sense, but when death come, sense don't matter none at all. Addis sitting there in the hot stillness and release every bit of wonder and all hope of this world. She got no more questions for it. The world been watching her burn all her life anyhow. Seem right to her that's the way it see her die.

Addis right eye all but swole shut with blood so she close them both and everything get quiet. She don't hear Haynes yelling, the watchmen retreating from the fire or the crackling wood beneath her. She hold fast to the tree and in the silence she hear it: the ocean rising up behind her.

--The water brought you. The water will take you home!

Addis hear the deep, hollow whisper of Eboe plain as day, if she don't hear nothing else. The wind carry them words direct to her ear. The mighty wave come to take her away from here, like her dream tell her, she thinking, and she ready for it.

Addis look behind her but see nothing but burning trees. Then she look down and see her skirt on fire and scream. Addis burn her hands beating the fire out and scream again when a gunshot boom and knock out the branch just below her. She hold her skirt in one hand and leap for life to the tree behind her. Another blast keep her hopping tree to tree, her sack banging against her backside with every jump. The ocean getting louder and she chase it, feverish, fire and bullets following from below, and she just keep jumping to the next tree.

Haynes shoot out a branch from underneath her and she scream and fall. Addis hold on to a branch and swing a moment and see Haynes beneath her reloading him musket. She pull herself up and get her footing and start again, jumping to the next tree. She hear Haynes firing behind her but she don't stop til she reach the edge of the woods. She almost slip off her branch when she see in the moonlight there aint no ocean at all below her, only cliff and rock and a running stream a steep way down.

She look back and see Haynes drop him empty musket and begin to climb her tree. --The water gon take me home, she say, but in case it don't, she rather the rocks take her than Haynes ever lay him hands on her again. She close her eyes and jump.

When Addis hit that water, it feel like whips lashing her whole self at once, out for blood. It cut so deep she forget the pain that run cross her face as she sinking to the deep and sweeping away with the river. Her mind caint think of nothing but the hurt her body in, no room even to wish for death. She want to cry out but when she open her mouth it fill with water and it shock her back to life. She try to swim up but don't know the way; below her and above her looking both the same.

Then she start to wonder if she should even try to leave the cloak of this dark shadow; Haynes caint find her now if she just stay put, let this water wash it all away. She start to numb to the pain and let the river push her farther and farther still from the fear of straddling two worlds: flesh and spirit. She know that be the only part to be fearing anyhow, cause she felt it when she dream of her Gran Gran Dido on the execution block. Addis membering that the musket digging deep in Dido's neck were the worst of it, cause after that blast, Dido feel like whatever coming be leaps beyond what here in this world. Addis thinking on this as the water get up into her nose and burn all down her insides. After the blackness of the stream, even if what coming be only more blackness still, what a joy and what a rest she got coming.

She think of the black after and it warm her. She feel her wounds healing as the water keep its swirl all round her. In the darkness, her eyes too heavy to open, she see her pap's face, chestnut and chiseled, smiling down at her, arms open. It make her smile too to see him looking so happy and whole. She reach for him too and kick her feets to get closer, but the river thick and she slow. He open him mouth and speak Eboe to her.

--The water will bring you back to me!

He tell her this and she swim harder, faster to him. But the more she reach for him the farther away he go, smiling and drifting away. Addis want to beg him don't leave her, not again, but her tongue heavy and her mouth won't open. She swim and reach and swim but the moment she break the river surface her pap disappear. She cough up water and suck in air as fast as her body allow and she fight to stay above the river current.

In the moonlight, she see a strong branch swing low in the

distance and she swim with the current to get to it. When she reach it, she grab it with all the power she got left and pull herself up, half out the water, and with every move she closer to the river bank. She crawl and claw toward the base of the tree once she hit land and collapse on the roots, into a feverish, dreamless sleep.

Addis wake on top of tree roots, sweating and shivering in the sun. She go to open her eyes but her right one swollen over worse than before. She squint with the other to take in the morning, but even that be a strain on her throbbing face, so she rest her eye again. She want to move up off the thick roots what making ridges up and down her back but she caint move. Her head feel full of water. Her throat be hot and dry but her whole body be a freezing damp mix of sweat and the river. For the first time, her body feel like her insides been feeling all her life, forever at death's door.

The sun beat down on Addis and she open her eye again. She know she far too out in the open for a oji girl, let alone one who done what she done. She prop herself up on her elbows and pull herself back, over the roots and stagger away from the bank, deeper into the woods. She wore out in no time and just rest herself against another tree, praying her head at least gon stop its pounding so she can think what to do next. The river sound almost like a distant lullaby in her ears but she knowing it be deceiving. What new evil this river gon carry her way?

Addis stop and think she might be the evil. In the whole of her life she never thinking she might could kill a man, but she done it now. Burken warn't even half as bad as other massas she hear of nearby Wellesbury. Ole man Bush been known to burn him name into the flesh of him slaves and cut off toes of the ones what try running away. Warn't nothing to hear bout Bruce Herbert letting him wife line up all the womenslaves he done laid with and beat them for entrancing him with they obeah magic. Herbert hisself kill the boy the missus find him with, but that little less known, cept round House Farm at Wellesbury.

And Burken aint never done what him own mam done, spiking Dido and thems heads and such. But Sheriff Turner do it. Just up the way from Wellesbury, Sheriff Turner known to do all manner of evil to him slaves he find up North where they free and bring them down to Virginia to work him fields. Bout 15 of him slaves try fighting back a few years back, what with them not being born slaves and all, and Sheriff Turner have them all butchered and hung out to dry. Addis aint hearing nothing more bout slaves fighting back since then, though Burken did cut short the times they all could gather after working days was done. Addis aint mind that none cause warn't none but Ekwueme and Nnene she want to pass time with anyhow. Warn't no one else she could pass time with, what with her pap dead and mam snatched and Gran Gran Dido spiked.

Addis get to thinking, aint it enough? Aint it enough Burken take her pap from her and then her mam? Aint it enough he lurk round her and get her to fearing the day he gon come for her like he done her mam? Aint it enough he take her life away, even if he never snatch her from a different world hisself? Never mind he were gon take her body from her too. Never mind what he letting him wife do, what he letting Haynes and him watchmen do. Aint the world she born into, the world *he* ruling, aint that enough to kill him over?

All them thoughts make her keel over and vomit in her hands, on the side of her dress. She cough it all out of her then stop dead when she hear rustling in the grass. She look straight ahead and see worn boots and tattered knickers. She look up a little and see some no-color hands coming straight for her. She scream, then pass clean out.

-27-

ADDIS

Addis come back to herself slow when she smell burning eucalyptus in the air. Her face feel tight and hot, burning like she aint never felt. She open her eyes and the white lights she been seeing dim a bit so she can see clear again. She feel soft cushions beneath her but itchiness all on her skin. A high wood ceiling rest above her head with bales of straw sitting in the rafters. She see cinnamon color brick walls in front of her, a iron stove in a far corner and a heavy door with a thick wooden latch cross it.

Wouldn't take much to throw it open and run, she thinking. She don't stop to think where she might run to, she just sit right up. But Addis head bring her unthinkable pain at that sudden motion and she fall right back down on the bed. She go to cry out in agony but something restricting her mouth.

The muzzle! She thinking as she try and fail again to move her jaw. But when Addis lift her hands up above her, she see they all cleaned up and bandaged. She bring them down to her face and feel cotton rags, not a muzzle, tied up all round her head, leaving only holes to see and breathe.

--She's awake!

A gruff, tan no-color man with hay color hair and a short beard come running into her view and she close her eyes and shiver thinking bout what this man done to her while she sleep and what he gon do next.

--Thom Terry, you scaring her! Back up, now.

That second voice, though stern and loud, to Addis, run smooth as tree sap out a maple. She feel her body start to relax and her heart slow to normal.

--You all right, Addis. You safe here.

The tall man with the voice come into her view and sit on a stool next to the bed and the first thing she see is him hair. Long and coiled, it hanging from him head like glory, with cowrie shells and kola nuts tied to some of him locs. Addis never seen nothing like it.

Every slave man she ever seen got to keep him hair cut low, manageable. This warn't no managed man. Her chest get warm and her throat go dry. She try to talk again, but the rags wrapped too tight round her mouth. She careful not to whimper. Even in this tied-up state she thinking: show no fear.

--Careful, now, the man say and reach for the rags. He unravel them slow and gentle, but Addis still wince, pain shooting through her face everytime a rag get caught up in dried blood. --Sorry, sorry, he say and keep unwrapping. It scare Addis to see how much blood cover the rags he taking off her and putting in a sack by the bed. But he don't scare her. Him eyes be as gentle as him voice and she caint shake the stirring in her gut what tell her she know him.

When the man finish, he touch her clamy forehead with him sturdy palm and say,

--Your fever coming down; that's a good sign. You were out in the cold night, soaked to the bone, in nothing but a dressing gown. We put some wool coverings on you.

She suddenly aware of her itchy skin again, scratching up against the wool. She think of these men undressing her but caint imagine the kind eye man bringing her to any harm. She loosen her jaw and it pain her, but not so much as before.

Addis go to ask him who he be and where she end up at, but then she catch the hay color man staring at her from the corner. Addis thinking he looking menancing, over there in the corner, muddy boots and knickers patched round the knees. How brave she thinking the kind eye man must be, who can command action and the hay color man go right to the corner and aint say boo since.

Still, she whisper to the kind eye man in Eboe,

--Who are you? What is this place? How do you know my name?

He lean back from her a little and look surprised. --You are Eboe, he say.

--Yes. And you?

--No, not me. We all speak it here. Even Thom there, he say, pointing to the man in corner. Addis scrunch up her face. Caint have nothing, she think and shoot Thom a look to say what she aint saying. Thom's tan face turn red and he turn him head away. The kind eye man grin all the way to him ears, laugh a little while he say, --There is no need to worry yourself about Thom. I won't let him hurt you.

Thom swallow hard at that and then leave the hut quiet and it make the kind eye man to laugh harder.

--We have hurt his feelings. Poor Thom. He is nwanne. Meta ya ọfụma.

But Addis don't want to hear bout no Thom and him feelings. She don't care that Thom be called brother. She just want to know who this man in front of her be. This straightback man who look a no-color man in the eye when he speaking and don't fear death.

The man hair move like wind over the Potomac when he grab a clean cloth and dip it in a washpan of warm water, then begin to clean her face. She feel her face get hot and a chill run up her. This smoothskin man got the gentlest touch. She barely feeling any pain at all in that moment, not the gash in her face or the burns on her body from the fire Haynes set, the bumps nor bruises all over from colliding with rocks in the running river and sleeping upright atop tree roots. Her body were in no kind of shape at all, but while this man cleaning her wounds with one hand and holding her chin steady with the other, she feel something like joy.

--Thom has been by your side since he and his partner Bartemus brought you here to me. I am Tembu, I should say.

Tembu, Addis thinking as she catch and hold him name between her fingers. She don't know what it mean or where it be from but she know she not ever going to let it go, not if she can help it. Addis get flushed when she think it, so she break the Eboe to talk other things.

--You talk funny, Addis say. She understand him fine, but him Eboe still sounding so different from Wellesbury or even how Rit Greene speak it. Addis were used to a bowed and whispered Eboe, a slow, heavy drip off the tongue. Tembu's Eboe had a quick skip to it. It jut out of him mouth. Him Eboe warn't like a sorrow song Nnene teach her; it were loud and light as cotton in the wind. Him Eboe had its own song to it and it were soaked in happy. How did he get this way? She wondering.

    --You don't talk like no menors I know, she tell him and he laugh again and follow her lead, breaking Eboe.

    --That's cause I aint no menor, Addis. You neither. Not up here, anyhow.

    --Where we at? Why that man bring me to you? Addis start to get right anxious and she move her face out of Tembu's hand til he answer her.

    --Caint imagine what you been through, Addis. I know you scared, but you safe here. You in my ụlọ ọgwụ, in a place called Meroë, Addis. It's free and oji land. No one gon harm you.

    --How you know my name?

    --Saw your free pass in your sack.

Addis panic at this. --Where's my sack? What you done with it? Tembu hold him hands up in surrender and walk to a near corner and hold up her sack.

    --Set your map out to dry, but I aint take nothing from you, I swear on it.

    Addis close her eyes and breathe out a little easier while he stand there with him hands open for her to see.

    --I promise you, I aint gon hurt you.

    Addis think back on all the men she done known in her life and reckon it be more than likely he a lie, but what she can do bout it?

    --I can finish cleaning you now, if you feel all right bout it.

    She hesitate at first, cause she don't know how she feel bout nothing no more. But he do got kind eyes, she decide, so she settle herself again and he get back to dabbing at her face with cloth. She reach up and touch her stiff, swole face and feel thread in spots from her forehead down her jaw and start breathing heavy, eyes widing.

    --What you do to me? What you done? Tembu put the cloth in the washpan and hold him hands away from her face, palms open, so she know she safe. He speak Eboe to her.

    --I am a doctor, Addis. That's why Thom and Bartemus brought you to me. I know you're in pain. I am trying to help you. Believe me, you are *safe* here.

    Addis feel paralyzed listening to Tembu. That word, *safe*,

warn't nothing she ever know, and after what she done, she aint gon never know it. But him voice, steady and sure, quiet her. She breathe like normal and don't struggle no more. He go on.

--When they found you down the river, your face had a terrible gash. I stitched it up to stop the bleeding and put a balm over it to ease the pain, but you gon always have that scar. I am sorry about that.

It all come rushing back to her. The yolk easing out the side of Burken's skull. The burn of Haynes knife cross her face. The blast what kill her mam. The fire what kill her brother and almost her too. Getting lost in the river. Dreaming of her pap. Was it a dream? She aint got time to think it all through. She kilt a man. She kilt the most powerful man and she got to get out of here.

--Well, thank you for your kindness. I sure appreciate it. But I best be moving on.

She try to lift herself up out the bed again but her head get to swirling and she have to close her eyes to make it stop.

--All right. That's enough for one day, Addis. Take a rest now. Lay on down.

Addis' mouth still protesting but her body stay still. --No, I got to leave here.

--Let's get you well, then you can go wherever you like. Where was you headed anyhow?

--My map aint tell you? Addis snap. --Say, how soon fore I can get to moving on from here?

Tembu's face shine a little less the more she insist on leaving and it make her wonder if she might could stay, maybe never leave. She start to picture what Meroë could be like, outside the walls of this room, where ojis living free, growing they hair long in coils, crowning it with glory beads, doctoring, growing food for theyselves and theyselves alone, sailing with no-color folks whose feelings they could hurt. Don't make not one bit of sense to Addis. For one always dreaming of things she aint never seen in waking life, she caint seem to picture what this new world might be like or what she might be like in it.

She like the thought of Tembu, though, and think she might could stay here, in a house like this one, with a warm fire in the cold months, air heavy with the eucalyptus and aloe she bringing him out her garden that he crush into ointments like Nnene do. She could be Adaeze in Meroë, she certain of it. No more Addis. No more agụ...

--I want to watch you a week or more, Tembu say, --Just till you get strong again. Caint have you out here fainting in the woods again. Infections could set into those wounds too. I gotta clean them every day, at least a week, maybe a month...

Addis here it outloud and know it simply aint possible. She don't belong here and she caint be sullying up Tembu and this lovely place, Meroë, where ojis live free.

--Do what you can in two days, Addis tell him. --Then I be on my way.

--Addis nobody know what you done here. You aint got to worry!

Addis eyes get to wideing and her throat go dry. --What you know bout what I done?

Just then, Thom and a taller, strong man bust through the door and set Addis on her nerves. Tembu stand up quick to shield her fore he see him friends.

--Thom, Bartemus, what has happened? Tembu ask them in Eboe and Bartemus answer the same.

--What we feared.

Bartemus walk toward them slow while Thom peek outside the door then close it quick behind them. Bartemus pull a paper out the back of him trousers and open it up slow for Tembu to see. Addis watch the brilliant brown of Tembu's face drain away to a ashen gray as he stare down at the paper. Addis gripping the bed with her battered hands and say with a rhaspy voice,

--Tell me, Tembu!

Tembu look from the paper to Addis to Bartemus, who nod. Tembu hand her the rumpled up paper. It shoulda been what Addis were expecting, but still it warn't. Addis see a sketching of her own wild eye face glaring back at her from the paper, flaps of hair sticking out from her braids, skin like chestnuts roasted and crushed, and that hideous gash cross her face, that scar Tembu say aint never going away.

Addis don't see her own hands shaking til she try to read

149

what the words say round both sides of her head. Tembu reach out to steady her hands but she pull away, pain shooting up her arms and cross her chest and face.

WANTED: DEAD OR ALIVE
MURDERER OF OUR BELOVED PRESIDENT BURKEN
ON THE LOOSE
Negro slave called Addis, aged about 17 years. 5 ft. 8 inches tall,
deep scar forehead to jaw.
$50,000 REWARD!
DANGEROUS. Be warned.

She read the story below the picture too, bout how this feral menor shewolf sneak into the sacred bedroom of the president of the United States and him angelwife while they sleeping and bash Burken head in with a rock then scatter when Missus Burken get to screaming. She read how the beastly Addis mighta escape unscathed if not for Rutherford Haynes, the president's childhood friend, fellow soldier and overseer, who caught her and sliced her to kingdom come fore he is ownself were attacked by a circle of menor dogs, all since dead and dust. A treasonous attack on Amerika by a small band of cowardly, untamable menors.

The writer say that Stanton Thompson, Secretary of War done issue the reward on behalf of Amerika and done appoint Richard Lawrence, Adjutant General of the Virginia Army and confidante to the Murdered President, to take the place of Burken as the new president as soon as possible. No word from the new president on just how the no-color man can stay safe from the rabid menors, but the writer warn all them that menors can seem harmless but they nature be of the beast and can transform at any time. Though this only be a small band, most all since kilt but the girl Addis, men ought still to bear arms and protect him family and him land from any threatening looking menors, free or slave.

Them last words stick to her insides like bad meat. Free or slave. The declaration were out in print for all to see; any oji what look threatening to a no-color man were to be nullified by musket, *free or slave.* Men and women, like her pap and mam, boys like Basil

Lee, girls like her and girls nothing like her. It all be too much for Addis and, swimming head aside, she got to leave.

She raise up out the bed, slow this time, and look round for her sack. --Where my bag? She ask Tembu who come and hold her arms to try and steady her. --Easy, now, Addis. Just lie back down.

--No! Give me my bag.

--We will protect you, Thom say and it take Addis aback and she fall forcefully into Eboe.

--I do not want anything from any of you! I want to leave and be left alone!

Tembu let go of Addis but say, --You are not yet well. Let us help you. You can trust us.

--Trust you? All of this time you have known who I am and said nothing. You seen my free papers is all what you said.

--I did. But, yes, we had heard about the president's death and a description of the killer. We have ears all over Filadelfia. We are not so far away. I did not want to alarm you because you need to get better, and we can and will protect you. Nobody knows you are here in Meroë.

Bartemus step forward. --May not be the whole truth, Tembu. And even so, we gotta tell Mama Biny. We caint keep this from her, not when trouble coming this way, not when she can help.

But Addis don't wait to hear who Mama Biny be or how she gon help. Addis put her tender feets down, slow and soft, one after the other. She see her sack in a corner and go to walk towards it. Tembu, Thom and Bartemus all get out of her way.

--We will not keep you here if you don't want to stay, Addis. But you are a wanted person now. People are looking for you, looking to *kill* you, and we don't want that to happen.

Addis stop at the door and turn to Tembu to ask, --And why is that?

Tembu smile at her and shake his head. His Eboe strong when he say,

--You don't know? You are a hero, Addis! It's one thing to strike down a master, but *the master*, the symbol of this corrupt nation...it means more to so many of us than you can know.

--How do you know what it means? How many days have

151

past? Who even knows what I have done, *really knows*, because that paper does not tell the truth.

--It has only been two days, sure, but I believe ojis in Filadelfia and right here in Meroë understand what this means, that maybe change will come for the rest of the ojis outside this state.

--What do you know of the ojis outside this state? You live here in your oji village, a oji doctor in your own world. I have brought trouble onto you and all the rest. Can you not read? *Free or slave* will be killed now. We are at war.

--That is one man's word in a paper, Thom jump in to say, Eboe clunking round him tongue but strong enough. --We will all protect you from any who come against you. We can help you escape to the lands beyond the Falls or to the western territories. Whatever you want to do, we will help you do.

--Once you are well, Tembu say. --Biko, Addis. Please lie back down, have some water. Let us fetch Mama Biny. She will know what to do.

--If she is wise, she will collect the $50,000 since you all are too foolish to do it, Addis say fore she turn again to the door, open it and walk out, crisp air filling her chest, freeing it from the hold of the suffocating eucalyptus. She look round on both sides fore she drop down into the dirt.

-28-
TEMBU

When Tembu get Addis back in the bed, he hold a damp cloth over her forehead as she slip in and out of sleep. He look at her swollen face and trembling hands and think how she one of them peoples you know right off bout. He don't know much bout who she be or where she come from. He don't know much sides she wanted for killing a man.

She say it warn't true, the way they say it were done, and he believe her. If she did kill him, he decide, she got to have plenty good reason. And he know certain that she were a special person and that he got to protect her.

He put him hands on top her hands as she sleep and wonder if this special woman ever have that: protecting. He find it hard to believe she never did, even being on the run alone and near death. He caint imagine no seeing person could come round Addis and not just know sure enough she be somebody God-given.

Anointed, him ole massa used to call it fore he die and set Tembu free, so many years ago. Him ole massa were a doctor what taught Tembu all he know, and were a God-fearing man. He used to tell Tembu bout the patients who live when all else die from the same cause, that it were God's anointing what keep them patients breathing, that a doctor who listening, who really seeing people the way God intend it, could see when a person have it. Warn't no halo round the head could alert you to it, nuther. Maybe the eyes though.

But Addis eyes were closed when he first hold her face in him hands, when he numb it and stitch it up. When she whisper out her name in her sleep. When sweat pour from her forehead and soak up the bandages and he have to re-wrap her. All the time her eyes closed up and still he knowing that when the time come for it, he gon give him life for her.

He look over to Thom, resting quiet in a chair in the corner holding a ready musket, and know Thom see it too. Even Bartemus, often quiet and deep inside him ownself, jump quick to fetch Mama Biny once Addis were safe in bed. If she could stir up three men as they, what this slight woman caint do?

Tembu think all this and it scare him like he aint been scared in awhile and he know he wise to be fearing. He hold her hands a little tighter and pray to Jesus for her total healing. And when Tembu pray, he pray with sureness, knowing God caint be through with this one yet. She got a destiny. He want to be a part of it. When he see that in hisself, he let go her hands right away and busy hisself burning the old blooded up bandages in the fire. Even at this distance, staring into flames, smelling the cleansing odor of burning blood, he feel hisself tying him soul to hers snd he don't like it one bit.

--There is no God but God, Tembu mutter into the smoke, girding him loins against Addis. Right off, he ask forgiveness for it. Addis know nothing bout him thoughts or how these three strong men done changed just for being round her. It warn't her doing necessarily. Whatever he put on her, fault or power, that were him own doing. Warn't no one else to blame.

Just then, the door creak open and Tembu whip round to face it and Thom jump up with him musket in hand.

--MotherFather God!

Goliwe say, frightened. She drop the basket of biscuits and fish she bringing and some fall onto the ground.

--So sorry, Go, Thom say and lower him musket, breathe out and sit on back down.

Goliwe turn to Tembu, shaking, and demand in Eboe, --What is going on, Tembu?

The look on Tembu face alert her danger be present and she lower her voice right away. --Who are you guarding with guns at the ready? Goliwe say from the doorway, craning to see a still-sleeping Addis.

Tembu breathe out, full of relief to see Goliwe at the door and not no one else. Goliwe warn't gon tell a soul bout Addis hiding in Meroë. Others he warn't so sure bout, even though he tell Addis they all prolly thinking she a hero. Times be good enough in Meroë; plenty food for everybody, houses and land for all the families right on the Delaware, trading on market days, steady work for good pay,

154

all right there in the village.

And that don't even mention the deal Mama Biny get with the state to be left alone with they prime river lands, so long as the village keep to itself and don't go meddling where they don't belong, trying to vote and trade and set up shop in the cities. Tembu don't blame Mama Biny for this none; warn't like he wanting to go doctoring on sick no-color folks or nothing, and plenty ojis warn't safe outside the village, even if they warn't slaves. But he know it make what they say bout Meroës being free not so at all. They all like best not to think on it much.

But a $50,000 reward? That could buy off any weakling itching to curry favor with the state, be a hero to the no-color nation, calm down they fears with a *see, all menors aint the same!* goodwill gesture that could get them a pass to be more than a hired hand in the city. Maybe get to be a friend! $50,000 were dangerous.

--Who is this girl, Tembu?

Goliwe ask, though she and Addis were round bout the same age. Goliwe voice were low and steady; it never fail to calm Tembu. He like a lot of things bout Goliwe, like how she twist up her hair in a thousand teeny coils, then weave them up into all sorts of patterns, like tapestry. He always have to touch her hair just fore he kiss her, caint help hisself. But the peace she put him in, the unwavering steadfastness just with her voice, were him favorite thing. She don't scare him.

She were a plenty serious woman, managing the only large farm in the village, owned by the sisters Kosi and Lotanna. Goliwe live alone and like it just fine that way, though she always think to bring him by some supper from the farm or herbs from the garden he use to make remedies he sell in Kosi and Lotanna's shop.

He were happy to see Goliwe, happy to hear her voice, just then when he were worrying bout what he might do for Addis, if she wake up and ask him. Goliwe were too grounded and too grounding for him to ever fear placing her up too high. She warn't a god-danger to him. She warn't any kind of danger to him and he like that very much bout her.

--She was attacked and has come down sick. Thom and Bartemus found her like this.

155

--Mere nke ọma, Thom! Looks like you saved her life.

Goliwe step over the food she spill on the ground and go sit down in the chair next to Addis bedside. Tembu shift on him feets a little. He know Goliwe warn't going to hurt Addis, couldn't never, but still he want to ask her to get up, to leave them be, just a few days. Maybe a month, til it all blow over. At least til Bartemus come back with Mama Biny and they know what they gon do with Addis, where she gon go.

Tembu look up from him thoughts and catch Goliwe staring straight in him eyes. He swallow and smile slight.

--Who this girl to you, Tembu?

Tembu think fast and careful and decide warn't no sense in lying to Goliwe. He know the woman. He trust her. Addis change a lot of things for him, but she don't change that. So he confess all to Goliwe while he putting the food she dropping back in the basket and setting it off in the corner. He show Goliwe the article in the paper. Tell her that Bartemus gone to get Mama Biny so they know what to do next, and the part he know she already know, that caint nobody else know Addis were in Meroë.

Goliwe were stoic, breathing slow and deep when she turn from Tembu back to Addis. He realize he holding him breath when Goliwe brush her thin fingers against Addis swole up cheek and say, --Poor girl.

All the air escape him at once. He feel something like shame at that relief, the realization that he could doubt Goliwe, even just a little, after seven years in Meroë, seven years knowing her. Good, kind Goliwe.

--Will she be all right? Goliwe ask, a hand on Addis hand. Tembu feeling dizzy hisself now. He need air, need to think. He all shook up inside.

--I hope so, Go. Just a fever. Got to watch for infection and just let her rest awhile. Stay with her?

She nod, ring out the cool cloth into the tub by the bed, then place it back on Addis forehead. Tembu give Thom a look he understand and Thom get up and say, --I'll keep watch outside, and the two walk out together and close the door.

When they a small ways from the ụlọ ọgwụ, Thom stop

him.

--Hold, now. You look like you been caught doing something much worse than harboring a fugitive. You looking as pale as me now. What's happening to you?

Tembu laugh a little. --I wish I knew! Just need some air, I reckon.

--It's the girl, aint it.

Tembu feel blood rush to him face. What a stupid, stupid reason for a grown man to fall suddenly ill, the spell of a sleeping person.

--How long you think we can keep her here with no one knowing?

--Depends on how many more women you got hanging round your hut.

--Well the next fugitive that come, we stash at your hut. Nobody ever find em!

They laughing together.

--It's gon be all right, Tembu. Mama Biny will know what to do.

Tembu breathe in and out deep while Thom look round and say, --We ought to get back. You standing?

--I'm standing, Tembu say and place a hand on Thom shoulder fore he turn to go back to the ụlọ ọgwụ.

When they set foot inside, Addis sitting up, eating some stew Goliwe bring for Tembu's supper. Tembu smile to see it. She looking better. He come stand with a hand on Goliwe shoulder and she smile up at him and hold him hand.

--Kèdú, Addis?

--Better. Not so dizzy.

--Good, Tembu sigh. --Very good.

Addis look past them both to Thom back in the corner, holding strong to him musket.

--I aint thank you yet for saving me, Thom. You and Bartemus. Thank you.

Thom tan skin turn a funny orange color and Tembu almost laugh cause he never seen Thom in such a way in all the years they knowing each other, cept Tembu don't laugh cause he know just

157

what it feel like for this stranger to come in and flip everything on its own head.

Just then, the door slam open and Thom point him musket right at Bartemus.

--Easy, killer, Bartemus smirk and Thom start to smart mouth him back, but then Mama Biny step through the door and everybody kneel.

--Kèdú, Obi! All cept Addis say as Mama Biny walk to the center of the ụlọ ọgwụ.

--Kèdú, Oba Achebe! They say, still kneeling when her partner Achebe walk in behind her.

Mama Biny walk closer to Addis and Tembu have to clench him toes in him shoes and squeeze him fists at him sides to keep from moving him feets to stand in between her and Addis. He look to the side and see Goliwe looking right at him, her thick eyebrows at attention. He look down, embarrassed. Mama Biny warn't gon hurt Addis, he know that.

And even if she were, Mama Biny, in her wisdom, know what be best for Meroë, that be why she were chosen and Achebe chosen to be her help, cause they honor the laws of the ancestors, they honor fairness and justice. Whatever Mama Biny choosing to do with Addis warn't none of him business, he know this, he know this, he just got to keep telling it to hisself in him own head. Still, a chill go down him when Mama Biny walk right up to Addis and say in her slow-dripping Eboe,

--Well, now, Miss Addis. What will we do with you?

-29-
ADDIS

To Addis, Mama Biny seem to float. The sound of her voice were ethereal, even if her words, *What are we going to do with you?* seem menacing. Addis don't know if the woman they call mam meaning her any harm...she can barely see why they call her mam at all, when there aint no way she birth someone old as Bartemus...but she can see right away why they call her Obi.

She were regal in a way that Nnene coulda been regal. Both having the same kinda strength that don't need to announce itself, the same kinda eyes that say I been somewhere and been through things you caint never in your life know. A natural grace they both having, and Nnene were the only queen Addis ever knowing. It sting Addis to see what Nnene coulda been, unshackled.

It make Addis mind fill up with Nnene, what she would think bout what Addis done, what they might do to Nnene cause of what Addis done. It sink her heart.

Mama Biny reach a hand up to touch Addis along her scar line and Addis don't flinch. She look Mama Biny dead in her eyes. It warn't that she warn't fraid of this woman who wield so much power over this place she in, strong people like Bartemus and Thom and Tembu.

It strike her how these men revere Mama Biny, kneel to her, call her the center of they world. It were one thing for a man in love with you to do it. She seen that before. She know what that feel like. These men, these no-relations to Mama Biny, no lovers but Achebe, it seem to Addis, look upon her with a fierceness, and she think how it warn't right that Nnene never know such feral love herself.

--You bring a lot of trouble on us coming here, Addis Agụ. That name, the one Ala give her in her dreams, shock Addis to hear from Mama Biny mouth, and Addis frown up and breathe in quick.

--Why you call me that?

Achebe start to protest the disrespect Addis show by not addressing Mama proper, but Mama grab him hand and he quiet hisself. Mama reach her hand back out to Addis face and speak to her in gentle Eboe.

--This stripe across your face, like a tiger's. You are not a child anymore. You are woman and warrior now. This scar is proof. Your name should reflect that.

--My name is *Adaeze*, Addis answer in Eboe. --Everybody names me what they want to name me my whole life. But my name is *Adaeze*. Daughter of a king.

Achebe start again and Mama quiet him again with a touch of her hand, but break the Eboe.

--It matter little what folks call you when you know who you are or when you dead. While you living, you gon always belong to something else, whether for good or evil. Your life aint never gon be just yours. Meroë folks know that well. I know it well. And you gon learn it sooner than you think. Which bring me back to where I start with you. You done brought a lot of trouble on us coming here.

Addis inch herself up in the bed and everybody seem to hold they breath and get ready to act, should it come to it. Addis notice and nod her head low when she say,

--Begging your pardon, Mama Biny, but I aint *come* nowhere. I were brought here. And I been ready to leave but my body and Tembu over there keeping me from it.

Addis see Goliwe flinch a little but Mama Biny smile at this. --You do seem to have some kinda roots on my men here, Addis Agü. They tell me you are special. That my hundreds of warriors of Meroë must protect you from the scarred-up no-color man what done this to you, and all the troops in the country what marching to find you. Prolly coming this way right now. Is that what you thinking we should do?

Addis get hot with questions. How she knowing bout Haynes and the scar on him face? How she knowing if troops coming for her in Meroë?

--I never ask nothing of nobody! I just want to leave.

--And go where? Tembu say, distressed.

Addis feel herself get dizzy again and lean herself back against the bed. Mama Biny bring back the calm of Eboe.

--Do you know we have an accord with the state? They do not bother us if we do not bother them. We live in peace, free from hunters, we have our own land and our own farms and our own riverways. We are our own people here, free from trouble. Did you know that?

--I don't know nothing bout you people. And I don't want nobody doing nothing for me. I want to leave and make my own way.

What she want were her Nnene, to crawl back into her arms like she done when her pap were kilt. What she want were to lay in the field under willows with Ekwueme and have him read the stars to her. That be what she want. But it finally come to Addis that she aint never gon see them again and that she aint long for this world her own self.

Mama Biny don't take her eyes off Addis and Addis don't take her eyes off Mama Biny.

--Achebe, Mama Biny call, eyes still on Addis, --What do you think we should do?

Achebe step forward and say with a booming voice,

--Binyelum, the girl must see The Eboro.

Mama Biny keep staring in silence, the whole ụlọ ọgwụ silent, barely breathing, waiting for something to live or die.

--The Eboro, Mama Biny repeat. --It is so.

Tembu step to Mama Biny's side and say, --I will take her, Mama Obi.

--Oh? I thought you swore off *Eboe debilment*, as you call it. Swore you never again go see The Eboro after what she tell you, Mama Biny say over her shoulder.

--Yes, Mama. It's just that Addis is not well yet.

--In the morning, then. Achebe should lead you. Bartemus will come along, and Thom too.

Now Thom stepping forward. --Forgive me, Mama, but I wonder if there is something else I should do first, before morning.

--And what is that, Thom Terry?

--It's the picture, Mama.

Thom take the newspaper copy with the drawing of Addis on the front and put it in Mama Biny's hands.

--People are scared. The article says it was only a small band of ojis who did this and they are all dead except for her. But what if we change that? This picture could give them hope. I could take it to my brother Cliffe. You know he print up the oji paper, *Eziokwu*, for The Tunnel folks, and he could have it in the *Eziokwu* by morning, send it all up and down the coast, all the way to Virginia. *Hero slays President*, it could say. Every reading oji ought to know what she done, and not the way they telling it. It could mean something.

Addis tense up at this, *what she done*. She don't like the thought of it, folks seeing her in the paper all the way in Virginia. Nnene hearing bout it. But she done what she done, and it were foolish to think Nnene warn't gon know all soon, anyhow. It were already in the no-color paper, and all of Wellesbury prolly know of it soon enough.

Maybe Nnene see it and be proud, she thinking. She know Ekwueme gon be proud to see it, and know that he were right bout there being a oji paper where folks write in Eboe. She know he gon be proud that she aint let Burken get away with what he done to her or what he were gon do. If she warn't never gon see them again in this life, she were glad they might could see her like that, blazing scar of battle cross her face, eyes wide open and daring.

She like the picture, though it warn't nothing how she looking when she done it, and sure not how she looking now, swole up and bloody. But the girl they painting like evil looking strong to Addis, like she done had it out with the Debil and won, even just this one time. She see now what Thom see when he look at that picture, what he think that picture might could mean to people, a tiger-stripe conqueror on the loose! It's all Addis can do to keep from screaming, --Yes! Yes, Thom! Do it!

--You do not think it will point anyone to Meroë to have Heathcliffe print this picture in the oji paper?

--No, Mama. I will make certain of it. We just use the picture they sending out everywhere anyhow. It will not get back to Meroë, that she is here or that we are involved.

Mama Biny don't look sure of that. --Hard to say when your brother the one putting out the paper. Still, it gon be so.

Mama hand back the paper to Thom. --Use the picture, but Thom?

--Yes, Mama?

--Make sure the paper call her *Addis Agu*.

-30-
THOM

What you thinking bout, Thom Terry?
When Bartemus ask it in him low growl, a smirk on him face, it knock Thom out him head and back into the small riverboat Bartemus rowing while Thom daydreaming. Thom look up to the setting sun just above the trees and think bout lying to Bartemus, but don't see the point and just say,

--I'm thinking bout what's gonna happen. What this could mean if we get this picture out. If people get scared enough, angry enough, things gonna change round here.
Bartemus laugh as loud as a person could who trying to row downstream unseen.

--What, you think slaves aint plenty scared, plenty angry right now? Lawd! That's all it take? Why you aint tell us sooner!

--A mụ na m amụ!
Thom saying, and Bartemus turn from laugh to smirk. Thom hate that, when Bartemus laugh at him. Just when he think he in, he as much a Meroë as anybody could be who come and go as much as he and Bartemus do, something always happen to let him know he aint really. A laugh, a word, a look of fear, of disgust, like what Addis cut him with while ago, something always there to tell him that he not really the same.

Cause the truth were, he warn't the same. He don't see the world the same, and it warn't him fault necessarily, but he know he ought to know better sometimes. He knowing now what he say were a dumb thing to say, but he shoulda known it sooner. Wishing he'd a known it sooner. Wishing Bartemus aint rowing this boat they in for a reason. Specially now, when folks all hot bout Addis and the president, Bartemus got to act like he Thom's property even more, when they out in the world.

That be how they get together in the first place. Bartemus were a seller of stolen things, secret things folks caint get nowhere easy, after the Great War: china, tea, sugar, butter, *weapons*. So

Bartemus selling all manner of things he get him hands on, up and down the coast in a boat for awhile, til things get too dangerous for a oji, especially one as massive as a tree trunk, like Bartemus. He stop for a long while til he meet Heathcliffe Terry and him partner Leo.

Leo write up a paper for ojis who read Eboe and Cliffe got him a printing press and together they making *Eziokwu* and they ask Bartemus to start up again, selling on the coast and giving the paper and weapons to the folks what run The Tunnel along the way. Bartemus tell them he caint get no crew, that it be too dangerous for a oji to captain a ship when Sheriff Joe Turner out of Virginia and him watchmen always on the prowl to steal free ojis and sell them as slaves. That's when Leo come up with the plan. --Take Heathcliffe's little brother Thom with you. Won't nobody try to steal you if they think you Thom's.

Thom were just turnt old enough to look like he could own somebody and when Leo say it, near 7 years ago, it excite him. The look on Bartemus' face change everything, though. Bartemus aint want nobody to think he were Thom's or anyone else's. Thom feel bad right off for being excited bout what he thought were a game. It warn't no game and he were old enough to know that.

Still, they laughing bout it, when Bartemus got to bow him head and say, --Yessir, Massa! in certain places, certain towns, most everywhere, really, cept when they alone in a boat or on they ship or in Meroë, which aint often enough for either of them. Even when they pillaging a war ship, it come in handy, cause Thom get instant respect when folks see he got him a slave, and they let Thom and Bartemus and they thieving crew on board easy. Laughing bout it be just how they got through the ugliness of it, make em like brothers, almost.

Thom knowing Bartemus would die for him and Bartemus knowing he do the same, any time. And the roles they play saving both they lives more times than they can count. But Thom know even a little time playing Massa and Slave gon stick a wedge between souls caint nothing close.

So Thom need things to change. He need to live in a world where all him brothers can sail they own ship, row they own boat in peace. He knowing that day far, far off, but maybe Addis might could make it come faster, he want to say. Instead, he just say,

--Things *got* to change.

--I know, nwanne, Bartemus say, and keep rowing on to Camden.

They coulda been there by now if they gone on horseback, but it were too hard to see who were lurking in the woods at night. Hard, too, on the river, but at least you might could see somebody fore they right up on you and you could move more quiet, if need be.

--You really think she a hero?

Bartemus ask and Thom don't pause.

--I do think it. We got to make sure other people think it too.

--I think the more you stir shit, the more it stinks, Bartemus say. --I do believe she got something special in her though. I don't know if it be what she done or what she gonna do, but I knew the moment we saw her she were somebody.

--I felt it too, Thom say. Then he grin and ask, --You ever think that bout me when we first met?

--Nah. I always knowing you aint shit.

And they laughing again.

Fore long, they seeing a big boat off in the distance with the Amerikan flag flying near the lookout deck, oil lamps all round it, and another boat heading they way.

--Get down! Thom say, and Bartemus bow hisself and start rowing toward the bank. When they get close enough, they hop out the boat onto the bank and pull it up out the water and cover it with brush.

--We just try walking the rest of the way. Not much farther.

So they walk in near dark, sticking close to the river. Just fore they hit Camden, they see a line of men with torches and guns.

--Take the bag, Thom, Bartemus say and Thom take the sack from him, what got the newspaper of Addis face in it, and sling it over him other arm that aint got him musket swinging from it.

Thom keep him hands free so he can reach for it, should occasion call for it. Bartemus got pistols hidden near him waist and he keep him hands at the ready. They both get in they positions.

Thom walk with a straighter back, a higher chest, and Bartemus bend hisself a little, at the neck, the waist and the knees.

--Halt, there!

A soldier say it, musket at the ready, and they pause with they hands up. Bartemus get behind Thom.

--What is your business in my town, soldier?

Thom ask and the soldier lower him musket. The rest of the regiment follow suit.

--Your town, sir? State your name.

--My name, soldier, is Thomas Terry, and I do not take kindly to threats with guns, especially not in my own town. We have a Constitution to protect against this now.

--No need to be alarmed, Mr. Terry, these are just precautions. There is a murderer on the loose, after all. We are checking every town. Who is this menor you brought with you?

Thom feel him neck getting hot and sweaty.

--He is mine and not your concern, soldier. Now I ask that you let us pass in peace before I start to take this very unpleasant interruption personally.

--It's only for your safety I ask, Mr. Terry. These menors are known to riot, you know, especially one as big as that. And after what that brute did to our fine president, God rest him, we must all be on our guard.

--God rest him, indeed, but you have nothing to fear from this one. He is quite gentle, I assure you, and, as I said, *mine*. Good evening, soldiers.

--Good evening, the soldier say and step aside so Thom and Bartemus can pass.

It aint long fore Thom can taste the bile rising in the back of him throat. The back of him neck be soaking with sweat and a shiver inch its way him up him back.

--You did good, Thom. Just keep walking. You did good, Bartemus whisper, and it steady Thom.

They walk in silence into the town, hickory smoke wafting into the cool night air. Thom breathe it in and feel a bit of comfort. The smell of venison remind him of him pap, of going out hunting for deer with him as a kid, when he were blissfully unaware that some folks hunting people, too, and one day, he gon be one of them. Thom and Heathcliffe only had they pap growing up. They mam die just as soon as the Fever hit big in Filadelfia. Then they pap got in with Quakers, talking bout freeing slaves…crazy stuff for a no-color man with a bit of money to him. Warn't no time fore somebody take him out and leave Heathcliffe to raise Thom. Course, Heathcliffe done the best he know to do, but it warn't much for a boy barely a man. Thom and Heathcliffe learn quick how to look after theyselves.

What Heathcliffe caint teach him, he learning from Bartemus these 7 years, and he think he turn out all right. Thieving from a nation of crooks warn't no crime, he figure. (That be what him pap used to say, *a nation of crooks*.) And Bartemus make sure whenever they go back up coast they take whatever slave wanting to be free, in secret, surely. They warn't fighting no war or nothing, but it were something. It were a start of something, at least. Might could even make him pap proud, he thinking, if they get this picture of Addis out to The Tunnel.

Might could stop the swell he get in the pit of him stomach every time death be near. If he say the wrong thing and make a man with a gun suspicious, he were gonna have to kill somebody or be kilt, and he warn't bout to die.

When they first starting out stealing, him and Bartemus kilt plenty folk who test them, folk who catch them when a pillage going wrong. When he do it, he feel all the blood rush everywhere through him, from him toes and fingertips, to the top of him head. He get real trance-like. All the fear of death, the waiting for it to come, mix up with the victory of living another day, and only in that space between life and death, heaven and hell, he feel him pap close by.

The way he kill and how much scare Bartemus, though. --You not killing cause you got to, Thom. You losing yourself, nwanne!

Bartemus say it whenever it happen and get so worked up he confess all to Heathcliffe. The two sit Thom down to say the killing must stop. So Bartemus and Thom deciding to get better at lying, better at thieving so nobody got to die, least of all them.

--You killing yourself, too, when you kill, don't you see it?

Bartemus tell him that and Thom agree outloud, but don't

believe that it be so. They think the good in him dying. He think hisself a plenty good man, plenty loyal, kind enough. Just another part to him like to do whatever it take to get back to that in-between space. He long for the feeling always, that power over life and death, but he learn to control it, for Heathcliffe and Bartemus sake.

--Home, at last, Thom say when they reach the low, wooden gate surrounding a log cabin dripping with cottonwoods. Thom unlatch the gate and hold the door open for Bartemus, who he feel eyeing him, though it be too dark for Bartemus to get a good look at him face, see if Thom really all right.

--I'm all right, Bartemus, go on, Thom say and Bartemus walk on up to the door and knock with Thom trailing behind.

--Who is it?!

Heathcliffe sound agitated, nervous, like a beast who know he bout to be prey.

--Your brothers, Cliffe, open up.

First, Heathcliffe swing the latch on the peep hole open, then the door, and Thom see him brother look just like he sound. Unshaven were the way Thom and Bartemus carry theyselves, but never Heathcliffe. Him eyes were wild and him grasp firm when he close the door behind Thom and Bartemus and hug them both, in turn. Thom and Bartemus look to each other with worry fore Thom say,

--What's happened, Cliffe?

Heathcliffe were pacing the floor of him cabin, him silver-toed boots clicking against the wood floor. It were too warm in the small cabin, the fire raging in the pit big enough to heat up a three room house.

--Didn't you see them? The soldiers have been occupying towns up and down the coast for days! How can I work like this?

Thom come and stand in front of him older brother, towering a bit, and Heathcliffe stop pacing.

--You must find a way. I brought you something.

Thom reach into him bag and pull out the print of Addis' face.

--You think I don't know about this girl? Of course I do! Why do you think the troops are here? All over any place within twenty miles!

--Yes, but we need to give our people hope, Bartemus say. --This is not a time for fear, it's a time to fight! We get this picture in the *Eziokwu*, send it out to The Tunnel, who knows what might could happen?

--I'll tell you what will happen! We'll all be slaughtered! Heathcliffe rip away from him brother's grip and go sit down at the kitchen table and take a long swig of port. Thom and Bartemus share another look fore Bartemus go sit cross from Heathcliffe. Thom stand nearby.

--They want us to be afraid right now, Cliffe. They want that. We send this picture out, tell them Addis Agu is a hero, a warrior, who won this first battle of the war, and people will rise up with a new hope of what's possible. She is living proof we can fight and win! Don't you see that?

Heathcliffe laugh at this and shake him head.

--Do I look like a fighter to you? We hide people, we feed people, we help people, we speak out at town meetings, we write papers. We don't go to *war*, don't you see that? Don't you see that at least half of our people on The Tunnel want slaves free so long as it won't impact too much of their spoilt lives? One at a time, they want. Slow change, they want, not revolution! This is a pastime for most. I'm the one they'd kill, not the unmarried Quaker women helping on the Tunnel who can still be saved yet, with a good husband.

--The ojis will fight for ourselves, Bartemus boom out. He membering the troops and instantly lower him voice. --We don't need nobody to fight for us. We just need the right folks to know, all up and down the coast, what this tiger-woman done, and that they can do the same cause they not alone!

Heathcliffe put him head in him hands. --You must not have heard. The *war*, as you so eagerly put it, brother, has already begun. The slaves at President Burken's plantation have rioted and killed every watchman, both the no-color ones and the ojis. The same has happened at six plantations near Wellesbury, and all of the ojis from all six plantations are occupying Wellesbury, for now. Privately, the soldiers are saying it's a coordinated attack, but they won't say it in the papers. They don't want people to be too fearful, especially after the loss of the president, and some unknown Virginia general taking over the post.

--This is just what we need, Cliffe! We've got to get it out that the tiger-woman led this attack, that we're winning! People must know, Thom say.

--Brother, by the time these papers get to them, the slaves at Wellesbury will be murdered. So will you and so will I.

--Maybe, Bartemus say. --But maybe not. We should try, Cliffe. We should try.

Heathcliffe get up again and pace the room. --This is madness. This is madness, he repeat.

--Only thing is, we need a new way to get it out. Bartemus and me, we got something else to do. Something real important.

Cliffe laugh, --Something more important than this death mission you are sending me on?

--Yes, Bartemus say. --If you print the picture and the story, can you get it out without us?

Cliffe stop pacing again and sit down cross from Thom.

--I have men and women with horses and ships at the ready. This story about Addis Agu, the calculated attacks, the picture...my people will get it out by morning.

Thom get up and go to hug him brother and Cliffe lay rather limp in him arms, a spirit in defeat. Thom stand fully upright and put him hands square on him brother's shoulders. --In the morning, ride for Meroë. It's not safe here anymore.

Cliffe silent, wobbly-kneed, when he rise. He hug Bartemus and whisper, --Look after him, Bartemus. You are his brother. You know, when the killing starts...how he gets...

Bartemus leave one hand on Cliffe's shoulder and promise to look after Thom and tell him, don't worry. It were all going to work out. He gon see. Cliffe smile weak and sit back down. He grab him fountain pen and paper and begin to write the copy as Bartemus and Thom creep out the door, looking every which way for soldiers.

-31-
GOLIWE

When Tembu come to Goliwe's cabin to tell her that they warn't gon wait til morning to see The Eboro, that Addis were feeling better, that really, it were urgent and they caint wait for Bartemus and Thom to get back, Goliwe feel in her pit a deep and strange sense of loss. It warn't just that Goliwe know right off that Tembu got something like soul-level love for this warrior woman who fall into him lap. She get that. Addis got something even Goliwe feeling drawn to. But Addis coming here were a sign things warn't never gonna be the same again. She been sitting in the rocking chair Tembu make her ever since he leave her, warming herself by the hearth, fighting off the chill she feel coming on.

Goliwe like her life in Meroë. She warn't born a Meroë or nothing, but life in this village be all she know. At 7 years old, after slave life in the New York harbor, her mam give her up to a woman heading North for the borderlines during a revolt where near 100 ojis getting killed. Goliwe don't member the escape none, don't member her mam none, just bits of what Mama Biny and Oba Achebe tell her bout it when she were older. Somehow or nother, she winding up in Meroë, left by the fleeing woman, and she aint necessarily belonging to nobody as a chile. The whole of Meroë raise her.

She spend much of her early years following behind the sisters Kosi and Lotanna on they farm, learning bout healing herbs and how to plant and harvest. They teaching her how to braid and twist up her hair in all kinds of glorious ways like the Meroë do. Warn't but one time Goliwe mention to Kosi how Lotanna built like every man she ever see so Lotanna got to be one. Kosi hush her up quick.

--Lotanna say she a woman, so that just who she be. How you think you know better? Goliwe say she aint know no better and that were the end of that. Warn't long fore the sisters open up a shop and put Goliwe in charge of it, when she were old enough.

Goliwe spend her days trading the crop, woven baskets,

quilts, and Tembu's healing salves. That were how they meeting the first time. He come into Meroë a few years back saying he a doctor, though he look too young to be knowing much of anything, to Goliwe's eye. He sure were fine, though. Tall and broad built with gentle eyes, a dimple in each cheek.

--Never trust a man with dents in him cheeks, yeah? Lotanna tell her when she see him. --That mean a woman done slap him so much the skin stick together!

Goliwe laugh but don't believe a word of it. Not bout Tembu. He come to get peppermint, lavender, oils, yams and such from her and come back at week's end with all sorts of salves to heal a cold in the chest, a pain in the stomach. Soon, she were stopping by the ụlọ ọgwụ he set up for hisself to treat the sick. She bringing him supper, cause once he mention he were working so hard he forget to eat. He never ask her to do it, but he never ask her to stop nuther, so she keep on. She like to do it. She take the kola nut beads traded in her shop and thread him locs with them and rub oil from coconuts deep in him scalp.

Soon, he teaching her how to make salves too and they making and trading twice as much. Then, he holding her and kissing her and making all feel right with the world. He say he would have come to her sooner, but a prophecy The Eboro give him make him stay away. She beg him to tell her what The Eboro say, but he refuse her. He say she The Eboro just a witch. Eboe magic brought over from Afrika, staying too long in the new age.

The new age were bout Christ, he tell her and anyone who listen. He learning bout Christ from him massa, what teach him medicine and set him free. But the source don't make Christ no less true, he telling her. Read for yourself, he telling her. Ị dị njikere ị zute ya? He always asking. A gbaghara go mmehie gị? And she were always unsure cause she not even sure what sin be. Warn't it a sin to own people? Warn't it a sin to steal land and rape and kill? Yet these sinners sitting way on high, and they hiding away in Meroë just to live safe.

Tembu don't know none of the answers to her questions, but soon they reading the Bible together when market days are done. And she surprise herself, how quickly she believe: a loving God who forgive all, a Christ who saves, who wash all sins away, if you just believe. She find Chúkwú in the Christian God easy, though. Chúkwú don't battle with Christ in her mind the way it do for Tembu. She like the ways of her ancestors. It be the only thing she have left of her mam. It were worth holding on to, just as much as the Eboe tongue.

She never quarrel with Tembu bout it none though. She were happy to share Christ with someone else, since some bow to Allah like they ancestors done in they homelands and others just live by what The Eboro prophesy anyhow. She use to think like Tembu did, that Christ come from no-color men teaching, til Oba Achebe set them straight bout Christ in the Afrikan north. Tembu were eager to learn from Achebe, and she like that best bout him. He listen, to her and others. He like to reason and he don't think he know everything, like other folks in Meroë.

Cause he warn't nothing like the others. Most the men was warriors of Meroë, but not all the warriors was men. Training were still a pastime for all the warriors, when they warn't doing they other trades: carpentry, blacksmithing, farming, weaving, potting and such. The warriors got the outdoor smell of long-working on them always and Goliwe like its sourness. She respect the warriors, to be sure; they keeping Meroë safe, in case the governor change him mind bout the deal they striking with Mama Biny to leave the town be. But Tembu protecting them in a different way. He were a healer and he smell like sweet peppermint and coconut, always.

The first Meroë he ever save were a baby boy name Uzo. He have the Fever and The Eboro caint do nothing for him, so him mam finally let Tembu work, and within two days, Uzo were laughing again. That were some years ago now. And in that time, Meroë grown into a place she were quite comfortable in. She only been to Filadelfia a handful of times, with the sisters or sometimes with Mama Biny, when she go on business with the governor. But never once do Goliwe wish to be a part of that world where she got to walk bowed and cross the street when a no-color man coming. No-color children spit at her and laugh and they mams smile or act like nothing happening at all and Mama Biny act the same while they in that town. It were a dizzying thing for Goliwe to be a person up until she cross the town border. She caint hardly keep her balance moving tween two worlds, so she avoid going all she can.

But it warn't so much she avoid Filadelfia as it were just that she don't want to leave Meroë. She love the blacks and browns and tans and creams of the people. Even the ojis like Kosi who been born with all the color drain out they skin and hair, Goliwe find so beautiful, like all of Afrika come to life in Meroë. It were something sweet to her, something she treasure, something that lift her up to see so many glorious people. Good people she live among. It were a easy life, where nets set up in the rivers and fish to feed the whole village just jump right in em. Don't even take but two folks to watch it during the days and nights. Leave so much time for folks to do what they want in the plentiful season.

All the peoples do what feel right. Some call theyself mens some call theyself womens some call theyself everything and nothing at all. Don't matter none to nobody. Everybody just together, singing and telling stories and fashioning copper pots and painting and making music and dancing. Folks free to retreat on they own and come back into the world when they ready, and no one blame em none.

What a burden it lift off them all when nobody got to worry bout proving they got a right to be alive. More joy, more love, more time to be more when you aint got to get nobody off your neck. She know it aint that way for everybody and she happy she be one who get to live here, who get to just be.

Here, she have the respect of the people and the sisters for the way she running the shop. It come natural to her and she don't let nobody walk over her none. The ones who got eyes for her still knowing not to mess with Goliwe, that they paper charms don't work on her cause she only got eyes for Tembu. But now, they bracing for something bigger than what her eyes seen thus far.

It coulda made a lovely distraction to be sour with Addis for splitting Tembu's heart, but if Goliwe were anything at all, it were practical. Maybe Tembu love Addis and maybe he only love the cause of Addis, and that part, she repeat to herself, she could not fault him for. When you helping people only one at a time, like Tembu, winning some, losing some, it burrow under your skin like chiggers, and puss up. The heart know that one at a time aint nothing at all. One at a time be the real distraction, one of Tembu's healing salves that smell nice and hold you over till the doctor can fix you right.

Now Addis come and Goliwe know the sticky smell of cedars all these years in Meroë were a false comfort. Sturdy trees that circle the town warn't gon hide them. The river that flow on the edge of Meroë were an escape route, not a lifesource, not a guarantee.

The acres of farm, the hope in the store she run, the hundreds of warriors, the bevy of little children, both born free and made free, and Harold the Bronzer who making bronze pots just for the beauty, for the joy, and Linus, the cook, who painting beautiful pictures that remind Goliwe of another world possible; Goliwe know it all mean nothing cause none of them, not one of them really be free.

She never think to hate Addis for setting fire to they lie. Goliwe feel something like relief. Here it were, right in front of her, what she been fearing, what been lurking behind the shadows of her mind ever since Mama Biny and Oba Achebe tell her bout her mam and where she come from. It had come, at last, the moment of truth, and she were ready, though she not sure what for. Ready to fight? Ready to die? Ready to live without fear? To Goliwe, Addis were all of those things. If Addis could be, why not she?

-32-
ADDIS

It were dark in Meroë when Addis, Tembu and Achebe set out to see The Eboro. Achebe and him oil lamp lead the way and Addis follow, with Tembu at her heels, sucking in him breath every time she stumble a little. It make her chest feel heavier every time she hear him.

At first, she like to be near him, she like the way he look at her with what she think were longing, but then she see the same look on all they faces...even Mama Biny. At first, she grateful none curl up in horror at the sight of her wounds, none staring, transfixed. She feeling a deep sense of pride when Thom calling her a hero, wanting to put it in the oji papers. But her fever gone now. She still a little dizzy, but she thinking clearer and surer. She don't understand what they think of her and she don't like it and she wanting none of it. She feel them all, when she were laying there, helpless, and they looking like they mouths filling up with spit for they pig to fatten and reach the appointed hour...all but Achebe.

Achebe mouth were clean, him eyes not glassy. He were an upright man, with a speckled beard what hang past him neck. He want to know what be true, so he say, --Take her to The Eboro. Whatever they was all hoping Addis gon do for them, she see Achebe don't believe it, so it were him she trusting now. She quick up her feets to be closer to Achebe and farther from Tembu's sighing.

--Oba Achebe, Addis start the Eboe just to hear again how it drip from him lips. --I have never been to a village governed by a woman.

Achebe look to Addis out the corner of him eye, duck under a low tree branch and keep moving uphill.

--Been to many villages, have you?
Him words fall like winter rain. Addis feel a rush of heat fore she answer soft, --No, Oba Achebe.

She slow her feets down again behind Achebe and trip a little over a crawling root.

--Careful, Addis! Tembu say in him loudest whisper,

176

reaching out to her.

--I am fine! She say back, pushing away him hand and keeping pace. --Tell me, Tembu, what do you mean, calling The Eboro *Eboe debilment?*

--I am a Christian, is all, Addis. I do not believe in fortune tellers.

--Do not speak ill of The Eboro because you did not like what she had to say to you, Achebe say, keeping stride, but with a voice so commanding it make Addis shiver.

--No, Oba. Of course not.

--What did she say to you that you did not like, Tembu? Addis ask, more than curious. She get the sense that what The Eboro tell him change the whole course of him life and she must know of it. Tembu say nothing. Achebe answer in Eboe.

--What The Eboro says is for you to do with what you please. You need not share her words with others. As for the Christian, you would do well to know the role of the ancestors and heed the teachings preserved at all costs in the wretchedness of this world. That's for your own sake, Christian or no.

Tembu continue on in silence but behind Addis back she can feel him brow furrowing. She do not like it, how comfortable she feel with Tembu's face, etched in her memberings in such a short time. She think of Ekwueme just then and know what he might think of a Eboro. *Sssk!* He say to such things. *Your Gran Gran had her a Eboro, too, or caint you member it? Sssk!*

Slowly, Addis own mouth start to fill up with salt water. Her face get hot and she start to feel dizzy. --I am fine! She answer nobody's question. But she warn't. Her legs get shaky and she feel Tembu behind her, holding her steady.

--Oba! She needs water. We have to stop.

--Just for a moment. We must keep going.

Tembu lean Addis up against a tree and give her him pouch of water. She take it and mutter, dālụ́, between gulps, but don't look at him, grateful for the dark so she don't have to look him in the eyes. They still such kind eyes but she thinking now he don't see her when he look at her with them. He see somebody she not and somebody she might could never be. She know it, even if he don't yet know it. And one day he gon look on her just like Ekwueme done, betrayed. She not wanting that at all. Not again.

--It is time, Achebe say. --We cannot keep The Eboro waiting.

Addis push off from the tree slow and regain her foothold. Steady, she follow behind Achebe and ask, --How The Eboro know we coming?

Addis get hot again on the back of her neck that she ask such a fool fool thing, but Achebe don't make her feel bad for long.

--It aint that she know we coming necessarily, but she know something coming. The gift of The Eboro be in the knowing, but not necessarily knowing something specific. But even I feel it. There be a shifting in the earth. Got to hurry so we can be back by dawn.

Addis want to ask Achebe what it mean, a shifting in the earth, and when she caint think of the answer on her own, she do.

--Movement, Addis. People coming this way. It may not for long be safe in Meroë. That be why we seek The Eboro now, while we can.

--And bring her rations? Is that what you have in your sack?

--Yes, Addis. We take care her and she take care us. And we gotta be quiet now and move as quickly as possible.

Addis fall silent and try not to think of who all Achebe feel coming on the wind. She fix her eyes on the flickering flame in the oil lamp Achebe got stretched out in front of him. She look to everything the flame touch...the bending trees up the hillside, the yellowing leaves in they path that fallen fore they time.

She suddenly smell rich earth, like she hadn't been smelling since she were laid up. Her body seem to be coming back to itself, though she warn't in no hurry to see her reflection in a mirror. She stiffen thinking bout what Haynes done to her face, to her. She were born of a hunted people, and now she sure she look the part, a prowling beast.

It make Addis swallow hard down her dry, scratchy throat. She don't want to think bout what they make her. She think instead bout the smell of the sap-covered leaves she walking on and the fresh, turned-over earth. She hadn't seen none of Meroë since she come, and she aint seeing much of it now in the night, but Addis know it warn't nothing at all like Wellesbury.

Still, in that moment, she sure all she need to smell be dirt and leaves and she could find herself at home just bout anywhere. She could leave Meroë tonight and keep running til she hit the lands beyond the Falls. Long as she get there fore winter come, she might could make it alive. She aint need The Eboro to tell her it were time for her to go away from these people and they watering mouths. Achebe warn't gon miss her none.

Addis look up to the faint outline of the trees above her, they sturdy branches. She could climb these trees and be lost to Meroë forever, she were certain. All she need were the strength to get up the first trunk...

--We here, Achebe stop and say and Addis trip and slam her face right into him strong back. Her face feel like she running through a maze of jagged branches and she gawk like injured fowl.

Tembu rush to face her but she turn from him and press both hands against the sides of her face, fraid it might slip clean off her head if she don't. When the stinging get softer, she look up to see a log cabin covered in brush in front of her, on the rough side of the hill they was climbing. It have no windows from what Addis seeing. Achebe set him lamplight down and Addis caint see clearly no more the house of The Eboro.

--Go in when you ready, Achebe say and hand over him sack of rations to Addis. --She know you here.

Addis want to ask Achebe more questions but she don't. She pick the bag up and walk to the door. She go to knock but the door creak open and Addis got to shield her eyes from all the light coming from the oil lamps all round the cabin. Addis walk in and her eyes adjust to the light and focus in on a timeless woman. Skin like sable, big silver hair in tight curls round her head. If ever again Addis dream of what Ala earth angel of Chúkwú might could look like, she gon see The Eboro in her cabin, this night, surrounded by oil lamps, smelling of pressed olives.

--A clever crab what escape from a trap with all her legs in tow, The Eboro say and Addis draw closer to the satin voice.

--I know you, The Eboro say in a Eboe unblemished by strife. It make Addis stop where she stand, out of the trance of The

179

Eboro. Addis try to match the strength of her voice and the perfection of her Eboe.

--Great Eboro, I assure you, if we had met before, I would never forget it.

--Your grandmother, Dido. She is alive in you.

Addis walk to the table, float more like it, and sit down across from The Eboro.

--What do you know of my Gran Gran? You cannot be much older than my mother, and my Gran Gran never traveled up to these parts.

--A clever crab, indeed. You know how to survive, I will grant you that. But what you do not know of, I would speak far less assuredly about.

--Then tell me. Did you know my ancestor?

--Think carefully about the questions you wish me to answer. My time is precious and my patience thin. Why have you come?

Addis push the sack of rations across the floor to The Eboro.

--Great Eboro, I have brought you gifts. They told me...

--They?

--The ones I came with. They said you would know what to do...what *I* am supposed to do.

--Do about what, child? Speak clearly.

--I killed someone.

The Eboro laugh heavy and low and her body shake in a way that tell Addis there were nothing heavenly bout her. The Eboro were as real as she and it make Addis angry at first, then sad. Warn't no magic gon save her.

--You will kill many more before your life is over. What else? These words make Addis gut cave in on itself.

--You have seen this?

--I have.

--Then you have seen wrong. I am not a killer.

--No?

The Eboro look amused and it make Addis angry again and she break the Eboe.

180

--You know I aint mean to do it? What they celebrating me for? I aint saying it don't fill me with joy that that man don't breathe air no more. I aint saying that at all. I kilt him. I done it. But it warn't on purpose. I aint my Gran Gran. I aint no warrior. Not really.

The Eboro stare so deep into Addis it make her soul shake. The Eboro laugh long fore she bring back the Eboe.

--What did they teach you on that plantation? A warrior is more than what they tell you in stories.

--I do not want to fight or kill. I want to hide, and I want to live.

--Purpose does not stand at your door and ask you if it can come in. It does not ask you what you want. It reshapes your life to fit itself. Purpose is to be lived, not chosen.

Addis get up out her seat then.

--You are wrong, I can say no to this death.

--You try my patience.

Addis sit back in her chair, drained and dizzy.

--I am not myself. I am sick...

The Eboro start again.

--Indeed, you can say no to a revolution, but you cannot say no to death. Death will take what belongs to it, despite what you have to say about it.

Addis start to believe it and lose hope.

--You have seen this...that I will kill again?

--You will kill and be killed, Addis. Yes, I have seen it.

--And what you have seen, can it be changed? Can I change it?

--Why would you bother? Everyone must die.

--But not at my hand! Tell me, who are these others I will kill so that I can change it?

--Death follows you wherever you go and in its pursuit of you, it will swallow whole those who love you. They will bend their ear to your voice and they will die because of it.

--Then I will hold my tongue and run! I will run far from this and live in secret for the rest of my days.

--The rest of your days are soon spent.

Past tired, Addis feel relief to hear this.

--Death is a release I can bear. It is a life with guilt that I fear.

--Well then, rest well. Your guilt will not eat at you for much longer.

--Eboro, I beg you! Speak comfort to me.

--I cannot speak what I do not see. Comfort was never in your future. You are a fugitive killer. The way for you is grim and lonely. Though many men will love you, they will pay the cost for it with their lives. Though many will stand with you, you will shoulder their corpses on your own.

--Then you must tell them! Now, you must go out there and tell them that I am not the one they want. You must tell them not to start this war!

--You killed the president of Amerika. The war has already begun. They've chosen you, Addis Agụ, and they will follow you. You are lady liberty, the very fragrance of freedom, she laugh. --They will not abandon you. They will fight for you and they will die for you. To them, this is worth dying for.

--So I will run. I'll tell them I'm not the one and then I'll sneak away and run alone. I'll keep North until I reach the Falls. Then the war will end and no death will be on my hands.

--Why have you come?

--For answers! To know what I'm supposed to do!

--Then, I'm afraid you have come to the wrong place.

--What is this game you're playing? Tembu was right; I never should have come here.

--Tembu, she coo. --Another who did not like what I had to say. But I only say what I see.

--You mock me when I have come to you for help!

--No person can help you. Whether you stand and fight or flee and hide, your burden is yours alone. No one can really know it. You will make choices that cause others to die and because of your choices, you will die.

--No. I do not accept that.

--And whose world depends on what you accept?

Addis clench her fists in her chair, a hot tear streak down her face and sting her wounds.

--Addis, you bear far too much guilt inside you. Shouldn't a mother die for her child? Shouldn't a lover die for their beloved? Shouldn't the wicked people of a just God be made to tremble? If this life has taught you anything it ought to have been that death is a mercy, even for the evil. You can flee if you like, and yes, they will find another champion. Hearts are fickle...you do know that, don't you? And yes, that champion might win or lose, just as you might win or lose. The end of the cause I do not see. But it will be just as it was meant to be.

The Eboro rise out her chair and hover over Addis. She place both her hands on either side of Addis face, close her eyes and hum. Addis watch her swaying side to side in fear, not knowing if The Eboro blessing or cursing her. Then The Eboro just stop. She open her eyes and take her hands off Addis face and say,

--The swelling will go down in a few days. Take that comfort with you as you go.

Addis want to speak her anger, want to say she feel cheated. This hiking through the woods and uphill when Achebe felt a stirring in the earth, for what? Addis warn't healed, didn't have no good answers, felt no comfort. But she say nothing. She get up from the table and start for the door. She don't turn round when The Eboro say, --Careful, Addis. When everyone seeks to mold you into what they need, you must be certain of who you really are.

Addis walk out on The Eboro and all she prophesying. Achebe don't speak when she come outside, he just readying hisself to move on, but Tembu run to greet her. --What did she tell you? Tembu wanting to know and Addis be silent.

--What The Eboro sees is for you and you alone, Addis, Achebe repeating. --Don't feel compelled to tell it.

Addis look Achebe in the eye and say, --Nothing.

Achebe nod him head and set out on the path downhill. Tembu follow behind him and Addis come a few steps after. When Achebe get far enough ahead, she grab hold of Tembu's arm and ask him to tell her what the old witch said to him to make him so angry. She feel him arm shake with a small shiver. He don't turn to her, don't look at her, just keep walking and say, --I hope I never have to tell you.

-33-
HEATHCLIFFE

HERO KILLS PRESIDENT, STARTS REVOLUTION. It were treason to write it, (in Eboe or not) let alone publish and distribute it, but here Heathcliffe were, doing all three. And why? Heathcliffe warn't no warrior.

Never shot a gun in him life nor wield a knife. Him pap never teach him or him brother violence, yet here Thom could slit a throat without a single thought, crush a man's skull in him hands and wipe the slop on him pants after. Heathcliffe been fearing for Thom many years now, what he turn into after they pap were kilt, the blank whiteness behind him eyes. Now, Heathcliffe were sinking into despair for him own self.

He were a dead man. One of him closest eight folks in Camden were a rat, he just know it. Rarely any ojis at all in Camden, yet the soldiers come here to camp out, to watch and wait. He hear a soldier say, --Someone's helping these menors. They must be! Heathcliffe know he bout to give them what they waiting for, deliver it right into they hands, and it make him sweat something fierce. He scratch at him beard as he read and read again what he write in plain English for all to read bout the girl they calling Addis Agụ.

The Wellesbury Rebels have risen up under the command of Addis Agụ, in a coordinated attack on the corrupt nation of Amerika. Working on two fronts, she ordered the slaves of Wellesbury to attack the overseers and masters of every plantation within a 20 mile radius while she, in Philadelphia, killed the country's first president, William Henry Burken. Though she was briefly accosted by President Burken's overseer, Rutherford Haynes, who gave her a deep gash across her face, she outwitted him and escaped alive and is now known by her followers as The Striped Woman, Agụ. The Wellesbury Rebels now occupy Wellesbury and her armies across the states grow in number daily.

Addis Agụ makes it known this day that there is no peaceful response to the violence of slavery, which includes the abduction, rape, murder, forced labor and dehumanization of Afrikans. Addis Agụ makes it known this day that all ojis and freedom-loving warriors of all races should join them in defeat of the barbaric institution of slavery and its champions. Addis Agụ makes it known this day that she and her warriors will not surrender, but will continue to fight

184

until this nation makes good on its promise that all people be treated equally under the law, starting with the abolition of slavery and immediate full citizenship of all who live in this land, with restitution paid for generations of stolen labor, pain and suffering.

Again and again he read it and know it be more than him own death sentence he writing. Countless ojis will be slaughtered for these words, even those with no knowledge of Agụ or what he done fabricated in this article to fan the flames of war already burning. And why? And why?

Maybe it will help, he hope. Maybe ojis and allies really will line up side by side and take to task a nation of thieves. Maybe it gon fail and Agụ gon be slaughtered fore she ever make it out Amerika. Maybe the time of war be so short it gon slip quietly from the minds of the children, so much so that when the time comes for membering, nothing will be membered save a wild soul who kill a president and were swiftly put to death for it, leaving all they efforts in vain.

Heathcliffe want to do what him brother ask him, want to follow in him pap's footsteps, want to die someone who done something for the good of him people, all people. But it warn't lost on him that he were gonna die, if he print one more paper or not. It make him to thinking bout how he start printing this paper for Leo so many years ago.

Leo were him friend, sure enough, a good fella married to a smart woman named Zora. They come to Heathcliffe in the cover of night, asking for a life and death favor. Along with the town paper Heathcliffe printing, maybe he can print a oji paper Leo and Zora gon write, called *Eziokwu*, and Heathcliffe scoff. --How can you ask this treason of me?

He want no part of it. Leo were him friend, what did he know of the others? Were he to give him life for them just like him pap done? He had Thom to take care of. It were too much for Leo to ask of him.

Heathcliffe membering them times now, the right and the comfort to say no, to say it don't involve him none, if he don't want it to. Leo promise to pay for everything, to no avail, so then ask Heathcliffe to at least forget he mention it, spare they life, and

Heathcliffe say of course and they go on as friends, like nothing changed, though Heathcliffe know everything done changed. It make him sick to know it.

But nothing worse than to see Zora so low as when some no-color men in town finding out she were a reading oji. They chase her down and knock her over with her baby boy in her arms. Baby hit him head on a rock, caved in one whole side. He cry and cry for days, dying, til Leo have to take a pillow to him. The day they bury that baby, Heathcliffe say, --Write the paper. I will print it.

So Leo and Zora staying in Camden, when many other ojis fleeing to Meroë. Leo and Zora staying and they writing the paper together, anonymous. Some parts they writing in Eboe, some parts in English, and through the years, it helping many ojis and allies on the Tunnel learn a common Eboe. It spread out the word *oji* far and wide, for those who aint want to answer to menor no more, who warn't quite Eboe or at least warn't sure.

It give them something to be that recognize all parts of theyselves, Afrikan and Amerikan. It helping the Tunnel organize theyself up and down the coast of the country, making a coalition of folks helping oji slaves escape to freedom and Heathcliffe getting to be a part of it, even if he risking him life and Thom life to do it. Then, all the sudden, they warn't just surviving another day no more, they doing something what matter to people. They giving hope. They shifting the earth for a new harvest. And it feel good.

Until Leo done something he shouldn't. Heathcliffe warn't never sure what Leo done zactly. Walking, talking, reading, breathing in a black body. A year back, some no-color men in Camden finally done had enough of it. Heathcliffe found Leo and Zora charred up inside what left of they smoking cabin.

Heathcliffe were wrong to think he could protect him friends or hisself. He want to run to Thom, but Thom out at sea with Bartemus, and Heathcliffe were all alone. He pack up some small stuff and think of some places he might could go. Maybe Meroë would take him. Maybe he go to the lands beyond the Falls. Maybe he just drift in the sea til it take him away from here. But when he digging under the floorboards of him bed for the box with him gold pieces in it, he see in tact the first *Eziokwu* they ever done.

Heathcliffe sit in front of the fire and cry while he read front page to back.

The mission of *Eziokwu* read like so, *To give the Oji people, a sense of somebodyness, while working to establish liberty, equality, justice and community, under the law, in word and deed.* Heathcliffe could not let *Eziokwu* die with him friends. He start making him own connections with nearby folks on The Tunnel, getting some to write articles the coalition need to keep going. He learn to write Eboe since he been speaking it so long with Leo and Nora, and even learning how to write Eboe.

Most of all, he got him 8 no-color Tunnel men and women to take the papers up and down the coast, since he aint hearing from Thom and Bartemus in some time. That make him all the way in. He get to exist inside *Eziokwu* in a new way that fill him with promise and equal terror for what were sure coming.

And now it were here. Heathcliffe take one last look at him words, then the picture of Addis, take a long swig of port, then head to the printing press set up in the side room of him cabin. He take til just fore dawn to print one hundred and one copies of the last *Eziokwu* he ever print. He make eight stacks of thirteen papers, wrap them in brown paper, tie them up in sturdy twine and carry them out two at a time to him small buggy. He make nine stops in the twilight hour. Tell him crew of 8 each to deliver they papers to they usual stops, being sure not to get stopped by no soldiers. He give them each gold coins…more than usual under the weight of the occupation…and then he make one more stop to a Camden no-color journalists and leave a copy on her doorstep. Then he ride off as quiet as he can back to him cabin to wait.

Just as the sun were waking up over the mountains and he finishing up the last of him port, the soldiers come and break down him door with torches. The captain waving *Eziokwu* with Addis face cross the front, but Heathcliffe don't hear what they saying. He be in a dream with a swaying Addis smiling at him. And he smile back as the torches come down on him, him printing press and him log cabin.

-34-
BARTEMUS

I t were the most unsteady night Bartemus ever spend in Meroë. After all they pillaging up and down the coast, Meroë were him resting place, healing place. That were til now.

After he and Thom make it back unscathed, he go straight to Mama Biny and tell her bout the soldiers afoot in Camden and what they say bout soldiers going town to town in search of Addis. He were glad to hear Addis leave without them to see The Eboro. Time were not with them. He never seen Heathcliffe so fraid or Thom struggle so much not to kill them soldiers in they path. Things were getting out of hand and whatever word The Eboro got to say could only help.

He and Thom taking first watch with a line of warriors round Meroë. On second watch, he and Thom lean up against a tree and nod off a bit, but Bartemus don't never take him hand off him blade and Thom stay steady on him musket.

--Whew! Looka here, a woman say and Bartemus and Thom jump up at the sound. --Never think we gon catch these fools sleeping!

Bartemus see quick it were Amadi talking and the rest of they pirate crew laughing; she the one they leaving in charge when he and Thom got other business.

Damas like to joke round like Amadi, but he were deadly as anything moving with a arrow. Newby handle the money. He were runty and folks don't pay him much mind, which make it easy for the fella to rob anybody blind. He could add up any number in him head, quick as flash lightening. A honest thief, so they all trusting him count. And then Louis. Louis were quiet and have him a good mind for plotting, and him tricks saving all they skins more than once. After Thom, if anybody Bartemus wanting on him side, it be quiet Louis.

--What's the word on weapons, Amadi?
Bartemus asking after they all had them a quick laugh.
--Pick up bout 200 hundred guns. We aint test em, though. Don't know what work and what don't.

--That's real good, lady, Thom say, --Real good.

--Left em out on the ships with the rest of the crew a ways off in the bay, Amadi say.

Thom nudge Bartemus just then and they see Achebe coming down through the woods with Addis and Tembu. Bartemus get up to greet them and Thom follow, telling the crew to wait there. Bartemus and Thom meet Achebe and them at the heart of Meroë, then go inside Mama Biny's cabin.

The spicy smell of roasting cinnamon hit Bartemus right off and he breathe it in and out. The energy in the room bounce back to him and he feel him blood pulsing through him veins. Mama Biny were getting ready for something, he know it by the smell, and him whole body ready now, too.

--Bịa ebe a, Mama Biny say to Addis and the girl come to her in the middle of the room.

--What will you do, Addis Agụ? Mama Biny ask and he want to know too, what The Eboro tell Addis, what word she have for them all, but he stay silent.

--I will try to go North, beyond the country lines. Alone. Bartemus feel him throat tighten at the words. This were not how it were posed to be.

--No! Tembu yell it and surprise them all. Mama Biny don't look to him, just put up her hand to silence him and he quiet.

--You are Eboe, Adaeze. Daughter of kings. Fear does not become you. Make your choice. Mee ya ọfụma.

Addis look away, upset, ashamed, Bartemus caint tell.

--Tembu, Mama call him to herself. --You will help gather rags and salves for Addis to take with her to keep wounds from infection.

--But, Mama...

--Go to Goliwe's hut and see that Addis has some food for traveling.

--Addis, you caint go...

--Tembu!

--Mama! She don't even know what happened at Wellesbury!

Addis lift her head at this.

189

--What happened at Wellesbury?

Tembu turn to her and tell her how the slaves revolt, killing all the watchmen, whether they no-color or oji. He tell her that the same happen at plantations all round Wellesbury and how all the slaves from miles over hole up there now, preparing for war.

Bartemus see Addis chest drop, but she say nothing. She don't look to Tembu or Mama Biny or anyone, she just run past them, out to the heart of Meroë, a wide open field. Then she shrink and rest on her knees.

Tembu start to go after her but Mama Biny voice boom in the wide room.

--Let her go. She will answer when her name is called, and not before.

Tembu stand in the doorway in front of Bartemus, frozen for a moment. Then he leap out the door after Addis and Bartemus call after him. Bartemus caint believe he would disobey Mama Biny so, but looking out the doorway, he see what push Tembu to defy her.

Out from the woods, a no-color man were creeping toward a hunched-over Addis. Tembu were yelling for Addis to run and Bartemus break out of the cabin toward the man, wishing he had him ax handy...the man would bleed where he stand. Bartemus hear Thom breathing close behind him and all a sudden, warriors of Meroë running up from all sides and the no-color man drop to the ground with him hands in the air.

--Thom! Thom! Help me! I am just looking for Thom!

The man yelling and Tembu stand between him and Addis. The warriors stand with Tembu and Bartemus stand back and let Thom break through, musket slamming against him back.

--What's your business here, Grant?

Thom pacing when he ask the man on the ground. Bartemus get a hallowing in him gut and walk closer to Thom, but don't touch him.

--Bad news, Thom. Real bad news.

The man begin to cry and Bartemus see Thom's fists ball up at him sides and Bartemus get that tightness in him throat again.

--State your business and be on your way, Bartemus say in a way that make Grant shake.

190

--It's your brother, Thom. Cliffe is dead.

Bartemus drop him head and feel the air escaping him. Him head get to pounding, him mouth dry up. Bartemus know he hear fear in Heathcliffe voice when they was speaking, he know Cliffe seen death coming for him. Bartemus know it been years coming, too, working that paper so long, working with the Tunnel. He begin to regret ever going to Camden last night, asking Heathcliffe to risk him life like this, what with soldiers all over the town. It were selfish. It were wrong. It were cruel. And it were all for nothing.

Bartemus hear nothing for a long time but the *click click click* of Thom's musket butt banging against Thom's back as he pace. Bartemus swallow hard and wonder how it feel when the urge to kill get to pumping through you like he see it doing in Thom. That be what making him pace so. Bartemus seen it one too many times and he know it warn't gon be long now fore Thom swing that musket off him shoulder and get to it.

--When. How did my brother die.

Thom aint asking no question. Grant begin to blubber again.

--The soldiers at the port. They caught me with the papers Heathcliffe ask me to carry. I didn't look at them. I never look at what he tells me to carry. I just do what he says, that's all I do is what he pays me for, I swear on my life!

--How did the soldiers know my brother.

Grant sink lower into the ground, head in him hands, shaking as he cry. Bartemus yell,

--Speak up!

--Everybody knows it! Everybody knows it's Heathcliffe who print all the papers that come out that part of town, everybody! The other seven Cliffe gave the papers to must've got away. It was only me they caught. They didn't know bout the others. Still don't, I swear it. And even if they find out bout the seven, they're long gone by now. They got sense enough not to ever come back to Camden. But they caught me and they would've killed me. They would've killed me, Thom!

--Did you tell them where you got the papers, Grant? You can tell me.

All the commotion draw a crowd of Meroës in a circle to

the heart of the village, in the open field, warriors, grown folk and children. Most the village were awake and watching Thom and this no-color man who got him brother kilt.

--Say it, Grant.

--Yes! But they knew already, Thom. They knew. And I had to tell you. With all the other seven gone, nobody knew where you were, nobody could tell you what happened to your brother except for me. I could've run when they let me go, and I will. You'll never see me again, I swear it. But I had to tell you what they done to Cliffe.

Thom quit pacing and stand right over Grant. The back of Bartemus neck get real hot and he begin to brace hisself.

--Oh, Grant. You should've run.

Before Grant could scream out the *No* that were forming in him throat, Thom throw off him musket and lift Grant's head up by the neck. Punch after punch Thom landing and everybody still, everybody quiet while this man do what he can to scream with broken jaws, broken teeth, broken eye socket.

Bartemus ears fill with cries and fists and breaking and Bartemus don't move. He watch the man grow limp and quiet, life drained out. He watch Thom kneel over the body and spit fore he push back him hair with him bloody hands and still Bartemus don't move. The warriors of Meroë stand at attention. Addis stand quiet. Mama Biny, Achebe, Tembu, all stand with the crowd and watch Thom judge and execute.

Some of them in the crowd too young to know bout the Great War of the no-color men, but they seeing firsthand what war look like now. There be sides to this thing. If the others straddle the fence, they gon be spit out. If they choose they own self at the cost of what they fighting for, they gon die. Now everybody know it and they stand in the silence of the lesson.

Bartemus look to two young warriors near him and say, --Bury this traitor in the woods.

The warriors look to Achebe and he nod and they jump to it. Bartemus look round at the stone faces of the children, of the warriors, of Thom. All is still, cept for the oozing wound cross Addis face. These be the scars of war, he thinking. He know it be the end of Meroë. Maybe the end of them all.

-35-
ADDIS

Addis stand watching through the wall of warriors as Thom walk away, straight-backed. She feel something like pity for him for the loss of him brother. Something like kinship for what he just done. She caint right fear him like her mind tell her to, cause she were a killer too, though she sure Thom meaning to do what he done. Still, a dead man were a dead man.

And Thom's brother were dead helping put her face on the war she aint want no parts of in the first place. But she decide then, Thom were a powerful ally and a frightful enemy. She might could call him nwanne, one day. Not today, though.

She watching Bartemus, who moving slowly behind Thom so as to give him space but not so much that he wander off and be gone in grief for good. And then her eyes rest on Tembu. Somewhere in the madness, Goliwe show up and he were holding her. Now, he release her to come to Addis and ask if she all right. She start to say how she fine. How she not even worried bout the revolt in Wellesbury, cause Ekwueme gone out West and she sure he taking Nnene with him.

She ask him to take Chima, like she promise Chima's mam, but now that she think bout it, she knowing he caint leave Nnene behind, not when she mean so much to Addis. And her mam say Billy Lee were going with Sayzare too. Ekwueme got to take him. So, yes, she start to say, she fine. But then she see Tembu aint fixed on her no more but behind her. Addis turn to see a man on a brown, clopping horse with a blue saddle with gold tassels what hang over the edge that she recognize anywhere.

--It's Reuel, she say calm. --He come for me. They found me, she say. She thinking bout running but she don't move, and not cause Tembu holding her arm or the warriors standing behind them.

--Steady! Achebe tell the warriors and they stand at the ready.

Reuel stop him horse and ball him right fist up, pound it to him chest, then up to the sky in the salute they all knowing.

--People of Meroë, Reuel say in a silky Eboe that surprise

Addis with its elegance. --I have brought refugees from Wellesbury in need of sanctuary.

--He is lying, Addis say to Tembu. --He work for Burken's kin. He turn me in to Burken when I was trying to escape. He here for me.

--Steady...Achebe say.

Reuel look behind him and motion with him hands and the refugees start they slow crawl out the woods...near forty of em.

--Wait, Tembu say. --I see Sayzare!

--Sayzare? Addis hear the name and then hear Ekwueme's voice tumbling far away in her memberings. *Sayzare got the caravan. He taking 12 people. They going West.* This warn't West. Something gone wrong. She don't want to think bout it though, not now. Ekwueme in this crowd. Nnene in this crowd. Billy Lee in this crowd. Got to be!

When Tembu get to running toward Sayzare, Addis follow. He stop and embrace Sayzare.

--Alo! Sa fè lontan!

They say to each other, gripping each others arm at the elbow. But she run right past them, past Reuel to get closer to the refugees, scanning the crowd for Ekwueme. He were bigger than most of these, should be easy to spot, but she look and look and don't see him.

--Addis?

A voice to the side of her cry out and Addis turn to see Chima running toward her. Chima. Her heart start pounding.

--Addis!

Chima say as she throw her arms round Addis. Addis hug her back and a tear leak out from her. No Ekwueme. No Nnene. No Billy Lee. Addis break the embrace and ask Chima what happen to Ekwueme and what she know of Nnene and her brother.

--All I know is, one night bout a week ago, Ekwueme come to get me. He say you send him and that I got to run right now. So I follow him and we meet up with all these, Chima say and point to the women and some children from Two and Four Farm who come along with her. --We meet Sayzare in the woods and Ekwueme leave me. He say it were not safe to stay. It warn't til yesterday I hear bout the war, that my pap prolly dead now in it. I hear what you done. So glad you all right, Addis!

--What bout Nnene? What bout Billy Lee? Ekwueme warn't never gon leave them in danger.

--Awful sorry. I don't know nothing bout your Nnene or your brother. We was heading West til there were word a war were breaking out tween the First Peoples and the soldiers out that way. So Sayzare switch the route, say we go to Canada instead, til it were safe to go West. Then we hear bout the soldiers in Filadelfia and almost get caught so many times, though we got our papers. Mine say Addis Agụ on it, so I don't reckon they any more good for traveling safe.

Chima stop all her talking and put her hands to Addis face and near cry. --Look what they done to you. Look what they done.

Addis take Chima's hands in hers and say she just fine. She hug Chima, squeeze her hands and say, --So glad you safe.

Then she turn to the rest of the crowd and see the others who come with them. She see a wide, stocky man and know it be Lew. She look just behind him and there she see her. --Rit! Addis scream it. She run to Rit and recoginze them all from the cellar. She throw her arms round Rit and Rit laugh in return. --How did you get out? How did you escape from Hamilton?

They all start walking towards the heart, refugees and warriors alike.

--It were you who help us, Addis. Hamilton lock us back up while he waiting to figure what he gon do with us. Then, when he hearing what happen to Burken, he flee that night to be by Missus Burken's side. Sabine go with him, of course and he leave Reuel to go bout our killings. We was ready to take him out and run til he say they warn't no need. He fetch us and meet us up with the Wellebury folks he hiding and bring us here. Look like we aint going nowhere for some time though, what with the soldiers and all.

Addis nod and walk on. --Yes, it look like it, she say. But Addis know she aint gon stay. Not with Nnene and Ekwueme and Billy Lee holed up at Wellesbury. How they'll be after Billy Lee, now! The only Burken blood heir. How they'll burn him up like they done Basil. She member her vision, Billy Lee sitting still and smiling in the pit of Hell. She caint allow it. Not her loves. Not her mam's chile. She have to go back for them.

When they all reach the heart, Reuel climb down off him horse and say to Addis, --Forgive me.

But Addis don't hear none of it. *Did you know they was gon take my body from me, the fools you leaving me with? They massa too?* She want to demand it of Reuel but she don't. It were done now.

--Sabi all right? Addis ask instead.

--Quite all right, I assure you, he say. --Master Hamilton would not ever hurt her.

--She look hurt last I saw her, Addis say.

--I come with news for the leaders of Meroë.

Addis gesture to Mama Biny and Achebe and Reuel greet them.

--What news have you brought us from the Burken house?

--Mama Biny, he say, --The news is not good. The new president has authorized the secretary of war to send troops to all nearby villages in search of Addis with instructions to kill or capture. Troops are also preparing to sail for Wellesbury and take back the plantation from the rebels and put them all to death.

Addis hear this and it knock her breath away.

--Troops should be there in a week or less and the rebels must be near out of ammunition. I fear these brave acts were all for naught, he say and look upon Addis face.

But she don't hear nothing else he say. She gone some other place that be warm, a place where she float. She hear the wind whispering to her, Za afa gị ngbe a kpọrọ gị. She open her eyes to get back on the ground and she look to the stunned silence of the people all about her. They hear it too.

Za afa gị ngbe a kpọrọ gị!

Someone in the crowd yell in Eboe, --Addis has brought a curse upon this nation! Hear how the ancestors cry out! Look what she has done to us!

Some rumble low in agreement. If there be any protest, Addis caint hear it.

Addis head get to spinning all a sudden. She filling with the prophesy of Ala, that the horrors to come gon make her a tiger of the people. Her heart be a drum of war and she get to believing what

Ala say to her. She reach her hands up to the sky to receive it. Then Addis move to the heart of Meroë and speak Eboe with a stirring in her spirit she aint never felt this side of living.

--People of Meroë. Hear me!

The buzzing of her doubters fall silent and the silence give wings to Addis words.

--Yes! War is at your doorstep, but I did not bring it to you. Do you think you are safe here? That this bargain you have struck with the no-color governors will stand forever? I tell you, it isn't so.

--The prosperity of the Meroë will always be threatened as long as the law insists that the ojis can live in chains anywhere in this land. What is to stop slave catchers from mistaking any of you Meroës for a slave and dragging you to where you say you don't belong? Your northern tongue? Your place of birth? Your free papers? I tell you this: My Gran was born on the soil of the ancestors, in the seat of Mama Eboeland, the daughter of a king, rich in cattle and land and it did not stop the slave catchers from dragging her onto a ship when her back was turned. These things you love, these treasures you hide behind, this place will not save you!

--If you believe there are two kinds of ojis, the free and the foolish, you are wrong. The luck of birth or the good fortune to escape with your life does not mean your kind of freedom was earned or deserved. In a dirt hut on Wellesbury Plantation, *still* I was born free! And they took it away. And if you do nothing about it, you will forever look over your shoulder for the time when they will take it from you and they *will* take it from you!

--Unless we fight. The war has been here all along and the time has finally come for the Meroë to choose. You can live this illusion of freedom in shame, or this night, you can reclaim the gift that was yours at birth, the power to ensure the truth of freedom for you and your children's children. And in our efforts we cannot fail, for if we die in our fight, all we forfeit is this living death. And if we live, we live free, standing upright, knowing full well that this night we reached the limit on what we would could stomach in silence. Stand with me, people of Meroë, and stand with yourselves!

--AAAYYYA! Mama Biny cry out, pounding her chest with her right fist and raising it to the sky. She move to the center next to

Addis and take her hand and say, --The warriors of Meroë are yours.

--We will fight with you!

Oba Achebe say it and all circle round Addis and begin they war cries. Tembu and Bartemus, Rit and Thom, Amadi, Damas, one then another and the next come right behind. Newby, Linus, Chima, Louis, Goliwe, Harold the Bronzer, Sayzare. The market sisters, all the able bodies come and stand with the warriors of Meroë. Those aint able sit and shout or wave they hands.

--Ike! Addis yelling.

--Mba! The people answer.

--Ike!

--Mba!

--Ike!

--Mba!

And on and on they chant it as the dawn breaking, preparing theyself and they houses for war. *Power through God to the people! Addis Agu will lead us! Chúkwú will not fail us!*

END OF PART THREE

PART FOUR

Isi Kotara Ebu Ka Ebu Na-Agba

It's the Head That Disturbs the Wasp That the Wasp Stings

-36-
REUEL

I t were well into the afternoon the next day when Sabine corner Reuel in the parlor room alone. --I take it all is well? Sabine ask him and he know she meaning to ask what become of Rit and the others. --Yes, my lady. All is well, thank you. And yourself? --The same, thank you, Reuel. And your daughter? How is she faring today?

Reuel know Sabi don't think he kilt Rit and them in the cellar. Aint got to be too smart to know that Rit and Lew warn't gon let one man take them all and live to tell it. But here Reuel stand, nary a scratch on him. So Sabi asking him bout him daughter, instead, and she meaning Addis. But now it were too late to join up with Sabi.

Maybe if he'd a known bout the Tunnel and that she were part of it, that Addis warn't stealing, things coulda been different. He were just a man tryna live good and be good to a man who been good to him, paying him well all these years and treating Reuel like a person. But then here come Hamilton asking him to do something a man aint never gon ask another person to do: kill people in a cellar like rabid dogs to put down. Well, Reuel warn't gon do it.

Reuel gon do what a person ought to do. He never have no desire to go to Meroë all the years he knowing bout it. He have him a nice house on the oji side of the city, good food from Hamilton House and him own earnings; he have him books and write him own poetry and a woman who stop by when she please, and it all work for him just fine, fore all this happen.

But he caint keep them people safe in him own cellar forever; they have to go some place. And he caint just let them wander or Hamilton gon know he aint do what he say he done. Then this man Sayzare find him in the square, ask him the way to Meroë, say someone tell him he a upright man, and he wonder who? He wonder if he aint fooling nobody, if everybody know them people be in him cellar. He decide they got to get out right then. He tell Sayzare he take him and him kin to Meroë if he keep quiet bout it and they all go together. But he aint gon tell Sabi none of it.

What for? Sabi been cut off from her finances and with Hamilton watching her so close, Reuel aint seeing no point to working with Sabine or telling her nothing she caint do nothing bout, no way. He don't even wanna be seen talking to her, lest he mess him own self up. --A daughter, my lady? I have no daughter. I am an unmarried man. You must be confusing me with another.

--Oh. Yes, of course, she say with a sadness that mean she understand she been caught and her role in this here fight be quite over.

--May I ring the kitchen for you, my lady? Have them bring you some tea?

Sabine don't raise her head to look at him. She only say, -- No, Reuel, thank you. I suppose that will be all.

Reuel nod to her and leave her in the parlor, staring down at her empty hands. It don't take him long to find Scott Hamilton perched in him cabinet poring over a stack of letters. --Pardon the intrusion, Lord Hamilton, sir, I have a brief report, Reuel say and Hamilton look up from him letter-writing.

--Yes, go on, Reuel.

--The mischievous stable boy has been released and I have put out word for a new one, immediately. I have prepared your horse myself, should you have any need to go to town today.

--Thank you, Reuel, though I will not be going out today. Haynes and President Lawrence...my, will I ever get used to that?...they will call on me here, later.

--Very good, my lord.

--I cannot say what I would do without you these past few days, Reuel. Not to mention your discretion regarding that awful incident in the cellar...In fact, close my door. I have a bit of a proposition for you.

--Of course, Lord Hamilton, Reuel say and feel him blood rising with anticipation of the task as he turn to close the door.

--I am worried about my wife.

And just as quick, Reuel sink with disappointment, but swallow it. --Of course. She seems quite devastated over the loss of her uncle.

--But with her trickery, the stealing, the lying, she is most

201

unwell, I see it clearly now. She could quite possibly bring this family to ruin with her deception. I had hoped to take her away to the Caribbean, but I am needed here, now. Still, I need her to be watched.

Reuel think quickly. --Lady Sabine wears the face of utter heartbreak, my lord. I assure you, whatever thrill she was getting from the games she was playing prior to her uncle's murder has been quite stamped out by his death. May I be so bold as to suggest you might send her to her aunt's? They can comfort each other. And seeing her aunt's pain will be both punishment for crimes past and assurance against any future ones.

--Hmmm, Scott Hamilton say, furrowing him brows. Reuel get nervous, not sure if he gone too far or not far enough, so he try a final time.

--My concern is for you, Lord Hamilton.

--Ah! Reuel, I am quite all right.

--But these are dangerous times and you are a very powerful man. You should have your own body man. I am surprised you do not have one already, my lord.

--A body man?

--Yes, of course. More than a valet, my lord. An armed man who can protect you.

--You sound as if you have someone in mind, Reuel.

--I do, my lord. I served in the Patriot Army during the Great War in the 1st Rhode Island Regiment under Colonel Varnum. I am very good with a shot, and more important, very dedicated to you and your safety. You are a very good man, Lord Hamilton. I would hate to see you not properly cared for in these trying times.

--You flatter me, Reuel.

--On the contrary, my lord, I never flatter, and as it stands, good men are dropping by the wayside.

--To be sure. A soldier, you say? I never knew this about you, Reuel. It appears everyone in my life has hidden talents. It appears I don't know anyone at all.

--Times are perilous, my lord, not like they were before. I never dreamed my life as a soldier would be of any use after the Great War was won. I assure you, my lord, all skills I possess, both known and unknown, are at your service, as they have always been.

Hamilton look him over awhile, look deep into him, even through him fore Hamilton say, --And so it seems.

Reuel let air escape him slow, through the nose, and he clench him fist behind him back when he realize him hand been trembling.

--You have been a most trusted footman for my family for many years. I have not forgotten.

Reuel nod him head at this.

--I had rather hoped you would take watch over Sabine and keep her out of trouble. But you have raised some valid concerns and I will take them under consideration.

--Thank you, my lord. Shall I ring the kitchen for you on my way out?

--No, no, Reuel, thank you. That will be all.

--Good day, my lord, he say and close the door behind him. Reuel walk off toward him horse with a grin on him face.

-37-
GOLIWE

T he world seem rather quiet to Goliwe, though near three hundred folks traipsing through the woods alongside her and Tembu. Then she realize it were just quiet tween them two. It were decided: Tembu were going with the warriors who gon fight to save Wellesbury. He were going with Addis.

Tembu were certain the warriors were gon need a healer and he were likely right. Goliwe were going up North beyond the Falls with Mama Biny, the children and those men and women who don't want to fight. The njems, Mama Biny call them. Mama Biny ask her special to come along and Goliwe were happy to go where she were asked to go; where she were wanted.

She coulda help Tembu with the injured but he never ask it of her and she were tired of being just a help to him anyhow. So this were good bye.

--Won't be forever, Go, Tembu say soft to her when he reach for her hand as they walk. Goliwe let him, but don't feel no way bout it when they hands intertwine. She caint member when exactly it happen, maybe when she seen him look at Addis, but she already done start to let him go. That way, he warn't leaving her, she were releasing him. To her, that feel better.

--You gotta take both Bartemus' ships? Seem like one ought to be plenty big enough.

--That be Oba Achebe's doing. Guess they hoping to pick up many more at Wellesbury, if they can do what Thom say they can and head off the army marching that way.

--And then what?

Goliwe ask it and don't expect no answer for it, at least not from Tembu. This warn't no well-thought out plan on him part. This were him believing in Addis and needing to protect her, though he warn't no kind of warrior.

To Goliwe, he were on a fool's mission. He gon fight brave and die quick, like the rest of the poor souls at Wellesbury. The point already been made; slavery warn't right and it warn't fair. It warn't *mmadu*. But it also warn't nothing new that no-color folks got no knowings of what be mmadu and what aint, specially when it come to ojis. But were this gon solve all? Everybody signing up to die? Tembu signing up to die? And for what? To prove The Eboro wrong...or maybe to prove her right? She know it were whatever the old woman say to him so long ago what driving him crazy now.

Maybe it don't matter no way. They all got they reasons to fight and she got her reasons to survive. Mama Biny leading all who aint fighting, from the just born to they gran mams and paps. Nobody get to go on living in Meroë. And those who aint budging one way or the other, well, they laying out in the sun all in a row, like Oba warn them. Goliwe tell Oba, --Don't do it! She tell him, --We caint be ones who kill our kin! But Oba only doing what the village agree need to be done; too many risks with the reward on Addis' head; the kin who warn't gon choose a side now be the first to sell them all down river. It were most likely true, but still, she aint never think less of her people in all her life.

She start to wonder why she aint speak up when Thom were beating that no-color man to death. That were the time they all deciding who they gon be. Did she speak up? She caint member it clear, just Tembu saying, --That man saw Addis. He gotta die. And she fine not thinking bout any of it at all. She gon push it out her memberings, she deciding.

Goliwe gon focus on Mama Biny who do listen to her and Mama Biny say Goliwe got to keep them safe, get them to a free place where they can start over and not be looking over they shoulder waiting for soldiers to drop down on them. That were Goliwe's new commitment, and she warn't gon rest til she done it.

--You aint mad, right?

Tembu ask it with a bit of urgency in him voice and it bring Goliwe back into herself and she almost laugh at the question. If she ever feel such a simple feeling as mad, she gon lay down on the ground to die. Like usual, she feeling every feeling there be.

Goliwe turn to look at him now. --I meaning what I tell you while ago, Tembu, she say. --We all got our own path to walk and they aint always going in the same direction. Aint nothing to be mad bout and aint nothing to be done bout it.

She see in him face something be off with him. Maybe he

were mad hisself cause she warn't mad. Maybe he were disappointed. She will herself to be mad at Tembu, to feel something like betrayal at him leaving. She know by the look on him face that be what he wanting. A passionate scene, maybe, like Lotanna and her warrior seem to make at least once a week in front of the store. But she aint never ask Tembu to be more than Tembu, and she aint never gonna be more than Goliwe, not even for him sake, so she turn to him and hug him and say, --Be safe. May Chúkwú guide you.

Up ahead, Goliwe hear the splashing in the water of four of Bartemus crewmen pushing two rowboats out the bushes. She watch them rowing toward the two ships they got stashed far off in the deep of the bay. It take the crowd no time to catch up to the edge of the lake and Goliwe start counting the minutes it take the crewmen to reach they ships and scale up the anchors.

She watch in silence as each team of two haul more row boats into rope harnesses and lower them down over the side of the ships. While the crewmen ready the ships, Achebe call Mama Biny, Bartemus, Thom, Sayzare, Rit, Lew Tembu and Addis to him. Mama Biny call Goliwe to her, and they all gather close to one another out of hearing of the people.

Achebe ask Mama Biny in a low voice, --What you planning? Where you gon go?

--I leading them up beyond the Falls.

--You been there, Rit Greene, beyond the Falls? Achebe asking.

--Yes, Oba. I been there.

--Haps you play a different part in the war. Haps you go with Mama and Lew come fight with us.

--Rit don't go nowhere I don't follow, Oba, Lew saying and nobody object.

--I go with Mama and Lew come with me, Rit say.

--It be so, Achebe say.

Achebe turn now to Mama Biny and hold her a last time and whisper the tongue of they love. --I will find you, beyond the Falls, my light.

--Peace, my heart. I will wait for you, she say, and Goliwe turn from watching them to see Tembu next to her all a sudden.

Tembu holding her mighty tight. He smell her neck. He pat her teeny curls, an angel's hair, he always say. --I love you, he tell her and it crack something in Goliwe. She hug him tight, like it be the last time and run her fingers over the creases on the back of him neck. She count each one in her head and impress the feel of him collarbone against her cheek, deep into her memberings. He kiss her neck then the line of her jaw then her lips fore he back away. --I will see you again, Goliwe, he say to her and she nod and turn from him to draw her tears back into herself.

The next touch she feel behind her be Mama Biny's.

--Name the number who come with us, Goliwe, Mama Biny say quiet.

--We are forty-eight njems strong, Mama Biny. Two hundred and twelve go to battle.

Mama Biny nod her head. --Write them numbers down. They caint be forgotten.

Mama Biny hand Goliwe a long black pistol with a gold butt and some bullets and powder. It feel heavy in her hands and just for a moment, she overcome with the feeling of dying embers, of the endings of things. But she know she got to swallow it.

--You take up the rear, Mama Biny say, and Goliwe tuck the gun into the belt of her dress.

-38-
ADDIS

I says we snake round the Potomac, Sayzare saying. --We dock in the bay behind the Great House, ou konprann mwen? They never suspecting us cause the dock at Five Farm on the other end of Wellesbury be much deeper, made for bigger ships where they sending out they harvest and such. That be where the Amerikans gon be sailing to, for true.

Addis hear Sayzare speak of the lay of Wellesbury like he live there and it take her aback. --How you know so much? She ask him and he shoot her a look like pity or guilt, maybe both, she caint decide, but she know she don't like it.

--I been all up and through the place, on land and sea, Addis Agu. Awful sorry bout Maman Taddy. She were a bon kinda woman. The best kind.

It shake Addis deep inside her to know Sayzare had dealings with her mam. But what? She want to demand it, stop everything til he tell her just what he know bout her mam, but she just nod her thanks. This warn't the time.

--Good plan to come in by the Great House, Addis say instead. --That be where Burken keep all the cannons.

All they eyes flashing at this. --How many cannons, Agu? Achebe saying to her.

--Seven cannons, Oba, but they from the Great War. Don't know if they even working. They been sitting round like dressings all these years.

--I can get a cannon to work. Seven gon do just fine, Achebe say. --Since Sayzare and Bartemus both knowing the way to Wellesbury, aint no sense in both being on the same ship. Sayzare, you go with Thom and Bartemus lead the way with me. We needing equals on both ships in casing something go wrong. Sayzare what you membering from the revolution on your island?

--Membering all I need, Oba.

--Amadi been in the Great War too, so she go with you and you train these warriors every day what to be expecting. Take my lieutenants Landover and Harmon, they know my signals. They gon help train them for war. I will take my two strongest, Malium and Dober. Addis and Tembu gon come with me. We got us another healer?

Achebe asking Tembu and Tembu say Goliwe were the next best, but now she gone. Addis face fall a little by the way he say it, like he so full of regret. Then Lotanna come forward.

--Oba, forgive me for listening. I will work as a healer.

--Lotanna, you were posed to go with the njems North, Thom say, angry to see she done stayed behind. --Does Mama know? Or your sister?

--Aint no safer traipsing beyond the Falls with winter coming than getting on these ships. I stay cause my man going with y'all and you needing a healer on your ship. Everything Tembu get he get from my farm, so if Oba allow it, I going.

--You going, Achebe say and it settled. --Aint nobody we don't need.

Just then come a no-color man dressed in black riding up on a horse, out from nowhere and too close. Achebe loose him pistol and aim dead at the man. Soldiers on the shore see Achebe and aim with him. But Addis see the blue and gold tassels on the horse and cry, --Wait, Oba!

The man pull hard on the reigns to stop a ways from the warriors and climb down off the horse with hands raised and reigns in one fist. --Please! The man say in a high and trembling voice. The man take off him hat and out come spilling the straw-color curls. Addis cry again, --Wait! It is Sabine!

--I mean you no harm, Sabine call out as she walking forward.

--Izuike! Achebe call out and the warriors on the shore lower they weapons but stand at the ready. Sabine back away, unsure she safe. Achebe hold fast to him weapon and Sabine seem to know she aint no more welcome than any other no-color rider.

Achebe step forward between the people and Sabine.

--Why have you come? Were you followed here?

--No one has followed me, she say with a straighter back and reigns on her tongue this time. --I have come to go with Rit Greene.

--We know no Rit Greene, Achebe say and tears find the corners of Sabi's eyes. She search for help in the crowd and spot Addis among them. When Addis meet Sabi's eyes, she step forward.

Sabine caint hold in her relief. She run and hug her. --Addis! You are alive!

Addis smile and hug her back. She want to tell Sabine she sorry bout her uncle, but she aint, so she saying nothing.

--When Scott caught me I thought sure enough all of us would die. But I've gotten away from him now. I'm free!

--Why have you come here? Achebe say short of patience.

--Please. Take me with you! I have knowledge of the Army shipping out in the morning.

–We have no need of your knowledge, Achebe say.

--I have food and weapons here, she say and go to her horse to show them.

--We have no need of your food and weapons, Achebe say.

So, Sabine just cry out, --Have mercy!

Tears come and choke her while she speak in a panic, voice so thick with French she almost caint be understood. --I cannot help with the Tunnel any longer. My money has been cut off. I am a prisoner at Hamilton House and in this country. Rit promised me she would take me from here when I have done all I can and I have! I just want to go with her, like she promised.

Achebe look to her sternly. --How long you helping on the Tunnel.

--Over a year I helped, sir, a year! Money, food and hiding! It is my turn to get some peace!

--Peace!

Achebe scoff. --How much money did your family give to fund the Amerikans in the Great War of the no-color people?

Sabine face fall, she seem confuse and stuttery. --I...I don't know. They gave much money, went bankrupt to do so. It is why I am here in this country, married and slaved to Scott Hamilton, to restore the wealth that was lost. But it's all gone now! Can't I stay with you now, for some rest? My life is in danger!

Oba shake him head low at this sad woman and Addis get to fearing. Sabine done seen her now, she done seen the ships, the

210

warriors, the weapons. She no different than the other Meroës what lose they life for seeing what she seen. If they kill they own kin as protection, warn't nothing to stop them from killing Sabine. She mean well enough, poor fool, Addis thinking.

--How you figure you safe with us or we ought to protect you? Name the no-color fool what gon hang the niece of the president? We the ones in danger. And you the one still got room to do something bout it. Your money help corrupt it. Maybe your voice help right what never been right. Clean your house fore you come crawl to ours. Work with your own people to end what they done destroyed. That be the way we work together.

--I have been a friend. I have risked my life!
Sabine start to say for Achebe interrupt her.

--And what of your own house? Bring your house to the table, clean. Then we can eat with you and call you friend.

Sabine grab at her head. --Where will I go? What will I do?

--We have our own course to chart, Achebe say. --Best you be on your way.

--Addis...Sabine start but Addis thinking of the Meroës who not surviving this very day while Sabine getting to live and Addis got no comfort for Sabine. Addis say, --You say you wanting to help, well this how you help us and your own self. You don't want your daughters sold? Work on your own people, free your own self. Our pain aint your bridge to freedom.

Sabine stand in bewilderment of it all. --That's not what I am meaning to do! It's not what I am meaning to say!

She try to say but Tembu cross over her to speak to Achebe.

--We losing the sun, Oba.

--It be so, Achebe say back. --Go now, he tell Sabine who linger just a moment longer hoping they might could change they minds. When she see they aint, she back away, near trot to her horse. Addis just yell after her,

--Sabine! Get rid of the colors. They gon see you a mile away.

Sabine get to her horse and rip the blue and gold saddle from it. She take out a knife from a sheath in her belt and cut all her curls in a felling swoop. She wrap the hair in the colors and throw them behind a bush. --My colors are gone, she say. --My allegiance is to God and the people of Meroë and to myself. I will do what you ask.

She jump back on her horse and ride on.

--That might could come back to haunt us, Oba, Bartemus saying and Thom nodding.

Achebe turn to them both and say simple, --Might could.

But Achebe don't dwell on it none. He turn to Amadi then and tell her --Split the army! Linus, split the rations! Dober, split the ammo! And they all doing it. He turn to Thom and tell him once they get out the bay into the sea to man the oars, that they gon need the wind and muscle to get to Wellesbury fore the Amerikans do. Tembu go to split medicines and salves with Lotanna but she already empty out the store in her sack. So he guiding Addis into a rowboat they piling in by the twenties and heading out to Bartemus ship.

She climbing the rope ladder up the ship like a tree and feel at home right away on the sea, though she aint never swam but that once when she almost drown not long ago. When she land on the main deck, she feel a rush, but not the kind she getting right fore she have a vision. It be the kind what tell her the vision be real life, and all round her.

This ship were magnificent, a beauty like she never known made by hand. It warn't like Hamilton House, the intricate prison for dolls, or the Great House at Wellesbury, what hold the bones of them kilt, in body and spirit. To Addis, this ship, with its cannons on every side, were a weapon against evil. A harbor from danger. A dream from Ala that all gon be well. She don't know nothing bout ships or war. Soon, though.

--Agụ, Bartemus call to her and she snap from her reverie. --You still having that map, what lead to the Island?

Addis unsteady when she see him outstretched hand waiting for her to pull the map from her sack. --What of it, Bartemus?

--Oba wanting it, just in case.

--In case of what?

--*In case*, he repeating and him eyebrows raise with a knowing Addis understand enough to be fearing they aint necessarily shipping off to Wellesbury afterall. She thinking maybe it were best they not go; maybe it were a fool's errand to fight a war with two hundred warriors and whoever still standing at Wellesbury. She hear the words of the Wellesbury preacherman in her ear just now.

Meaningless! Meaningless! Says the Teacher. Everything is meaningless, preacherman say. It warn't nothing to Addis in this moment to think a war were a waste of time and life. Who could win against forces so evil and so big? In case they wise up, in case they fleeing to the Island instead, Addis give Bartemus the map out her sack but don't look him in the eye when she do it.

At first, when they sail out the bay, she were wanting to stand on the upper deck and breathe in all the freest air she ever breathe. But now she follow others down to the lower deck and set herself up on a hard bunk to rest. In the cold belly of the ship, she close her eyes and wrap herself in a cotton quilt and will herself to dream of her Gran Gran, of her mam as a chile, of the promise of the Great Thing her mam were to do. But behind Addis eyes were nothing but white and she wake after a short while with her face throbbing.

-39-
ADDIS

Ajerk in her head were what wake Addis and she hit it square on the narrow wood slate of the bunk above her. It hurt but not like the rest of her face, which she hold on to with both hands, lest it jump clean off her bones.

--You all right, Addis?

Tembu jump up from the bunk below her and ask it in a way that comfort and enrage her. She want to be cared for, she want to be cared for by Tembu even, but she don't want Tembu to fix her. She warn't no broken thing. Battered, yes, and confused and afraid and alone, but she cast herself down to the depths of the sea fore she let Tembu try to fix her. She long for Ekwueme in that moment. Ekwueme who just let her be.

--Yes, Tembu, she say quiet. --I fine.
Tembu reach into him bag and pull out a dulling salve. He try to rub it on her wound but she block him with her hand.

--Thank you, I can do it, she say and rub the salve on slow. It sting at first then she feeling nothing but cool and breathe in the eucalyptus like fresh air.

--You feeling dizzy? Can be a bit rough your first time on the sea.

--How you know it be my first time?

--A hunch, he say with that smile that make Addis smile then swallow hard and look away. --Chew this, he say and hand her a cluster of roots.

--Ginger, she say, and he nod and say, --It gon keep your belly still.

--I know what ginger for, she say and he laugh at her.

--All right then, he say and offer her him hand. --Come down from there. Go with me to the main deck. You ought to see the sea.

Truth were, the only time she seen the sea were in her dreams, the one where Ala drowning her with a wave. She fearing it. But Tembu have him hand outstretched to her and she take it and jump the short ways down from the bunk stead of using the ladder.

Him hand linger in hers fore she move hers to her side. She reach back up to her bunk and grab her sack off it fore she follow him up the stairs to the main deck.

Without the food and the map and her beautiful silk dress, the sack feel like nothing on her shoulder, but it were all she got in the world. It were the sack Sabine giving her, then her mam, then Tembu, each after they saving her in they own way. It were a reminder of what she never get to do for her mam and what she got no choice but to do now.

--Tembu, she ask fore they reaching the main deck. --You sure we heading to Wellesbury?

Tembu turn back to her, puzzling. --Caint be more sure, Addis, why?

--Bartemus come and ask for my map. The map to the Island.

Tembu put him hand on Addis shoulder and they slow rock like they dancing as the boat sway side to side. But aint no lightness in Tembu eyes.

--Folks who warn't gon fight or flee to the Falls, *Meroës* who warn't gon stand with us getting kilt this very day, Addis. Our own brothers and sisters, who mighta turn you in for half of the $50,000 on your head, let alone all. Not to mention how much more a traitor might get for turning all us in! Aint no place but Wellesbury we going. Aint no other place.

Addis nod, knowing she ought not have thought otherwise. Tembu turn and climb the stairs up to the main deck and Addis follow behind, wondering how Agu just come and go inside her when she please, gifting her wisdom and courage then taking them away. Addis feeling every warriors' eyes on her when she climb up to the main deck and she wish Agu would come to stay. Addis just straighten her back in they presence tuck the fear away as she meet they eyes. She gon stand straight-backed til the Tiger come again, she deciding.

A strong wind catch Addis in the face and bring her out of her thoughts into the now of this great ship she standing on. She look above her and the clouds in the sky matching the big white swabs of cotton she standing under. She lift up her head to breathe new life in herself. All round her be stormy blue water and cloud and

215

fog. For a moment, the fear just blow away. She never feel so free.

--Agụ! Achebe calling out to her from the fog on the upper deck at the back of the ship. --Meet me at the stern, he say. She don't very well know what the stern be but she climb up the stairs to the upper deck on the back of the ship. She pass Bartemus who steering on the main deck and him crew who taking him orders.

Achebe be alone when she catch up to him, staring out into the fog what settling over the sea. --It is beautiful here in the middle of the world. I never want to leave, she tell him in quiet Eboe.

--Careful what you say on a ship, Agụ, he say. --Ala may here you and grant your wish.

--Yes, Oba, she say. Addis look to him and long to understand him, this great elder of Meroë, who spilt blood in the name of Amerika, what hate him, what shackle him and him people. --Will you tell me of the Great War, Oba? I have never known an oji who fought there. My guardian told me Burken put a stop to ojis fighting to get their freedom.

--Your guardian speaks the truth, Agụ. But I had been fighting for months by that time. The *colored guard*, they mocked us with.

--Why did you do it, Oba? If you were already free?

--I was thinking of more than me, Agụ. My wife was not free. My children, not free.

--Mama Biny?

--No, he say, and offer nothing more and Addis know better than to press him.

--What is it like, Oba? To fight a war?

--It is like no other thing. Gunfire and the clanging of swords and bayonets. The burning plains. Grown folk screaming like infants. The dropping of bodies right in front of you, right behind you, right next to you. In all my years I have never seen as much blood as what ran through the fields in the Battle of Fort Mose. War is a thing to be survived but never overcome. If you survive, it is a terror that sits in your chest til the day you die.

--Why do it again, Oba? Why go back to this?

--You ask it as if there was a choice.

--Don't we all choose our paths?

--To a degree, Agụ, yes. But when Chúkwú commands, you

216

obey. And I heard Chúkwú when you spoke. I heard Chúkwú enough to kill my own people to protect us. It is just as you said. We were at war whether we would go on to Wellesbury or not. We were always at war. Some run and hide, some survive, but the warriors, we fight.

Addis turn from Achebe. She want to tell him she aint even meaning to kill Burken. Course she thought on how it could be done: A slip on the stairs, a fall off a horse, a trip in the garden, the roots coming to life and wrap all way round him and open up the earth to swallow him whole. Course she thought on it. But who woulda thought a 17-year-old woman chile with iron in her hand would do in the legend of Burken, in him skivvies no less? Not even Addis ever thinking this.

She walking far from Achebe, to a corner of the stern and looking over the edge to see how fast the waters moving behind them. She look over the other side and see the oars sticking out into the water from the lowest deck, rowing like mad, the whole length of the ship. Watching the oars move in harmony make Addis all a sudden feel the fastness and it make her dizzy. She can almost hear the ocean singing, *Bïa, Chineke*. She reach in her pocket for the ginger root and suck it desperately until she calm. All the while feeling Achebe's eyes on her.

--A prophet is not an angel, Agụ, he say to her, full of the calm missing from the sea.
She turn back to him at last.

--What do you mean by this, Oba? She fearing when she ask it, like she know he done seen all through her mind.

--I mean that Chúkwú has sent the earth angel to speak to you, bathe you in the spirit. But Chúkwú has not cured your imperfections or your personhood. You are mmadu, Agụ. Fully so. That means there is strength and weakness in you, wisdom and folly. Do as Ala guides you and you will continue to inspire. Do not concern yourself with the things you are not. Chúkwú performs the miracles. You are the blessed vessel. Do not forget it.

Addis feeling almost delight at these words. She look round though and see the warriors and crew still eyeing her while they working, with that hunger in them, like she the only one what could fill them. They aint hearing Achebe's words. They aint knowing she be no kind of angel. Worse, they aint knowing what The Eboro done seen, that all who follow her gon die. That *she* gon die, and soon. Whatever delight she were feeling gone away with these memberings. Still, she don't hesitate when she asking,

--Do you believe everything that The Eboro says?

--I believe that The Eboro is another kind of vessel of Chúkwú. There are many kinds. I believe The Eboro sees and knows things I cannot see or know. That is her gift and I honor it. But she is not Ala and she is not Chúkwú. What she sees and knows, she offers freely to those who seek her, but with all earthly vessels, she has her limits. She is not the magic. You are not the magic. Only Chúkwú is magic.

To hear this overcome Addis. It break her and she break the Eboe.

--What if I don't believe, Oba! What if I don't accept The Eboro or Ala or Chúkwú! What of this God who could stamp out all evil long ago but instead sits still? Leave *me* to kill evil. Leave two hundred warriors to fight a battle with *thousands*!

She say it loud and bold and immediately get to fearing who hear her. She wonder if Achebe fearing too, wonder if she keep talking so loud, they gon go on and right the ship, send it back to the bay at Meroë, bring back to life the bodies spilt in the name of war and honor.

--You suggest that Chúkwú has left us and I say it is not so. Chúkwú can withstand your doubts and questions. Your frustrations and fears neither harm nor disarm Chúkwú, Agụ.

--My name is Adaeze! It never were Agụ!

--I have my own questions, Achebe continue in Eboe, not paying her no mind. --Why use a child with so little sense of herself, let alone the world, to do something so great? Why not me? I have served Chúkwú faithfully all my life. I have protected the people Chúkwú gave me to protect. Even while at war for a country that does not love me, I have fought in the name of Chúkwú. I have led Chúkwú's army in Meroë and have kept the peace with the state. All this I have done.

It is too much for Addis to bear and she got to say out loud,

--The Eboro tell me folks gon follow me blind and they gon die for it. I gon die soon. Aint nothing I can do bout it. She couldn't a been more clear bout that. I am sorry, Oba...

But he just keep right on talking Eboe. --I have the heart of a warrior, the mind of a leader. I do not doubt Chúkwú. I never doubt Chúkwú. So why not me? Then it comes to me simply, Agu. Never would the president accost me into his bed.

Addis look away from Achebe, shaming and confused, but he looking straight at her now when he speaking.

--Chúkwú sees and knows. It must be the least of these to fell the giant. It must be the womanchild, tormented from womb to womb. You must swing the sword and I must die protecting you. It is so.

--I am a warrior and a servant, Agu, he say. --That has been my role. I have served Mama Biny and now, I serve you. But you want me to lead you. You beg for it. To be led is all you have ever seen. It is all you have ever known. A symptom of the illness you never knew you had, but it is there and it must be rooted out. I will not lead you.

--The evil the no-color man put on the oji woman for many generations, Chúkwú has seen fit to use it to bring about the freedom of all people, he say. --You are the reminder that we are all mmadu, especially our chained up brothers and sisters. You are the reminder that we have knowledge, that we are wise, that there is a truth and a freedom worth fighting for and without all of these things, there is no beauty. People cannot be less than mmadu. We cannot allow it.

--Do not fear, Agu, he say. --It is not you whom we blindly follow. It is not you for whom we sacrificed those who would not stand with us. That weight is not on you. It is Chúkwú in you that we see and respond to. It is Chúkwú in you that we follow, even unto death. I have heard it said that a child will lead us. It is so.

Addis cannot hold back her sobs when she asking him, --What do I do, Oba, Father? What do I do?

--I will not lead you, Agu. Know the difference between counsel and surrender. All you know is a man's will over your life, so you seek it out in me, but I will not do that to you. Be greater than what you have known. You already are. And do not break your Eboe simply because you are angry. Eboe can withstand your anger.

At these words her heart come flooding out at Achebe in groans that tell it all and Achebe go to her and hold her like him daughter longsince dead and the father she straining to member. And just in time for night, the fog lift.

-40-
TEMBU

Nightfall come and Tembu see Bartemus sitting in him quarters up deck, watching as Achebe and him best two warrior lieutenants Malium and Dober slipping through Bartemus glass and wood doors. The leaders take a seat in the velvet chairs Bartemus got circled up in him parlor. Tembu bringing up the rear and catch a puzzling look what mean Bartemus don't like Tembu being there none at all. Tembu aint a man built for war, he know it. But Achebe saying nothing and Bartemus saying nothing, so Tembu saying nothing too.

--What of Addis, Oba? Bartemus asking.

--Resting, Bartemus, resting. And we will let her.

--Very well, Oba, Bartemus saying and he get him a pen, a inkwell and a long roll of paper off him wooden desk in the corner. He begin to map out Wellesbury. --The Amerikans gon enter down through Five Farm way out here, Bartemus say, pointing with him pen. --So, we gon have to draw them up to House Farm, here, in range of the cannons.

--With our backs to nothing but the sea, Bartemus? We will be trapped should those cannons not fire, Achebe say. --The fight will be over before it begins.

--We must get there first. We must test the cannons. We will push them out as far as we can with time we have, but those cannons are our only salvation. The Amerikans will never suspect that we could use them.

--And what if they hear us, Bartemus? What if the testing gives away the surprise? It is too much to risk, Dober say and Malium agree. Achebe ask Bartemus,

--How many miles between Five Farm and House Farm?

--It is a great distance, Oba.

--Impossible. Impossible, Achebe say with him hand stroking him chin as he think.

--Not impossible, Oba. We just have to surround them. We will not be the only ones with our backs to the sea. And do not forget, the rebels at Wellesbury have done fine on their own. We come to help them, not lead them.

They all sit in Bartemus' spell as he spinning a battle plan what might help the rebels. When Achebe finally agree to it, they letting out a sigh. It warn't the best laid plan, but it were something. They warn't going in so blind. It were decided that Malium and Dober gon begin training the warriors with the bits of the plan they needing to know in the morning, but it all warn't sitting well with Tembu.

--Oba, what about Addis? He asking.

--She will train with Dober, Achebe answer.

--Shouldn't she stay on the ship, where we can protect her?

Bartemus cut him the same look from when he first joining this meeting of strategy. Then break the Eboe and say, --This a *war*, Tembu. Aint nobody safe and aint no place safe. Fool fool to think it otherwise.

--But you seen what she do for the people! They fighting for her! They ready to die for her! She is the Agụ. You know how it will break them if she dies.

--Seem it gon break *you* if she dies, Bartemus saying. --The warriors gon fight with they Agụ or fight even stronger to revenge they Agụ. Do not mistake it, Tembu.

Tembu caint believe what Bartemus saying, and worse, that nobody stamping it down.

--Oba? Tembu pleading for the intervention of him leader. After a deep sigh, Achebe say,

--Bartemus speaks the truth, Tembu. Addis has done her part to incite in the warriors a sense of duty and a need for freedom. Her bravery in killing Burken alone is enough to give our warriors hope to win. Do not be confused, Tembu. Our mission is not to keep Addis alive, but to fight til every oji is unshackled and restored to the full power of mmadu. Do you understand?

Tembu see him leader peering into him with earnest, waiting for the answer they all need to hear, the answer that mean Tembu got the mission, that he know it bigger than just one person can hold, that he aint gon do nothing foolish. Tembu knowing what they all needing to hear and so he tell them, --Yes, Oba. Yes, I understand.

Bartemus' eyes cut into him but Tembu don't look away. He

need to make them trust him, respect him. --I said, I understand, Tembu say direct to Bartemus. A long pause happen for Bartemus say back.

--Good. We done here for the night.

Tembu get up to leave but he notice no one else do but they all staring at him. He stare back a moment, catching each of they eyes, fore he turn and leave Bartemus quarters.

Outside in the raw, cool air, the night feel to Tembu a safe place. The sky aint never been so clear, the stars too great to count. The mystery of the whole world seem just within him reach.

Inside that cabin, in the light, that be where the danger lay waiting. Those men who seeking to use Addis. Those men who don't love her. Those men who not caring if she live or die. To Tembu, those men, him friend Bartemus, him leader, Achebe, those men be just as much the enemy. Right away he knowing what he have to do. He knowing he the only one what could do it. He settle on a plan of him own in moments, breathe in the clear air and head below deck to the sleeping quarters.

The warriors aint all sleeping when Tembu walk past they bunks, but Addis, in her middle bunk, were breathing slow and steady. He stand there and watch her awhile, til he notice warriors round him watching him. He climb into the bunk just below hers and lay awake and waiting, listening, counting her every breath. He warn't no warrior, for true. He warn't no killer. He were a healer, always been so. But he knowing what he have to do if anybody come near Addis to harm her. He know what he have to do and he know he not gon hesitate to get it done.

--Sleep well, Addis, he whisper to her in the dampness. --I am here, he say, and hope she hear him.

-41-
GOLIWE

Never in her life Goliwe thinking she gon kill someone. She were far too young to member much from being slaved with her mam or the bloody revolt that make room enough for her to escape to Meroë with a fleeing woman. If she really think on it, she see blood and death be what change her whole life, but she never did think on it fore now.

What were Mama Biny thinking giving her the gold-butt pistol, telling her, *Take up the rear?* What she seeing of her time in Meroë been a time of peace and contentment. She have a job of note, the respect of the leaders and the attention of Tembu. She have everything she think she need, for a time. A long time, even. So how she even getting here?

Goliwe were just a storefront worker, not a hunter. They barely eating meat in Meroë; warn't no warriors out killing animals for food when Meroë so rich and easy with fish. Animals get kilt only to keep theyselves safe, only when it were necessary. Still, Goliwe knowing nothing of it. She were a seamstress by night. No killing in that nuther. She warn't never ever posed to be no kind of killer.

She were just doing what she were told to. Keeping her ears and eyes at the ready for any sign of trouble. Her hand were wandering all on its own to the pistol in the belt at her waist. It keep resting there on its own, any time a squirrel run up a tree or snap a twig. She were jumpy. She were fraid. Mama Biny shoulda known it, Goliwe thinking. But now it were too late.

She never thinking what she gon do if her eyes and ears do catch something amiss. If a no-color man on a horse come riding up behind them, hair wild and short and spiky like a animal, face scrunched up, determined to catch them. Goliwe warn't thinking up no plan of defense. Mama Biny aint tell her no plan if a no-color horse-riding short-stature man come galloping up behind them waving at them, yelling at them.

Goliwe aint hear what the man were saying, she just see him scrunched up face, him fist in the air and him riding, riding, getting closer and closer to them. *Take up the rear*, Mama Biny tell her, and she aint never done nothing against what Mama Biny tell her.

It were her hands what move faster than her mouth in that instant. It taking no time at all for Goliwe to grab that gold-butt pistol out her waist and cock it like she been taught. She aim that pistol square at the mad man shouting at them, waving with him fists, shouting, and everything go quiet to Goliwe ears. She don't hear the shots what come out the gold-butt pistol, but she feel them coming out.

But they aint come out one after another like Mama Biny saying they would. Them shots come out all at once, then the barrel catch fire and burn Goliwe hand so bad she dropping the gun and seeing the fire sop up dead leaves near her but she aint move. She watching the fire then she hearing the screaming at last and she look up from the fire, from her hands and see the horse down, the man down underneath and both creatures swimming in blood.

Someone pushing past her but she not really feeling it cause she floating, looking down on herself, the blood and the fire. She see from above it be Rit and Lew right behind her, Mama Biny, others trying to get the horse off the man that warn't no kind of man at all.

--Sabine! Sabine! Rit yelling and all go quiet for Goliwe again. In the silence, she stop and think bout the time fore Addis got possessed by Ala and start speaking them truths. Thom were killing some no-color man what made the wrong choice in asking Thom for mercy. Tembu were rushing to Addis aid. Nobody were paying Goliwe no kind of mind. If she'd a left right then and there, who woulda been the wiser?

Maybe she coulda gone West, til she reaching the land the First Peoples still control, then keep going more west still. She hearing bout the First Peoples out there. The originals. She hearing how sometimes they joining together with the ojis and living in peace together. She thinking she coulda join them First Peoples out West, where no no-color man done set him foot of death and destruction.

She caint reckon why she stay back then when every pulse in her body beating for her to move. Maybe she stay for Tembu. Maybe for the only home she ever knowing. Maybe cause she have nowhere else to go, no how. All she know is she regret it, missing her chance. Now she wandering through the woods with a group too big to hide in case of trouble, babies too unknowing to quiet theyself, children too young to have the sense to be fraid, old ones who caint fight, young ones who won't, and those, like Goliwe, who have pistols and rifles hanging from they person but knowing nothing at all bout fighting or shooting or killing or what it cost.

Someone pulling her away from the fire. Other folks stamping it out. --What's her name? A girl asking. --Goliwe? Goliwe, can you hear me?

The girl saying it to her looking into her eyes but Goliwe eyes a haze. --My name Chima. You all right now. Can you hear me? Goliwe?

Goliwe watching Chima shake her but don't come to herself til Chima slap her twice. Goliwe let out a big gasp as she look at Chima who holding her shoulders. --You gon be all right. You gon be all right, Chima repeating and Goliwe shaking her head no. --Mama tell me hold up the rear. She told me! I done it.

--Shh, shh, now. You right. You done just what you were told.

Goliwe wake from her empty sleeping to the sound of coyotes in the night. She find herself on the ground of a tent she aint pitch. A small lamp outside give her just enough light to see the outline of the tent and the shadows of those sleeping in they own tents, nearby. She hear the soft snoring of chiles, sleeping so peaceful, like nothing at all happening today. She wondering what gon happen to chiles like these, who done just today seen more than they ever should. Who they gon grow up to be? What the world gon be like for chiles who so quick getting used to seeing what she done that they can go on and sleep soundly? Goliwe don't want to know. She don't want to stick round to see what horror she bringing upon these chiles, let alone what she done to the man that warn't a man afterall. Sabine. A friend of Rit. A friend of Meroë. Goliwe don't want to know nothing at all.

--MotherFather, God of all, she whisper. --Forgive what I done. I shaming and it weigh me down. Show me what I got to do. I want to leave here and never come back. But not what I want, what You want gon be so.

Her voice fall as silent as her tears, and she lay there waiting for the comfort of total darkness, waiting for Chúkwú to answer or take her for what she done. But she laying for what seem to her like hours, and nothing stir, not even the lamplight getting any dimmer. If it would just burn out, she could run. She feel round for her sack and it be right beside her with all she needing to survive awhile. She gon go where she caint hurt nobody else.

Just then, a figure with they own lamplight come near her tent and Goliwe close her eyes and feign sleep. She feel the figure enter and she look up into the lamplight and see who it be.

--Chima?

--You member me, eh?

Chima set down the lamplight in a corner of the tent but away from the cloth and the tree it were tied to.

--You been out like the dead a long while, I just came to check on you again. Got some water here for you, and some bread.

Chima give Goliwe a pouch of water and the bread wrapped in cloth and Goliwe eat and drink quickly.

--Not so fast, you make yourself sick, Chima saying and Goliwe slow. --You looking better. How you feel?

Goliwe wipe water from her mouth with the back of her hand fore she answer. --I feel like a killer, Chima, how you thinking I feel?

Chima smile a little and take Goliwe hand. --There are other horses. Fool fool for her to run up on us like that, no how. You done just what Mama Biny tell you to do. You protecting us. Everybody know it.

But Goliwe not understanding. --Other horses?

--Yes, Goliwe. We burning the meat so no one eat the panicky spirit, and we sending him off proper.

--But the woman? She lives?

--Oh, you poor thing! The woman, Sabine, yes, she lives.

--God of all things!

--She were startled, no doubt. And it take four folks to get that horse off her, but sides some bruises and whatnot, she gon be all right. You aint seen us take her away?

--I seen...

227

Goliwe get to thinking and plain caint recall what she seen, and what she hadn't.

--You aint no kind of killer, Goliwe, not today.

Goliwe jump up and hug Chima who laugh a bright and wonderous laugh.

--I thought the Lord were gon take me out sure enough o'er it.

--And what for? Begging your pardon, but if God aint take these no-color folks out for what they done to us all these years, I think you safe enough. Sides, you shooting the horse quite square, I tell you! If we'da been in real danger, you'da save us all with your shooting!

--I warn't aiming for the horse, Chima.

--All the same...

--I never gon shoot again, Goliwe say and feel certain of it.

--Not with that pretty pistol, no how. Don't know what gone wrong but it look like it plain blow up in your hands. Lucky your hands aint go with it! It were sure something to see though. What a day, what a day.

--A day I spend thinking I kilt a woman.

--I so sorry no one tell you she were alive. I aint know you aint know. They pull her from under the horse right in front of you. But you just went some place else. Your eyes was all empty. And you been sleeping all the day. We had to pitch a tent round you, afterwhile, when we making camp. You warn't eating or drinking. I were sure one of the njems tell you everything were all right. I so sorry, Goliwe.

--But it aint all right. Don't you see? I look a woman dead in her eyes today and aim a pistol at her. I fire it with hopes to drop her. That aint never gon be all right with me.

--Fine, it aint all right. But what part of war you thinking all right? This our life now, Goliwe. They got $50,000 on Addis head. Who knows what they gon throw in to take the folks who help her escape? We warn't in real danger from Sabine...not from what we knowing so far, anyhow, but after she hug up on her friend Rit, she go on her way, and aint no telling what she gon do, you know? Still, we in real danger every minute we stay in Amerika. Not til we get beyond the Falls can we breathe easy. Don't you see that? Lots of folks lost they lives today. I aint know them, I aint from Meroë no kind of way. But you knowing them, the ones what caint be trusted not to sell us all out. They die for real today. And lots more gon die and it caint be us, you hear me? It caint be us.

Tears welling up in Goliwe til she almost caint see but she swallow them, won't let them spill. Chima lay a gentle hand on Goliwe's neck and look her straight in the face when she saying, --Get you a better aim next time.

-42-
ADDIS

The first light of the morning touch down on Addis as she drinking greedy from her fresh water gourd. Sweat were pouring from her just as fast as she were drinking, so she getting no relief as Dober yelling at her to stand up and fight her again. --Come at me, Agụ! It be death to move so slow, Dober saying and Addis put her gourd down and come again at Dober, fists raised at her chest and getting blocked again at every jab, til finally, Addis land a firm punch on Dober's chin, what send the warrior backward off her feets.

Since the darkest hours, Dober been training Addis in the art of gunplay, how to reload a cannon with no light, to shoot at long range and to defend herself with nothing but her hands. It be a sight to behold for Addis, who aint never seen women lieutenants like Dober, nor any other such lieutenants in action. But now as Dober getting back to her feets and breathing deep, the lesson be over.

--Good, Addis. Enough for now, she say. The two grab they drinking gourds and sip deep as they lean against the side of the ship, breathing heavy.

--Say, how you end up a woman warrior anyhow?

Addis ask it and Dober shrug. –You the first to ever call me that. We just warriors or aint warriors in Meroë. How you end up one?

--Warn't on purpose. Warn't no way for women to train to fight out in the open. Only mens training to be watchmen. That were bout the only job women warn't allowed to do. Every other labor be just bout the same. Doubt if I aint left Wellesbury I'd be a warrior of any kind.

--Well everything been done the way it posed to be, I reckon, Dober say as she get up to leave. --Keep your hands up and your eyes open. Don't let em catch you with your back turnt.

Dober walk back down below deck and Addis finish the water in her gourd fore she make her way to the stern of the ship. She look out towards the sun and Thom's ship, not so far behind. She catch her breath and take in the morning and a calm settle over her.

She were feeling almost content when Tembu climb the steps to the stern to see her.

--Something aint right, Tembu say near a whisper.

The first wave of warriors come from below deck just then and Achebe's lieutenant Malium lining them all up to train. The routine of it all were starting to bring her comfort, peace even. But here Tembu come with him wrinkled up brow. It unsettle Addis.

--What you mean, Tembu?

--Bartemus. Oba. They got them some kind of plan, don't sit right with me, Tembu lean in and whisper. --Don't sit right with me at all.

The first row of warriors kneel just below the edge of the ship and the other rows stagger making windows in the air to shoot through. They fire air so not to waste bullets.

--Reload! Igba!

She hearing Malium, thick and shirtless on the starboard side, yelling commands through him sweat to the men and women warriors with they guns in they hands and weapons strapped all over they body. They practice reloading, getting faster and faster, and they rifles clicking empty once they firing to the sea.

--What you hear?

--I thinking when we hit land, we might not be fighting after all.

--Tuh! Go on, Tembu! All this training we all been doing.

She brush him off and watch the warriors at work but he keep going, raising him whisper.

--I mean it! You might coulda been right, I tell you. I thinking they gon turn you in when we gets to Wellesbury. Kill you even. At least let you die.

Addis frown up her face. She don't want to be so disappointed in Tembu but that be just how she feel. Maybe he been sensing it, her pulling away every inch they get closer to Wellesbury. Whatever were drawing her to Tembu, whatever feeling she had that she could trust him, she wanting none of it now.

She aint never been one who want to be needed by no one. Never. She don't like it. She don't want it and she don't want to need

231

nobody else nuther. She were sick back then. Delirious, even, and feverish. She were weak back then, but now her face healing and her body healing. She were getting her strength back, getting back to her old self. Those few days of needing Tembu done drowned in the sea.

--Fool fool thing you saying, Addis say and turn to leave him.

--You take me for a man with no chest, Addis Agụ.

Addis stop but don't turn back to him.

--You wrong. You wrong by far, she saying, but still don't turn.

--I tell you, Addis, I don't know what, but they mean you no good thing. They say you already done the one thing they needing you to do and that were kill Burken. They saying your life don't matter no more. And when I saying something against it, they shutting me out the meeting altogether.

Now she turning back, looking all round her as she walk close to him. Then she lean over the back of the ship so not to seem suspicious or angry, case anybody she don't see be watching.

--Anybody in those meetings you trusting?

--Fore last night, I woulda said Oba and Bartemus, with my life. The rest be Bartemus' crew and Oba's lieutenants.

--How we gon learn what they up to if we on the outside?

--Leave it to me, Addis. I swear to you I protect you and I gon do just that. Just you be on your guard. Keep your ears in this ship and out that sea, he say fore he walk back down to the main deck.

The first line of the warriors come running up from below with they weapons in hand and strapped all over they bodies. They line up quick in four perfect rows cross the deck and stand at attention. She see Achebe come out Bartemus chambers to inspect the line. He smiling proud, saying they was a fine lot of sons and daughters of Meroë. He salute Malium fore he stop the exercizes with a long blow from a shell horn.

Three men Addis don't know come up from below deck with cloths in they hands. They winding round the warriors and saddle up to the foremast, the mainmast and the mizzenmast, each. Like worms, they inching up the masts with the cloths. It aint til they reaching the top that Addis see what they flying on the foretops of the masts.

The first be a black flag with a slash diagnal through it, right to left. Below it be the Amerikan flag upside down. Achebe were standing back to let Malium work and to observe the men raising the flags. Achebe climb to the stern to meet Addis and Tembu, like a satisfied pap. Achebe signal to the man up the mizzenmast and the man blow a mighty horn of him own. Addis look over her shoulder and see on Thom's ship men snaking up the masts and raising the same flags, slashed black, upside down Amerika.

Addis feel heat rising off Achebe and she don't know whether to back away from it or bask in it all. Achebe just turn back to the warriors on the main deck and raise him right fist straight up above of him, finger pointing to the glory of Chúkwú fore he pound him right fist to him chest then to the sky in salute. --A ghọtara m gị!

He yell it and all the warriors echo the salute with one voice --A ghọtara m gị!

Malium's voice cut through the silence that follow. -- Gbá na áká èkpè!
Malium say it and all the warriors turn to face up at Achebe at the stern of the ship.

--Mighty warriors of Meroë! Look, brothers, look sisters, up at these flags. Below, is the corrupt order of Amerika. The land which steals us and steals from us. We will turn it right-side up til the God of justice makes the unjust answer for their crimes! Eboe kwenu!

--Aeee!
The warriors cry, thrusting a quick fist in the air.

Achebe look to Addis now and Addis look to Tembu as Achebe saying,

--Look brothers, look sisters, upon the black flag slashed from right to left. It is the face of our Addis Agụ! Our tiger woman who will not be tamed or silenced by the weapons of the enemy! The bravery of this daughter of Ala gives us strength and courage. She rises above the corrupt flag and as she rises we will rise! Kwenu!

--Aeee! They saying with another fist in the air, finger

233

pointing to the glory of Chúkwú, tapping that finger to they left shoulder. Addis swallow her uncertainty and smile slight at Achebe as he come to her and put her before the warriors. Addis fill with all the warmth what come from all over Achebe and she stand upright in front of them and say with a loud voice, --Ike!

--Mba!

--Ike!

--Mba!

In no time, she hearing the chanting behind her all the way from Thom's ship and she know they with her. They all with her. She look to Tembu and shake her head and he tight lipped but she pay it no mind. Tembu were wrong, she know it now like she always known it. She hate that she ever doubt it. These her people here. Her people meaning her no harm.

-43-
REUEL

It warn't no time at all fore Scott Hamilton knowing Sabine done run off and warn't likely coming back. The grief were eating him whole and Reuel knowing this were him only window. He climb through it with both him hands, but careful. Hamilton been on edge and aint no telling which way a man gon go when he brokenhearted.

--It is my fault, Master Hamilton. I was concerned with your safety and in guarding you, I left her free to go.

--*Left her free to go?* Hamilton scoff at this. --She is not my prisoner, Reuel, she is my wife!

Reuel wince as Hamilton sit down behind him desk with him head in him hands.

--Of course, my lord, of course. My apologies.

Hamilton waive a hand at Reuel but don't look up when he say,

--No, no, Reuel. Forgive me. This is not your fault. You have been very good to me. Loyal. Hard to find in times like these, and I am appreciative, despite my recent outbursts.

--I am at your service, my lord.

--You don't have to call me that anymore, you know. My wife is gone. It was her title I bought in this marriage. It is not my birthright.

--My lord, if you were only judged by what was your birthright, how much less would your fortune be? By birth or by work, my lord, you have earned all that you have, lost wife or not.

Hamilton give again the look of bewilderment at Reuel, at him capacity to reason and to comfort Hamilton. Reuel keep him eyes and head slightly bowed to be sure Hamilton don't get unsettled by him strong words and gaze.

Hamilton put him head back on him desk and Reuel look up at the clock and get a bit of a panic when he see the time.

--My lord? It is nearly noon. Surely you cannot be late for the president's advisers meeting.

Hamilton look up at the clock and then over at Reuel in a way that fill him with a sort of dred. He pushing too hard, him intentions seeming too clear. He try to think of something else to say but nothing come to mind. He just smile at Hamilton, a worried smile but firm, an uneager smile, he try to manage.

After a long pause, Hamilton finally say, --Yes, of course, the meeting. An honor I did not ask for and do not want.

--President Lawrence needs your wisdom, sir. He is a military man and knows nothing of the Capitol; not the way you do. He will be lost without you.

--How you speak flattery to me as of late, Reuel.

--Never, my lord. I was raised to speak in earnest, and the time compels it now more than ever.

Hamilton look Reuel in the eye and begin to rise. Reuel don't look away and keep him smile steady.

--So you have said. Speak in earnest to me now, Reuel. Mrs. Burken has found her way into the advisers' room, as well, surely a result of Burken's absence of legitimate sons, and nothing more than a symbolic honoring, not to mention the vast wealth and public support that comes with the Burken name. But when I see her, *and I will see her*, and she asks me, *and she will ask me*, why her neice hasn't come for her, what am I to say?

Reuel swallow at the test and think quick.

--A few words come to mind, my lord.

--Go on.

--Yes. Of course, you could say that your wife abandoned you and has fled to God knows where, probably into the arms of some colored gang or another. You could tell them all of her treason, of the shame that she's brought on your family and herself.

Hamilton get to looking uneasy, get to shifting on him feets and leaning into him desk. Hamilton drop a hand below the desk where Reuel caint see. --Is that the truth of it, Reuel?

--Not the way I see it, my lord.

--No?

--The way I see it, Lady Sabi was overcome with grief by the murder of her sweet uncle, the one who saved her from the clutches of certain death. She was unreachable for many days in her grief. You did all you could, of course, my lord, but she was just sick. She began to fear that the revolution in her home country had followed her here, cornered her. That Death was chasing her across oceans and would not stop til it had her. This time, with her uncle unable to protect her, she would not escape. Then, last night, or, perhaps tonight, if it better serves, she became so undone that she ran out to the cliffs. You chased after her, called after her, did all you could, of course, my lord, but my lady was ill.

--And she fell?

--Right off the cliff, my lord. Into the water. In the moonlight, you could see her tumbling against the rocks.

--Ghastly sight. The worst night of my life.

--Indeed, sir. You tried to go in after her, of course, my lord...

--But how could I without meeting my own end?

--Impossible, my lord. Truly impossible.

Reuel stand firm and smile straight. Hamilton nod.

--It would save me much embarrassment, for sure. Certainly would spare me criminal prosecution. But what if she comes back?

--She will not come back, my lord.

--She has no money, no resources. Took nothing but a horse, from what I could gather. That, and a map to an island to which she never wanted to go.

--My lord, Reuel say firm and look Hamilton straight in the eye. --She will not come back.

Hamilton drop him head and balance hisself against him desk and nod.

--I could say she was kidnapped by vengeful menors.

--You could. But that would be very messy. Of coure, you could not have been present when it happened or you could never live it down. We would need other witnesses.

Reuel see Hamilton bristle at the we, like they in it together, so Reuel ease off.

--All resources, including our soldiers, must be used to stamp out this rebellion in the South and any others that might rise up. None can be spared on a pointless mission to bring back a woman who does not want to be found. Instead, my lord, let her be a symbol of what this great nation has to lose, the peace of mind of the meekest and gentlest among us.

Hamilton sit back down, head in him hands, and Reuel

know to be silent and still. Not a word, not a creak of the wood by him feets while Hamilton thinking it all over.

--You are right, Reuel. The cliffs. It's the only way.

Reuel nodding and Hamilton pausing still, looking down at him hands. --More trouble than she was worth. She was always more trouble than she was worth. I loved her, though, Reuel, I really loved her.

--Of course, my lord, Reuel nod, him voice carrying the right amount of solemn.

--It will happen tonight. No need to make a fuss during the meeting of the advisers. We'll all need our senses about us.

--I'll call the coach, my lord, Reuel say and begin to leave.

--Nonsense, Reuel. We will go out together. You will take me. Surely, I'll need my bodyman at a gathering of the president and his advisers.

--Of course my lord, Reuel say, and wait til Hamilton walk out the door in font of him fore he get to grinning.

When Reuel pull the coach up to the Capitol building in Filadelphia, he feel a sense of something shifting. He temper him joy with the truth of the volatile nature of grief. He playing with him own life more now than ever, and a shift go both ways. He open the coach door for Hamilton, who step out and straighten him hat and coat once him feets hit the ground. Reuel tip the valet, who take the coach away to the Capitol stables.

Reuel look all round at the guards posted all over the outside of the buiding in twos. He say, --It seems they're learning to protect what is precious, my lord, and Hamilton say, --So it seems.

Reuel lead the way up the Capitol stairs past two guards who seem to recognize Hamilton and make no fuss. He hold the door open for Hamilton and follow close behind him. --Third floor, Lord Hamilton, a gloved valet say inside, pointing to the north stairwell.

--Do you know the way?

--Yes, good man, thank you, Hamilton say, almost spritely, as he take the stairs two by two, like a man unburdened. Reuel smile at this and hope it mean Hamilton see him as a help, one to trust, one who make him lighter. Time gon tell all, he thinking as he climb the stairs close behind Hamilton.

Guards pacing the halls on the third floor, and one stand firm at the meeting room door where the cabinet were already assembled. At the sight of Hamilton, the guard jump a little and knock at the door before opening it.

--Lord Hamilton, Master President, the guard say and open the door wide for him. Behind Hamilton, Reuel peek inside. He see the new president, the war secretary, Stanton Thompson, Missus Burken and the scar-up man Haynes. He look down quickly fore he meet eyes with that man and say soft to Hamilton fore he enter the room, --I will be just outside the door, should you need me, my lord.

--Very good, Reuel, Hamilton say, without as much as a glance backward.

--Master President, you're looking well, Hamilton say as the guard close the door on Reuel. --I hope I have not kept you.

--Not at all, Scott. Thank you for coming.

--I serve at the pleasure of the president.

Reuel hear Hamilton's steady voice through the door and feel him hold slipping already, but there were nothing to be done at this moment. He already pushing too hard as it were. And Scott Hamilton warn't no fool fool man. He were born into wealth, sure, but he triple what him father gave him flipping cotton.

Scott Hamilton were a businessman above all else and he know how to read people and they intents and whatnot. Grief mighta slow him down a bit, but obviously not for long. It get Reuel to thinking it were just the shame, the fear of the loss of power Hamilton were grieving all along. Sitting in a room with the president, though, give him just the power Hamilton fear gon die along with Burken.

But soon, Reuel start to thinking, what if he set him own self up with Hamilton? Don't nobody know the truth bout Sabine outside Hamilton and he. Sabine were gone, but Reuel warn't going nowhere. It were a risk for Hamilton to trust him and warn't no need for Hamilton to risk nothing. With Reuel out the way, Hamilton be a bird flying high.

Reuel thinking this and get to fearing he gon have to kill Scott Hamilton. Then where he gon go? What he gon do? Reuel catch the guard eyeing him suspicious like, so he turn from the guard and walk a few paces away but not so far he caint hear through the walls.

--How is my niece, Scott?

--Sick with grief, my lady. Sick with grief, of course. She is quite unlike herself.

--I will go with you to her after our meeting is done.

Reuel perk him ears to this but try not to seem like he listening when two guards get to eyeing him. He do what he been taught, he shrink hisself a little, step away from the door some, hold him body loose. The guards whisper to each other, but after a short while, get back to they pacing.

--She sleeps, Aunt. Won't you give her the night? I will bring her by after you've had your breakfast in the morning.

--Very well, she sigh.

Reuel breathe out soft what he been holding in and back hisself closer to the door.

--Time to get going, a gruff voice scratch out in the somberness and Reuel know it be the scar-up man.

--Yes, of course, Lawrence say. --Secretary, what of the troops arriving in Wellesbury?

--Tomorrow at the latest they should arrive, Mr. President. I've sent two fleets of federal troops, near a thousand men. They will bring the animals to justice then secure Wellesbury for the state. They will stand guard day and night, on land and sea, and Mrs. Burken can return home soon.

--We shall see, Missus Burken say, and nothing more.

--Very good. And how many slaves remain at Wellesbury?

--Hard to say, sir. There were three hundred in President Burken's care, and then there were those who joined them from the surrounding plantations. Many of them had small numbers of slaves, but Sheriff Turner had at least two hundred on his own, God rest him. Without casualties, no more than six hundred, and there's no telling how many of those are female and children. Certainly there are not six hundred ruffians for our armed troops to handle.

--We should stomp this out very quickly, then.

--I am not so sure, Master President, Stanton say. Troops

down in Camden have sent word of a treacherous, degenerate newspaper publisher who printed hundreds of copies of a menor paper with the drawing from our advertisement utilized.

--The drawing of that beast? What did it say? Missus Burken speak up.

--Forgive me, my lady. I am told it read, *Hero Slays President*. Reuel hear them through the cracks, gasping. --Treason! Conspiracy!

--It is half-written in some menor tongue, but a translator says they are calling her the Tiger Woman, Master President. Because of the stripe Mr. Haynes gave her face.

--To hell with them all! Lawrence cry out and knock him fist against the table. --I called the Virginia troops to me when I arrived here, hoping to create a hedge of protection around the president. Virginia was unguarded in the attack and our absence has given wings to these brutes. They must be crushed. Any sign of the girl, Mr. Haynes?

--A week I been searching for the wench and nothing, Master President.

--We have gotten some unreliable tips to the war office, Stanton say. --Mostly any menor woman with a misshapen face is being brought in for the reward, dead or alive.

--Heavens! Lawrence say, but Stanton finding it all amusing.

--No need for alarm, Master President. Every menor girl they kill does bring us one step closer.

--Except it does not! Missus Burken shout. --My husband, *your* president's killer has not been found and there is no trace of her and we are no steps closer to finding her.

--Yes, of course, my lady. Forgive me. Forgive me, Master President. We will work harder to find her. But I must say, based on all Mr. Haynes has shared with us, the girl's wounds, the burns from the fire, the fall from the cliff into the water and the rocks below, I would surmise she is quite dead. And that our resources might best be spent stamping out any more sparks of uprising her cowardice and treachery have lit under the menor slaves. It is my recommendation that we drudge the river behind Morrison House tomorrow at dawn, recover her body and be done with it.

--She ain't dead! Haynes spit. --I feel her breathing. The

wench lives, I bet my own life on it. I will not stop until I slit her throat and pull her limbs from her jezebel body.

--Do what you must, Haynes, Stanton say. --But we just need any menor girl body for now. We'll shut them up with it, put them back in their place when they learn what we have done to her body.

--And what of the reward?

--We drag the river, Master President, maybe find a body and maybe take a body, if we don't. It surely would make for a better show if it were a live one. The word would spread fast and wide, knock the hope out of these rebels. *Tiger Skinned Alive,* we'd tell them.

--No! We are not barbarians, Lawrence say. --We will not spill innocent blood to cover up our own blunders. We let her get away and we will find her. Haynes, you will assemble a team and drag the river tomorrow. If she is not found, use one of the girls dumped at Thompson's office and get the word out in the paper of her capture and killing the following day. Then get back to finding her.

--I will need help, Master President. I'm a Virginia man. Sides Hamilton House and Morrison House and the Capitol, I don't know much about the city or who might be hiding her.

--The free camp, Hamilton speak up.

--What are you saying, Hamilton?

--Master President, there is a camp some miles out that is inhabited by free menors. My wife speaks about it often. Meroë, she tells me, is the name. That may yield some answers.

--Very well. Do you know it, Secretary?

--Heavens no. I am a Virginia man, like yourself. This whole state is a mystery to me.

--Could you take Haynes, Master Hamilton? Lawrence ask.

--Not if I wanted to! I haven't the slightest idea where it is. A silence tighten round Reuel throat as he listen outside the door. This be the moment. This be the time or it won't never be.

--But my bodyman, Reuel, Hamilton speak up. --He could show you. He must know all about the menors whereabouts nearby.

--You think I'd let a menor stand next to me and live? The words be a tense, low grumbling, slipping through Haynes gritty yellowed teeth. --Are you such a fool to keep them in your employ, even now?!

--You will be very careful with the way you address me from now on, Mr. Haynes, Hamilton say, calm, fore he turn to assure Lawrence. --Reuel has been my faithful servant for many years. He is not my slave and can leave at leisure, but yet he stays with me. His skill and loyalty are unmatched. He will be of great help.

Reuel swallow all he fearing. He were in now, no doubt. He back even farther away from the meeting room door, so when Hamilton come out, he have to call to him.

--Come, Reuel. We have need of your assistance.

Reuel turn and come closer. --Of course, my lord.

When they both enter the room, it were all Haynes could do not to shoot Reuel on the spot. --I tell you, it aint right, Hamilton!

--Once more, my good man! Once More! Hamilton say.

--Mr. Haynes, that is quite enough! Lawrence say and Haynes crack him knuckles against the edge of the table, but grit him teeth to keep him mouth shut.

--Reuel. Lord Hamilton believes you may have information that could help us in pursuit of the slave girl, Addis.

--Murderess devil! Missus Burken spit.

--Whatever I can do to help, Master President.

--Reuel, what are the odds that she is hiding on the free menor land, Meroë?

--Not likely, Master President.

--He lies! The menor devil!

--Silence! Lawrence raise him hand and Haynes swallow back him spit. --How do you know this is not likely?

--I went out on assignment for my lord Hamilton just last night in pursuit of...

Reuel hesitate, careful not to say Sabine. --...a stable boy suspected of stealing from Lord Hamilton. I rode as far east as Meroë and saw the camp quite deserted, disheveled I would say.

--Disheveled? How so? Lawrence ask.

--Huts were burned, bodies were lined up and burned, men and women too. I believed it to be the work of the Army, though I dare say I did not stick around to investigate further. There is nothing at Meroë, least of all your slave girl.

--We will see if you speak the truth, Haynes say. --You will ride with me to Meroë, show me these bodies and pray you don't join them.

--You will cause neither hurt nor harm to my bodyman or you will live to regret it, I sincerely swear it, Hamilton say. Lawrence speak up too.

--I assure you, Lord Hamilton, Mr. Haynes will do no harm to Reuel and Reuel will take him to Meroë.

--But Master President, if I may ask, who will look after Lord Hamilton in my absence?

--I'll be quite all right for the evening, Reuel. I will do the looking after for myself and my wife.

--Very well, my lord.

--Fetch my horse, Haynes say with a nod of him head and a grip in him fists. Reuel give him a nod of him own and walk out the room toward the stables, hand ever so close to him gun.

-44-
GOLIWE

Goliwe's load getting heavier now that she got a tent packed among her things and a rifle slamming against her side. Her back and legs beginning to cry out to her. She never walk so far with so much on her in all her life. The warriors were going to battle, sure, she thinking, but at least they riding on a ship.

--How you doing? Chima fall back a little to ask her.

--Fine. Just fine, Goliwe say, and put on a smile. Chima smile back and reach her hand out to Goliwe. --You let me know if the load getting to heavy, now. I got plenty room in my pack, Chima say and Goliwe nod.

--Thank you, she say with a new smile, a true one.

Goliwe never thought much bout having a sister round her own age, but Chima make her wonder what it might be like. Kosi and Lotanna have they own sisterhood, and though they bringing Goliwe into they business and trusting her with they store and they private lives, they always seeming more to Goliwe like young aunties than her sisters.

It warn't even they age what done it. Kosi and Lotanna warn't much older than Goliwe be. It were a matter of having things. Being equals. Kosi and Lotanna giving her rewards for working hard and being smart and having sense. But the store were still they own store, not hers. They giving her a job and letting her earn wages and helping her build a home of her own in Meroë. To Goliwe, it making all the difference. When money get into it, it make true sisterhood seem near impossible.

Maybe to Kosi and Lotanna, they seeing it different; maybe they thinking of the home they lending her, the store they letting her run as proof of love. Maybe they think giving money to women for any ole thing be as sisterly as a woman get. Maybe that were the right way to look at it, Goliwe decide.

Goliwe thinking over her life and wonder how, after so many years in Meroë, she not really knowing what a family posed to feel like. Maybe she shut down them feelings when she losing her mam or when she getting dumped in Meroë to begin with, like she shut down her feelings when she seen the way Tembu look at Addis. It make her to wondering if she been seeing the world wrong all along and never know it. Who say she getting dumped, anyhow? Who say those what leave her in Meroë aint save her? Who say Tembu leaving aint to free her? She think on these things and get to feeling more alone than she feel in a long time.

--What you thinking bout over there? Chima asking and Goliwe happy for the chance to ask her.

--You ever have any sisters, Chima?

--Me? No. I were the only one of my mam. My pap had more, to be sure, but I aint never know much bout who was who. Never gon know now.

--Why you say that?

--My mam be dead, not too long ago. She were kilt by the same man what cut up Addis face and kill her mam and pap too. My pap be dead too, but he were kilt in the rebellion. Fighting on the wrong side, he were.

--Oh. Awful sorry, Chima.

--Death be just another bridge to cross, Chima say and it strike Goliwe.

--Reckon so, Goliwe say and it take her off track. Instead of wondering what it mean to be a sister and if she ever could be, she get to thinking bout what death be. She like the thought of a bridge, another path to connect you to another path. Chima were clever. Goliwe like that too.

--You a real good sister, Goliwe say. --How you get like that when you aint never had no sisters?

Chima shrugging fore she reckon, --Maybe that be why. If they got any sense, folks get real good at giving what they wanna get back. Nobody ever looking out for me, sides my mam. It what made me love Addis so, even fore I met her. She having this legend of a gran gran by the name Dido who coming straight from Eboeland.

--True?

--True. But that aint even the best part. Dido poisoning Burken's father to death to save her daughter from the raping and then the daughter grow up to have Addis and Addis father die too trying to save him girls from the raping. She got a man of her own, too, Ekwueme.

--Addis do? Goliwe ask and wonder if Tembu know any of it.

--Oh yeah. He a fine man, too. Beautiful and proud. A blacksmith. He would choke a massa with him own whip to protect her, everybody know it bout him. I just never have that, you know. Someone who think I worth dying for. It what make me want to know Addis, even long ago.

--Get on, Chima. Aint you ever heard of Chúkwú Christ? Don't you know Chúkwú Christ die for you already?

--Course I knowing it! But seem to me Chúkwú Christ dying for just bout any ole body. I want someone who be a little more choosy when it come to dying, you hear me?

Goliwe holler. —I aint never heard nothing so silly in all my life! She laughing.

--Aint it terrible? Chima say and they laughing together.

Goliwe stop laughing when she hear a commotion way up ahead. He far off, but it look like Lew running back downhill toward them. —Something's wrong, Goliwe say and take hold of her rifle so it won't slam her when she get to running through the crowd toward Lew, Mama Biny and Rit. Chima run right by her side and the sea of folks part for them.

--How many you counting? Rit asking Lew when Goliwe reach the crowd circling round them.

--Seven armed overseers for near fifty slaves, mostly women and chiles, but a good number of men. Twenty, what it look like. The master got him a wife but no chiles there from what I gathering. Looking sure we can take on seven men.

--Why we got to take on any of em? A elder asking. —Why we caint keep traveling on til we reach beyond the Falls?

--We could, Mama Biny say. —We could keep moving and act like Lew aint seen what he seen, near 50 of our brothers and sisters tied up, mostly women and chiles, some men.

--And so we got to free them?

--Caint no one free another, Rit saying. —We been born free. We gon teach some people that.

--If we do what y'all saying we do, word gon get out, a

woman with a baby sucking at her breast say. —Amerikans gon be on our trail more than ever if they aint already. We not just gon be heading to beyond the Falls then, we gon be fleeing there!

--When we do this, Rit say in strong Eboe, --captives will go free. When we do this, we buy time for Addis Agu and the warriors who fighting in the South. We send a message to other captives that they can be victorious in battle and to Amerikans that the fight is on all fronts. When we do this, Amerikans will know their time to plummet the earth is near a bloody end.

--It is decided, Mama Biny say. --We will not leave these people behind. We will split the camp into the able-bodied and those who will stay to protect our children. Rit and Lew will take the able-bodied deeper into the woods and train them at gunplay. The rest will make camp here with me. I will stand guard over our babies and the unable. And we will loose the chains off these people this very night! Kwenu!

--AEEE! The njems shouting.
But something well up in Goliwe and she got to speak.

--Mama Biny! Please!
Mama look down to Goliwe, surprise on her face.

--Yes, chile, speak up.

Goliwe start to wonder what come over her, what she got to say or do with any of this. She warn't no agu. Ala never visit her with nothing. Yet here Goliwe stand with a fire in her what gon choke her if she don't speak out. She don't want to seem like she against self-defense...and that be all the killing of any slaver was, self-defense, but she plain and true don't want to be a killer. She got herself a taste of it and bitter it were on her spirit. No way they could win with bitter weighing down they spirits.

--What if we asked them if they want freedom?
The crowd began to scoff and cut they eyes at her and hiss at her to be quiet.

--Let her speak! Chima say, and the njems mutter quieter.

--Rit Greene never taking with her to freedom no man nor woman nor chile who don't wanna go. Once they come along, she hold them to it, by force if necessary, but only once they chose to come along. Now we caint have with us nobody not wanting to come. It's dangerous to all us. So we surround that plantation, guns at the ready, and we silence those slavers, sure enough, but we ask the people do they want to come. If so, we defend them with all we got. If not, we leave them to their prison and go on our way.

--She right! A man say and others start to agree.

--Yes, chile, you speak wise, Mama Biny say. --We will do as Goliwe says. No one will be forced into freedom. At the end of daybreak, we will go.

--For Addis Agụ! Chima say.

--For Addis Agụ! The njems repeat, fists in the air.

Rit look to Lew and she smile and he smile and nod back, but Goliwe caint think of nothing else but that she aint now, and never gon be, ready for war.

-45-
ADDIS

Addis were kneeling down at the stern of the ship sipping from her gourd and hiding from the blaze of the morning sun. Dober leave her sore, soaking in sweat, and tired as she ever been, but better, much better. Addis were reloading her rifle and the cannons like she were born to it. She were landing punches much more than one. Her aim were getting better and better and Dober tell her as much.

She were just getting used to the choppy waters and the steady rocking of the ship, using the ginger less and less, when she hear a warrior cry, --Land! Land! The horn get to blowing and the warriors jumping up out of they bunks and running up the decks in swarms, guns strapped up at the ready. Addis hop up to the edge of the ship, she caint hardly believe what she seeing.

There in the distance be the circle of waving willows she knowing anywhere. Her heart ache for Ekwueme just then and if she could swim, she sure dive straight in and float to shore. She look all round, eager for Achebe to command the warriors. While Bartemus steer straight for the grove, she see Thom's ship circle past them heading for the steeper waters of the dock of Wellesbury on the far side of the plantation at Five Farm. She see Bartemus at the helm of they ship, him voice rising above the murmers of the crowd.

--DROP ANCHOR! LOAD THE ROWERS! LINE THE DECK!

--FIRST WAAAAAAAAAAAVE!! Malium commanding. First wave get to lining up in front of Malium and Addis get to searching for her captain, Dober, but Dober finding her first.

--Addis, Dober say. --You to join the first wave with Malium.

It don't sit well with Addis. Dober been her command. --Malium? Thought I were fourth wave under you.

--Achebe order it, she say and turn from Addis to help ready the rowers that gon take them all to shore. What Addis care? The sooner she get to land, to Ekwueme, the better. She pull her rifle back on her shoulder and go quick to join the first wave.

--Wait, Addis! She hearing Tembu call out from behind her and turn to him. --Your armor. Come with me below, I'll fetch it for you.

--I aint got no armor, Tembu, they calling me to join first wave, she tell him.

--Ain't gon take but a moment, Addis, trust me. I hate to see you caught out there with no armor on you.

--Nobody else got armor on, Tembu.

--You mean the warriors been fighting all they life? Come on, now!

She hesitate a moment then take the hand he offering her and they slip down below deck while Bartemus stay yelling commands and the people dance tween being warriors and sailors.

She follow Tembu down to the farthest place she been on the ship all the days they been at sea. Addis get to feeling uneasy and don't know if it be from the energy running off Tembu or the ship rocking harder now that it been anchored and the waves crashing up against it.

--Where we going?

Tembu don't answer, just keep walking back and back through the narrow hall to the stern of the ship. Addis see out the windows ocean meeting bay, nothing for miles and it unsteady her.

--Tembu!

--This way, he say and open the last door on the hall. --Here, he say, and point her through the door. --Tembu, where we at? She ask as she walk on through. She barely cry out when he knock her over the back of her head. Addis touch her hand to the tender spot, then lift it up to her face enough to see drops of red painted on her fingers. She turn to look at Tembu who standing there with a plank in him grip. --Awful sorry, Addis. So, so, sorry, she hear as he close her up in the cell. She want to speak but nothing come out. She just slip to the floor and all the world go white.

-46-
REUEL

R euel were covered in sweat, as much from him thick jacket in the sun as from the bad nerves Haynes giving him. He'd kill Haynes dead if he have to, no question. But that warn't a part of the plan. That sure would ruin all, and just when he were getting where he want to be! He praying all the time Haynes don't act the fool out here in these woods. Reuel done peep it all. Haynes were a hotblood no-color man. He don't think. He don't plan. He just do. Sure, a no-thinking no-color man kill a oji just as fast as any other, but a man like Haynes, Reuel prefer. He like him danger where he can smell it.

It were the civilzed ones Reuel fearing most. The good Christian men. The lords and their ladies. Warn't nothing more fearsome to Reuel than a genteel, good-natured no-color man what could make a law for the common good. What could string together words of pearl to justify torment.

They kill a oji in flesh or spirit, for *the good of the whole* then hide they bloody hands beneath white gloves. Might even feel sad for the oji, think they do what they do cause it gotta be done. Nothing cruel, nothing unusual, mind you, but necessary all the same. Dead ojis, all the same. And the no-color man hisself getting to decide what be what. Deciders. Reuel could spot a Haynes a mile away and know to take hisself down another road if he got to. But warn't no road a oji could take to outrun the law.

Reuel know what horrible death the law say await him if he kill a no-color man and get caught. He were in no mood to die a horrible death, and he sure warn't itching to get caught. He look to the sun as he ride a short ways in front of Haynes and know for sure aint no way they making it back to Filadelfia fore sunset hit. Anything could happen in the cover of dark.

Soon, they riding up on the grove of cedars what mark the entrance to Meroë. Warn't no fence or nothing cause warn't never no need. Warriors be the fence. --We are here, Reuel say yielding him horse and climbing down to walk through the grove to the heart of the village where the bodies still laid out, rotting, picked at, shamed.

Haynes climb down from him horse too and walk over by the bodies, nose nestled in the pit of him elbow to escape the stench.

--Just like I told you, Mr. Haynes. Men and women were killed here. The village is abandoned. Surely a great force has been here and wreaked much devilment.

Haynes ignore Reuel and walk through the heart to the cabins. He kicking in the doors of deserted homes, crushing they handmade goods, they high-skill crafts.

--How could they? How could they? Haynes walk through the village, marveling and muttering. Sturdy cabins made of wood and brick. Paintings and pottery. Multi-color tapestries, --How could they!

Reuel hear the sound of the rushing river and know Haynes going straight to it. He walk not far behind Haynes and come upon the giant fishing wheel, still sitting in the river, full of trapped, fat fish. It were enough to make Haynes fall into him rage. Reuel watch, silent, as Haynes kick and rip apart the wheel with every appendage getting a go at it, til the wheel lay in ruins, half-live fish flapping desperate out of water. It were then that Reuel see what could end everything. Reuel see it before Haynes do, but not fast enough to do nothing bout it.

--What the devil? Haynes say and creep closer to the blue and gold cloth what caught him eye, stuck in the bushes near the shore. He pull at the tassels marked with the crest of the House of Hamilton and out fall locs of straw-colored curls, Sabine's unmistakable hair. Reuel think of nothing better to say than,

--Best be getting back. Dark soon, Mr. Haynes...

Haynes turn quick on him and pull out a pistol. --Not so fast you menor dog. You best tell me what you know bout this.

This were it. Haynes got the drop on him. Haynes ready to kill. What choice Reuel have but to kill the sucker? What choice at all?

--Easy now, Mr. Haynes, easy. Don't shoot, now, Reuel say, him hands up and empty. --I don't know any more than you bout what's gone on here, not any more than you, I assure you!

Haynes spit at him, pistol cocked and ready.

--Just where you learn to talk so proper! *Bodyman to a lord,* simple menor like you, just where you learn to do it!

Reuel look down at Haynes gun hand and see it shaking and Reuel see how hate vibrate the body like music. Then, Reuel see the fear in Haynes, pouring out him eyes molasses-thick. Cause Reuel exist in him skin, a shiny black mirror for Haynes to see hisself thru and all he done and it serve Haynes right to fear. A time soon coming when Haynes warn't gon get away unjudged; not much longer bodies gon lie there under him feets, unrevenged. Haynes time were up and Reuel can tell Haynes know it just by the look in him eyes.

Fore Haynes even sense it, Reuel got strong hands on the gun, twisting Haynes hand til a shot ring out and a cry of anguish more piercing than a bullet leak out Haynes mouth as him cracked hand go limp and get to swelling. Haynes crumple to the dirt, holding him hand breathing quick and heavy.

--That's the last time you'll ever point a gun at me and live, Mr. Haynes. The very last time, Reuel say. He tuck Haynes' gun ino a strap at him waist and leave Haynes turning pink and grunting on the ground. Reuel make off on him horse for Hamilton House and he don't look back, even as Haynes curse him name.

Reuel riding like the Debil be in him. It warn't safe for him to be out alone with raging no-color men on the loose. He would be safe at Hamilton House, safe as could be, til Hamilton hear what Haynes know bout Sabine. Through the gates he riding, straight up to the house, not even stopping to tie him horse. He leaping down and, forgetting hisself, he running for the front door and walk right in, crying, --Lord Hamilton! Lord Hamilton! He echoing all through the great hall, the only answer back he hearing.

--Lord Hamilton not here, the new stable boy call out to Reuel from the front door the boy dare not enter through. Reuel come charging out at the boy.

--Where? Where is he!

Frightened, the boy say, --He at him Aunt Burken's house. Some awful done happen to Miss Sabine. I saw the whole thing, really.

But a chill come over Reuel just then and he don't hear the boy speak no more. He were too late. It were too late for him. He were good as dead, by Hamilton or Haynes, and for what? Now it were too late to join the Meroës, wherever they done gone. But it warn't too late to run. Not just yet.

Reuel rush back into the house and close the heavy doors behind him. Fore he know it, he find hisself in the kitchen, filling water jugs and loading up on biscuits and chicken meat. He throw it all into a sack and be out the kitchen door, so lost in him own panic, he don't even see Scott Hamilton standing before him, eyeing him curious-like.

--...in God's name are you doing, Reuel?

Words turn to ash in him mouth and all else dry up inside him. Reuel drop him sack, look Scott Hamilton square in the eye, and ready hisself for whatever gon come.

-47-
TEMBU

Tembu get sick thinking bout what he done to Addis as he row out to shore with the first wave, gun and powder and bullets at the ready. He know she gon hate him forever for it. But she gon have a forever, Tembu thinking, and to him, that were enough. Warn't that him job, to protect her? Hadn't he swore it?

Deep down, Tembu know that aint the reason he done what he done. He know what he really want from Addis. He want to keep feeling how she make him feel. He need her alive so he can keep on feeling alive and for the first time in him life, like things were worth hoping for. Like things were gon really change.

But she scare him too and he don't like it. She were a bright, beautiful being and if he could have her, if he could make her yield, he would always be bright and beautiful too. It make him sick to know what he done, why he done it. He know when Achebe find out it gon make him spit, at least. Achebe don't never try boxing in Mama Biny or forcing her hand none. Aint no way to, no how, but Achebe don't even want to. He let Mama be, like Goliwe let Tembu be. So why Tembu caint let Addis be?

It were just like The Eboro warn him all them years ago. --You gon love a woman more than God and love yourself more than her and it gon kill you both, she tell him. Fool fool not to listen. Now it were too late.

Tembu begging God for more life for Addis, for him so he can make it right with her, just as the first wave were hitting land and pulling they row boats up on the shore.

A warrior up near Malium and Achebe sounding the horn just as the second wave joining them on land. They forming ranks and marching behind Achebe.

--Listen! Achebe say it and hold up him hand and the warriors all fall silent. They hear it: drums beating quick and heavy nearby, a Eboe warning.

--Ready your weapons. Fire on my command alone!

Tembu march on, weapons near both him hands, him healing kit slung on him back, unsettled and unprepared for this paradox of war. Him whole body tense up to every new sensation, the sweet smell of fruit and willows, the sharp blow of the wind off the river, the anxiousness of every warrior he marching alongside. They all wanting it to be over with and all wanting to come out alive. Sides Achebe and a few others, most too young to know anything bout warring or how very long a second feel when the bullets starting to fly and there aint nowhere to run. They gon know soon enough.

When the warriors round they way out of the willow grove away from the Great House, they come upon a group of oji rebels, a young sturdy oji man leading them, a rifle strapped to him chest and two pistols at him waist, a pouch of powder and enough bullets to kill a herd of cattle. He come forward to Achebe and say in a loud voice,

--We heard the call of calvary in your horns. Name yourselves, brothers and sisters. Who sent you?

--Brother, we are the warriors of Meroë. Our sister, Addis Agụ calls us to your aid.

--Addis! Where is she now?

Tembu speak loud and out of turn.

--Safe, brother! She is safe.

Achebe give Tembu a look that mean he know Tembu done something aint right. Addis were posed to be there now, not the medicine man. But they all got more pressing matters and Achebe take back command.

--Brother, the warriors of Meroë are yours. How can we serve?

Ekwueme break the Eboe. --Drums done sounded in the southern farms. Amerikans must been spotted by the rebels at the watch. We got hundreds of rebels spread out over five farms. We got all our chiles and invalids up in the Great House being kept safe as long as we can. What we got to do now, we got to meet the Amerikans at the docks and beat them back, fore they even make it to land, if they aint already here.

--A ship of Meroë warriors down at your dock. We will fight them on two fronts. We hear you got cannons and cannon fire.

--Leftovers from the Great War. No telling if they even working.

--No time to test them out. We bring them with us. Who can show my lieutenant and him guard to the cannons?

The young rebel leader point to a solid woman who Malium and the first wave follow close behind back up to the Great House. The drums start up again and the young rebel raise up him voice above the troubled thumping.

--We caint wait for cannon fire! We go now to meet them!

The leader and him rebels get to running towards the drums, Achebe right behind, and Tembu and the warriors on they heels. They run a long ways through a clearing that feel to Tembu like no time at all. Warn't no time that the rebel man next to the young leader drop off and get trampled by the warriors behind him. Tembu aint even hearing the gunfire at first, til a few more drop off.

--Make for the trees!

The young rebel yelling to the warriors to get out of the open fields and Tembu dive into the forest with the others and find him mark cross the way. The Amerikan look to be bout him own age, maybe younger, aiming at them all with shaky hands. Tembu aim, eyes wide open, and shoot that man square and dead. He warn't born to this life and warn't grafted into it nuther. Meroës warn't no hunting kind. They make no practice of taking life what aint fish or plant. Only to defeat death did they kill, and Tembu find it all maddening. Then he member what the Bible say bout seasons for all things, a purpose to killing. A time for it. That be enough for him to shut off a part of hisself and shoot another. Then another. Then another. And all round him, warriors dropping.

Tembu don't even realize when he been shot. --Fire! He yell to everyone and no one, but there aint no fire cept the one through him shoulder where a bullet pierce clean through and send the burning all up and down him whole left side. It knock him flat back and he lay there a moment, like the roots of the trees all sprouting up and tying theyself round him whole body so he caint move, caint breathe, caint think. He lay there, swimming in him mind, still in him body, for he don't know how long, just listening as the world get real quiet and cloudy. He blink him eyes to make sure he still alive and caint really be sure til he hear the most glorious sound he ever hearing. Close behind him be the booming of cannons.

-48-
ADDIS

In all her life, Addis aint never hear cannon fire. When she hear them, she think she were skipping past Burken's statues of glory on her way to the gardens, trying as she might to imagine they sound, what the Great War musta been like, what kinda greatness could ever be born of war. She were a chile then and were a chile all along, til she hearing the unmistakable sound of cannons bursting through her unconsciousness. She hear it and the screaming of the warriors left on the ship above her and she jump herself up. The battle aint waiting for her.

Addis grab the sides of her head what hurting her all over. She feeling so different, not just dizzy, but lost. She know what been done to her, she know who she be and where and why, but still, she feeling a part of her done slip away while she were sleeping.

Addis gather herself and feel her way to the wood door. Warn't no handle to be felt. She push and pull against it with no victory. She beat on the door til it splinter her hands and she cry out for help, but only her own voice echo back to her. Still, she hearing the dying cries of warriors above her and wonder what horrors Tembu done.

She lift her foot to kick at the door but when she lower it back to steady herself, she feeling something cold splash against her legs. Addis sink her hands in the darkness round her feets and know they taking on water.

Warn't no time fore the water rising to her ankles. She fight the door like mad, but it hold. She feel round in the darkness for anything what could help her til she stumble upon her gun. She lift it out the water, aim it at the door and shoot, but the water done jam it all up something good. So she flip it round and use the butt to beat into the wood. Harder and harder she thrust the gun through til it making a hole in the door and light bust in. She beat at the edges til it widen and widen and widen so she can fit herself through. She throw the gun out first and it splash into a pond what almost half the height of the door. She climb herself out, dredge through the water low, both hands on the ground til she reach the ladder.

When she go up a deck, she see a woman warrior sprawled out on the stairs, eyes wideing, body still, fingers loose on the trigger of her gun. Addis close the eyes and disarm the warrior of her gun and bullets and Addis make her way to the carnage on the top deck.

Bodies strewn all round on the main deck and it fill Addis with a sickness she aint never known. She see it now, a great navy ship before them, the uniformed men all in straight battle lines beneath a steady Amerikan flag, Wormwood emblazoned cross the ship.

But Addis ship were rocking from the cannons flying and bullets hailing down on it, and the waves be just as violent. The warriors running round, covering they heads, some even get to jumping overboard and trying to swim they way to the war on shore. A running woman knock into Addis and snap her back to the chaos round her.

--You! Addis say it and the woman stop.

--Who remains on deck?

--Fourth wave, and fifth, the woman answer, ducking down.

--Where be Dober? Who be the lieutenant of the fifth wave?

--Dead! All the lieutenants what aint already gone to shore in the rowers be dead, Agu!

Addis swallow quick and ask the woman, --What they call you?

--My name Fania, she say.

--Stand with me, Fania, Addis say, and Fania nod to her. Addis raise her voice above the cannon fire for all on board to hear.

--Warriors of Meroë! Stand your ground! Don't you dare to leave this ship til the enemy be sunk!

--Look! Agu! She lives! Some looking up and whispering to each other.

Addis point to a cluster of 20 warriors nearest to her. --You! Below deck! Load the cannons! The warriors humble at her command and move swift to get below deck.

--Fania! Lead the cannon fire! Fania nod to her and fly below deck with the others.

--Guns at the ready! She yell to the warriors ducking on deck. They scrambling on they knees to duck down along the edge of the ship with her. The one on her right be just a boy, she can see in him slight face, with him big gentle eyes. He knowing as much bout war as she knowing. She smile at him a little and he smile back.

--I am glad to be with you, Agu, he say, and she hold him hand tight. She peek over the edge at Wormwood, the Debil ship what must be sunk.

--Warriors, on my command, she say with back against the edge. --Igba! She yell it and the warriors raise up, just over the edge of the ship, aim and let they bullets fly.

When they out of bullets, they squatting down again, backs against the ship. --Reload! She yelling. --Igba! And off they go, on they feets again. Cannon balls start making dents in Wormwood, Amerikans start flying off its edges. All round her, she hear her warriors crying out, falling back, too. Still, with her back against the ship, she yelling, --Reload! --Igba! And the warriors firing more shots still, more cannons still. Aint no end to it.

Cries and shots be so deafening Addis don't rely on her ears no more. Her sight alone tell her they caint stop. --Reload! Igba! The warrior next to her fall, the young boy with the gentle eyes. She see him go down off to the side but she keep her sight straight, though her stomach get to tightenting. She peering over the edge of the ship in time to see the sun exploding at the edge of the water, sending its last light up and down the sea. Warn't gon be long now, she thinking. --Reload! She yelling. --Igba!

-49-
GOLIWE

When night fall, only three armed njems stay behind with Mama Biny at camp, to protect the unables. The rest, twenty-five in all, taking up arms and sneaking they way toward the orchard plantation just through the woods.

It were decided. Three at a time, the warriors gon stand guard at the four little white houses what mark where the slavers living, two gon stand guard with Rit and Lew at the master house. And the rest going to each little cabin where the slaves be held and letting them choose. All who were ready were gon come, all who warn't were gon stay behind, and Goliwe praying warn't nobody gon die this night.

--And what of the enemy babies? Lew ask it while they was plotting.

--We leave the children be, Rit say, firm.

--Rotten fruit grow from a poison tree, Lew saying and Rit grab hold of him arm. --We leave the children be, she saying and Lew shaking him head. --What say you, Mama Biny?

Mama Biny breathe in and lift her head to the sky in reverence, but her worship be brief. --We will show they children what they never showing to us. We will teach them mercy.

Rit nod and Lew swallow and warn't no more said of it. With the plan in place, the njems descend as silent as fog on the orchard plantation, only moonlight shining on the slavers row, they all white houses shining bright just for the njems, the children of the moon, to see. Goliwe hold tight to the musket strapped to her body. Her fingers shaking and she grip her weapon tighter to silence them. Her heart beating in her ears, sweat forming at the top of her forehead though the night wind bring a chill with it. She feeling hot all over and she got to talk to herself on the inside.

--Fifty men, women, chiles in chains. Fifty souls enslaved, she tell herself. It don't stop the tingling in her hands, the thumping in her ears. Nothing gon stop that. But it steady her. Give her bird-like focus. She and the two with her, a big man named Edrus, a tall, thin woman name Mya, get set for the white house at the far end.

She see the clusters of three forming all to the right of her behind the trees, Rit and Lew front and center of them all.

--Agha! Rit whisper and lightening spring from all they feets as they running toward slavers cottage.

Edrus reach the door first and break it in with him foot in one kick. Mya and Goliwe following and find the overseer sitting up in him bed, candle light bouncing off him ashen face. He reaching for him longarm next to him bed, but he don't get no chance to touch it for Mya get to shooting, red splattering all on the man white sheets. What she don't finish, Goliwe do with one final shot that set the man head back against him headboard, what left of him face twisting in surprise as much as Goliwe's at her own strength. She stand there staring as Mya fly past her. Edrus yell to her, --Goliwe! Come now!

She grab the man longarm, cock it and carry it out with her behind Edrus and Mya. They starting in the slave cabins, saying, --Do not fear, free peoples! It is time to leave!

Screams of chiles all down slave row rising up as scared ones waking up to the sight of these warriors with guns in they hands, the sounds of shots, of grown men crying out. --Do not fear, free peoples! They saying at every slave cabin. --If you want to be free, move quick!

Goliwe get a high when she see the looks of fear mixing with joy on the people's faces. Mams and paps packing nothing but they chiles, and shoes for they feets as they piling out the house behind Goliwe and the others. She leading them to the woods over two fallen and still njems whose names she not knowing, til she hear a crack through all the noise followed by the screams of the brokenhearted. Goliwe stopping cold.

--Follow them to safety! Goliwe yelling to the orchard folks and they keep fleeing behind the other njems. Goliwe turn back and run straight for the great house. She stopping at the stairs of the redbrick home to reload and get uneasy when she hearing nothing but creeping silence. Then, a yellow figure come bursting out the front door and down the steps straight at her. Goliwe got her gun at the ready but then the chile scream and keep running and Goliwe stop herself just fore she shoot. She let what look like a boychile run off into darkness. She breathe out, and everything in her fill up with gratitude.

Goliwe then take to the stairs, bound through the door and up more stairs to the top floor, where she see two njems, guns by they side, in the doorway of a bedroom. She see the splatterings of the man and woman, still tucked in bed, candles burning bright as ever. Then she see the back of Rit slumping on the wood floor of the room and her heart stop beating there in her throat.

Goliwe squeeze past the njems at the door and get closer to the crumbling warrior. She see Rit breathing, her body rocking, doubling over with gasps and sighs. --Rit? Goliwe call out soft, but the closer she get to Rit, she see what Rit hunching over. The gasps coming from Lew, sprawled out on the floor, head in her lap, struggling to breathe. The chest of him shirt were soaking with red, blood were spilling from him front and back and Goliwe know he been run through.

--You all right, Lew. You all right, Rit telling him, cradling him in her arms.

Goliwe feel a welling up in her spirit. The high she were on that have her thinking she could do this, she could be at war and live, start fading faster than Lew. She turn to the njems at the door. --Why did this happen! Why did this happen! She yelling at them, not asking.

--We was handling the masters, all us. Chile came in here outta nowhere.

--Chile?

--He aiming for Rit and Lew go to stop him and get run through with bullets.

--A chile, Goliwe say, breathless. It making no sense to her. She standing there, barely a scratch, and this warrior been felled by a chile. It making no sense to her at all. They finest warrior. She think on it and wonder what ever were the point of it anyhow.

--I don't understand, Goliwe say. --This warn't posed to happen. Warn't posed to be like this, she say and every part of her shaking when she see Lew done quieted and stilled. --What do we do now, Rit? What do we do?

Rit bend down to kiss the lips of Lew a final time. She take off her headwrap and wrap him face in it. Then she lower him head off her lap and stand.

--We bury the dead, Rit say, steady as iron. --We bury the dead and we move on.

Goliwe fall to her knees, never taking her eyes off Lew's empty body. For a moment, he look like Tembu do when he sleeping, peaceful as a chile. It draw all her tears out and they be silent only cause she forgetting, for that time, how to make a sound. Rit motioning to the njems to come and they carry what left of Lew up out of that room.

--Get up, Rit say, but Goliwe don't move. --Now. On your feets, daughter.

Goliwe rise up slow and wipe her face with the back of her hand, and they walk out the house together. By the stars, they run for the camp in silence.

When they reach the camp, Rit telling Mama Biny what happening to Lew and Mama Biny hanging her head. She whispering to Ala to take Lew into the earth and him spirit on to Chúkwú with the ancestors. Then, Mama Biny calling Goliwe to her and Goliwe come, heavy.

--I didn't want to say, Mama. I didn't want to say it warn't right to kill them. That we gotta find another way. I didn't want to say cause they killing us, even when they not killing our bodies, they killing our minds, they killing our souls. They crushing us from the inside out and so I aint wanna say it warn't right to kill them. If anybody deserve to die it be the slavers and any who help them and any who stand by while it happen to us all. But I don't want us to be the ones to do it, Mama! This who they be! This aint *us!*

Mama take Goliwe in her arms a moment and let Goliwe rest there.

--We caint never win against them, Mama. Never, she saying, too numb to sob. Now she know what be true and what aint. Truth were that ojis caint last in no real war. Warn't enough willing to die. She look to the orchard folk they helping escape and all them looking just as solemn as she and she wanting to yell at them, *We freed you! Yet you weep? We give our best warrior for you, yet you hang your*

265

head! But she don't do it.

She swallow her disdain. Maybe she know it aint a fair thing to think, let alone say. Maybe she know she don't know nothing bout these folks. Mama Biny just keeping her eyes trained on what matter.

--Name them, Mama Biny say. --Name the number fallen, name the ones what march beyond the Falls.

--We still loosing in the end, Mama, she say, despairing. --We still losing, when it all be over...

--Name them, Daughter.

Goliwe look up and see Chima among the surviving njems and she breathe out thanks to Chúkwú.

--Three fallen, Mama. Lew, the traveler, Wayne the potter, Dana, the seamstress. Ninety-six surviving. Ninety-six now marching beyond the Falls.

--Write it down, Daughter of the Sun. Don't forget it.

Goliwe dropping her last tear for Lew and all what fallen and know she warn't gone forget none of it.

--Dawn coming soon, Mama say to all. --We best be moving on.

-50-
ADDIS

Addis call on the warriors once again. --Reload! She yelling and squat back down behind the edge of the ship, til she search all on her person and see she aint got no more ammo. The fallen all round her aint got no ammo nuther. She look down the row at her warriors, bleak in they faces, no more bullets tween any of them. Addis peer up over the side of the ship and see the Amerikans jumping into the water by the dozens, the Wormwood done for. Addis squat back down and look to her warriors on the wall of the ship. She member the commands Dober teach her in the last days. The farewell.

--You have fought well and brave, sons and daughters of Meroë! Addis yell to them and salute them as cannons fire. --Chúkwú smile upon you! Make for shore! Abandon ship! Abandon ship!

A warrior at the port of the ship get to the bell and begin to toll it for the warriors below deck. --Abandon ship! Abandon ship! They all cry out, jumping overboard. Addis stand up to see they aint so far removed from the water theyself, the ship done took on so much. She see Fania leading the cannon firers up from below deck and Addis run behind them. Fania grab for Addis hand and the two plunge into the deep together.

The water were warmer to her than she were expecting, but the taste were bitter with blood and death, and it choke her. Through a haze, she could see Fania and her lengthening crown of hair being made to curl at the command of the sea. A fat bass slip past her ankle and slap its tail against her leg, all to let her know she warn't dreaming, that dreaming for Addis were over. She were still alive.

Addis look back to Fania who done roll herself up into a ball then stretch herself out straight, kicking her legs and slapping her arms through the water like a frog do. Addis try it herself, til her chest burn her. Then, she swimming back up toward the last light of dusk and taking in the biggest air she can once she reaching the top. She looking all round her, seeing bodies in the water, Amerikans and Meroës alike.

On shore, what seem like a lifetime away, she seeing Meroës.

267

Nearby, she spotting a chunk of the ship hull floating and she kick and splash her way toward it. When she secure herself on it, she push the water back from her and will herself toward shore. Addis try not to think of what gon meet her when she reach the edge of the land she swore to never set foot on again. For now, it be her only mercy.

While she paddle herself amongst bodies and ship pieces, she not knowing what part of her she leaving in the hull of that ship, in the dark room Tembu lock her in. She aint felt what make her Addis Agụ since that moment. Ala abandon her. It be her own tired arms and drained, battered body what pushing her nearer and nearer to shore. Maybe it always were, she thinking. She aint seeing her pap face in the stars this time. She aint hearing the whisper of the ocean. Nothing chanting, nothing singing, cries of Amerikans drowning be all what ringing in her ears. That and the words of The Eboro.

Addis think on them words and see the faces of the warriors strewn round the ship, near the bottom of the Potomac by now. She see the eyes of the boy fighting next to her, the eyes, once big and full of wonder, frozen into a empty stare and Addis make peace with the debil what come for her life. She done all she could. Why Addis caint slip off this piece of wood and sink into the deep like she done in her dream? If she aint done all she could, Addis thinking she done quite enough.

When Addis were little, she thinking often of what it were like to die. Always she membering how Haynes shoot her pap through the gut, and she imagine her pap's spirit floating out the hole the gun make in him, smiling as he go, like he walking up some stairs at first, then just lift him head up and disappear into gold light. He aint wanting to leave her and her mam, sure, but praise MotherFather! He were free. It were what they always singing at every homegoing she ever go to her whole life, the beauty in death for a slave. And now she done face death more times than she can count, waiting on the beauty that aint never come. How many more times she got to ready herself for it to sneak away from her?

At least another, she thinking now, cause fore she know anything at all, with the waves at her back, she see the moonlight shooting down on the rocky shore. Addis sink her feets down below her, and sure enough, she touching the bottom, water just under her chin. She nearly walking herself up to the rocks of shore. She pull herself up and sprawl out among Meroës, coughing and spitting out the bitter sea.

--Agu! Some cry, weak, and she answer them the same when she catching her breath. --I am here. I am here, she say it to herself, as much as any other, her back against jagged rock and dirt. The more she ready herself for the release of death, the more it slip through her fingers, she thinking. Addis roll onto her side and smile when her eyes meet Fania's. --I am still here, Addis say, and right then, she glad bout it.

Then Addis mind start to focus. She hear the drums nearby and know they drums of the warriors of Wellesbury calling to her. They giving her strength. Addis stand with full force in her body and count what remaining, some 45 of them still! --Warriors, she tell them, her Eboe fierce as it ever been. --Rise! Our people need us. Those who cannot stand, call out to us, and we will carry you.

And all the able-bodied stand and carry the fallen and follow Addis toward Wellesbury. The closer they get to the Great House, the louder the drums getting, and Addis hear what sound like yelling. She pick up her pace and the warriors follow her lead. They making they way down through the circle of willows, through the garden walls to Slave Row. When she reach it, she see hundreds of warriors, Meroë and Wellesbury, singing and chanting and dancing praise to Chúkwú round a fire. The first face she see in the firelight be that of Thom running up the path from the Farms, warriors behind him, and when he see her, he run to her.

--Addis! He yell to her. When he reach her, she manage a tired smile and he hug her close. The warriors stop to cheer, --Agu lives! Agu lives! Praise Chúkwú!

--We just got word the ship was sunk, Thom say. --When Tembu told me you were still on it...

--Yes, she say, and hold her hand out to the people standing behind her. She don't want to talk nothing bout Tembu. --But we survive.

Thom count the number. --So few return, he say. Fania come forward and say, --Our Agu saved us. She were mighty in battle. We were not the only ship what fall into the sea! The

Wormwood what carry Amerikans sunk to the depths and bittered the water with its fallen!

All the warriors cheer at this and Addis find her place among the people. She smile and breathe. More and more warriors running up from the Farms shouting victories in every corner of Wellesbury. --We laid them straight into the grave! They yelling. Thom telling her they even taking over the Amerikans' ship at the docks at Five Farm. Hundreds of them celebrating, joining together round the fire, --Addis Agụ lives! Wellesbury is ours!

Addis stand before them now, full of the blood of Taddy and Bernard. On the planks where Dido, Turk and Pompey were slaughtered, full of their sacrifice, full of Eboe, Addis stand and speak to her people.

--This day is for the ancestors! Ripped from their villages, stripped of their tongues, their pride, their bodies, their past and their future, our ancestors have cried out from beyond. Too long they have laid, unavenged, until this day!

--KWENU!

--This day is for our children! No longer is their future out of our hands! No longer will we weep and pray while the no-color man plots to sell them away. No longer will we chew the bitter root not to know the pain of stolen children! Of forced futures!

--KWENU!

--This day is for us! The warriors, the fulfillment of the ancestors' dreams! We will die before the no-color man takes another thing from us! And we will take them with us when we go!

--KWENU!

--This day, we take back our mmadu! This day the Amerikans learn what it means to feel the wrath of Chúkwú and tremble! This day, on land and sea, the Amerikans learned we can reason and fight and win! The blood of our fallen was not shed in vain. This first battle of the Mmadu Revolution will stand as the beginning of the new age! The dawn of all power to the people!

--Ike! She yelling

--Mba! They crying back.

--Ike!

--Mba!

Addis look to all the faces among the crowd and see friends. Achebe bow to her, Bartemus salute her, Sayzare as well. But one face in the crowd make its print on her. She step down off the planks and come closer as the warriors and rebels dance and sing praise to Chúkwú.

--Ekwueme? She call out, not certain if he be ghost or true. He run to her. He lift her up. He kiss her scars and hold her and she cry with joy. --I found you! I found you, she keep saying against the joyous chants of the people.

When the rapture of holding him again, the joy of knowing he survive melt from dream to true life, she back away from him to hold him hands and look him in the eyes. --Tell me, my love, she say in Eboe. --Where did you hide my Nnene? Where did you put my brother?

He hold her scar-up face in him hands then take her bye the hands and say, --Come with me.

They leave the warriors dancing and chanting round the fire and those still coming up from the battle at the docks and the farms joining in.

When they reaching her old hut, the fire light growing dim and the chanting seem a distant hum. She feel some kind of way to be seeing it again, the place where she were birthed. It make her shiver, but she don't turn from it. She swallow and set her mind to getting inside, to holding her Nnene again, in this very same place where she saw her last. Addis get towards the door but Ekwueme stop her with him hands and gentle Eboe.

--I am sorry, Addis. Nnene is not here.

These words fill Addis with joy and she hug him tighter than before. --You sent her West with Billy Lee? Thank Chúkwú!

--No, Addis, please listen. Billy Lee went missing when the caravan came. And Nnene...I did not save her. She was unprotected during the first attack. She is dead. No one saw it happen. She was felled and tangled in roots when we found her.

Addis back away from him not understanding how joy could turn sour so quickly in her mouth. --We did not bury her in the mass grave, after. We buried her just behind your hut, near your garden. Come, I wil show you.

Ekwueme reach for Addis hand but she wrench it back from him, reeling, her head pounding till she caint see clear. She don't look at him when she ask him,

--What do you mean you did not save her? You let them kill her?

--Addis! I mean only that I was not here to save her. I was not here when she died. No one was. It was near a week ago in the first attack. All of us were fighting at the docks where the watchmen had just gotten off their ship.

--Did you do this to hurt me? Because I left?

Ekwueme step back from her shaking him head and put him arm out to keep the distance

--Addis...

--Did you!

She demand of him.

--That you could fix your lips to say it twice! I did my best to keep your mother's uprising a secret for months and to execute it in her absence when the time came. I rescued Chima, like you asked me to. I tried to get to Billy Lee. I could not find him in time. Nnene was dead when I found her and I am sorry for it. But do not ever say I let her die to punish you for leaving me.

--My mother's uprising?

The words stick to Addis like a sweaty shift. They don't feel right. They don't sound right. Her mam have nothing to do with this. But Ekwueme too mad to keep the Eboe.

--Two years Taddy been working with The Tunnel through to the North to get weapons to Wellesbury and the other plantations close by. Every homegoing, the drummers beat out plans for folks at the outside plantations to hear. Your mam the one tell me bout Sayzare, say to meet him in town when I go to the smithy. She tell me to round up 12 able-bodied to travel and make sure you was one of them.

--No. It don't make sense! How she could do this? Two years?

--She tell me what I need to know to do my part and no more. That year she were in Filadelfia with Burken when they was setting up the nation, something happen to her, she say. That be all

272

she say. She call it a thing she got to do.

    --NO. She warn't to do nothing without Nnene. Aint no way she tell you all this and not tell you to protect her above all us! My mam love her.

    --You love her too and we was gon leave her behind, you and me.

    --No.

    --We was always gon leave her, Addis!

Aint that always the way, her mind say when it turn on her. No matter how good, no matter how loving, they still be some folks don't nobody mind leaving behind. She membering what The Eboro say, how she set people up to die for her, and it burn her in her chest.

    --No!

    Addis take off running behind her hut to they garden and stop cold when she see the grave in the moonlight.

    A stone what mark where Nnene lay, and a mound of fresh earth stretch out in front of it. Addis start to shake. Her ankles buckle first, fore she even know what happen, then her knees go, and she kneeling, then collapsing in the dirt, laid out like Nnene, the side of her face smushed into the ground. The breathing be the first thing that hurt, like being slashed cross the face a thousand more times. The harder she breathe, the less air she take in, the more it cut her. Then the tears come like they never gon stop. She try to speak Nnene's name, pray Ala bring her back but nothing come from her throat but bottomless wails.

    She rub her hands in the dirt as she moan, then her hands, of they own accord, make fists and start pounding the ground, then she get up out her body and watch a fragile soul clawing away at what separate them. She aint never been more separate from herself than this moment, in a world with no Nnene. It were a nonsense world, a stale world with shriveled flowers, a dry and barren land and she dig it all up. She watch herself digging a circle round herself til she start to sink but keep on digging and wailling, blinded by tears and torment. Only when Ekwueme come and scoop her up out the grave do she come back into herself.

    He carry her a ways away from the site and she fight him

at first, then lean into him with her sobs. He sit down on the ground and lean against the hut with her in him arms, cradle her, kiss her and she want to speak. She want to do so much more than cry. Ekwueme don't shush her. Don't tell her it gon be all right. He never were the lying kind. So he just rock her and let her cry. -- Nnene! She cry out but Ekwueme answer. --She free now, Addis. Caint nobody ever bring her back to this place. She free now.

Death were something a slave were aching for, sometimes so quiet it burned the insides, sometimes so loud it might could set you deaf, then sometimes soft in moans, but always, always the ache for death. Addis take slow, deep breaths and quiet herself when she think on these things..Her pap were dead, her mam, at least one brother, and now Nnene. Dead as slaves.

But Addis look round her and see no slavers. They done fled with they chains or drowned with them at the bottom of the sea. Warn't nothing anchoring her to herself no more. She feel free, but not like Nnene. Warn't no joy in it. It were a hollowed-out free. The kind of free that come when you stop aching for death and start chasing it like a house on fire.

She lift herself off Ekwueme and start to walk away. She don't turn or stop or flinch when Ekwueme calling her name. She know just what she gon do. In her path she see Tembu, who call out --Addis! but he a ghost to her and she walk straight through him, blood in her eyes. She see Thom among the others and call to him. --Come, she say, and he don't ask no questions. --Help me, she say to Fania who walk abreast with Addis, torch in hand.

It aint no question what Addis set fire to first. She head straight for that greenhouse and find a full can of oil just inside the Upper Garden walls. She go inside the greenhouse like she done near a thousand times and she douse that house like Haynes done Basil Lee, her brother who aint knowing nothing, aint hurting nothing and dead now, like nothing. She thinking this as she drenching every miscegenated plant, the seeds of rape and torture and every quiet corner of that hopeful structure. This were Burken's future and pride and joy and every bone in Addis body meaning to break it.

When it empty, she put down the oil can and pick up a

potted sapling by the stem, wielding it against every window near her and they shatter. Addis screaming when she do it, screaming nothing. That be what good Burken's smarts done him in the end. That be how much it profit him soul. He were a thief what stole from other lands and prop them up where they don't belong for him own pleasure, to marvel at him own self. Now he dead like nothing, too.

Addis scream and scream breaking glass with every blow til the pot shatter and she start to use her fists. She don't feel the blood sweating down her fingers and wrists, licking the hair on her arms. She don't feel the welts the glass making when it bite her. This feral, rabid house leave her with nothing and she cannot let it stand. Thom with her, smashing out what windows left, throwing potted plants against the walls until there aint nothing left to break. Addis catch eyes with Thom and motion toward the door with her head. He follow.

--I need the light, Fania, she say when they both back outside the house in Upper Garden. Fania hand the torch to her. Addis turn to the greenhouse and spit as far as she can fore she throw that torch inside and watch it catch ablaze quick.

Addis eyes light up with the glorious fire in her face and she feeling the burning deep inside her skin. She need more. She need more for her mam, who were held prisoner on this land, her pap who were slain through the belly like a dog on this land. She need more for Chima's mam who spent her last breath in agony on this here land. And Nnene, the forgotten chile of war, it were high time she were lifted up. Addis look round at the rows of warriors, Wellesbury and Meroë, what standing behind her and tell them, --Burn it all to the ground.

Slave Row go up in no time, the willow circle where her and Ekwueme used to hope they empty hopes, burn as quick as dry paper with no breeze. But Addis pick herself up another torch for one place in particular. Thom it seem were handling the Great House, getting everybody out who hiding in there. She got to get to the loft. She walk up through the kitchen and stick the torch in the keep on the wall and start climbing the ladder.

When she reaching the top, she see a candle flicker on the

table in the corner and give her light to see the bed. --Billy Lee? She calling out but the room be still. Addis walking toward it and catch a corner of paper what sticking out from underneath. She hold it up to the candle and read *Eziokwu* cross the top, and the date, just a few years back. Three rebellions in New York, she think it say, significant Amerikan casualties. Addis run her fingers cross the wrinkling paper and spread it cross the bed like a cover. While she stretching out over the bed, her foot knock against something underneath the quilt and she kneel down to see what it be.

Addis touch her hands on a book with leather binding to it. She bring it out from under the quilt and open it by the candle light and see Taddy scribbled in the inside cover. She flip through the book and see it be filled, page after page, with writings from her mam and it near stop Addis heart. She sink onto her knees to take it in, this treasure she finding.

--Best you take that and get on out of here, a small voice say in front of her. She look up to see Billy Lee standing in the shadows on the far side of the bed.

--Billy Lee! You alive! She jump up to come to him. She want to hold him, tell him they safe now. They won Wellesbury, everything gon be all right, but he put him hand up to her.

--Stay back, he saying, and it catch Addis off guard.

--Come on now, Billy Lee, we gotta get from here. This whole place set to burn up any moment.

But Billy Lee don't move. He staring off. Him face dirty like he aint wash hisself in weeks. He look thin and sick as she ever see him. It like he aint there.

--Billy Lee, you hearing me? We gotta get out *now*, Addis say and come toward him. She grab him arm but he yank it away so hard she trip and drop her mam journal on the ground. It shock her; him size don't match him strength. She pick herself and the book up and tuck it under her arm.

--Billy Lee, you listen to me now. We not safe here. Folks coming to kill us.

--They coming to kill *you*, I reckon, Billy Lee say, cold, still staring straight.

--You thinking they gon spare you cause you aint me, Billy?

--They aint spare my mam. They aint spare my brother nuther, from what I hear. I reckon they take me long with em.

--You right, Billy Lee, you zactly right. So you coming with me. We getting out of here. We gon go some place safe.

--I don't reckon I will, he say, looking her in the eye at last.

--If you think I'mma leave you here, brother...

--This pistol say you will. Billy Lee pull the long gun out from behind him, slow. The silver barrel shining against the candle light. Addis chest get tight. She think on it now, all the times she survive, just to be run through in the end by her own brother. Meaningless! Meaningless, says the Teacher, she thinking.

--What you gon do with that, now, Billy Lee?

--Whatever I got to, I reckon.

--I aint leaving you here! She yell it, she clench her fist, she look him dead in the eye and get to tearing up.

--You go away, now, or so help me I start shooting.

--Billy...

--You go away, now, he repeat. Him hand shaking but he close enough to Addis with the gun it don't matter much. So Addis start to backing away.

--I going, Billy Lee. Just how you want it. But, I tell you this place bout to go up in flames, nobody gon be left here. You gon be all alone.

--That be all I ever been!

--I'm sorry. I'm sorry Billy Lee. Nobody wanting to leave you here, I promise. You promise me you get out while you can. Addis feets catch the ledge of the loft and with the journal pressed under her arm, she climb down the ladder til she caint see none of Billy Lee no more. Outside the kitchen, she hear Thom calling for her and she run to him. --I here, Thom.

--We gotta go, now! Gunpowder all over this house. Make for the ships at the Five Farm dock!

Addis look all round her and everybody running away from the flames, straight for Five Farm, setting fires at Two and Three and Four as they go. Addis watch it all in glory Not him house nor him harvest, nothing at all gon stand! She running and running til she hear an explosion, like all the cannons going off at once and she trip over.

Addis look back to see the Great House, the kitchen, the Loft, the gardens all in flames as tall as the willows. Her heart cry out to Billy Lee and she get no answer. *Never shoulda left him alone*, she thinking, from the day they leave for Filadelfia. *Never shoulda left him alone.* The poorest souls always full of shoulda dones.

Addis get back to running to Five Farm with the others and don't never again look back. When she reaching the docks at Five Farm, she see the warriors on both Thom and the Amerikans' ship preparing to make birth. Warriors running down the docks and separating theyselves tween the two ships. Addis and Fania make for the Amerikans' ship and watch as warriors tear down the three flags what flying on the masts.

--We got to move now! We making for the Island, Thom! Achebe yelling out and Thom run down the docks toward him own ship and get at the wheel. When the sails and ships both ready, deckhands ringing bells, lifting anchor and pulling up the lines what tie the ships to the docks and set sail into the night by lamplight, silent as the dead they leaving behind. She see Fania watching the whole of Wellesbury going up in flames as they sailing away, but Addis seen all she ever needing to see.

-51-
ADDIS

Out at sea, the air send a chill through Addis, but going below deck to sleep warn't even something she could think of. Not after all what happen. So she just lean over the stern of the ship they take from Amerika, the wood more beautiful, more newly assembled than their last ship were. Addis stare out into emptiness, but know better than to take any relief from it. The fog were getting thicker and any ship sides Thom's could be nigh.

Turned out, it warn't ships in the fog what sneaking up beside her. It were only Ekwueme. But she don't have nothing she ready to say to him.

--I know you are angry, he say, in low Eboe, too close to her person.

Addis put her hand up and say --Hafum áká.

--I won't touch you, but Addis, please forgive me. Yes, I would have sent you West alone and I would have stayed behind and fought this war. I wanted you to be safe and happy and away from the war that was coming. But I was always going to come and get you when it was over.

--Don't you see it doesn't matter? I left *you*. All your plotting with my mam about where you were going to send me was for nothing.

--Your mam was the only reason I didn't come for you when our plans changed. She swore to protect you and asked me to swear to the rebellion and I did.

--And so did I. You take me for someone you used to know, Ekwueme. But I have spilled blood. My blood has been spilled. And you have led a rebellion. We are strangers to each other.

--It isn't so!

--I spoke to you in grief and for that I am sorry.

--Which time? The last I saw of you when you were pushing me away or today when you accused me of killing Nnene?

--I'm sorry I hurt you. I don't want to fight with you. *We*

279

don't fight each other. We never have.

She turn from him and face the sea and as she do it, the sun get to rising, just where the sea and sky meet. As the heavens open, so do she. Addis and all her cracking scars turn to face Ekwueme.

--Yes, I left you, but I came back for you, to *save* you, she tell him. --I brought them all here to save you.

--I know, he say and everything bout him soften. --And you did save me. You saved us all.

--For now.

--That's all we have, he say and she caint stop herself from throwing her arms round him and breathing him in, kissing him fiercely and resting her head on him shoulder when she were through.

When she open her eyes, she see Tembu on the deck below them, looking straight at her, like a man apart, and something like ice shoot through her. She shiver and it make Ekwueme hold her closer. Tembu turn from her and go back to binding up the wounded with him one good arm, and Addis close her eyes again.

There gon be plenty time to worry bout Tembu and Ekwueme, bout where the ship gon take them and if the Amerikans be close behind. Plenty time to wonder if Rit and Chima and the rest of the njems make it beyond the Falls, and how long it gon take Haynes to meet him end by her hands, Chi kwe. There be time another day to know if all who done pass away in the Battle for Wellesbury be all who gon pass following her lead. Time still to see if The Eboro speaking true and death still clawing away at her heels.

But right now in time, she surrounded by the ones her heart love. With the sea at her feets and the sun on her face, she feeling peace. She honoring her mam and her Gran Gran Dido. She done a great thing of her own. What she done be greater than freedom or truth or love alone. It be all those things at once. It be revolution, and it warn't gon end with her.

ISE

NOTES

The italicized text on page 24 references the book from which Addis learns to read, the 1762 version of the *New England Primer.*

Parts of Burken's letter to Richard Lawrence starting on page 37, echo a letter George Washington wrote to Martha Washington on June 18, 1775.

The editorial written about William Burken in the *Massachusetts Gazette* on page 112, is from an actual article published about George Washingon in the *Massachusetts Gazette* on January 25, 1788, page 95.

Eziokwu's mission statement on page 187 is from the Black Parisian paper of the Négritude movement, *Revue du Monde Noir.*

Many of the sayings used by The Griot, Nnene and other characters are things my grandmother Chestina Obie used to say before she passed away and are things my grannie Hattie Ward still says.

All other events and characters are a combination of historical record, Igbo myths and legends, and fantasy.

ABOUT THE AUTHOR

Brooke C. Obie is an award-winning writer who explores the intersections of Blackness, faith and spirituality. She is a graduate of Hampton University, *summa cum laude*, Mercer University School of Law, where she served as the first Black Eleventh Circuit Survey Editor of the Mercer Law Review, and The New School's Master of Fine Arts in Creative Writing, Fiction program, where her novel proposal, which became *Book of Addis*, was a finalist for the Fulbright Fellowship. She's attended Columbia University's writer's workshop in Paris, France and will attend the writer's workshop for Callaloo Journal of African Diaspora Arts & Letters at Oxford University. Brooke lives happily in Harlem.

Made in the USA
Middletown, DE
04 October 2016